House of Rose

A MAGIC CITY STORY

T.K. THORNE

CAVEL
PRESS
Kenmore, WA

For more information go to: www.camelpress.com
www.TKThorne.com

This is a work of fiction. Names, characters, places, brands, media, and incidents are either the product of the author's imagination or are used fictitiously.

Cover design by Aubrey Anderson

House of Rose
Copyright © 2018 by T.K. Thorne

ISBN: 978-1-60381-758-5 (Trade Paper)
ISBN: 978-1-60381-767-7 (eBook)

Library of Congress Control Number: 2018950036

Printed in the United States of America

This book is dedicated to my husband and friend, Roger Thorne. We shared a career in law enforcement and a love that has weathered life's storms. Thank you for being there for me in so many ways and always supporting my need and passion to write.

Acknowledgements

Many thanks to all those who helped make this book happen. To extraordinary coach and story editor, Barbara Kyle, who first gave me confidence that I could write a crime novel. To Kristen Lamb, Nathan Bransford, and D.P. Lyle's 2017 group at Master CraftFest for the helpful critiques of the novel's beginning. To author Carolyn Haines for her kind and helpful response to someone she didn't know. To author Thomas Lakeman for his great twisty suggestions. To Adriano Viganò of Cappuccino Books for his belief in Rose, and Greg Hendrick for his enthusiasm that this story would make a good TV series—that didn't happen (yet) but it was a boost when I needed it!

To the professionals who offered technical advice—Birmingham Deputy Chief Henry Irby; Dan Katz, communications engineer at Johns Hopkins Applied Physics Lab; Pat Curry, homicide detective and medical examiner investigator; Dr. D.P. Lyle, medical forensics expert; Sally Reilly, Esq., and David Brody, Esq., and Jefferson County District Attorney, Brandon Falls.

A special thank you to my super literary agent, who is now also my friend, Kimberley Cameron, and to Dorian Maffei for her excellent suggestions. To all the support staff at Camel Press, especially my story editor, Jennifer McCord who made certain the story was the best it could be. To David Ivester, my publicist, for his work behind the scene making sure you knew about this book.

To my beloved beta readers and editors: Jimsey Bailey, Clarence Blair, Robin DeMonia, Stephen Edmondson, Debra Goldstein, Lee and Fran Godchaux, Scott Godcheau, Rebecca Lipscomb, Dan Katz, Laura Katz Parenteau, Harriet Schaffer, Janet Wallace, and most of all my husband, Roger Thorne. If I have forgotten anyone, please forgive me.

To my parents, Jane and Warren Katz. Neither got to read this book, but their pride and support of me never waivered. They are my foundation.

Chapter One

"Rose" is a difficult name. For one thing, it made me a target throughout childhood for "smells the same" taunts. For another, it sets up an assumption that fails to describe any part of my nature, conjuring an image of a tiny gray-haired woman. I am neither tiny—standing barefoot at 5'8"—nor gray-haired—dark curls minimally tamed per Birmingham police uniform regulations—and I'm more prickly thorns than soft petals.

Setting two to-go cups of coffee on the table, our waitress beams at me. "Just the way you like it, Rose."

I pry off the lid to check anyway. In my world—the world of a patrol officer—a peaceful moment can flip into crazy without notice, so I always order the coffee to-go in case we get a call. I learned this from my partner, who is also my training officer, Paul Nix, only he doesn't drink coffee. He drinks milk.

I can't go there. And besides, by 10 p.m. I need the caffeine to make it through the remaining hour in the shift.

"Thanks, Becca," Paul says. "I'll bet mine is just the way I like it too." He grins and leans his chair back against the wall. We always sit at the same table, the one that gives him the best view of the restaurant, including the door.

"Of course, Officer Nix." She rises to his tease. "Although I'm tempted to make it chocolate milk one night just to surprise you."

I can't help noticing that I am "Rose" and Paul is "Officer Nix." I also can't help wondering if her real motive in being so friendly with me is to get Paul's attention. Almost a decade older, he is a solidly built man, just shy of 6', with a disaster of red hair and pale blue eyes that see right under your skin. I frown.

She wouldn't be the first woman to flirt with him. Not that I'm jealous, just suspicious.

"Lighten up, Rose," Becca says, smoothing the checked apron they make her wear. It's incongruous with the tailored pink shirt, gray skirt and heels. She probably had no time to change clothes between jobs, but knowing her, it wouldn't matter. I don't think she owns a tee shirt. The heels make me wince and grateful not to have to worry about fashion choices. Mine is the same every day—navy blue uniform and black lace-up shoes. And for special occasions, a hateful hat that is a size too big in order to fit over my wild hair.

"What?" I say. "Lighten up from what?"

"You're so serious and grim. It's like you're in another world."

I start to snap something back, but bite my tongue. She means well and maybe she's right. Lately, I have been grumpy, distracted by strange adrenalin spurts not related to anything, as if my body is warning me I'm going to step off a cliff. No idea what that is about.

And maybe Becca does just want to be friendly. Since the diner was robbed two months ago, she always makes sure she waits on us. Unfortunately, Paul and I weren't here when that happened, but we were the first responders to the call. When we arrived—despite having just had a gun stuck in her face—Becca blurted, "Your eyes can't be that green. Do you wear contact lens?" Before I could respond, she added without taking a breath—"You don't look like a police officer. You could be a model, you know. I would die for curls like that!" Her hair, as straight as mine is curly, is a striking ash blonde and cut in a stylish angle at the shoulder.

She talked nonstop, which, at the time, I attributed to nerves, and she didn't back off at my cool answers to her personal probing. Undeterred, she discovered, by dint of direct, random questions that we were both orphans with no siblings and invited herself to be my friend. I don't do friends, but she is difficult to detach.

With a glance over her shoulder to see if her manager is watching, she slips into an empty chair and tilts her chin at the overhead TV that is replaying the local news.

"I just heard about the verdict," she says. "Did you know the officer?"

I shake my head. "It happened before I got here. I was still in college."

Paul's square chin sets. "I knew him."

To her credit, Becca doesn't say anything stupid, just, "I'm sorry," to Paul.

He grunts. "Hoffman is a good man."

The news flashes a photo of the man Officer Hoffman shot. It's a typical happy pose with his wife and son. I am sure at his trial the jury also saw that picture and his grieving family in person.

"Today," the newscaster says, "the jury was out for only two hours and returned a verdict of guilty for Birmingham, Alabama police officer James Hoffman on a charge of manslaughter. The family's reaction was anger that the verdict was not murder."

"Can't you change the channel?" Paul asks, gulping a swallow of milk like a chug of tequila.

"We're not supposed to," Becca says, "but consider it done."

She bounces from the chair with an energy I find amazing at this time of night, not to mention this is job number two for her. Before she can change the TV channel, the dispatcher calls our unit number and gives us the code and address for a domestic.

"I'll drive," Paul says.

I throw him the keys and slide into the car as gracefully as one can with a belt crammed with ten pounds of bulky gear. When we pull out of the lot, I flip on the blue lights and continue the argument we haven't had time to finish and wouldn't discuss in front of a civilian.

"I don't get it," I say. "Hoffman shot a man *in the back*. How could that possibly be justified? Department policy says lethal force is only justified if you or another person are in imminent danger."

Paul doesn't answer. I hate it when he does that.

"How can a person running away present an imminent danger?" I insist, knowing that as my training officer, he will give me an answer, eventually.

He rubs a hand across his mustache, a thick red that matches his hair.

"They don't, normally."

When he stops for a red light, I automatically check my side for oncoming traffic, not bothering with the siren since the street is empty.

"Clear." I say.

Frowning, Paul pulls through the intersection and picks up his end of the discussion. "According to Hoffman, when he decided to shoot, the man was pointing a gun at him. Then the guy suddenly spun around."

"What about the witness?" I ask. "I don't buy how that could happen. The witness said the suspect was running away and *then* the officer shot."

"Of course he did. They see what they think they see. They've never been in a situation where a split second decision is life or death."

I want the officer to have made the right decision too, but I don't see how that could be.

"What about his body camera?" I ask.

"Wasn't working. They don't half the time, but there was that pesky bullet in the guy's back. Hoffman never had a chance of winning that one."

"Well," I say, exasperated, "what do *you* think happened?"

Paul sighs and is silent for a moment, before answering. "I don't know. I wasn't there."

The domestic call is in my own neighborhood, just a few doors from the house I rent in Birmingham's Southside. The back of my house nestles against the wooded flank of hills that divide the city proper from the "over the mountain" suburban municipalities to its south. In daylight, shades of autumn crimson and gold, interspersed with the green of pines, dapple the slope of Red Mountain, the last ripples of the Appalachians. Rich seams of iron oxides stain the heavy clay soil, giving the mountain its name and spawning the mining industry that created the new city of Birmingham in 1870.

Our call is to a cedar-sided house a half block away, but in sight from my front porch. Thankfully, I don't know the combatants. I don't know any of my neighbors, actually, and like it that way.

The Southside streets of Birmingham are pretty much deserted and dark. Several streetlights are out. Others battle the branches of live oaks and hickories. A few blocks north, everything changes to the red bricks of the university, but this area was built between 1890 and 1920, before the university existed. The wedged-together houses are home to an eclectic bohemian mix—from students and professors to artists and dopers. A resurgence in redeveloping older homes has gentrified it some, and I was lucky to find a house I could (barely) afford.

Porch-sitters and dog-walkers have gone inside. The warm, mid-October "Indian summer" air carries just a hint of crisp promise. Fallen leaves congregate on the sidewalks and gutters, and the crisp, smoky scent of an unseen pile burning triggers childhood trick-or-treat memories—sticky hands and unmitigated terror of false vampire teeth.

There's no parking available on the street, so Paul pulls into the narrow alley that runs beside our destination, a perk that comes with the marked patrol car. A walkway leads to the steps and raised front porch. Patches of dirt and yellow grass dot the small front yard, evidence of the season and the long dry days of the past few weeks.

The fact that domestic violence calls are one of the most dangerous encounters for police was drummed into our heads at the Academy. It's hard to get worked up about them, hence, the "drumming." By habit, Paul and I stand on either side of the door, in case bullets are involved in the "hello."

A woman pulls open the door. Pole thin with pale skin and raccoon smudges under her eyes, she blinks at us as if trying to register who we are in the yellow porch light. The waft of alcohol-evaporating-from-pores means she's been at it for multiple hours. Clinging to her pants leg is a boy about five years old. He stares up at us, one fist in his mouth.

"Hi," I say to the woman. "We got a call on a disturbance here."

I feel Paul's eyes on me, evaluating how I will handle this. Tonight is my last night on the three-month patrol training car under his supervision. After tonight, if he passes me, I will stay in patrol for years, probably on the late shift at some precinct, not necessarily this one. I don't want him to say I'm not ready. I like this job. It feels right.

The woman's hand tightens on the door latch. "No problem here," she says. "He's gone."

"Mind if we come in and make sure?" I ask.

The child looks up with frightened, dark eyes fringed in a thicket of lashes.

"I do mind," she slurs. "Nothing for you to see."

Paul offers no assistance. This is my call.

I'm not sure what to do. If there is someone inside, we need to keep him from hurting her or the child, but we can't go in her house without permission unless he is there and is a threat. And, of course, if he is, the odds of violence are high, from him or her. That lesson sank home on my first domestic disturbance call when a woman jumped on my back while we were trying to arrest the man who'd just beaten her bloody.

"You called us for help," I say carefully. "That's why we're here."

"Go away now," she says.

"We can't go away until we make sure you are okay, and there's no one inside threatening you."

"So you're not going away?" She seems to be processing this through the alcohol fuzz.

"That's right." I jump on her logic. "We're not going away until we can come in and make sure no one is here who might hurt you." I look down at the child and add, "Or your son."

Her eyes follow mine to rest on the top of his dark tousled head. Her shoulders slump and she steps aside.

For all Paul's "women have to carry their own weight" talk, he makes sure he is the first to enter. I grew up in a military foster home, but we spent several years based in the South. If a man wants to be gallant, it doesn't bother me. Besides, I am his rookie. He doesn't want to get me hurt or have me make a mistake that gets him hurt.

Inside, we focus first on making sure we won't be ambushed. Paul and I draw our guns as soon as we're out of the woman's sight and work through the house, clearing it room by room. As always, my pulse does a stutter at the bathroom door. *Old demons.*

Nobody jumps up out of the bathtub or the linen closet. But the rear door in the kitchen has been forced open.

Returning to the living room, I start to sit on the couch to take the report, but it is nasty, so I remain standing. The burn holes on the sofa arm add to my concerns for the little boy. Drinking and smoking can be a lethal combo.

"Can you tell me what happened?" I ask the woman after I've gotten the basic info on her.

She shrugs. "This man just burst in the back door."

"A man? You didn't know him?"

"Never seen him before. A white man with a dark blue ball cap."

This changes things from a domestic violence to a burglary and maybe an assault.

"What did he want?"

"He seemed surprised to see me, like he thought I wouldn't be here."

On the other side of the room, Paul squats on his heels and gravely accepts a plastic toy soldier from the little boy.

"What did you do when you saw him?" I ask, turning back to the woman.

"Went after him with a kitchen knife." She sniffs. "He won't be back."

I frown. There is no guarantee of that. "Did you cut him?" I hadn't noticed any blood anywhere.

"No, but scared the crap outta him." She lights the cigarette and belatedly glances at me. "You mind?"

I do, but it's her house, so I just try to take shallow breaths and hurry us along.

Paul hands the boy back his soldier, eliciting a shy smile. I wonder what this woman's real priorities are—her son or the bottle she obviously has a close relationship with? If there is evidence of neglect, we can take custody of the boy. But it's not an easy call to make—to leave a child in what could be a nasty environment or to snatch him away from the only family he knows.

"So," I say, "you ran him off with a knife, but he didn't threaten you or hurt you?"

"Nope. Didn't get a chance."

I'm not sure I believe she didn't know him, and I try again. "Who was he? The boy's father?"

"Lord no. He's been gone since before Daniel was born. I told you, never seen this man before."

While I finish writing the report and get a case number from the dispatcher, I try to think of some reason to go look in the refrigerator to see if she feeds the kid. He is very thin and his shirt is filthy.

Before I can pursue the thought, the dispatcher gives out a residential burglary-in-progress call less than a block away with a description—short, white male wearing a dark ball cap. Adrenaline jazzes my pulse. There is nothing routine about an "in-progress" felony call, and it's on our beat, close. It might even be the same man who broke in here.

Paul is on his feet. He glances at his watch and nods at me to answer.

Startled by Paul's abrupt movement and the voice over the radio, the little boy draws back into his mother's shadow. I hate to leave him, but I don't have a choice. There's not enough evidence to take him. I pull out the radio on my belt while we head for the door.

"Three-two-four," I say, giving the dispatcher our car. "We'll get it. Give us a 'A-alpha' on this call."

"Sorry," I say to the woman, laying a card on the coffee table with the case number for the report. "We have to take a call."

In the car, I glance at Paul's grim profile, ghostly in the glow of the patrol car's dashboard lights and computer screen. He doesn't look at me, just guns the accelerator straight down the alley. The address is in the block behind this street, and the alley will put us out halfway there. I snatch the mike from its hook on the dashboard.

"Three-two-four, we're close."

At the alley's end, Paul turns right onto the street, slams on the brakes and jerks his head. My gaze follows. A man barrels out of the night, pelting toward us on the narrow sidewalk. A short white man, he's wearing a navy ball cap pulled low and running from the direction of the burglary. No time to tell more.

Apparently seeing us at the same time we see him, he abruptly changes course, sprinting down the same alley we just cleared.

"Stay with him!" Paul says. "I'll cut him off."

Without questioning, I jump from the car. Tires squeal behind me.

For a moment, I hesitate. It seems a safer bet to stay at this end of the alley and seek cover, rather than run down a dim passageway after a possibly armed suspect. But Paul said, *Stay with him*, and I trust him implicitly. He's always had my back.

I draw my gun and plunge forward.

On my left, a fenced back yard gives way to the two-story house we just left. The long side runs almost the length of the narrow alley. I hope the little boy stays inside.

Along the alley's opposite side, thick bushes form a barrier. A heavy tree canopy patterns the pavement with intermittent patches of darkness. At the far end, the single working streetlight dimly exposes the suspect needling through broken shadows.

As I run, my focus splinters between him and the gun in my hand, my forefinger stiff along the smooth side just above the trigger, as per Academy instruction, to keep from accidently firing. It would be my luck to trip and shoot him … or myself.

Midway down the alley, I hang back, hugging the house on the opposite side from the bushes, my shoulder brushing a wall that smells of old cedar. Neither side of the street offers cover, but the shadows pool deeper here. If Paul can get to the end of the alley fast enough, he will trap the suspect between us.

Using the shingle-wood siding to steady my body, I bring up my gun, cupping it with both hands and locking my right shoulder with pressure from my left hand and arm, as I've done in target practice drills when the distance is far enough to aim. Over the last months on the training car with Paul, I've pulled my weapon a few times, but never had to actually point it at anyone. My heart pumps harder than the short run demanded.

Without stopping, the suspect flings out his arm in the direction of the bushes. With his sudden movement, my finger drops and curls around the trigger. Even in the adrenaline rush of the moment, I think about what happened to Hoffman. What if this guy I'm chasing turns with a gun, and I shoot as he spins back around? Suddenly that doesn't seem so unbelievable. I don't want to shoot him in the back. I don't want to shoot him, period. I don't even know for sure if he's committed a crime.

I start to yell, "Stop! Police!" but I'm in a vulnerable position, so I don't. Any moment now, Paul should pull our patrol car in front of him and take control of things.

Closing my right eye, I focus down the clean line along the top of the gun barrel, lining up the stubby front sight between the two back ones and leveling them all square in the guy's back. The dispatcher didn't say anything about him being armed, but I've only seen one hand. If he does turn with a gun, a split second will matter. The voice of the Academy firearms' instructor echoes in my ear—"*Forget all the TV cowboy fast-draw stuff; the person who decides first has the advantage.*"

Wrapped around the cold metal grip, my fingers feel … odd. I try to focus, but a weird warmth gushes from my feet to my head. *What the—?*

What happens next has never happened to me before and challenges everything I thought I knew about reality.

Reaching the glow from the streetlight, the suspect stops, looking back over his shoulder, though the ball cap is pulled low and I can't see his features. Can he see me? Around him, the air wavers and shifts. I blink hard, but his image ripples like a desert mirage. While he stares in my direction, a dark smudgy version of him peels away and turns toward the alley's end, leaving the original version still looking back.

A patrol car, also rippling out of focus, stops at the head of the alley. It takes a moment to realize the sound of squealing tires is missing. In fact, no sound of any kind reaches my ears, as if I am deep underwater. Before I can absorb what this could mean, the car door slowly opens—

That's not right. Paul should be moving quickly. Somehow this seems more important than the real question—*how can there be two suspects?*

Locked in a paralysis, I watch beyond the sights of my gun as the shadow version of the suspect lifts his arms in slow motion. Paul, now partially out of the car, seems either frozen or moving slower than I can detect. A puff of gray smoke rises lazily over the suspect's shoulder and a small object spins through the wavering air, straight toward Paul. Even at this distance, I know what it is. I want to move, to do something to stop the bullet headed for my partner, but my body seems mired in the same molasses as his. Slowly, the projectile buries into Paul's neck, leaving a sluggish bloom of blood in its wake, and Paul crumples, bit by bit.

The air stops rippling. The shadow-figures and shadow-car disappear. Tires squeal. The "original" suspect turns his head toward the sound as the "real" patrol car pulls up, blue lights flashing.

I have seen all this before, an endless moment before. That's impossible. But I know what happens in the next seconds, what will happen if I let it. I don't have time to figure out how or why. Paul opens the driver's door on the patrol car, puts a foot on the asphalt to bail out … and I pull the trigger.

Chapter Two

My throat feels like I just swallowed sand; my ears ring and the sulfur stench of gunpowder fills my nose. As a topper, my head is pounding with the worst headache I've ever had in my life. Air goes in and out of my lungs, but someone else is breathing, not me. Blue lights stutter across the cheek of a dead man. A man who lies sprawled on the asphalt, two bullet holes in his back staring up at me like accusing eyes.

This can't be real. But it is real. It is the words that just came out of my sergeant's mouth that aren't: *"You're a hero; you saved your partner's life."*

A hero? Is this how heroes are supposed to feel? I'm in denial—I did not fire my gun for the first time at a person instead of a cardboard target. I did not kill a human being.

But I am here, and I *have* shot someone, because that person's body is now lying a few feet away, the centerpiece in a rectangle of bright-yellow police tape. Just beyond the tape, the staccato flicker of blue from several patrol cars illuminate the close-set houses, the man's lifeless back, and Sarge's beefy face.

His breath onions and cigar, Sarge grabs my shoulder with his burly hand, turning me away from the body. "Rose? You gonna be okay?"

Okay? What an idiotic thing to ask.

"I'm okay, Sarge," I hear myself say in a thin, shaky voice.

"You did what you had to do. You made a tough call in a bad situation." He squeezes my shoulder.

Did I? How would I know? I don't think there is precedent for killing a person because you saw him shoot your partner in a vision, and it begins to happen in real time.

Am I losing my mind?

A few feet away, a guy in plainclothes is talking to Paul. My partner's right elbow rests on his gun butt. To an outsider, he looks relaxed, but I recognize the tension in his stance. Still, seeing him nearby helps.

Paul shakes his head, pulls his gun, and hands it to the guy in plainclothes, but I can't hear the exchange. *Damn it.* What are they saying?

"Who is that guy Paul is talking to?" I ask Sarge.

"IAD."

IAD—even a rookie dreads those initials and knows they stand for Internal Affairs Division, the detectives who handle internal police investigations and determine if a shooting is in-policy or not. This guy holds my career in his hands, maybe the rest of my life, if it goes badly.

Sarge keeps his hand on my shoulder, an anchor to reality in a world gone bizarre.

"What happens next?" I ask.

"IAD will take your weapon."

Rookie that I am, even I know that's standard operating procedure—SOP—for any police shooting.

"It's SOP," Sarge says, like some kind of echo of what's playing in my head.

"Great."

Am I going to prison?

Sarge moves off to brief the chief, who has just arrived at the scene. If this were a ball game and I weren't a woman, he'd probably give my butt a pat of encouragement. But it's not a game. When a cop shoots a man in the back, plenty of questions will be asked … and I'm not going to be able to answer them.

When the IAD suit takes my gun, he says, "Be at Admin 9 a.m. tomorrow morning."

I nod, only vaguely registering what he is saying, fighting the pull from behind me—a dark hole sucking me into its maw. I know I shouldn't, but I turn back to face the body that should have been alive, would have been alive, except for the two small bits of metal spewed from my gun lodged just below his shoulder blades. *Double tap. Always shoot twice. Aim for center mass.*

The man was DOS, dead-on-the-scene, by the time paramedics arrived, so they left him as he lay, on his stomach, head to the side, his skin already waxen, eyes glass marbles immune to the world, a gray revolver clutched in his hand. His ball cap, so low over his eyes as he ran, now askew, exposes his face. It's a face that has seen less than twenty-something years—only a few years younger than I am.

According to the *Criminal Investigations* textbook, a dead person clutching a gun results from a spasm, the shock of death, and means the person was holding it at the time of death. You can't force a corpse's fingers to hold anything. It's one of the ways to distinguish between a homicide and a suicide. A fact that might save my bacon.

I can't stop staring at his body, noticing things. He's not bleeding. From the same book, blood coagulates when the heart stops pumping. Common sense, but somehow ... wrong.

A woman wails. "My son! My son!" Her keening slices through the shock that has buffered me, and I turn to throw up into the bushes along the edge of the alley.

"Rose!"

A hand on my back is a muffled pressure through my Kevlar vest. I've never been more grateful for a man who carries a handkerchief. Paul's hand guides me away as I wipe my mouth.

Thank God he doesn't ask me if I'm okay.

"You saved my life," my partner says quietly.

I want to cry. I want to scream. I want to go somewhere and be alone. I don't ever want to be alone again.

Chapter Three

Paul's strong hand is now on the back of my elbow, guiding me to our patrol car and sitting me in the passenger seat. My head feels light, as if all the blood has drained into my queasy stomach. It's been two hours since the shooting.

Birmingham's chief, the shift lieutenant, officers to block traffic, officers to knock on doors and find potential witnesses, evidence technicians, and investigators, both Internal Affairs and Homicide, came to the scene, as well as state investigators, who brought their own forensic personnel to take their own photos and collect their own evidence. Everyone wanted our stories about what happened. And of course the media. Reporters, TV cameras. Fortunately, the chief and the public relations officer fielded them. Paul says our names will be withheld for a while to protect us.

Protect us. I turn those words over in my head. From the media? Or from vengeance seekers?

Paul turns and speaks to one of the Birmingham detectives who hands him his gun, which he re-holsters. They have examined it and determined he did not fire. Closing my door, Paul moves around the car and settles into the driver's seat as if we have just cleared up from a routine call, but my elbow encounters the empty holster at my hip like a missing tooth.

"Where are we going?" I ask.

"I'm taking you home."

"That's silly," I manage, the taste of my vomit in my mouth. "I can walk from here." In fact I can see my house only a few doors down the street.

"Shut up."

Paul drives right by my house, which is only a half block away. I bite my tongue. He knows good and well where I live. The one thing I am picky about is where I use the bathroom, and since my house is on our beat, he usually just drops me off and waits for me in the car.

Instead of taking me home, as he probably told the IAD detective he was doing, he drives along the crest of Red Mountain. I have come to think of the spot where Paul stops as "our" place. It's too early for the people who come to park and make out, so we have it to ourselves. Our viewpoint overlooks the city's center. I've seen lots of sunsets here, and Birmingham has some spectacular ones. The smog from the lone furnace still in operation in the western part of town creates a filter that sometimes burns the sky a deep orange. But it is past midnight and only the glitter of jeweled lights below are visible.

I take a ragged breath. When I first looked out over the city like this, I felt like a guardian, like maybe I did the right thing becoming a cop. But tonight I can't find that sense of rightness. My insides are jagged and jittery.

"What's going to happen?" I ask.

Paul leans back and echoes what Sarge said. "Internal Affairs and Homicide investigates and the chief can make administrative decisions—"

"Like firing me."

"The state investigators will make the call to the D.A." Paul says.

"The call?"

"On whether it's a criminal case or justifiable homicide. Then the District Attorney either decides to go with that or send it to the Grand Jury."

"Why does the state investigate? It's not their jurisdiction."

"It's how Birmingham does it, to keep outsiders from saying the internal investigation is a cover up."

It never entered my mind that the Department might try to cover up what happened. A snort of ironic laughter escapes my mouth—I'd been too busy covering it up myself.

The moment of humor fades as quickly as it appeared, and I look down at my hands, which are knotted into fists and still clutch Paul's handkerchief. I would give it back, but I doubt he wants it at the moment.

"What am I supposed to do?" I ask.

"Just stick to what you told them tonight. You thought he was going to shoot me and you shot first. Keep it simple."

My stomach feels like I ate a nest of ants for supper.

"Then what?" I ask.

"Wait."

"I'm not good at waiting."

"I know, but you're on administrative leave."

"That sounds dire."

"Paid vacation," Paul says lightly. "Take advantage of it."

I steal a glance to see if he is smiling. He's not, but that doesn't mean anything. He's a man of few words and fewer facial clues. It took forever to learn to tell when he employed his very dry sense of humor.

With a start of surprise, I realize that regardless of what happens, I'm going to miss him. I've been so anxious to pass the training phase, I haven't thought about it, even though I knew he was first on the sergeant's promotion list and rumor has it Homicide asked for him. I bite my lip. I am just feeling vulnerable and shook up. I don't need people. I don't even want their company.

Even if Paul had stayed in Patrol, I am subject to transfer out of the South Precinct. They could send me to North, East, or even the Wild West, assuming I don't end up fired or in prison.

"Rose," Paul says, "it's going to get nasty. Don't do anything stupid."

This startles me out of my reverie and reminds me I am in a pile of shit.

"What do you mean?"

"I mean, just let them all do their investigation. Sit tight. Stay out of trouble. It'll blow over."

Why does he think I would do anything different than wait for the investigation? Does he have any idea what I saw, what happened to me? Did he see it too? My mouth opens to ask him, to get some kind of confirmation that I have not lost my mind, but I think better of the idea and snap it shut.

I AM NOT A MORNING person, but it is not hard to be at the Admin building at 9 a.m. for my prearranged appointment since I didn't sleep any of the three hours available. For thirty minutes, the IAD Detective Jenkins keeps me waiting. If he thinks it will make me more nervous, he is wrong. I can't get more nervous.

Finally he interviews me or interviews me again, as he was at the scene last night. "Tell us what happened in your own words," he says. I've lost count of how many times I've told this.

"It was a burglary-in-progress call, and my partner and I were nearby. We saw someone running as we approached."

"Was there a description?"

"No, but he was running from the direction of the scene, and he fit the description of a burglary suspect at the call we had just prior to this one. He ducked down an alley. I jumped out, and Paul drove around the block to see if he could intercept him."

"So you didn't know the man was the burglar?"

"No, not really."

"Then what happened?" he asks.

I close my eyes, my mouth dry, as I relive the moment for the hundredth time.

He is waiting for my answer.

I clear my throat again. "I followed the suspect, and the patrol car rolled up, blocking his path."

I don't dare say aloud what I felt and saw next. What I say is: "Paul pulled up and started to exit the car. The suspect pulled a gun from his waistband and pointed it at Paul, and I fired my weapon … twice." The last word comes out almost a whisper.

"I see," Jenkins says. "Why didn't your partner shoot?"

"I … he didn't have a chance. It happened so fast."

I wouldn't have had a chance either, even with my gun trained on the guy's back, if I hadn't seen what was going to happen … *before* it happened. I'm waiting for the question: *How did you see the suspect pull his gun if his back was to you?*

"How did you see the suspect's gun? Wasn't his back to you?"

Now I am in shaky territory. If I tell them something my body camera didn't "see," it won't be good. My throat is almost as dry as it was last night.

"He, um, turned slightly while I was running." I pause, mouth dry, praying my body camera was jiggling. "And I glimpsed a gun. Then when Paul pulled up, I saw the suspect raise his arms."

That is a lie. I never saw a "real" gun until I saw it in the man's lifeless hand.

To my relief, he doesn't say anything about the body camera. He must have reviewed the video by now and probably the Homicide detective and the state's detective have as well. I don't expect any of them will ask if I had any visions. So what else is there to say? But when I think we're finished, Jenkins casually says, "The only problem, Officer Brighton, is that your partner told it differently."

"What do you mean?"

"He said the man never raised his weapon."

For a moment, I am speechless, then I look him in the eye, a flush of anger burning my earlobes. This is a cheap trick. Paul would never say that, no matter what he saw or didn't see.

"I can't speak for him," I say. "I saw what I saw."

He takes another hour asking me the same questions in different ways. *Keep it simple*, Paul said. I try. But how can I explain what happened when I don't know, myself? If they put me on a polygraph, it's going to be dicey. I did see a gun, but it was a shadow gun in a vision. Will my body decide that is the truth or a lie?

Chapter Four

Restless, I pace from room to room of my small house trying to occupy myself ... every room except one. There's no point in going in there.

Becca, the waitress from the diner, wanted to come over. How did she know? The Department hasn't released my name. Paul must have told her, thinking I needed a friend, I told her thanks, but I wanted to be alone.

For an hour, nursing a glass of red wine, I try to do some sketches, but everything just comes out as doodles, the same intricate rose I have drawn since I was old enough to hold a pencil. I assume because of my name. Disgusted, I put aside the pad and switch on the television, distraction of the last resort. On the local news, front and center, is the photo of Zachary Fields, the person I shot, a young man with a lopsided grin. Then the camera scans over street protests where people hold signs chanting that I should be fired and prosecuted for murder, signs they probably had left over from Hoffman's trial. Watching the universe tilt and time spill out was not more surreal. They can't be talking about *me*.

But they are.

Desperate to shut up the voices, I run through the channels, again. What I end up watching is a documentary, something about baleen whales having a newly discovered sensory organ in their jaws that helps them coordinate feeding. When the program is over, I try to read, but after going over the same sentence fifteen times, I slam the book down. Not even an old movie can engage me, and I am a movie buff.

I know I am trying to keep from thinking about what happened. Am I an unhinged person who killed someone? Drugs always scared me, so I don't know what it feels like to hallucinate. Could someone have slipped something into my coffee at the Waffle House?

For the second night, I can't stop my whirling brain, so the next morning, it is with a mixture of relief and trepidation that I keep my obligatory counseling appointment, applying a generous amount of concealer to hide the dark circles under my eyes. Maybe it will help to talk about it. That's what they say, but how can I tell anyone what happened? They'd take the badge with the gun and stick me in the cuckoo's nest.

Counseling services for department members is privately outsourced and located in an old house in the same Southside neighborhood where I live. Access is through a back door, the servants' entrance. I check in with the receptionist and take a seat in the front parlor, filling out paperwork and thumbing mindlessly through magazines until my assigned counselor descends the *Gone with the Wind* staircase. She's middle-aged, with a carefully made-up face and a scarf that matches her blouse. I am underdressed in my jeans and a tee shirt picturing the image of a stern-faced cop with a caption that reads, "Looks Like You've Had a Bit Too Much to Think."

She gives me a scarlet-lipped smile, introduces herself as Sandra Faulkner, and leads me upstairs to her room, which is filled with knick-knacks and children's drawings. With another smile, she sits in a flower-patterned chair next to the desk. I've never been to a counselor, but, obviously, I'm supposed to sit somewhere. I figure this is the first test. If I pick the high-backed cushioned chair with arms, am I insecure? Does the couch mean I want to spill my guts? Maybe choosing the spare plain chair is a sign of confidence? I eye the hard seat—or perhaps a wish for self-punishment? I chew my lip. I have a shining new degree in psychology that imparts just enough knowledge to create anxiety. Biting my lower lip, I settle at one end of the couch because it feels more open. I don't like being penned in.

Faulkner consults the paper in her hand. "This is your first time here, isn't it?"

"Yes." I notice my hands are clasped together, my forehead is damp, and my earlobes are burning, something they do when I'm under stress. I think I'd rather face an armed burglar … *no, wait—I did that, and it was worse.* I take a deep breath. *Pull yourself together, Rose.*

"How would you like me to address you?" Faulkner asks.

I filled out the form downstairs as "V. Rose Brighton," which is how I've done it since I was old enough to hate my first name, Veronica. Everybody calls me Rose.

"Just Rose, please," I say.

"Rose. That's a name I haven't heard in a while."

I'm willing to bet she hasn't heard of an old-fashioned "Veronica" since the

Archie comic books, either.

"I see this is a mandatory visit," she says. "I want to make sure you understand that everything you say to me is confidential, although I can make recommendations."

Recommendations. I interpret that to mean she has the power to send me back to work or keep me penned up in my house or have me fired. My stomach clenches. To my surprise, I like being a cop, having the power to help people without getting personal with them, to do something about bad guys other than read about them in the news, and maybe, if I'm honest, I'm a little bit of an excitement junkie. Not everything happens in an hour like the TV shows. Stretches of boredom are normal, but the next moment can turn on the adrenalin spigot.

On the shifts when Paul was off, I worked with other officers who didn't hesitate to let the rookie (me) know I was not to drive or touch the radio in "their" car, but all the grouchy acts were just part of testing a rookie. Maybe I received an extra dose because I'm female, but I get that it's important to know if I'm tough enough. Not being as strong as a man is enough of a liability. If I'm going to wimp out when things get bad, it's better for everyone, including yours truly, to weed me out quickly.

I didn't wimp out, again to my surprise, though once I had to blow my nose hard in the ladies' restroom after a severe berating over an accident-report diagram I couldn't get right. It is little comfort that I may never have to draw one again.

"Why don't we start with you telling me a little about yourself?" Faulkner suggests.

I clear my throat. "What do you want to know?"

"Well," she consults the paperwork on her lap. "I see you are a recent psychology graduate from the University of Alabama and that you were an excellent student, graduating *summa cum laude*."

I nod.

"You minored in art?"

"Yes."

"But no extracurricular activities. No sororities or sports. No art club …?

"They're not required."

"True, but that is a little unusual. And to end up here as a police officer—is that something you always wanted to do?"

"It never occurred to me. I was just looking for a job and saw the opening. To be honest, I thought it would be temporary, just until I found something else."

"What were you looking for?"

Discomforted by the question, I uncross my legs and cross them the other way, realizing, too late, she will read that as a defensive posture.

"I don't know what I was looking for," I say honestly. This was my problem in school as well. I didn't have a clue what to do with my life. Picking a field of study felt like trying to draw in the dark. My career counselor almost pulled her hair out trying to get me to commit to something. Finally, when I absolutely had to declare a major, I chose psychology. Not that I had any desire to do research or be a shrink, but maybe to try and figure myself out.

"You were born here in Birmingham?"

"Yes, but my parents died, and I was adopted by a Marine sergeant and his wife, so we moved around a lot. College was the longest I stayed in one place my entire life."

"What about other relatives?" Faulkner asks. "Are they here? Is that why you came back?"

"I don't know why I came back. It just was always in the back of my mind that I would."

"Where are your adoptive parents now?"

"They're dead too. My father was killed fighting in Iraq, my mother in a car accident shortly afterward."

"I'm terribly sorry. Is there no one?"

There is no one, only the one-sided, wannabe friendship with Becca. That's pretty pitiful, but it doesn't make me a killer.

"I've always been a loner, I guess." That is somewhat of an understatement. Even as a child, I played mostly by myself. The few "friends" in high school I hung with tolerated me, but I always felt … different, as if there was some other meaning to my life that I just couldn't quite grasp. Sometimes the feeling was so powerful and frustrating, it was a physical ache. The things my acquaintances were interested in, primarily boys, were boring to me. I just pretended to be one of them and managed to dissuade most dating offers. Once, I overheard a popular guy say I was a "beautiful, frigid bitch." That surprised me. The beautiful part. I was gangly, tall for my age, all bones and elbows, which mostly stayed scraped and scabbed from climbing trees and falling off my bicycle as a child. But he got the "frigid" right. And maybe the "bitch." Why Becca wants me as a friend eludes me. Maybe she abhors a social vacuum, and I am her mission.

Faulkner's face clouds. "I imagine there's a good bit of … pressure on you and the department from parts of the community."

"You mean all those people who want to see my ass fired?"

With a slight smile, she says, "Yes. I'd imagine some pressure internally from fellow officers as well?"

"Not really. The officers think I'm a—" I can't say the word. "They think I did the right thing." Then I recall the IAD detective trying to break me down and amend that. "The street officers, anyway."

"And what do *you* think?" she asks softly.

For some reason, the question tightens my throat, and I feel my nose start to run.

She hands me a box of tissue.

What do I think? I have to tread carefully here.

"I did what I thought I had to, to save Paul."

She waits.

"But … it feels wrong." I can see Zachary sprawled on the pavement, his life shuttered too soon. Maybe he was a thug, but he was young. He could have been anything. I took his future from him.

"It feels wrong," I repeat.

"Rose," she says gently, "it's okay to grieve for him."

Chapter Five

I don't know exactly why I'm here, but I walk the alley and stop, staring at the ground where Zachary went down. Built in the late 1800s as one of the city's first "streetcar suburbs," the Southside area is now a hodgepodge of turn-of-the-century houses and churches nestled close on narrow lots. Unfortunately, the streetcar rails were long ago paved over. Old trees line the cracked sidewalks along my street, their branches clipped on one side to keep them clear of power lines, but the light poles are another matter and those that work have to compete with the tree branches. The houses are so close, I can hear the details of my next-door neighbors' disagreements from my bathroom.

Unlike in the movies, no homicide chalk mark outlines where the body sprawled in the alley. Since the man was DOS, the evidence technicians got plenty of photos. The techs and detectives have been over the scene carefully. I'm just a patrol officer, and a rookie to boot, so what do I think I'm looking for?

It's midday, and fortunately, most people in this neighborhood are at work, so nobody comes out to ask why a twenty-two-year-old woman in blue jeans and a tee-shirt is walking a linear search pattern in a little area between two houses. Under the bushes, the dirt is the reddish-brown of soil rich in iron oxide. I find a bottle cap, a piece of gum, and bits of glass.

"Hey."

Startled at the soft greeting, I turn to find a grubby boy in the alley, no mom in sight. I recognize him from last night—the shy boy who offered Paul a toy soldier just before we got the call on the burglary suspect.

"Hey." I squat, like Paul did the night in his living room, bringing us to eye level. "Where's your mom?"

He points at the house to his left—the one with cedar siding I leaned against when I shot Zachary.

I search my memory for his name, but before I can ask, he does. "What's your name?" He is clearly comfortable interrogating a stranger on his turf.

"Rose."

He frowns. "It yours?"

"What?"

He hesitates and holds out his hand, which is curled into a fist. A smudge of chocolate runs from the side of his mouth to his chin and a smudge of the red-orange clay across his other cheek. As he slowly uncurls his chubby fingers, I look down at his palm and suck in a quick breath. At first, what rests there appears to be just a small chunk of red glassy rock in an intricate tarnished silver setting with a circular loop at the top for a chain. It's about the size of my knuckle. Sunlight slides from a cloud's edge and catches it, revealing deeper crimson layers within the crystal in a pattern as multi-chambered as a … rose. Not just any rose, but *my* rose, the stylized one with sharp edges that I have drawn over and over all my life. When I put my finger on it, a golden fire flushes from my feet to my head, and my body thrums as if I'm a tuning fork.

What the hell? The only time I have ever felt something similar was last night, just before the impossible happened. *What is going on with me?*

The cloud reclaims its position covering the sun, and the stone in the boy's palm darkens to quiescence, the color of smoke. I feel normal again. Empty.

But I know that I want the jewel in the boy's palm. Oddly, he seems to know it, too, because he keeps his hand open for me to take it. I hesitate. What if this is some family heirloom he has filched from a jewelry box?

"Where did you get it?" I ask, controlling the deep itch to hold it.

"There." He points to a spot under the bushes.

In my mind, the dark outline of the man I chased flings his arm out. If he had actually thrown something, it might have landed near that spot. A chill spiders my spine.

"Daniel!"

In the doorway of the cedar-sided house, his mother appears. Her bones beneath the thin white shirt appear knitted together, and she tucks her hands under armpits in a defensive movement that belies her sharp tone. "How did you get outside?" she demands.

At the sound of his name, the boy's head turns, and I snatch the pendant from his palm.

"Come here right now," she says. "You're going in time-out!"

Daniel's dirt-smudged hand balls again into a fist, this time plugging his mouth, and he moves slowly toward her and the doom of time-out.

She eyes me with suspicion until recognition blooms. "You were here last night."

"Yes, ma'am."

"I'm worried about safety in the neighborhood. I never worried so much before."

I can't help thinking that her bluster has worn off with the alcohol buzz. She seems much more vulnerable than when she was talking about running a man out of her house with a kitchen knife.

"It was an unusual … circumstance," I say.

Apparently, she doesn't know I was the shooter. My name and photo haven't been released yet, though the media is clamoring for them.

"That man from last night died, didn't he?" she asks, and I wonder why she needs to ask. Maybe she doesn't watch the news or get media tweets.

I take a breath. "Yes, he did."

"Maybe it's not nice to say—" She tucks a bit of stringy hair behind her ear. "But at least he won't be back here."

I point behind her house. "He broke into another house about a block away."

"Nobody was home, I hope."

"No, ma'am. The house was empty."

She cocks her head at my jeans and tee shirt. "Are you here officially?"

"I live down the street." I point toward my house, barely visible on the corner, hoping I won't regret giving out that information. I should have asked her about the stone pendant, but instead I say, "I was just walking by and wondered what … Daniel was doing out here alone." Unobtrusively, I slip the jewel into my jeans pocket.

It's evidence. It has to be what Zachary threw when he was running, but I know I have no intention of turning it in. Great, in the space of a day, not only have I shot a man in the back and lied about it, now I'm a thief.

Chapter Six

I take a deep breath and knock on the door of the wood frame house, which is not much more than a shanty on the east side of town. I'm not supposed to be here. Protocol is for the homicide detective investigating my shooting to follow up. I'm supposed to be on "administrative leave," staying out of policing until the investigation is concluded. But I have to know what is going on. I may be putting my career at risk, but this is about more than my job; it's about my sanity.

I haven't ruled out that it was Zachary who caused that psychic event in the alley, not me. Who is he? And how did his mother arrive on the scene so quickly, even before the media? The name of the young man I shot was in the newspaper along with his mother's name. It didn't take a detective to find her address.

Driving into a section of the Avondale neighborhood beyond the recent gentrification and bustling restaurant/bar zone, the houses are old. Here, the cracked paint and fallen-in roofs are not necessarily signs of abandonment. People live inside.

This area wasn't our beat, but I worked here a few times when Paul was off and I was "utility," filling in for an absent partner. It wasn't easy. Some of the guys still have a hard time with the concept of a woman in uniform. But after a drunk swung on Paul and we wrestled him to the ground, the harassment stopped. I was labeled "okay." Being "okay" is a big deal; it's membership into a close-knit fraternity of blue. Now that I have shot someone in defense of my partner, that membership will never be questioned again. I am beyond okay; I am a "hero."

I want to throw up again, but a stout, middle-aged woman with wispy blonde hair comes to the door, eyeing me with caution.

"Hi, I'm Officer Brighton." I work my badge case out of my jeans and flip it open for her to see, tense against some sign of recognition from her. I don't get any, but I recognize her. She was at the scene, but apparently too horrified with her dead son to figure out who did what. She stares dully at the badge.

"May I talk to you about what happened to your son?" I ask.

"Po-lice already been out here," she says with the southern pronunciation that accents the first syllable. I can't see her well through the screen door. For a moment that door seems like a barrier between our worlds, riddled with tiny holes that distort our view of each other.

"I know," I say, "but there are a few more questions we have. May I come in?"

She shakes her head, and my heart sinks.

But she pushes open the screen and steps out. "We can talk on the porch."

That is fine with me. The inside of the house is dark, and I haven't gotten my gun back, and no one knows where I am—a good thing, since I'm supposed to be at home not-being-a-police-officer, but not a good thing if things go bad here. I know Paul told me to stay out of this, but I can't. There is more at stake than keeping a low profile, such as the matter of my sanity.

The woman sits in a metal chair with a scallop-shaped back that reminds me of shells. A sandy beach somewhere on the Gulf of Mexico sounds very appealing; however, I'm standing on a front porch with a woman who has just lost her son—the woman whose son I have shot and killed. And, like my experience in counseling, I am left to choose my own seat or stand. I sit on the edge of a two-seater swing, trying to keep it still.

For several seconds, neither of us speaks. She is not even looking at me. Dark patches half-moon her eyes, which gaze out into the narrow street and beyond. What kind of life have they seen? I have no idea, but I know something of what she is feeling. My adoptive parents are dead. My birth parents and sister died when I was five. It isn't difficult to find compassion and let it into my voice. I hope she won't realize that it is mixed with guilt.

"I am very sorry about your son," I say.

She looks at me. Maybe she wasn't expecting a cop—a po-lice officer—to acknowledge her pain, just to ask questions. She gives a brief nod. For a moment, we are just two women sitting on a porch. Then the connection vanishes, and bleakness settles back over her features.

"Could you tell me something about Zachary?" I ask softly.

"Not much to tell. He was always a quiet boy. Hung with the wrong crowd some."

"Did he work anywhere?"

"He worked at the car wash down the street. That's where he met them other boys. They got him in trouble with Juvenile before he turned eighteen." She darts a look at me. "My Zachary wasn't bad, but after he met them, he changed. He got into trouble, but he wasn't a bad boy. I told the same to the detective that was here, but he wasn't interested."

"I'm interested."

She considers me.

"Can you tell me who called you to the scene that night?" I ask.

I distinctly remember the paramedics saying there was no ID on Zachary. So, how did Mama know about it and get to the scene before the media?

She shrugs. "I don't know who it was. One of his friends, I guess."

I think she does know, but she's not going to tell me. She may blame Zachary's criminal activity on other men, but she's not about to rat on them, maybe because she's afraid, or maybe because I am an "other" in her world.

Chapter Seven

When my cellphone rings with a number I recognize as Internal Affairs, I almost don't answer. Even without a vision, I know it's bad news. On the fifth ring, I snatch it up.

"Hello?"

"Officer Brighton?"

"Yes."

"We need you to report to IAD this afternoon at 2 p.m."

I take a breath. "More questions?"

"A polygraph exam."

Jesus. The Fraternal Order of Police attorney has explained this to me. If I refuse to take one, I can be fired. If I take it and fail, they can fire me, but can't use the results in court. This is going to be a disaster.

"I'll be there."

HAVING RUBBER TUBES AROUND MY chest and stomach, a blood pressure cuff on my arm, and electrodes on my fingers is unnerving. It's not the first time. I sat in a seat like this as part of my hiring process, but there was just a job at stake. Today, it is *my* job, a job that has somehow become very important to me.

I answer the questions the operator asks, waiting for the big one. It comes.

"Did you see a gun in the suspect's hands before you fired?"

I focus on the shadow man raising his arms, on Paul falling.

"Yes."

It's not until the next day, day four since the shooting, that I get another call.

"Did I pass?"

"There was some discussion about your results, but, yes, you did."

Relief floods me. "What happens next?"

"Report to Burglary Unit tomorrow morning at 8 a.m."

"Burglary? But I'm a rookie. I just got off a training car."

"That's what I've got, Brighton. Report to Burglary. It's in the Admin building."

I'M NOT HAPPY REPORTING TO my new boss, Lieutenant Jake Fisherman, though I realize working in the Detective Bureau is considered a perk. In fact, it's an unheard of perk for a rookie fresh off a training car and bound to cause resentment. I am happy, however, to be back at work after days of stewing about everything. Transferring me to a plainclothes unit, I realize, gets me off the streets and keeps me out of the public eye ... and any further "trouble."

I'm not stupid. I saw the marchers on TV. The PD has wrapped up my case. The state is still investigating, but the chief has decided not to fire me, for now. He has sent the case to the District Attorney. It's in the DA's hands whether to pass the buck to the Grand Jury. If he does, they will decide whether there is probable cause to charge me criminally or not. But since only the prosecution presents their side to the Grand Jury, it is, for all intents and purposes, the DA's call.

Meanwhile, I have to deal with my own ghosts. *Zachary did have a gun*, I tell myself over and over. He *was* going to shoot Paul in that alley if I hadn't shot him first. I am *not* crazy ... *am I? How would I know? Does an insane person feel normal? What is normal, anyway?*

Crazy or not, I now work in the Administration Building as a burglary detective, the lowest rung of detectives. One of the first things drummed into us at the Academy was the difference between a burglary and a robbery, a distinction citizens often miss. Burglary involves breaking and entering of a building, and robbery is a theft by means of a threat, usually a weapon. The more violent the crime, the more status the detective has in the unofficial internal hierarchy. In addition to burglaries, my lowly unit catches most anything else that comes along that isn't a homicide, assault, robbery, juvenile, or vice/drug-related crime.

I knew I had to wear something better than my jeans and tee, so, in desperation I called Becca. "At least you get to ditch the uniform," she said. Even under the apron they make her wear, she always dresses in nice clothes and heels. For me, not wearing a uniform was no consolation because I hate shopping. According to Becca, this means something is wrong with my DNA.

However, having no love for or expertise in shopping, I was more than happy to take her with me. Other than my uniforms, I owned three pairs of jeans, a drawer full of tee shirts, a couple of other shirts I got at a second-hand store, and one drawer of sweatshirts for winter. I'm not exactly a social butterfly. My idea of relaxing is a hike in the woods, a movie, or sitting by the fire with a good book. After multiple rejections, the guys at the precinct assumed I was gay and left me alone. I'm not gay; I'm just not interested. Maybe the guy in college who called me a frigid bitch was right.

In any case, with Becca's help, I ended up with a tailored white shirt and navy jacket with matching slacks. She insisted I needed more than one outfit, so I bought the same thing in black and in brown with an off-white blouse for variety. She said I looked stuffy and had no imagination. We almost had a fight over the shoes.

"I cannot chase a bad guy in heels, Becca!"

We ended up with a flat-heeled compromise, not as comfortable as my boots, but workable. And one little black dress that Becca found on sale and insisted I buy because I looked "absolutely fan-tas-tic" in it, and "everyone *must* have a little black dress."

Finding a purse that could carry my gun was another adventure. Off-duty, I generally keep my duty weapon, which has been returned, on my hip and hide it with a light jacket or stick it in the fanny pack I carry, but now I'm going to be on duty in plainclothes, and the slacks I bought aren't going to work with a belt. I finally ordered a purse with a hidden inner pouch from a law enforcement specialty magazine and paid a fortune to have it shipped overnight. My gun fits inside and is accessible with a pull of Velcro, and I can shoot it through the purse if necessary. I desperately hope it will never be necessary. I don't trust myself anymore.

I feel awkward and strange reporting to the second floor of the Admin building and Lieutenant Fisherman. He is short and balding with a long rectangular face and prominent eyes that rarely blink. I am actually taller than he is, even with the flats. Paul says the detectives refer to him as "Fish" behind his back. Fish gives me a very cold look-over before showing me my desk. That shouldn't be surprising. The lieutenant is always the bad guy in the detective movies.

No one else inhabits the office, which has ten desks. "Where is everyone?" I ask, as he dumps a pile of reports in front of me.

"Out working."

"Oh."

"Here are this week's cases. Expect to get a hundred or so a month."

"Is there some kind of detective class I should attend?"

He snorts. "You think they're going to give a class just for you? Normal turnover isn't until after the chief makes promotions. Then they'll have a class, and you can go to that one."

"Uh, when might that happen?"

"Might be a while."

I know they made promotions while I was on administrative leave. I went to the ceremony to support Paul. Okay, I was also curious about his family— he has a sister in Idaho who didn't come and no girlfriend showed up. Not that he has ever talked much about personal relationships. He seemed pleased that I came.

"So, it's a year before the next promotions, right?" I ask.

"At least, unless there's another lawsuit over the tests."

"So, what am I supposed to do?" I point at the pile of paperwork.

"Call the victims or go see them; determine if there are any clues overlooked. If you develop a suspect"—his tone indicates that is a highly unlikely scenario—"take it to the screening DA … um, assistant district attorney." At my blank look, he adds, "At the county courthouse, to see if you have a case. They screen all felonies."

"Can I put in a request to go back to Patrol as soon as possible?"

He looks at me as if I ate a cat. "You want to go back to Patrol?"

"Yes, sir," I say respectfully and hopefully.

He shakes his head. "Not happening, *Detective* Brighton. Get used to it."

BEING A DETECTIVE DOESN'T AFFECT my rank. I am still a police officer, paid the same as I was in Patrol. Some of the detectives are officers, some are sergeants, like Paul. Internally, there is a cultural status ranking determined by where you work. Juvenile Unit is on the bottom, followed by Burglary, then Robbery, with Homicide at the top. Vice/Narcotics and the Tactical Unit are in a special class by themselves.

One perk that distinguishes a detective, besides working in plainclothes, is the use of a city car. Of course, I am at the bottom of the barrel and get the oldest, most ragged-out one in the department. It doesn't matter; it's newer than my own car. I take it to the car wash on 6th Street, paying for a detail job out of my own pocket. It's expensive, but I tell myself it's worth it to get the car clean. I'm lying to myself again. This is something I need to do.

I'm probably the first client the Echols Brothers' carwash has ever had that was shaking in her flat shoes when she turned over the keys. Feigning a concern for my car, I decline to sit in the inside waiting area and instead, hover around the workers. Rap music thumps while the shirtless youths wash and rinse the car.

I am operating on the hopeful theory that the weird stuff wasn't me at all. It was Zachary, the young man I shot. After all, he's the one that split in two. I just watched. But the young men laugh and joke with each other, and none of them exhibit any particular behavior that would account for Zachary's conversion to the dark side.

I am left thinking about going back to the counselor and asking for help.

But there is something else I need to do first.

Back at the office, another detective is there. Based on my one-day experience, this is unusual. He actually stands as I come in, towering over my five feet eight inches, and offers a big paw of a hand.

"Hi. I'm Tracey Lohan. You must be the new guy. Sorry, I mean—" He closes his eyes. "Maybe I should just stop right there."

"Maybe you should," I agree, but I shake his hand. His long fingers and hand swallow mine.

He smiles. It's a nice smile, and I forgive him. "How long have you been in Burglary?" I ask.

"Four years too long. But it's better than the street, I suppose."

"Is it?"

His mouth twists. "Actually, I hate it, but no one's ever asked before."

"I've only been here a half day and I already hate it."

"Well," he looks over his shoulder at the lieutenant's office and lowers his voice. "Don't let Fish bother you. He gets up on the wrong side of the bed every day. You may have noticed that people don't stick around in the office. That's one of the benefits. Nobody cares where you go or what you do, as long as you contact your victims and produce a court case every now and then."

"Then what are you doing here?" I ask.

"Well, I am rookie enough or stupid enough to require time to read through my cases."

His reference to himself as a rookie with four years in Burglary and an unknown number in Patrol makes me feel worse. There is no way I should be here. I should be in Patrol on the 11 p.m.–7 a.m. "morning shift" with Tuesdays and Wednesdays off, working utility—filling in when someone's partner takes off. Then, eventually, I would earn the privilege of having my own beat car assignment and maybe enough seniority to go to the day shift or evening shift or get a shot at detective. But here I am, a green-as-grass rookie, fresh off her training car. I know I'll be hated. I'm surprised Tracey Lohan even spoke to me.

I sit in my chair and fiddle with the stack of papers. "I guess that's no different than Patrol," I say, responding to his implication that most of the guys don't break their necks working hard. "Some people 'work' their beats, and some just answer calls and do the minimum to get by."

"True. By the way, we dusted for fingerprints on that burglar you and Nix ran down."

He has my complete attention now. "That's *your* case?"

"It's my case as a burglary. Homicide stuck their nose in it because of the shooting."

"Right."

"The prints matched the suspect's," he said. "I thought you'd like to know that."

I take a breath. So much has been whirling in my head, I hadn't even thought about whether the man I shot had actually been the burglar, or if there had even been a break-in. I was thankful, I guess, to know that. "Was, um, anything taken?" My fingers play with the strap of my purse where the pendant, wrapped in a plastic baggie, resides.

"Nope. He must have gotten scared off. The victim said nothing was missing."

Another breath. The jewelry had nothing to do with the break in. It was just something I found. A little weight lifts off my shoulders, because I know I couldn't have given it back. I don't wear jewelry. It's not that, it's something else. I feel connected to it somehow.

"Hey," Tracey says, opening the top drawer of his desk and offering me a chocolate chip cookie, something I have never turned down in my life. "I know you haven't had the opportunity to attend the classes for detectives," he says, "such as they are. Can I help you with anything?"

I take a cookie and glance at my purse. "Um, can you recommend a knowledgeable pawnshop jeweler?"

"Sure." He scribbles a name and address on a pad. His handwriting is a mess.

"You should have been a doctor," I say, squinting to try and read it.

I'm rewarded with a broad smile. "Maybe. Can you read it?

"Barely."

"Anything else I can do?"

I point at the computer that I apparently share with the person who is supposed to sit next to me. "Is this the same system that Patrol uses?"

"Yep".

The next few hours I spend calling victims and asking questions about their car or house break-in. They seem glad to have someone show an interest, but I figure out there's not much I can do for them. One burglary is fresh enough and has some items the burglar moved that might hold prints. I arrange for an evidence tech to go out and lift them. Then I realize there are no more cases. I've come to the end of the stack, so I access the computer dispatch logs for the night of my shooting.

After that, I go with Tracey for a cup of coffee. I like him. He hasn't once called me a hero or even asked about the shooting or given me the leer-look, though he is clearly interested. Even my stilted social skills can recognize that, but something about his manner puts me at ease. We talk about humorous things that happened in Patrol, and he tells me about his ex-brother-in-law and their camping trips, and we go our separate ways.

"My way" leads to a residence three blocks from where I shot Zachary. It's the origin of the second burglary call, the house Zachary broke into before running down the alley. Despite being a neighbor, I have no idea who lives here, other than the name, Alice Rhodon, which I got off the dispatch records, not wanting to push Tracey for the info. I don't mix much with the neighborhood. Even for gregarious officers, socializing with citizens is difficult, and it's doubly hard if you patrol the same area you live in, as I do. People want to talk about their problems or the time some officer pulled them over and gave them a ticket for speeding (which they weren't doing, and why weren't the cops out doing "real" police work anyway?). It's easier just not to participate.

The house is typical for Southside, with a miserly front yard, wide porch, and a façade of stacked, rust-colored native stone. Pots of herbs crowd the concrete ledges on either side of the front steps. From the top of the porch ledge, two cats idly observe me, only their tails twitching. One is completely black, the other is black with white paws, chest, tail tip and a trail of white down its nose. For no discernable reason, the hairs on my arms and the back of my neck rise, along with the feeling of being watched by eyes other than the cats'. A quick scan of the surrounding bushes and yards yields nothing. From inside the house, perhaps?

My knock on the door is answered by a silver-haired woman of indeterminate age. Smile lines feather the corners of her eyes and mouth, but otherwise her skin is smooth, the color of cream and her eyes a startling deep green.

"Are you Alice Rhodon?" I ask, digging for my badge. That was the name on the burglary report.

"I am. Come in, dear," she says in a crisp British accent without glancing at the badge. "I've been expecting you."

Chapter Eight

"You're expecting me?" I ask the petite woman at the door, as I step inside the house that Zachary broke into the night I shot him. "Do you know who I am?"

"Yes, dear."

"You know I'm a police officer?"

"That's not what I meant, but come in. Would you like a cup of tea?"

I find I would like some tea. Maybe it's the accent, or maybe I hope it will settle the chill bumps on the back of my neck. "That would be … nice."

Both the black and the black-and-white cat slip like shadows into the house. Unlike the city's therapist, the woman waves me toward a comfortable-looking chair. As soon as I sit, a third cat jumps in my lap, turns once before settling, and gently kneads my thigh. I have never been an animal person, and I'm not sure what to do, but I don't push it off. Instead, I distract myself by studying the room.

Books, wooden sculptures and nick-knacks crowd every space not occupied by a plant. The sculptures appear to be primarily from India and Africa. No paintings on the wall, though a lovely tapestry that looks like it might be Native American hangs beside the brick fireplace. It all seems cobbled together, but in an interesting and somehow familiar way.

She brings me a steaming cup that smells inviting and pats a stray strand of gray hair back into her neat bun.

"Thank you."

"Are you peckish? I have some biscuits."

"What?"

"Oh, sorry, I slip into old habits. Are you hungry?"

"No, thanks." I look down at the tea, which has real leaves in it and smells lovely. "What is this?"

"Ginger, lemon, and fresh mint. My name is Alice."

"Officer Brighton, I mean, Detective Rose Brighton." I don't normally give civilians my first name, but I am sitting in her living room having tea with her cat on my lap, and it just seems right. Not sure what to say, I look down at the occupant. It is a beautiful creature with unusual coloring, a light fawn color with dark brown points on face, tail, and paw.

"What kind of cat is this?"

"Charlie is a Siamese and very particular about laps. He must approve."

Tentatively, I run my hand across his silky back, igniting an inside motor.

"Rose, I am so glad you are finally here," Alice says. "And please tell me that another rose has found its way into your hands."

The moment of normalcy evaporates. The piece of jewelry that Zachary threw under the house. Had it been stolen from her, after all?

"Yes, I have it."

A flush of embarrassment that I haven't turned it in as stolen property steals up my neck to my earlobes, which I know flame scarlet because I can feel them burning. Fortunately, the curls that escape my attempt at controlling my mass of hair help hide that bit of evidence. *Why didn't I turn it in after I found it?* I just couldn't imagine giving it up, and, I remind myself, Tracey said nothing was taken. Was he wrong or had he lied? And if so, why?

"Are you talking about a piece of jewelry taken from your house?" I ask.

"Of course."

"Can you describe it?"

"I should think so."

She does. There is no doubt I have found its rightful owner. I dig it out of my purse and hold it out to her, unable to control the trembling in my hand this produces. *What is wrong with me?*

She barely glances at it. "Oh no, dear. It belongs to you."

My fingers close before I realize it. "Why do you say that?"

"I was just the custodian, waiting for it to find you, which it has."

"It?"

"The rose-stone."

I am getting more confused the longer I talk with her, and I'm not sure I want to know where this is going.

"I chased a suspect—the one who broke into your house and stole this— down an alley a few blocks from here. He ditched it under a bush. How does that make it mine?"

"Those are just the particular circumstances. It is yours."

I take a sip of the tea, trying to anchor myself on this tilting world of reality.

"I do feel some … attachment to it," I admit, "but I've never seen it before the other day. I'd like to know why you believe it belongs to me."

She sets her own cup on the cherry side-table. Another cat, the black-and-white one with green-gold eyes, lightly leaps into her lap, and she strokes it idly. "I've had the rose-stone for many years, waiting for you to come for it."

I try to absorb this. There has to be a logical explanation here.

"Is it a family heirloom?" This is a stupid question, given all the questions I could ask, but everything seems to be revolving around what Alice Rhodon calls a "rose-stone." It hits me that "rhodon" is Greek for "rose." I know this because my adoptive mother loved flowers, especially rhododendrons, which aren't true roses, but were named after the words for "rose" and "tree." Even my name seems mixed up in this.

Alice's head tilts a bit in consideration. "Much more than a family heirloom, though it has been in your family for many generations." She looks at me with concern. "This is all a bit much, isn't it?"

That is an understatement. "How do you know about my family? Who are you?"

"I'm just an old herb witch," she says with a quirk of her mouth.

I stand, dumping the cat, which lands predictably on its feet with a light *thump* and stalks away. If this woman is a nut case, fine, but if not, she's jerking me around.

"I shot a man," I say, with more emotion in my voice than I want. "A nineteen-year-old—in the back. There's nothing funny about this."

"I am sorry. I should have realized how this all must seem to you. It's just that I've waited so long to see you. But that's no excuse. Forgive me, dear."

The sincerity in her voice buckles my knees, and I find myself sitting back in the chair, embarrassed at my outburst.

"I may be able to help if you will tell me what happened," she says.

One part of my mind says this is too bizarre, but reality has already been shattered, leaving me in a carnival hall of mirrors with an image of an image of an image that reflects to infinity. All the way back … *to the impossible.*

To my surprise, I tell this woman I have just met what I swore I would never tell anyone. "I saw that man shoot my partner, only I saw it *before* it happened." I swallow and add, "If you tell anyone I said that, I will deny it."

Again, to my surprise, she doesn't seem surprised. In fact, she beams at me. "Wonderful. And so young."

"I'm twenty-two."

"I know, but everything is relative."

"So, you don't think I'm nuts?"

"Of course not."

"Then what happened?" *I need to know. Can she tell me?* "Start at the beginning, please."

She purses her lips. "The beginning is too far back, I'm afraid. I know this situation is very personal for you, but perhaps a little physics will help."

"Physics." I don't say it as a question. I am too stunned to get up and walk out, as I know I should. Her name is Alice. Perfect. I've stepped through the looking glass.

"Do you know anything about String Theory?" she asks.

I stare at her for a moment. "Not much." I try—with the part of my mind that is not bouncing around like an excited electron—to remember what I've heard about it. "Something to do with quantum physics."

She beams at me. "Good. That's more than most. It's a theory about what might be the smallest quantum of information, a vibration. You may also know the math for that indicates the possibility of multiple dimensions."

I have heard something like that, but it spins my mind whenever I think about it, and I don't have much call to think about it.

"That however, has been a bit out of favor lately," she says. "But what is interesting is the proposal that from the Big Bang, time moved in separate directions in two universes." Her gaze is bright. She blinks at my blank expression. "There is nothing in the fundamental laws of physics that says time has to move forward, you know. All the equations that best describe our universe—from Newton's gravitation, Maxell's electrodynamics, or Einstein's theories of general relativity or quantum mechanics—they all work just perfectly fine if time goes forward or backward."

"And this is related to me in what way?" My throat is a desert, and I take a desperate swallow of tea.

"Well, that universe with a backwards time-flow might be right 'next door,' if you will. Most of the time, people are completely unaware of it, although there are some who may pick up something out of the corner of their eye or a prickling on the back of their neck or a strong feeling about what is going to happen. Sometimes that means nothing, but perhaps sometimes they've caught a little bleed-over."

I remember my premonition of being watched just before climbing Alice's steps. What pops into my head next is the program I watched on baleen whales, which have a sensory organ no one knew about in their jaw. Do I have an extra sensory organ stashed somewhere? And while I am wondering such, what the hell was that rush of golden-fire thing the night of the shooting? I felt something similar when I first touched the stone pendant. Were the incidents related?

I shake my head at this silliness, reminding myself that I am dealing with a person who is off her rocker. But I plunge deeper down the rabbit hole.

"And how does this other-universe theory affect me?" I ask.

She fixes her green eyes upon me.

"Rose, you are one of those particularly sensitive to seeing through the gap between the universes, essentially through time. Your mother certainly was. You have a gift, an unusual one even in your family, our House."

The world seems to pause. My voice is hoarse. I can feel the pulse of my heart beating in my throat. "What do you mean? What do you know about my mother, my family?"

"I am your family. I'm your great aunt."

I am staring at her. "How do I know that's true?"

With a gentle smile, she pats my hand, which has closed around the rose-stone in a fist.

"Because I kept this for you."

This is the last thing I thought I would find when I knocked on this door. There *is* something about this house, maybe the woman, but it is all too much. I feel smothered, overloaded. There are too many things that don't add up. I need time to figure them out.

"I have to go," I say abruptly, standing.

She looks worried. "But there is so much we need to talk about."

"I can't talk anymore today. Maybe later."

"Rose, wait." Her voice has changed from sweet little lady to something else. "There is more I need to tell you before you go."

I take a deep breath. "What?"

"You must be very careful. I know this doesn't make sense right now, but you and I are the last members of House of Rose. There are people, the House of Iron, who do not want the rose-stone in your hands. I don't want to frighten you, but those people don't want you alive, either."

Chapter Nine

Shaken, I leave Alice's house without pressing her about being related. Family is something I have tucked away and packed down into the darkest part of my mind's closet. I know I'm going to have to dig it out, but I'm not ready. Besides, she might be lying. But why?

It is dusk and the autumn trees, glorious in daylight, are now dark finger-bones brushing in the wind. A light fog blurs everything out of focus. My brief time in Alice's living room has primed me to see monsters in every murky shape. I pull my purse to my chest and work loose the Velcro to the section that holds my gun.

Feeling the need for a little exercise, I had left my city car at my own house and walked the two and a half blocks. How had I ended up living so close to Alice? The pull of the rose-stone? That's probably what she would have said. It has to be coincidence.

Yet I feel the stone's presence in my pocket … and eyes on me again, and Alice's warning worms from my belly. *There are people, the House of Iron, who do not want the rose-stone in your hands, people who do not want you alive at all.*

I don't know about Houses, multiple universes, and time flows, but I believe I am being watched. The feeling is growing stronger. A glance over my shoulder confirms it. A man is walking at a quick pace behind me, and, up ahead, another has just turned the corner and is coming my way. My heart begins to thud, and I slip my hand inside my purse for the reassuring feel of the butt of my Glock 9mm. I don't like being sandwiched, and I cut abruptly across the street.

The squeal of brakes sends jolts of adrenalin into my body. Only a few feet away, a car stops, and the driver's door flies open. "Rose! What the hell are you doing?"

I recognize my training officer before my brain registers the car is a detective's.

"Paul!" I take a deep breath.

"I almost hit you."

"I know. My fault."

"Where's your car?"

"At my house. Give me a ride." I glance up. The men are nowhere, vanished. "Sure."

With relief, I slide into the passenger seat, reassured by his familiar presence. It wraps me in the firm, real universe, a place where witches and men-who-split-in-two don't exist.

Paul is also real, and I take in the familiar sight of him—the stocky, well-muscled shoulders, thick red mustache that matches his hair, and keen blue eyes that miss little. I haven't seen him since the shooting, though the homicide detectives are just down the hall from my office.

"So, how is the burglary detective business?" he asks.

I flinch. "Boring. Wish I was back in patrol."

"Are you kidding? You get a take-home car, plainclothes, day hours."

"I hate it."

He laughs. "I'm not surprised. So ask for a transfer."

"I did."

"And—?"

"And they said, 'No way.' They're not putting me back on the street, not for a long time. I'm going to dump my house phone. Even the city councilors are clamoring for my ass."

"They don't understand what it's like out here."

"Well, I did shoot a man in the back. I can see how that appears."

"The politicians don't care to look into what really happened. They just want to ride the wave. And the department figures to keep you off the street and 'hidden' in the Detective Bureau until the furor dies down."

"Paul, IAD tried to tell me that your story about what happened was different from mine."

He frowns. "They pulled that on you? I hope you didn't fall for it."

"I knew you would have backed me. But we did"—I tread carefully—"we did see the same thing, right?" I watch his face, looking for some sign that he saw something weird that night.

"I saw the gun, Rose. I came around the corner too fast, and I didn't have time to react. He would have nailed me."

"If he had shot," I say quietly.

"That's something you never know. You have to react in that split second, and if you choose wrong or wait too long, there's no second chance. That man made his choice when he decided to break into a house carrying a gun. He chose to run when he saw us, and he chose to point a gun at me."

I want to tell him that it is much more complicated than that, but I don't know how.

"Do you like Homicide?" I ask, changing the subject.

"So far. Haven't gotten a case of my own yet, so I'm just working with another guy to get back in the swing of things."

"Back?"

"Yeah, I worked in Narcotics years ago. That's a different world, but we built cases and took them to the D.A., same as any other detective."

He pulls to the curb in front of my house. "Not a long ride. You out just walking?"

"No, I was interviewing someone. The woman whose house was broken into when we chased that man."

His brows rise. "That's *your* case?"

"Not really."

"Rose, I told you to let it lie. You're going to get yourself in more hot water. They don't like officers under investigation to go around snooping into their cases. And yours is their baby until the D.A. decides whether to prosecute or not."

"I need to know … what happened," I say.

He shrugs. "What's to know? The little twerp broke in, the neighbors called, and he ran. He didn't have a chance to steal anything, but that was obviously his intent. Everything in the house was ransacked."

"Really? Who told you that?" *Did everyone know that but me?*

"A fellow homicide detective."

"The victim told them nothing was taken?" I ask, wanting confirmation of what Tracey told me.

"Apparently."

I bite my lower lip. So Alice didn't tell the police about the rose-stone. But if Zachary had been caught and had it on him, how could she have claimed it? It did fit with what she had said about it being mine, and she hadn't wanted it back. Somehow she knew I had it. *Curiouser and curiouser, Alice.*

"Rose?"

"Oh, sorry, I was just thinking about something."

"You're a born detective; you got good instincts. You'll do fine there."

This is high praise, not something he would have said when he was my training officer. The relationship has shifted, I realize.

"Thanks." I add, "Don't you miss Patrol any?"

He grins. "I miss your fairy tales."

That pulls an answering smile from me. The thing I remember most about my birth-mother is her voice reading to me. I would curl on one side, my sister on the other. Once, when Paul and I were patrolling a quiet street and passed a house with two massive climbing rose bushes, one red and one white, I made a reference to "Snow-White and Rose-Red," one of my childhood favorites. Paul had furrowed his brow and made me tell him the story. It seems no one read him fairy tales as a child. After that, while we drove around, he'd sometimes ask me to tell him one.

"I miss telling them to you," I say, and realize, to my surprise, I do.

As I dig into my purse for my house key, my fingers encounter a folded piece of material. "I almost forgot. I've been carrying this around, waiting for a chance to return it." I hand him the handkerchief he lent me when I upchucked at the scene of the shooting.

"Don't worry, I washed it," I add.

"Glad it was of service," he says, pocketing it. "You owe that to my father."

"I remember he was a policeman in New Jersey."

"Yeah. When I was a kid, I always wanted to be like him, and he would say, 'Son, if you wanna be a cop, you got to always be prepared—carry an extra set of handcuffs and a handkerchief.'"

"Well, tell your dad thank you from a lady in distress."

His mouth tightens. "My father's long dead, but that lady just saved my ass, so it was more than a fair trade."

Paul waits while I open the door to my house. I wave and he drives away. Inside, I turn on the living room lights, not wanting any dark corners, thinking about the sensation of being followed, when I realize I'm not alone.

"What are you doing here?" I say with a start.

A small cat is curled on my favorite chair. Observant cop that I think I am, I completely missed it when I came in. It considers me with unblinking gold eyes. There is no way a cat got into my house … unless I left a window open. I'm a lousy housekeeper, but I'm almost obsessive about two things—a clean bathroom and locking my windows. Okay, not "almost." I am obsessive, checking them all, sometimes twice. But if someone broke in the house and left a window or door open, a cat could have wandered in.

I pull my gun from my purse, holding it close to my body in case someone jumps out at me, and check all the windows and the back door.

The first time I had ever held a gun was at the police academy. In the beginning, the target had a fifty-fifty chance of a hole anywhere on it, but by the end of the three months, I was the best shot in the class. I liked seeing all those punctures in a close pattern on the target and the satisfaction of knowing I made the right choice in killing the cardboard "bad guys" that popped up in Shooter's Alley. What I didn't like was the noise and the sooty gunpowder up my nose. Now, I don't ever want to shoot anything again, even cardboard, but I will have to qualify twice a year, so that is a wish that won't come true as long as I have a badge.

The windows are closed. Locked. All of them.

When I return to the living room, the mystery cat is still there. I sit on the sofa and we regard each other. It is gray and very skinny, and the left ear has a piece missing from some recent mishap. Finally, feeling like a complete idiot, I say, "Did Alice send you?"

No response from the cat, thank God, and my cell phone rings. It's Becca.

"Hey, girl, how's the detective gig going?" she asks.

"Fine. What are you doing?"

"My nails. You?"

"I'm staring at a cat on my chair."

"Really? You have a cat? I didn't know you were a cat person."

"Well, I seem to have a cat, but I have no idea how it got in my house."

"Maybe it ran in when you opened the door. Cats do that. They're quick."

"Maybe."

"Wanna have lunch tomorrow?" she asks.

God, that sounds so normal. "Yes, I'll call you in the morning."

When we click off, the cat looks at me and blinks. I open the front door to see if it will leave, but it doesn't seem the least bit interested in the door or in leaving. I think about picking it up and putting it outside, but what if it "appears" back in my house? That would just be too freaky, and it looks pretty pitiful.

"Okay, you can stay, but just for the night."

I stretch out onto the sofa with my laptop and check my email. By the time I'm through reading a note from Becca telling me about a new outfit she bought and some unwanted attention from her boss at the attorney's office where she works days, the cat has managed to jump onto the back of the couch and from there onto the keyboard of my laptop, draping itself across the keys, as if that were the most natural spot in the world to lie on.

"Well, you're not afraid of people, are you?"

I ease it aside but let it stay draped across my upper leg, its heartbeat warm against my thigh.

My home phone rings.

"Hello."

"You're a murderer, a killer-cop."

So much for privacy. I hang up, careful not to slam down the receiver and startle the cat. There are claws under those little paws. "Well," I say to it with a troubled sigh, "looks like more people than Alice's House of Iron boogey-bears want my ass."

The next hour I distract myself on the Web looking up quantum physics and the nature of time. Both are as strange as Alice claimed—stranger. I actually find the proposal Alice mentioned—that time is an arrow that went both ways from the Big Bang, creating two universes. It appears to be running forward to those inside each universe, but from one universe, time in the other appears to be going backward. *Alice truly did jump through the looking glass.* Maybe what I saw was a glimpse into that mirror universe, in which time is going backwards, and it is slightly out of sync with our universe, sort of jiggling. In that universe I didn't shoot, and Paul died. In this universe, I did. But I shot because I saw what happened … or what was going to happen … or what might happen.

When my head begins to throb, I give up thinking and open a can of tuna for the cat, since I have nothing resembling cat food. It seems happy. By the time I climb into bed, I'm tired, but sleep dances just beyond my reach for what seems like a long time. When I finally drift off, the sensation of a body curled next to me wakes me in a panic, until I feel a soft vibration. I'm not accustomed to sharing my bed, but am too sleepy now to do anything about it besides roll over.

Between two more threatening phone calls, my dreams are dark and confusing. I open a box to find a dead cat that lifts her head and gives me a Cheshire smile. Shapes with red glowing eyes chase me down alleys. I don't have a gun, but Paul appears and calmly hands me a handkerchief.

In the morning, the cat weaves around my feet, and I trip over it and crash into the kitchen table. I'm not a morning person.

I give it the rest of the tuna and put down a bowl of water. Satisfied I've done my duty for the creature, but without the slightest idea how to carry a cat, I pick it up, legs dangling, and take it outside. "Goodbye, cat. Find your way home." Then I am back inside to take a shower and dress and try to act like it's just a normal day, and I am not lost in Wonderland.

Chapter Ten

By midmorning, my head is buzzing. Not that it has stopped since I woke up and almost broke a leg over a cat that wasn't supposed to be there. If—just what if—all Alice said was true?

It would mean I didn't hallucinate seeing Zachary shoot Paul in the black-gray world. It really happened … if "really" is the right word. As strange as that sounds, I almost want it to be true. There's some comfort in the idea that I might not be mentally ill and a menace to society. No, a logical, real explanation must exist, and I'm going to find it.

What all of this has to do with the rose-stone, however, is also a mystery. I put it in my purse before I left the house, loath to part with it. It's a family heirloom, as I had first thought when I saw it in that little boy's hand, but apparently mine, unless Alice was lying. I don't trust her or her motives. How does she know anything about me? That story about being related to me and knowing I would show up is just too convenient. I mentally fuss at myself for leaving before asking her more questions, but I was too unsettled or maybe—being honest with myself—I didn't want to hear what she had to say.

The other thing I want to know is why Zachary stole the rose-stone. How did he even know it was there? Surely there were other things of value in Alice's house, but nothing was found on him. Did he ransack the place looking for it?

Before I leave for my lunch date with Becca, I cancel my home phone line. Internet and TV use cable and I can do fine with just my cell phone. Then I take a detour to a pawnshop with a knowledgeable jeweler. The clothes purchases have cut into my budget but, perhaps infected by Becca's shopping enthusiasm, I purchase a sturdy silver chain for the pendant, one that has three hooks on it, making the length adjustable. I fasten it on the longest hook, so it nestles between my breasts, out of sight alongside the small handcuff key I keep in the same place on a smaller chain.

According to the jeweler that Tracey recommended, the stone is a rare red diamond and the setting is very old. If I decide to pawn it, I could live off it for a while. Keeping it out of sight seems like the best option since I don't want to be a walking target for petty thieves, not to mention whoever doesn't want it in my hands for more cryptic reasons. A safe deposit box is an option, I suppose, but I want the stone close. Can't explain that, but I suddenly don't trust anyone or anything.

Becca is waiting at the Pita Stop, a great Lebanese restaurant not far from my house. She is wearing a lovely suit, pink, with matching purse and heels. Who wears pink? She says clothes are her only vice. As a receptionist at a law firm, her schedule is tighter than mine, so she's already ordered for us. She moonlights at the diner where I met her and takes a few online college courses towards a degree. I don't understand when she sleeps. Apparently, nobody cares what I'm doing, as long as I work my cases and stay out of the office as much as possible, but I feel like a lazy slob next to her.

Plopping into the seat opposite her, I dig into my lamb kabob plate. All this thinking is using up calories, and cooking is not my forte. I survive on tuna fish and peanut butter.

Becca picks up the keys I set on the table. "What's this funny-looking one?"

"Handcuff key."

"Oh, better not lose it."

"Anybody's would work. It's one-key-fits-all, but I have an extra one stored in a strategic place"—I pat my chest—"just in case."

"Just in case what?"

I swallow and reach for the iced tea. "You have no idea what practical jokers policemen are. I have this fear someone is going to think it very funny to handcuff me to a pole or something."

"Right. I should have figured that out." Becca tilts her head and squints at me. "You look tired, Rose. What's wrong?"

Unaccustomed to people who can read me, I wince. "Just a little sleep deprived." I decide not to mention the phone calls. No sense worrying her. "I'm not used to having something in my bed."

For a frozen moment our eyes meet, and we both erupt into laugher. When Becca can talk again, her brown eyes dance with mischief. "The cat, I presume?"

"Yeah."

"If it's somebody else, you'd better tell me!"

"Tell you?"

"Rose, you haven't the slightest idea how to be a girlfriend. Sometimes, I think I'm the first one."

I consider that. "You are."

Her eyebrows lift in what I call the "golden arches" over her eyes. They are as prematurely white as her hair, and she feathers in light-brown pencil, because otherwise, in her words, "they would just disappear" into her fair skin.

"How is it possible that I'm your first friend?" she asks.

"Well, because my adoptive father was military, we moved around a lot. Everyone made fun of my Southern accent for one thing. It made me different, and it's hard to find friends when you're the newcomer all the time ... and besides that, I'm socially retarded."

"You are not."

"You're the one who said there was something wrong with my genes."

"I was just kidding; not everybody likes to go shopping. That doesn't make you a mutant."

Her choice of words makes me squirm. What would she say if I told her what I saw in that alley? I bite my lip. *Do you want to scare the bejesus out of your first real friend?*

Possibly sensing my discomfort, she changes the subject. "Tell me about this cat that appeared in your house."

"It was just there in my chair when I got home."

"Really? Well, she didn't just magically pop into your house. What did you do?"

"I gave it a can of tuna. It looked hungry."

"You fed her tuna?"

"How do you know it's a 'her'?" I ask.

"All cats are female until proven otherwise, but you'd better check that out and take her to a vet."

"Me? Why?"

"Rose, if you've fed a stray cat tuna fish ... you have a cat."

Chapter Eleven

After a fruitless search in the public library during my hour lunch, I take the recommendation of a librarian and make my way to the Reed's Museum of Fond Memories a few blocks away on 3rd Avenue North. A chime announces my entrance. From the moment I enter the store, the concept of witches living in Birmingham loses its absurdity. Anything is possible in this place. Old books line the high shelves, exhaling the smell of dusty pages-ink-binding. The stuffed shelves form a narrow, one-person-wide labyrinth of corridors. Stuck in every possible nook are assorted *things*—old copies of *Life* magazine, a Wonder Woman comic book, a faded wooden postbox, a jack-in-the-box. It is chaos, clutter, overwhelming, wonderful.

The proprietor, Jim Reed, looks like Santa Claus-on-a-diet and seems to know the incredible jumble as one knows the worn paths of childhood memories.

"Of course I have books on witchcraft," he assures me. "I have a bit of everything, and if I don't, I'll find it for you."

He leads me to the occult section, which lives below "true crime" and includes everything from UFOs to astrology. I find several books on witchcraft, including one with recipes, replete with bat's wing and tongue-of-frog. After thumbing through a few such tombs, including The *Dictionary of Witchcraft*, I find nothing mentioning a "House of Rose" or "House of Iron." I didn't think there would be, but it was worth a shot.

From behind me, someone says, "This is my favorite place in this city."

I turn at the deep male, velvet voice and look into a pair of intense blue eyes.

"Do you come here often?" he asks.

My earlobes burn when I realize several seconds have passed without an answer from me.

"There are wonders here," he says in a lovely accent I think is Italian, smiling, but his gaze remains locked on mine and my imagination has us both under some kind of spell. Maybe it is the book section I am in.

Mr. Reed intrudes into the vibrating space between us and puts a small, worn book in my hands. I sneeze violently from the dust on it, bent over double, and when I look back up, the man has disappeared. I start to ask Reed if he knows anything about him, but I don't. I am annoyed that I had a patently physical reaction to a stranger for no reason.

"What's this?" I ask, holding the book a distance away to keep from sneezing again.

"Something I forgot I had," Reed says. "It looked interesting, and I stuck it somewhere to look through and forgot about it. It seems to be a diary in another language. There are only a few pages to it, but I don't have the time to figure it out."

The faded red-gold ink on the cover seems to be in the shape of a star, which is an old occult symbol, possibly because it was originally the symbol for knowledge of the stars and Venus, in particular. That was a bit of information I picked up from a novel about the wife of Lot. Inside, in a scrawling hand and in the blackest ink I've ever seen, the first words say:

> Popeth yr ydych yn meddwl eich bod yn gwybod am yr ocwlt yn
> anghywir. Nid yw'r gwir i'w groesawu, ond byddaf yn dweud
> hynny, er bod fy nhŷ damn i mi amdani.

I look up at Reed. "What language is this?"

"Welsh, I think. I've got a translation dictionary here somewhere, if you're interested."

"I am," I say, and he is off to the hinterlands of the jam-packed shop, or perhaps museum is a better word. In a few minutes, he returns with another small book, *The Englishman's Guide to Welsh*.

What would have been the work of a few seconds with a computer takes about fifteen minutes with the book, but I am not about to wait to find out what this says and whether it is of any help. Eventually, I end up with a translation:

> *Everything you think you know about the occult is wrong. The
> truth is not welcome, but I will tell it, though my House damn
> me for it.*

My House. I carefully close the book. "I'll take them both."

When I return to the office after lunch, I'm a little leery at being late, although no one but the lieutenant is present, and he doesn't even look up. Sarge would have chewed my butt both ways to Sunday.

A new report is lying on my desk. It's a "Recovery of a Stolen Gun," and the suspect is in jail. Fortunately, Tracey comes in, because the only other person present is a sour-faced older man who looks like he'd just as soon spit on me as help me, and I'll be damned if I'm going to ask the lieutenant. I know he probably had somebody else in mind for this slot and resents the hell out of me for being in it, regardless of the fact that it wasn't my idea.

"Hey there," Tracey greets me. "How's it going?"

"Fine." I hesitate. "I have a question, if you have a minute."

He gives me his broad smile and a little bow. "My lady."

I can't help smiling back. "Is that supposed to make up for calling me a 'guy'? "

Behind him, Sourface rolls his eyes.

"What's up?" Tracey says, scooting a chair near mine.

I show him the report. "Any advice?"

"Well, you've got to interview him immediately because we're under this stupid court order that says we got twenty-four hours to charge him before he's released."

"Oh, that explains a few things," I say, chewing on the end of a pen.

He drags his eyes from my mouth. "Like what?"

I put the pen on the desk beside the report. "In Patrol, we notified detectives about arrests at all hours of the night. I thought they just wanted to know."

He laughs. "Not hardly. Somebody makes an arrest, you got twenty-four hours to make a case before they walk out of jail, so that's why we rotate on-call. When it's your turn, you may have to get up at three or four in the morning to interview someone. Sometimes you get home and just drop off to sleep and get another call."

I'm beginning to see why detectives don't feel guilty taking long lunches and running a few errands during their shift. "What fun. Doesn't sound like a perk to me."

"It's not, but we earn a lot of overtime."

"All right. I appreciate your help."

"Want me to go with you?" he asks.

"That's sweet, but I can handle it. Can I call you if I have a question?"

"Sure." He scribbles his number. "That's my cell. Got it on 24/7."

"Thanks."

When he returns to his own desk, I plug my suspect's name into the computer to see what I can learn about him before the interview. Darren Jones is a black male, twenty-three years old. He's got a record as long as my arm. I pull up the last case on him, a burglary. His alias is "Carrot Man," and he lives near Zachary, just on the other side of the tracks in Kingston Projects. My breath catches when I scan down to place of employment: Echols Car Wash.

The same carwash where Zachary worked and where I got my car washed!

Before I leave the office, I make sure the lieutenant has my cell number and knows my home number has been disconnected. He gives me a look that could possibly border on sympathy, but quickly covers it with a scowl.

"I'm going to the jail to interview a suspect," I say.

"Don't tell me where you're going to be every minute, for God's sake," he grumbles. "I've got enough to do without having to babysit you."

"Yes sir."

I've been in the city jail countless times, but never past booking. This time, after stowing my gun in a locker and getting buzzed through the layers of security, I'm shown the little interview room where I'm to wait for Mr. Jones. I'm not happy. I don't like close spaces, and this is tight. Four blank walls and a small table. Metal chairs. Fluorescent lights overhead. I can reach out and touch two of the walls. Until he arrives, I leave the door open and concentrate on my breathing.

The reason for my suspect's alias of "Carrot Man" is obvious as soon as his lanky frame blocks the door. Orange hair sticks up in spikes from his head. He was not among the men I saw at the car wash. I would have noticed. He's hard to miss.

I stand and introduce myself. He takes my offered hand but averts his eyes. I close the door to the interview room, which is more like a cell. Grimly, I focus on him to keep from thinking about the walls. When we both sit, I explain that I'm here because he was arrested for possession of a stolen gun, and I want to hear his side of the story. I've never been a detective, but I've learned something from listening to Paul interview people. Everybody wants a chance to tell his side.

Tracey gave me a stack of forms with the Miranda warnings printed on them. I read Carrot Man his rights and get him to sign the form that indicates he understands them. Then I refer to the police report. "It says that the police stopped you in Southside, and you threw something into the bushes, which turned out to be a packet of prescription drugs, 'a controlled substance.' They patted you down and discovered the gun. Is that what happened?"

"I didn't throw nothin' down. They lied about that."

"Okay, what about the gun?"

He shrugs, a sulky scowl on his face. "I got a right to carry a gun for my protection. How was I to know it was stolen?"

"So you didn't buy it from a gun store?"

"No." His gaze darts everywhere in the room except on me.

"Where did you get it?"

"Some white dude."

"Mr. Jones, you're going to have to do better than that if you want my help."

"I don't know his name."

"You know possession of a stolen gun is a serious charge, especially on top of your record. If you didn't steal it, do you want to take the rap for it?"

"I didn't steal it."

"Then tell me who did, so I can take the charge off you."

"I don't know his name. He comes to the carwash sometimes and gets us to do things for him."

"Echols?" I ask, keeping my voice matter-of-fact, but I can feel my pulse throbbing in my neck.

"Yeah."

"What kind of things does this white man get you to do?"

"Just odd jobs."

Like breaking into houses and stealing a particular piece of jewelry?

On a hunch, I ask, "Did you know Zachary Fields?"

Startled, he gives me a sharp look, his gaze meeting mine for the first time. "Why do you ask that?"

I make a guess. "You called his mother the night he got shot, didn't you?"

A widening of his eyes tells me I hit a home run, but his lips tighten.

"You were with him that night." I say it as a statement. Let him think I know more than I do. I'm winging it, but maybe Paul is right. Could be I'm not so bad at this.

He looks away. "Maybe. But I didn't do nothin' wrong."

"How do you know him?"

"Zachary?" He shrugs again. "He worked at the Wash."

"Did this white man ever get him to do 'odd jobs,' too?"

"What's that got to do with me?" he says evasively, shifting his lanky frame in the hard chair.

"Maybe nothing, but I can tell the judge you cooperated."

After a long pause, he says, "Zachary's dead, so I guess it don't matter."

I wait.

"Yeah, the dude hired him a few times."

"What does this white man look like?"

His face tightens. "I dunno; I don't remember."

"Why are you protecting him?"

With a deep breath, he says, "That dude, he's got a stony look in his eyes. He'd kill me faster than a snake bites."

Chapter Twelve

That evening, I pay another call on Alice. The black cat and a black-and-white one are draped along the top of the couch's back, watching me, their tails twitching. Charlie, the Siamese, is not in sight. I sit in the chair I sat in on my first visit. The pendant now hangs around my neck under my shirt. I pull it out and cup it in my palm to show it to her. "I took this to a jeweler. He said he'd never seen anything like it."

"Well, he wouldn't have."

"What is it, and what does it do exactly, and why is it mine?"

"Those answers will require more tea." She patters to the kitchen while I stew and returns with a little hand-painted teapot, pouring the hot water into my cup and hers. Then she settles back, and the black cat claims her lap. "This is Alexander," she says and the black-and-white boy, the tuxedo, is Boo."

"The stone, Alice?" I say, steering us back on track.

Boo jumps from the couch to the floor and sits at Alice's foot, swiping at Alexander's twitching tail.

"I wish I could tell you," Alice says, "but I was not in line for it. The rose-stone is worn by the *Y Tair*. I've always wondered if it might be something like a crystal radio in the sense that it vibrates at the received frequencies of energy used for our magic."

I look at her blankly and try to suppress the itch of frustration. "I'm sure that's connected somehow to quantum physics," I say, dryly.

She brightens, ignoring the sarcasm in my voice. "Most certainly, but we don't understand how it works."

I want to scream, but blow on my steaming tea instead. *Don't get angry.* She's making perfect sense to herself. I press my lips together and try to focus on why I am here. This is an interview. It's my job to bring the interviewee around to an answer that makes sense to me, even though I haven't had a lick of training at it. With great patience, I take a sip of the tea and burn the hell out of my tongue.

"Oh," Alice says, catching the expression on my face. "I hate it when that happens. Would you like a piece of ice?"

I take a breath. "No, I would like an answer that I can understand."

She sniffs. "Perhaps you are not asking the right questions."

Maybe she's right. "Let's take this from another angle. How did I 'inherit' this rose-stone?"

"From your mother, of course, as first born. And she from her mother, back into the mists of time."

The mists of time? I hold my scalded tongue from its craving for sarcasm. "What do you know about my mother?"

"She was my niece—"

"You're still claiming you're my great aunt?"

"Of course. I *am* your great aunt."

The implications of this float on the surface of my brain, refusing to sink in.

"The rose-stone is genetically coded or perhaps entwined to you," Alice says, her attention seeming to wander for a moment. "Do you know about entwined particles? They act as if they are the same particle—what you do to one affects the other, no matter what distance is between them. At least, that is the best explanation I've been able to come up with. Our ancestors have always called it magic, but they would have called telephones, the telly, and cars magic. Just because we don't understand doesn't mean there isn't an explanation, but we're not there yet, so we still call it magic."

"Genetically coded," I repeat flatly, ignoring the prattle about magic.

She nods.

"To *my* genes?" I want this clarified.

"Well, to what you've inherited from your mother's line, possibly in the mitochondrial DNA." At my blank look, she adds, "That's DNA inherited only from the female line, all the way back to the first mother." She taps a finger against her tea cup. "But that's just a possibility. I could be wrong about it. What I do know is that the rose-stone is yours."

I totally lack the background to understand this, but if I get bogged down trying to, I will never make it out of this morass. I decide to plunge into her world and see if I can catch her in an inconsistency.

"How did you happen to have the 'rose-stone' if it belonged to my mother?"

"Members of House of Rose are primarily healers," she says, "but your mother, Kathryn, could scry a bit. She saw little pieces of future happenings—a very rare thing. There hasn't been a real scryer in the family for two hundred years or so before your mother. On occasion, I have strong feelings about the future, but I've never 'seen' it in detail like she could. I don't know what exactly she saw that made her bring the stone to me, but she told me to keep it safe for you."

My mother—what an empty ache resides around that word. Of course, I did have a mother growing up. My adoptive mother was a kind woman, but I always knew there was another I was tied to, a presence beyond the reader of fairytales.

"So she gave you the rose-stone because of a vision?" I ask.

"Indeed, but just for safe keeping. It was always yours. I knew you would come for it one day when you were ready, and I had one of those strong feelings that the time was imminent the day before you showed up. That's why I brought it out of its hiding place."

I don't say anything, waiting.

"To polish it for you," she says. "The setting was tarnished, but when I went to polish it, I realized I didn't have any silver polish in the house. So I stuck it in a kitchen drawer and went to my yoga class. I go every Tuesday." She beams proudly. "I intended to get some polish the next day, but that man broke in my house." She sniffs. "He would never have found it otherwise."

"So, you did tell the detectives nothing was stolen?"

"Well, heavens, I did not want the police to report a priceless piece of jewelry had been filched and have the media going on about it! That would let House of Iron know it was out there in the world, ripe for plucking."

"I see. And nothing else was stolen?"

"That's right, although that man rifled through things." She draws her shoulders back in obvious indignation.

"I can't imagine you have nothing else of value," I say.

"I certainly do. My mother's china and, of course, my plants."

"I don't think he would have had any desire to steal your plants."

"Rubbish. Other than the rose-stone, they are the most valuable items in my house."

"Rare plants?" I hazard.

"Oh yes, many of them. I brought them from England long ago. They come from all over the world." Her eyes are bright.

My brain is fried. "Who are you really?"

She sighs. "Your great aunt, dear, as I said. But that's not the most important thing at the moment."

"And what would that be?"

Her green eyes meet mine. "House of Iron knows who you are, now that you've claimed the rose-stone. Every … um … member of the Houses within miles must have felt that hum—and I'm afraid they will try to kill you."

The "House" thing again. I haven't had time to translate more of the Welsh diary, but I did feel a rush of warmth course through me when I touched the rose-stone for the first time.

No! This is all absurd. I am dealing with a nut case. Psych 101 supplies a label—a paranoid schizophrenic—someone who has broken with reality and thinks they are in the middle of a conspiracy. Having a bachelor's degree in psychology barely qualifies me to recognize the symptoms, and I'm completely untrained in how to respond, so I put on my detective hat. "Why would people want to kill me?"

"Oh, that's a very long story. Have you ever heard of the War of the Roses?"

"Umm, sort of. I mean I know it refers to two royal houses in England who fought over the line for the king. That's about it."

"Correct, basically—the houses of Lancaster and York. Well, there are two Houses involved here. Three actually."

"Are you telling me you're royalty?" Another psychology label pops into my head—"delusions of grandeur."

She laughs. "No, I told you, I'm just a—"

She stops at the look on my face. If she says she's a *witch*, I'm out of here.

"I'm a member of your family, House of Rose," she says with a little clearing of her throat. "As I mentioned, we are the last."

This is too much, but I'm caught up in the intricacy of her fantasy. "And House of Iron wants to kill me. You said there's another House?"

"There is, House of Stone, but the important one is the House of Iron, the warlocks, we call them, though they don't care for the term." She ignores my frown. "Their heritage descends through the male line."

"And you know for a fact that the 'warlocks' are the people who want to kill me?"

"Indeed." She frowns. "Well, my niece, your mother, thought so and she was the one with prescience. Besides, it's the only theory that makes sense."

"So"—I cannot help the sarcasm in my voice—"the bad guys are guys, although I suppose there must be women in the House of Iron, or there would be no male children."

"Oh, absolutely. Identically for the House of Rose, except our power descends through the women, but we marry, of course."

"And what made your niece—I won't call her my mother—decide this Iron House is full of murderers?"

"Well, I don't know everything she knew, but she said she found a black rose on the doorstep one night—"

"Please." My head is beginning to thrum.

"Well, I'm sure that wasn't the only thing." She takes a breath. "To be honest, I don't know because I didn't grow up here. I stayed in England for much of my life, and she was very secretive about her personal life and the rose-stone. All I know is that the *Y Tair* wore it and that was always someone from the House of Rose. I'm sure she meant to tell you when you were old enough to understand, but … she never got the chance." Tears fill her eyes.

"The *Y Tair*?"

"It means 'The Three' in Welsh."

Welsh—that's the language in that little book I bought that spoke of 'Houses.' I haven't had the opportunity to translate more of it.

I try another angle. "So why are these Houses here in Birmingham, Alabama?"

She takes a sip of tea. "The ores, my dear. We are all here for the treasures in the earth. It gives us power, and we—along with the mining industry—have pretty much exhausted Britain's quality seams over the centuries."

I take a deep breath. "I think it's time for me to go." As if on cue, Charlie appears and rubs his head against my ankle and leaps into my lap.

"If you must, but there is one thing I must make very clear." She waits to be certain she has my attention. "It's the time of year for it, but you must not, under any circumstances, accept any invitation from the House of Iron."

I set my teacup on the table, wanting to laugh at the absurdity. "Invitation to what?"

"On All Hallows' Eve, it's an ancient tradition that the Houses put aside their enmity, and Iron always puts on the 'do.' "

"The 'do'?"

"The celebration, the party."

The cat on my lap digs claws into my thighs, and I jump. With care, I ease the curved daggers out of my pants leg and hold his paws, not knowing what else to do besides dump the creature on the floor again, which seems rude. Despite all this, I like Alice, though her namesake, the one who stepped through the looking glass, seems no more fantastical than this one.

"So," I say slowly, "you're warning me not to go to a Halloween party hosted by the House of Iron?" I suppress the slightly hysterical laugh that bubbles against my chest.

"You must not go, Rose." The pleasant curve of her mouth turns grim. "I know you will be curious, but please listen to me. *Don't go.*" Her eyes are moist. "I gave up so very much. It's been very difficult watching you grow up from afar."

A dozen questions spin through my mind, but the one that comes out is, "Why? Why did you have to watch from afar?"

"You were so young and vulnerable. I couldn't keep you," Alice says. "I put you in foster care out-of-state when your parents died, and signed off on the adoption, but I kept up with you all these years. I sent money." She looks down. "I know that seems a poor substitute for family, but you were able to have nice things and go to college, and I've been very proud of you."

I stare at her, stunned.

"If I had kept you," she continues, "it would have made you a target; they would have hunted you down. It was no accident that killed your family."

Her words catch me up in a wave that spills into the past, a place I work hard never to go—

I was four maybe five years old. It was night. I was in the bathroom when the shooting began—a muffled pop-pop. I climbed into the tub and hid, crouched at one end, clenched against the moment when the bad man or monster would rip back the shower curtain and see me.

A door slammed open. Booted steps, a man's tread, clicked down the hall.
More pops.

It seemed forever before I could move, much less climb out of the tub. Fumes permeated the house. Gasoline.

I had a Sleeping Beauty blanket. Amber had Cinderella. The Mickey Mouse nightlight bathed our twin beds in a soft glow.

I looked first to my bed, where the covers crumpled over the pillow. Small puncture holes riddled Sleeping Beauty. Blood dripped from my sister's bed onto the floor. Amber was tangled in her sheets ... so still. Cinderella's dress soaked red.

I couldn't wake her.

Boot heels from the hall. I climbed onto Amber's bed to reach the windowsill, tumbled through the open window to the ground and crawled into a row of azalea bushes. From my nest beneath the bush, I saw the slight billow of the curtain and a tall, thin man in a black overcoat jump out. He lit a match, holding the small flare level with his gaze and tossed it inside.

"I ran somewhere." With a start, I realize I spoke aloud.

"You came here, dearest." There are tears in Alice's eyes. "You were only five. You lived next door then."

Of all things, that feels the oddest. The house I lived in was next door, only two blocks from where I now live. Had my subconscious brought me to the neighborhood of my childhood?

My hands are shaking, my breathing shallow and quick. Those memories were buried so deep, I hadn't thought about them since ... since I went to see Zachary's mother. It is no wonder I wanted to be a cop, a hero, to have the power to stop that man, to back up time, to save my sister, my parents.

I catch my breath. *Back up time!* Is there a way to do that? To reverse time to a "when" where my sister and parents were still alive? Or some way I can, at least, find the man who killed them? My fingers clench the stone. For the first time, I feel something other than disbelief and confusion at the thought that I might have inherited something powerful—I feel hope, and a ridiculous, irrational determination that burns like a flame in my chest.

Chapter Thirteen

In the daze that seems to follow each visit to Alice's house, my feet carry me down the sidewalk. *Aunt Alice.* My hunt for childhood memories of her brings only vague images of a closet shelf with a black tin that harbored colored hard candies and a box full of buttons that seemed a treasure chest. I must have been in her house several times, which makes sense since it was just next door. It also makes sense that I would have gone there after the fire. Or maybe she came outside and found me. I'm fuzzy on the details. She told me she sent me away for adoption as soon as possible for my protection.

After the fire, Alice had my name included in the local obituaries and put a headstone at Elmwood Cemetery with my family. I don't know how she did it, but somehow she pulled it off that I had died in the fire. The house had burned to ashes. The murderer who shot my family got sloppy and apparently assumed it was me, rather than a pillow, under the covers. I still sleep curled around a pillow, but now I also have a gun under one too.

Was the killer in the city, and was he really a warlock or whatever, and if so, what was he thinking almost twenty years later when I touched the rose-stone and the world "hummed," signaling I was alive? Or is that story just a wild tangle in Alice's mind?

The whine of an accelerating engine breaks into my spinning thoughts, and I glance up to see high-beam headlights approaching from a cross street. *Why is that idiot going so fast in a residential zone?* Anger surges through me, along with frustration that I can't do much about it except report him on my cell phone. By then he'll be long gone.

In the next heartbeat, something *wrong* registers in my brain. This car is going too fast to make a turn, and *it's headed straight toward me!* I break into a run, but there is nothing but open space. Only seconds before the car bears down on me. My hand instinctively gropes for my gun, but there is no time for that; no time for anything except a stunt I have seen in the movies.

Just before contact, I jump up onto the hood, rolling, protecting my head with my arms. The *slam* of the windshield might as well be a brick wall—the lights go out.

VOICES FLOAT LIKE ELUSIVE BUTTERFLIES, unconnected to anything. A white light entices me, and I make an effort to move toward it, but it is a lot of trouble, and I'm too tired.

Darkness again.

This time my eyes flutter open, and I wish immediately for the darkness. It takes a while to identify where the hurt is. My foot and shoulder are screaming *pain*, and there seems to be a sharp knife lodged in my side.

"Rose?"

The blur that spoke focuses into Becca in a brown suede skirt and a green knit sweater that matches her earrings. Becca believes that dressing well in all situations is a matter of manners.

"Thirsty," I croak.

She plucks a cup from a tray. A straw pushes tantalizingly against my lips, which don't seem to remember how to work. My mouth doesn't seem connected to anything. Then I have it, and sweet, cool water flows down my raw throat.

"What happened?" I croak when I've had enough.

"A car hit you," Becca says. "A man saw it drive right up into his yard. He said you dove on top of the hood and rolled up the windshield and onto the roof, and then the car swerved and dumped you. He said what you did was amazing, and you would be dead if you hadn't jumped."

I feel only slightly this side of dead, but I remember bits—spitting out dirt and grass, voices around me, excruciating pain when I tried to move, feeling every jar of the ambulance, needles and tubes and answering stupid questions.

"It was awesome," Becca says, her eyes shining. "Just like TV!"

"How did you know what he—?"

"From the newspaper. They quoted him," she says, anticipating my question. "It happened yesterday."

One hand, which feels as if it belongs to someone else, lifts in slow motion and goes to my chest. "Where is my—?"

"That fancy necklace? It's safe in your purse. That's some rock, girl!" Her voice modulates to serious. "You have a broken shinbone, a dislocated shoulder, bruised ribs, and you've had surgery, Rose. They had to remove your spleen."

I try to remember what the spleen does and have no clue. Hopefully, that means I won't miss it.

"Oh," I say, still fumbling at my chest.

Again, with remarkable understanding of my ridiculously inadequate attempts at communication, Becca digs in my purse for the rose-stone pendant and fastens it around my neck. Why I want it there is as much a mystery as a spleen's function, but I do. She stuffs it under the front of the hospital gown.

"I bought some cat food and put it on the porch while you were in surgery," Becca says.

"Don't have a cat," I mumble. My eyelids close and I drift away, comforted by her presence and the pressure of the pendant against my neck.

THE NEXT TIME MY EYES open, Becca is still there in the same outfit, and I blink into focus the red-haired man standing next to her.

"You're a mess," Paul says.

Becca's hands settle on her hips in indignation. "That is not the first thing she should hear."

Paul ignores her. "We're looking for the bastard, Rose. The witness got a partial tag, and the feds are running it through NCIC."

I nod, sending a lance of pain into my head.

"Do you know anyone who might want to kill you?" he asks. "Somebody we put in jail maybe?"

"We put a lot of people in jail," I say carefully through my swollen lips. I don't think I can tell him, according to my long-lost great aunt, my attacker was a warlock from the House of Iron.

Paul inclines his head toward the hospital hallway. "We've got a guard on your door. South officers asked for the duty."

I know that normally guard duty at the hospital, which is usually for prisoners, is rotated throughout all four precincts. It makes me feel good that the South Precinct guys still count me as one of their own.

"He's just outside," Paul says.

I'm glad, and glad Paul is here too. I've never felt this vulnerable. My gaze travels over the room taking in a brown reclining chair and a coat and overnight bag, which have to be Becca's, on a cot beneath the window. Then I catch sight of the single rose—so dark red it is almost black—sitting in a vase on the windowsill. My heart skips. "Who sent that?"

Becca moves to the window and examines the flower. "No card." She pouts. "It must be from a secret admirer."

"No card?" I whisper hoarsely, although I heard her plainly.

She crosses her arms over her chest. "You *are* holding out on me."

I swallow. Alice mentioned a black rose left as a warning before the house was torched. That rose is not a message from a lover, though it is a message—a promise of death.

Chapter Fourteen

I am fairly certain Becca and Paul are in my room through the night, despite the officer's presence at the door. Sleep in a hospital is a relative thing, snatched between checks on blood pressure and temperature and pain meds. I have just faded out again when I hear Becca.

"I got her," she says. "Go get some sleep."

I open crusted lids to see Paul's back as he exits and Becca standing at the foot of my bed.

"What about work?" I ask her hoarsely.

"It's Saturday. Nobody says where I have to be on the weekend."

"You don't have to be in a hospital."

Time is a slippery thing for me at the moment, but her outfit confirms the change of day—slacks and a button shirt, accented with a scarf.

"You just don't *get* friendship, do you Rose?"

I ignore the question and eye the cup of water on the tray, wondering if my arm is going to work well enough to reach it.

She follows my gaze and is there before I can make the attempt, fitting the straw between my cracked and swollen lips. "I told you this last night, but I'm not sure you heard me. I put some food and water out on your porch for your cat. Don't want you to worry."

"Don't have a cat," I mutter stubbornly.

"Well there's a little gray feline with a missing piece of ear that seems to have adopted your front porch."

"At least she's not teleported inside the house."

"Does it hurt to talk?" Becca tilts her head sympathetically.

I think about this. My throat is a little sore, probably from the tube they stuck down my throat for surgery, but otherwise talking isn't painful. "Talking doesn't hurt."

"So, what can I do for you?"

I shake my head and stop abruptly. "Oh crap, now *that* hurts." When it subsides, I ask to hear everything she knows about what happened.

"The witness said there was no doubt the car—which, before you ask, was a black Buick—was bearing down on you."

Did they tell me this last night? I don't remember. "Who was the witness?"

"I don't remember his name, but he owns the house next door to the one where you were hit. The car came right up into the yard chasing you down."

"That's it? What about the car tag? Did anybody get it?" I vaguely remember Paul mentioning something about that.

"Part of it. Your detective friend, the big guy?

"Lohan? Tracey Lohan?"

"Yeah, he's been by while you were sleeping. He says they had enough for the feds to run it through their data base, and they decided the tag had been stolen hours before."

No help there. I don't know who the players are yet or how to begin figuring out who was behind the wheel of that car, but a resolve is forming in my mind. I will find out, and if there is any way in heaven or hell, I will find out who killed my family while I'm at it, because I am beginning to believe my Great Aunt Alice is right—they are the same person or people.

Another thought hits me. I can understand how Paul would know what happened. Police gossip would have spread that everywhere fast, but how would he know to contact Becca? I'd be willing to bet they didn't release my name right away to the news media.

"How did you find out about this so fast?" I ask.

"Paul called me. He said you never talked about friends or family, and he didn't know anyone else to call."

THE NEXT TWO DAYS I concentrate on getting out of the hospital. This involves obedience to the doctors and weaning myself from the pain meds, even though they assure me I can go home with some. Paul and Detective Lohan came by a couple of times. I'm grateful to them beyond words, especially Becca, who took two precious days off work and has pretty much lived in the room on a cot the staff brought in for her. She is at my side to help me go to the bathroom, saving me from having to call a nurse or the embarrassment of worrying about my butt showing in the skimpy hospital gown.

On day three, before the doctor thought I would be ready, I hobble up the walk to my house, sandwiched between Paul and Becca. I can only use one crutch because of my shoulder, and my left foot has a clunky plastic boot on it. As we open the door, a gray form streaks between our legs into the living room.

"Told you," Becca says.

Paul wants us to wait on the porch while he checks out the house, but I refuse.

"Rose, what the hell are you protecting in there? You are the singular most stubborn person I have ever met."

"You wait on the porch if you want," I say. "If there's a bad guy in my house, you'll know it."

"How?" Becca asks, eyes wide.

"The gunshot," I say with a grim smile, patting my purse.

"At least let me check the back door and the windows," Paul says.

"Okay." That doesn't involve anyone actually coming inside. I'm not the best housekeeper the world has ever seen, but more importantly, I'm not ready to show my amateurish artwork to anyone.

Paul finds no signs of a break in from the exterior, so I go in and check all the rooms. Then I report back to them.

"Are you sure you don't want me to stay with you for a few days?" Becca asks.

"I'm sure."

"Are you going to be safe?" Becca's lips are curled into her mouth, something she does when she's worried.

"The South Precinct guys will be watching out for me."

Paul looks like he wants to stay, too, but I run them both off. I want time to myself. "I'll call if I need anything, I promise."

When the door closes, I exhale in relief. They've been wonderful, but I crave peace and quiet and my own space. I am stubborn, I'll admit that, but I don't feel that bad.

A tiny meow from under the couch, followed by a pink nose, informs me the space is not totally mine. At least I know how the cat got in the house the night I met Alice. She must have slipped through my legs that first time, too. I hobble to the couch and set my crutch aside, lowering myself carefully down. Almost before my butt hits the couch, the cat is in my lap, circling until she finds the "right" place.

With mixed feelings, I run my hand across her head and back, turning on a motor that vibrates my thighs. How does something that small emit such a powerful sound?

That night, after I am in bed, I find her presence curled next to me a comfort, instead of the annoyance I thought it would be. Maybe it's the pain medicine that makes me so accommodating.

IT'S STILL DARK—THAT'S THE FIRST thing I notice. I am certain a noise woke me. At the end of my bed, the cat stands with her back arched and fur standing on end, hissing at the window, but I see nothing there. *Was someone there?* I feel under the spare pillow for my gun, trying to ignore the pit in my stomach. Maybe I should have let Paul stay. I think about calling 911, but I don't know if there is anything out there. Who knows what upsets a cat—a dog barking, another cat, a bump of a branch against the window? The last thing I want to do is call the precinct and get everyone excited about nothing. *I'll call them after he breaks the window, and I get a clear shot. They can come get the body.*

A flash of lightning illuminates the world outside the window.

Nothing.

I hold the gun fairly steady on the window until the cat's fur settles and she begins to lick a paw. With a deep exhale, I slip the gun back under my pillow.

But sleep does not return.

At 5 a.m., I stop trying and get up. By the time I dress and work a holster onto a belt that fits into the loops on my jeans and hobble to the kitchen, the cat is weaving between my crutch and legs, letting me know with plaintive *meows* that she has not forgotten the tuna fish. The cat may have eaten from the bowl of dry cat food while I was in the hospital, but it sits untouched in the kitchen. I dump the dry food, open my last can of tuna and put some in the bowl on the floor to shut her up.

It's a misty, wet fall morning. Probably muddy. I look at the cat. "Muddy. Hmmm. Let's check it out."

She glances up at me while scarfing down the tuna.

"I'll be careful," I promise.

Getting the one tennis shoe on takes a while, but I want something with grip. The last thing I need to do is slip in the mud and fall. I take two aspirin instead of the pain medicine and shove my phone in the back pocket of my jeans.

With more patience than I can remember ever having, I make my way with my crutch and bootie down the stairs, around the side of the house to my bedroom window. No signs of attempted forced entry on the window, but the wet ground holds a clear imprint. My heart skips. Someone *was* here last night at my window, someone who didn't want to make noise—because he knew I was home? Maybe he'd just checked to see if the window was open. Was this related to the guy who tried to run over me or the threatening phone calls or just an unrelated burglar looking for easy access? None of these possibilities are particularly comforting.

I place a quarter near the imprint for size reference and take a picture with my cell. Then I make my way slowly around to the back of the house. Outside the kitchen window is another partial imprint that seems to match the first.

Suddenly, it is difficult to breathe.

I am standing in the doorway of the room I share with my sister, a gust of air blowing the pink curtain. The smell of gasoline closes my throat....

I CALL PAUL, AND HE has an evidence technician come out to lift prints from the windows, something the police department would never do without at least a break-in. Paul arrives before the technician, and out of gratitude, I invite him in for coffee and biscuits or in his case, milk and biscuits. The biscuits are left over from a fast food haul a few days before the accident, but they smell okay, so I stick them in the toaster oven. While I'm puzzling over making the coffee—I just buy it at a fast food drive-though or a diner. I can't ever remember exactly how much coffee is supposed to go into the filter—Paul wanders through the house. I look up when he stops at the closed door to the study opposite the kitchen door.

"I'd rather you didn't go in there," I say quickly as he reaches for the knob. "It's a ... worse mess than the rest of the house."

His hand drops, but I know from the look on his face he heard something in my voice. Detective Nix doesn't believe my weak explanation, but he doesn't comment.

"I think it's ready," I say and wave him into the kitchen.

The cat jumps onto the counter and from there to the window sill behind the sink, where she stretches out to catch the morning sun breaking through the cloud cover, yawns, and watches us, probably hoping we will move on to something better for breakfast ... like more tuna fish. She looks glossier than she did when she appeared, but her rib bones haven't disappeared, and the tear on her ear is still raw. She'd probably eat herself sick if I let her.

"What's her name?" Paul asks, gesturing toward the cat as he takes a seat at the table.

I start to say she doesn't have one—"She seems to be my guard kitty, so I think her name is Angel."

"No offense, Angel," he says, after politely trying to chew the biscuit, "but I don't like leaving Rose here alone, even with a ferocious guard kitty."

I change the subject. "My mother made great biscuits, but I never got the hang of cooking. Did you break a tooth on that biscuit?"

He laughs. "Almost. Here, let me show you a trick." Ripping off a paper towel, he dampens it, wraps it around another biscuit and sticks it in the microwave for six seconds.

Amazed, I bite into a soft biscuit. "Wow, you are handy."

"I like to cook, too."

Somehow, I'm uncomfortable again. No, "uncomfortable" is not the right word, more like "panic." A man tells me he likes to cook, and I'm ready to run out the door ... of my own house.

When he leaves, I hobble to the bathroom, determined to take a shower. While the water heats up, I survey the damage in the mirror before it steams over. I've pulled my hair back but, as usual, several dark, corkscrew curls have worked their way loose. A deep purple bruise raccoons my left eye, and my upper lip is swollen. My eyes swim charmingly in a sea of broken blood vessels. I must appeal to some protective instinct in Paul, because it is certainly not my beauty that made him stay for stale biscuits.

For the first time since Alice's revelation, or assertion, that she is my great aunt, I see her deep green eyes staring back at me. I always wondered about my family, but I never dreamed there were witches in the woodpile.

People have commented that I look exotic and guessed everything from Italian to Native American, though the eyes throw them off. All I remember of my biological parents is that my mother had long, curly hair like mine, and her breasts were a soft cushion when I curled up for a story or scraped my knees or elbows and wanted comfort, which seemed to be often. My father smelled like pipe tobacco and would throw me in the air to my squealing delight.

My memories of Amber are clearer. Where my hair was dark, my sister's was light brown and fine. I climbed trees and she played with dolls. We fought over everything and bounced on our beds when we were supposed to be sleeping.

With my adoptive parents, I pretended I didn't remember anything about my birth family, because it was easier for everyone, but I knew they were all dead. Little by little, over the years, I think I convinced myself I didn't remember anything about them.

With a sniff, I turn from the mirror. Crying never helps anything, and I've never been able to cry, anyway. I'm sure I did as a toddler, but I overheard my adoptive mother say she was worried about it on more than one occasion. Perhaps it's another genetic defect. The closest I ever come to tears is a knot in my throat and a runny nose.

I unholster my gun and lay it on the toilet seat within easy reach and shed my clothes, moving stiffly. One advantage of the plastic cast on my lower leg is that I don't have to worry about getting it wet. Awkwardly, I climb into the shower, grateful for the rain of hot water.

Chapter Fifteen

Two days later, I am still at home per doctor's orders. When the doorbell rings, I check the window before opening the door. Alice stands on my front porch. I hesitate. Is it wise to let her in? Opening the door to her feels like allowing all the wild reality she represents to be … real.

The casserole pot in her hands decides me. I'm getting weary of tuna fish and peanut butter and even the pizza and the frozen dinners Becca has brought. When Alice steps inside, I know I've made the right decision. The smell from the pot is intoxicating.

"I brought you some chicken-and-dumplings. I'll put it in the kitchen," she says, eyeing my crutch.

I start to follow her, but she waves me to the couch. "I'll set it in the refrigerator and be right back."

Obediently, I sit in my chair. I'm moving better today. And the aspirin seems to be enough to knock off the worst of the pain. I can't afford to be lying around drugged up with someone stalking me.

When it takes her longer than it should to put a casserole into the fridge, I start to fidget. What is she doing? I don't like people in my house, especially out of my eyesight. But she returns with a steaming bowl and puts it in my lap.

"You're too thin," she pronounces. "I decided to heat some up."

My stomach grumbles.

"I would have come to the hospital, but I didn't know what happened to you. I should watch the telly more, but it is just so depressing."

"How did you find out?" I ask through a mouthful.

"My nosy neighbor finally caught me out in the yard and asked if I knew about it. Apparently everyone on two blocks has been buzzing about it. But the important thing is how are you feeling?"

"I'm okay." I squint up at her, a random stab of pain lancing through my head.

"Hmm. Mind if I take a look? I used to be a doctor, you know."

Of course she was and an Indian chief as well. "Why not?"

"I can't heal you," she says. "The Houses are immune to direct use of our abilities on each other, but I can check you out."

"Check me out?"

"Yes, think of it as a sort of scan." She runs her fingers lightly over my head and I feel a flush of warmth from her fingers, a sort of tingling that runs through my body. "No swelling," she pronounces after a minute. "That's the thing to worry about with a concussion."

"After this many days in the hospital?"

"It's rare, but it's happened."

She sits in a chair and Angel instantly claims her lap, kneading her belly. A twinge of jealousy surprises me.

"What's her name?" Alice asks.

"Angel."

"She's a young cat, but she's seen a bit of violence," Alice says, eying the torn ear. "But now, little Angel, you've got yourself a nice home, don't you?" Alice looks up at me. "Has she been much trouble?"

Before answering, I swallow. "She pulled an entire roll of toilet paper off the roll, scratched up the leg of the coffee table and put a hole in my toothpaste."

Alice laughs. "Welcome to the World of Cat. Is that all? We must get her something she can sharpen her claws on."

I just nod, busy eating.

"Well, I imagine you are full of questions," she says. "So now that you have me here, shoot away."

I have a list of questions, but the first one is about this diamond around my neck. "Assuming that burglar was after my—this stone. How did he know you had it?"

"If he's not connected to the Houses, I can't imagine." Her forehead wrinkles. "But if Iron knew I had it all these years, why did they wait until now to try to take it?"

"If all you did to make me 'disappear' worked," I say, "they shouldn't have even known I was alive at that point. Not before I touched it." I tell myself I don't believe a word of the magic part of all this. I'm just exploring the internal consistencies of her tale.

"True." Her frown deepens.

"So either they did know and wanted to keep me from getting it, or there is some other reason they wanted it …. Could they use the stone's power?"

"No, at least not from anything I've heard said about it."

I take a moment to digest this. Questions beget questions, but I yield to the one more pressing. "Speaking of alive, is there any ... *regular* way they could have known I was alive?"

"I never spoke directly to your adoptive parents," she says, pursing her lips. "All my communications went through the adoption agency I used, and they stake their business on keeping things absolutely confidential. Even the money I sent was handled through them. They are accustomed to dealings like that, apparently. Your birth name was April Rose Hawkins. I just asked that they keep the 'Rose' somewhere in your name.

I think for a minute; something doesn't add up. "But you said you were expecting me. That day when I showed up at your door."

"I knew you would come soon. There's no point in you having the rose-stone until you were, um, ready."

"Ready?"

"Did I not mention those of our House are, shall we say, 'late bloomers'?"

"No, you didn't."

"That's why I didn't seek you out, that and wanting to keep attention away from you as long as possible. Until you were ready for it, the rose-stone would have been just a stone in your hands, and you would have been extremely vulnerable."

I don't see how I am any less vulnerable, but before I have time to absorb this, she says with a bit of triumph in her eyes, "But, as soon as I saw you, I knew who you were."

"How's that?"

"Rose, dear. I can't explain everything. I just knew it. Everything was ... right again. I do have the blood of the House, you know." There is indignation in her voice. "Just because I am not in line for the stone does not mean I am deaf and blind and besides, you look very much like your beautiful grandmother, my sister Lilith."

"Okay," I say, although I don't have a clue what she's talking about. My brain hurts.

I offer her tea, which she accepts. She insists on making it herself, but I follow her into the kitchen to show her where everything is. Angel, who wants to be present and involved in everything going on, pads in behind us.

"We must get you a decent tea kettle," Alice says, wrinkling her nose at my microwave. "And some fresh herbs."

"Sorry."

"No matter." She holds up a hand. "We will make do for now."

While she putters, Angel stitches through her legs, leaning against each ankle as she passes. This is how she tripped me that first morning, almost sending me back in the hospital.

"What is she doing?" I ask, wondering if the cat had intentions to take Alice down too.

"She is just marking me with her scent. My pussies will be all over me wanting to know about it."

I almost choke. "Your what?"

"My pussies, my kitties."

"Right." I bite my lip and ask cautiously, "Um, you don't talk to your cats, do you?"

"Of course I do." She drops a tea bag into a cup, pours hot water over it, and sets it down before me. "Let it steep a few minutes." Then she glances at my face and laughs brightly. "Don't worry, they don't talk back to me … at least not in words."

Even if this person is not my great aunt, it is difficult not to like her.

"I am worried about you being here alone." She cocks her head at my boot-cast. "Especially in that condition."

"It would be helpful if you could give me an idea of *who* specifically might be trying to kill me."

Her hand pauses in mid-stroke of Angel's back. "I wish I could tell you more, but I have not associated with anyone in House of Iron for over two decades, though I get invitations to the Hallows' Eve party every year."

"I haven't gotten an invitation," I say. "If I'm 'outed' as a member of the House of Rose, I should get one, shouldn't I?"

"It will come, but you must not go under any circumstances." This is advice she has already given me, but she apparently feels compelled to repeat it.

"Why not?" I feel my back stiffen at being told what to do.

"You would be walking into their hands, Rose." Her tone is sharp. "Don't be foolish."

She's right, of course. That would be a pretty stupid thing to do. I'm still wrapping my mind around all this, but if I am totally honest with myself, the explanation for some of what has happened eludes me. I like Alice, but I do not trust her.

"I think we should report all this to law enforcement." I say. I have no plans to do that, but I want to see her reaction.

She pales. "Impossible."

"Why?"

"The secrecy of the Houses is of utter importance. It is imperative that people do not know about us."

"Why?"

She stares hard at me. "Do you recall the Salem witch trials? The Spanish Inquisition? Slavery? The Holocaust?" Her voice has lost the sweet airy banter of our earlier conversation. "Once there is a distinction between 'us' and 'other,' it is just one small step to label the 'other' inhuman. And then"—she shifts her gaze to the wall, but I know what she is seeing is not the wall—"then things can happen."

I jump at a loud knock on the front door. Fixing the doorbell was never high on my to-do list. Limping back into the living room, I glance out the window. A delivery truck doubled parked on the narrow street is partially in view. The writing on the side is obscured by the cars in front of it. A young man's back is turned toward me on the front porch. I crack open the door.

"Yes?"

"This the house of Rose Brighton?"

"Maybe."

He gives me a lopsided grin. "Then you're the lucky lady." He shoves a tablet in front of me. "Sign here please. Just the tip of your finger. Folks try to use their fingernail, but just the tip is what works."

I sign and he hands me a long slender rectangular box. When he is gone, I stare at it. Alice has joined me. She looks pale.

"Who is it from?" she asks.

I turn it over. "Doesn't say. Maybe there's a card inside."

"You aren't going to open it, are you?"

"It's too light to be a bomb." I give it a jiggle. "Or even a can of poisonous gas." She doesn't seem to appreciate my attempt at humor. I open the box and slide out the contents, which are wrapped in translucent, waxy green paper. Inside is a long-stemmed, single rose just opening. The petals are a deep, deep crimson, so dark at first glance they appear black.

Chapter Sixteen

Alice and I stare at the black rose.

I am seeing another rose in a vase in my hospital room. She might be seeing the one delivered to her sister's house before the arson. We are both seeing death, or a promise of it.

Into the long silence that follows, Alice finally says, "I want to ask you to do two things."

"What?"

"You are the only family I have now, and so there is no one to see to matters when I die."

"You're not planning that anytime soon, I hope." I don't know what to do with the rose, so I just stand there with it.

"Well, I am your great aunt and you were a late child, so I am a good bit older than you think." She goes to the purse she left by a chair, fumbles in it and produces an envelope. "It's my preference for internment, a funeral home I wish to use, and my attorney's name. If you suspect foul play, there is the name of a private doctor who performs autopsies. Do not trust the medical examiner. House of Iron has influence everywhere."

I won't have a choice if she dies under suspicious circumstances, but I don't mention that. Reluctantly, I take the envelope and put it in my pocket for transfer to my purse later.

"The house key is under the third pot on the right side of the porch wall," she says.

"How old are you?" I ask.

"Let's just say I'm over a hundred." Pride edges her voice.

"What?"

"That's not what my ID says, of course. The Houses' lifespans are longer than 'normal' people."

"Normal people," I repeat dryly. Conversations with this woman make the word "strange" inadequate, and I am, I admit, a little freaked by the rose thing.

I retreat to the practical. "So, how do people not catch on that you're over a hundred but look fifty?"

"Every so often, we change identities."

I'm staring at her. "Who were you before *this* you?"

"My name is not important, but we like to keep a 'rose' in there somewhere when we can, hence the surname 'Rhodon.' "

I continue to stare at her.

"It's not easy to leave people you've come to like," she says, "but it's given me the opportunity to expand my horizons. I was a doctor in England and a pharmacist once, and once, well, we needn't go into that one—"

I don't know what to think. "You were a doctor?"

"Oh yes, for several years. I am a healer, after all."

"A healer?"

"I'm not very powerful, but my skill makes up for that. Why do you look so surprised? It's the most traditional role for a witch." She narrows her eyes at me. "I know you don't care for that term, but you must tuck in and stop being in denial. There's just not the time for it."

I take a deep breath, thinking about the car bearing down on me. Maybe she is right. "You said we are the last of our House?" I ask.

She takes a long breath. "Yes, we are the last."

"How did that happen?"

"It's been a slow thing. Deaths that appear to be accidents, mostly."

"Why don't you fight back?"

She takes my hand and squeezes it. "How? By killing the entire House of Iron? You have no idea how powerful they are."

"So, you're willing to be annihilated?"

"Certainly not." Her nostrils flare. "Why do you think I hid you?"

I look at the rose in my hand and finger a sharp thorn. "I don't think hiding is going to work anymore, Alice."

THE SECOND THING ALICE HAS asked of me is more bizarre than taking care of her future funeral arrangements. Against my better judgment, I lower myself to the ground in my back yard. "Bum to the dirt," as Alice puts it. The simple movement is awkward with the boot cast, and I'm still stiff from the car-leaping thing, but I manage to get my butt on the leaf-strewn ground.

I have never understood the point of sweeping leaves when they are all replaced as soon as the wind blows. Might as well wait for them all to fall. And at that point, another theory takes over: Leaves are nature's way of fertilizing the ground, so why mess with all those millions of years of evolutionary wisdom by raking them?

In deference to her one hundred plus years, Alice sits in one of the wooden yard chairs, which are in reasonable shape, other than the peeling paint. There are two chairs. Not that I ever have company. The chairs came with the house.

Angel, who slipped out the back door with us, jumps into the empty chair and licks her paw, then uses the paw to wipe behind her torn ear.

"All right. I'm out here," I say. "Now tell me about the powers of House of Rose and Iron."

"It's simple, actually. We both draw power from the earth, they from the iron ores, and we from the living-green."

"The living-green." I sound like an idiot repeating everything she says.

"The plants, dear." She sweeps her hand in a half-circle to indicate the world. "All the wonderful, glorious life that is the counterpoint to ours, taking in our carbon dioxide, using it, and exhaling the oxygen. It's the synergy that makes all life work."

"How do you ... um ... 'we' draw power from the living-green?"

"I can't tell you how. You just have to do it. It's a personal thing for everyone. Many don't ever manifest an ability. They are still part of our House; we are family. So, you mustn't worry if that moment in the alley isn't repeated."

I give a little snort at the irony. Alice comforting me against the fact that I might be just a normal person.

"Tell me again why I have to sit on the ground to do this?" I ask grumpily.

"Because, dear, the closer to the power source, the easier and, for your first time, the safer."

I alert on the last word. "Safer?"

"Well, we don't want to pull from the *living*."

"Why not?"

"It would kill them." She looks horrified, but I'm confused. "If the living-green isn't the '*living*-green,' what is it?"

"I do see your point. We use coal for magic so we don't hurt anything alive. Coal is a condensed version of plants that lived hundreds of millions of years ago, a form of carbon, primarily, so in a technical sense, it isn't living now, but it once was."

"So, we're miners?" This strikes me as funny.

She smiles. "Yes, but we skip all the messy parts of having to bring it to the surface and ignite it to release the energy it contains. Much cleaner."

"It just seems so bizarre." Okay, I'm being nice. We have tipped the believability scale here, and I don't buy a word of this.

"People always underestimate the power of nature. Think of it this way:

Plants evolved to take in sunlight and make it an energy source; humans ingest plants—among other things—for energy; witches are humans with a special adaptation. We have all evolved to take and use energy in vastly different ways, yet at its heart, it is the same energy. E=mc2."

I blink. "So 'witches' have an ability to draw energy from coal without digging it out of the ground. How do you get it into you to 'ingest'?"

"Ah, that is the question! I'm convinced it happens in somewhat the same general way that plants use sunlight energy. I suspect we emit a kind of harmonic that creates a quantum pathway." She sighs. "But that is just a hypothesis. In actuality, I haven't the foggiest idea *how* we manage it." She barely takes a breath before adding, "Did you know that pepper frogs produce glycol that acts like anti-freeze and keeps them alive through the winter? I don't imagine they have any idea how they do that, either."

I blink at the introduction of frogs and try to keep us on track. "I've just never heard of witches using coal for magic."

"Well, what have you heard?" she asks, an annoyed edge to her voice.

I try to keep a straight face. "Only what I've read in stories. Witches use potions and spells."

"I see." She sits straighter. "'Potions' is just a word for a medicine made of various herbs and other ingredients."

"Yeah, but the ingredients seem to include bat's wing or eyeball-of-something."

"And I suppose," she snaps, "the witches are always old hags with long, crooked noses who wear black hats and fly around at night on a broomstick."

"Absolutely."

Her beryl eyes are flashing. "Nonsense. Those are stories told by ignorant people. I've never used a bat's wing or an eyeball in my life." She sniffs and adds, "Or even seen a recipe for it."

I can't help a laugh. She is so indignant. "What about the House of Iron? The sorcerers?"

"Warlocks," she corrects. "Their abilities involve manipulation, although we are immune to their direct influence. Obviously, they use iron."

"I don't know anything beyond high-school chemistry, but it seems like iron would be difficult to use as an energy source."

She sniffs. "Wolves couldn't digest grain until man came along, and they evolved into dogs who could."

When I look unconvinced, she adds, "There are billions of bacteria in the ground beneath you that take carbon from what you are breathing out now, carbon dioxide, and obtain energy from iron."

"Really?" I had no idea the world was so strange. Frogs that make anti-freeze and bacteria that eat iron and witches that drink from coal?

"Are you ready to try and draw the living-green?" she asks.

"One more question. You said this could be dangerous to plants. Is there any chance this could be 'dangerous' to me?"

"Of course not. Do you think I would ask you to do something that would hurt you?"

Somehow, I don't find this completely reassuring.

"You are House of Rose," she says, softening. "There is no way the living-green could harm you."

Something in her tone or the way she shifted slightly when she uttered this declaration makes me wonder if this is completely true. There is something she is not telling me. I consider calling off the whole experiment. On the absurd possibility I am able to access this living-green stuff, what will happen? I hadn't particularly liked the results the last time—if indeed, I am not mentally unbalanced and if I truly did see a young man shoot Paul in a different reality.

But if there is any chance she is right, and there is some way to use whatever I might have inherited, I need to find out. And if it doesn't work, I can figure out how to get help for my hallucinations.

Besides, I'm curious. I meet Angel's languid amber gaze. She seems to be thinking, *Curiosity killed the cat.*

At least there's a privacy fence in the back yard. If this doesn't go well, I don't want to freak out my neighbors. And if nothing happens—well, the worst scenario in that vein would simply be I end up feeling like an idiot, right? I take a deep breath. "All right, let's rock and roll. What do I do?"

"Relax," Alice advises, "and try holding the rose-stone."

I unhook my necklace and hold the pendant. "Now what?"

"Just look at it. My sister once told me that our mother taught her to 'watch the rock grow.' "

Watch the rock grow. I stare at the diamond. Rocks do not grow. This is ridiculous. Still, I dutifully stare at the rose-stone.

"Nothing." There is some disappointment mixed with relief.

"Patience, dear. Just wait."

I resume staring at the rose-stone, waiting for something magical to happen. I've never been the kind who can meditate. The whole point, I think, is to stop thinking, and for me that's like trying very hard to go to sleep. The more effort I put into it, the more I think about not thinking.

After several minutes of nothing happening, I am bored, but the rose-stone is quite beautiful, the way the red facets in its heart sparkle, especially when the sunlight catches them....

"Now reach down through the ground and find the living-green."

Alice's voice seems to be at a distance, and I wonder vaguely if she has moved to the other end of the yard. Without knowing what I am doing or how

I am doing it, I mentally reach down. Coal would be deeper than the topsoil. I imagine passing through layers of earth and roots, past the iron-laced red clay that seems to boost me on somehow, as if it has a repellant magnetic charge. Vaguely I know I am seeking the remains of foliage that died millions of years ago, liquefied and crushed into black seams of carbon by the building weight of rock and dirt.

The moment my awareness brushes it, I know I have found something, a seam of dormant energy. At my "touch," it ignites into a liquid-gold stream that flows upward faster than I can perceive it, flooding into me.

"Holy shit!" My eyes fly open.

Alice purses her mouth in disapproval. "No need for vulgarity."

It seems as if my whole body is pulsing with warmth. I look down at my hands, expecting them to be glowing, at the least, but they look normal, except they are shaking. I've dropped the rose-stone into the grass.

"I take it you found the living-green," Alice says with a smug smile.

Stupefied, I look up at her. "Guess so."

"How does it feel?"

"It feels as if I've been asleep all my life and just woke up. It feels … good."

"It's nice to see you smile for a change. You are far too serious for your age."

I lift my hands toward her. "What am I supposed to *do* with it?"

"Let's see if you have any healer in you." Alice lifts Angel into her lap and presents the chewed ear.

"What do I do?"

"Start simply. Touch it and visualize it growing to be like the other one."

Obediently, I close my thumb and forefinger on the cat's torn ear, trying to imagine it growing into the shape of the other ear.

Every hair on Angel's back stands upright. She arches into a Halloween caricature, her claws digging into Alice's thighs. Alice yelps as Angel leaps from the chair with a screech and disappears under the gate.

Alice and I look at each other.

"Is that normal?" I ask.

"Perhaps your gift is not healing. You mustn't be disappointed."

"I'm not," I lie.

With a profound sense of awe, I look down again at my seemingly normal hand. "At least we know where in my body this ability does not reside."

"Where is that, dear?"

"The spleen. They took mine out after the incident with the car."

She smiles. "Ah! Well, we are a step closer to solving an age-old mystery."

At that moment, I hear a familiar voice call from the front of the house, "Ro-se?"

"Back here, Becca," I shout.

In a few moments, she is at the gate to the back yard, wearing a wide-brim hat against the autumn sun, chunky, fashionable heels and carrying a purse that matches her yellow hat. Where do you even get a yellow purse?

"What on earth happened with Angel?" Becca says. "She flew by me like the devil was on her tail."

I am still holding the golden energy like a breath, not willing to release it. My mind is whirring from the whole thing.

Becca sits on the chair beside Alice that Angel has just vacated. Suddenly, in a visual overlay, a gray-black Becca exists in the same position, only this Becca wavers like an ill-tuned reception, wears no hat and sits on a cot in jail. She stares out toward me, her expression vacant, waiting—

What the hell? I release the living-green in a silent *whoosh*, and the vision fades, leaving only the Becca-in-a-yellow-hat sitting on a faded chair in my back yard.

Chapter Seventeen

When the invitation comes, the bruising has cleared from my face, but my ribs remain sore, and I am still wearing the clunky boot-cast that I've come to hate. I am not cleared to go back to work, but I am going to this Hallows' Eve party, and I'm wearing the pendant. It's time to meet these people, House of Iron, as Alice calls them. I haven't told her I'm going.

It may be a wrong move, but I'm going. Not just because Alice told me not to. The bum to the dirt experiment pushed me into believing her—at least until some better explanation surfaces. So if she is right about House of Iron, the answers I am looking for are there. I can either hide in my house and hope she is wrong or go find out what they are.

The doorbell rings just as I slip my gun into my purse. I no longer require the crutch, but I clomp to the door. Expecting Paul, as I've asked him to escort me—I may be stupid, but I'm not an idiot—I'm surprised to see Becca.

"Wow," she says eyeing me. "I knew you'd be a knockout in that black dress! But I thought you were going to a Halloween party."

"I am."

"No costume?"

"The invitation didn't say anything about a costume."

"Hmm. Sounds boring. How did you get all that hair up?"

I smile. "I've been wrestling with my hair all my life; it won't stay for long, I assure you."

"Well, it's awesome."

She seems particularly smug about something.

"What is it, Becca?"

"I see you don't have any earrings," she says.

This is too much. Why is she criticizing me? I'm about to tell her to mind her own business, but something makes me say instead, "I don't have a lot of jewelry, and I thought this would be enough." I touch the rose-stone that is hanging around my neck in plain view between the black "V" of my dress.

Becca produces a small box.

I stare at it.

"Well, open it!"

I do. Inside, on black velvet, is a pair of beautiful antique silver earrings.

"Becca, why on earth did you do that?" I know she doesn't have money to spare.

"I suspected you didn't have anything to go with that dress, even though your ears are pierced."

"I can't accept them."

"Sure you can. Don't worry. I didn't buy them. A guy gave them to me a couple of years ago."

"Oh Becca, I can't take them. They were a gift to you."

"Yes you can. He was an asshole. I don't want them." She eyes me critically. "Yep, they'll be perfect. They're simple, but elegant. You don't want to overpower that hunk of stone around your neck." She touches a finger to the pendant. "What is it anyway?"

I start to say it's glass, but I am reluctant to lie to her. "It's a red diamond."

She gasps. "Oh my God!"

"It's a family heirloom. The only thing I have from my birth parents. Adoptive parents raised me."

Becca immediately turns her focus from the pendant to me. "You've never told me what happened."

It's not her usual demand for information. I could blow her off. I don't know the meaning of the vision I had of her sitting in a jail cell. Is she a criminal? Was she in jail before I knew her, or was it something that will happen in the future? How can I trust her? I feel like I am walking the edge of a razor.

I suck in a breath. "A fire. It killed everyone. I was five."

Tears spring to her eyes, and her lips curl over her teeth in distress. "Oh Rose, I'm so sorry."

"I've never talked about it to anyone." I look steadily at her. "But you're my best friend."

She smiles, her eyes watery. "Now, you're finally getting it." With a sniff, she eyes my purse. "Do you have to take that purse? Don't you have a little black bag?"

"My gun wouldn't fit in a little black bag, and I don't have one, anyway."

"Oh yeah, the gun-and-badge thing. I forgot. You have to take them everywhere."

"That's right."

Her gaze travels downward and comes to rest on my unbooted foot. "And *that* doesn't exactly complement this dress."

We both study the sensible black shoe that I wear with my "detective clothes."

"You look like Mary Poppins from the knees down," she says. "But I suppose it wouldn't work to have heels, since you have to wear that 'club' on the other foot."

"No, it wouldn't," I agree.

Becca left only after I promised to tell her exactly what Paul's face looks like when he first sees me, but I am hard put to imagine how to convey his expression when I open the door. He looks as if he's been knocked on the head.

"Paul, are you all right?" I ask after a moment.

"Yeah, it's just you look—" He swallows and tries again. "You look … nice."

I swallow what I was going to say, which was that he cleaned up nice— irrationally irritated at his similar comment to me. "We're late," I say and clomp past him out the door.

The address on the invitation is to a house on the east side of the deep mountain cut that connects the north and south sides of Red Mountain. I live on the decidedly lower-income-class side to the west.

"Pretty swanky area," Paul says with a lifted eyebrow. It's clear he is uncomfortable in the suit and tie. "Is this family or friends?"

"Um, old acquaintances of my family. I've never met them, but they heard I was back in town and invited me." I am pretty uncomfortable myself. I don't like any part of this, but I have to have hard evidence, and I only know one way to get it.

"So, you won't actually know anyone?"

"Nope."

When we arrive at the enormous house on the mountain, Paul says, "I didn't recognize the address on the card, but this is the Simpson Mansion."

"Is that supposed to mean something to me?"

"It was owned by one of the first coal magnates in Birmingham. Watch out for ghosts if you believe in them. Simpson's wife was murdered here and is rumored to haunt the place. She was found on her bed with multiple stab wounds, and her son was arrested, but the case was dismissed. Not enough evidence."

I give Paul a hard look, not sure if he is pulling my leg. Reading him is something that plagued me throughout our months together on the training car.

"Well, it's a huge house," I say. "Maybe having a ghost brought the asking price down."

"The Simpson family left long ago, but I think it was on the market for a while."

I study the multi-gabled roof of the Tudor-style mansion that sprouts at least five terra cotta chimneys. The House of Iron may have found a deal. In any case, their home was far grander than where House of Rose had taken up residence, although I remember it as roomy, with a couple of coal fireplaces still intact and a small patio on the roof over the front porch.

As we top the front stairs, my hand in Paul's arm for balance, a slender man in a perfectly fitted tux gives us a slight bow and opens the door. "May I announce you?" he asks, as if I were Cinderella and this the castle ball. Despite his politeness, his dark eyes assess me and his movements suggest a coiled spring beneath the tuxedo. I hand him the invitation, figuring this is a fancy way of making sure only invited guests get in.

"Miss Veronica Rose Brighton," he says, reading the invitation, "and—?" He looks at Paul with cold evaluation.

"Paul Nix," Paul says. He glances at me and whispers, "Veronica?"

I ignore him and lift a finger to attract the doorman's attention. "Use Rose Brighton, please."

"As you wish," he says, enhancing the impression that I am stepping into a fairy tale. With a flourish, he opens the door, and we step inside. Since he doesn't follow and "announce" us, I assume my guess was correct. For all his airs, he's a bouncer, a muscle man.

Inside the foyer, a tall woman, drink in hand, greets us. She is blonde and stunning, her short green dress revealing long legs and heels that would unbalance even Becca. She gives me a surprised look.

"You must be April!" She has a British accent.

"Rose," I correct, my hand remaining on Paul's arm. "I prefer that."

"Rose, then." Her gaze slides from my face, drawn to the jewel at my throat, before descending down my body to my feet, and she frowns. "I heard about your accident."

I can't tell from her tone whether she is sorry it happened or sorry I survived.

"I'm Stephanie," our hostess says, extending her be-ringed hand.

I reach for it, and it rests for a moment draped in mine like a glove. I introduce Paul.

"Your house is beautiful," I say.

"Oh, thank you, but it's such a hodgepodge of décor, a poor version of ... where we lived previously."

I play innocent. "Oh? And where was that?"

"In England. The family had several estates."

"What brought you to America?" Paul asks politely.

Her face darkens. "It was not my idea." As if remembering her role as hostess, she smiles again. "Let me introduce you to Jason."

We follow her into a room with a large stone fireplace, leaded glass windows, and carved wood paneling. She winds us through a small cluster of people. Their gazes probe like hot irons. I try not to limp, but it is just not possible to be graceful with a hunk of plastic on one foot.

The living room takes up the space of my entire house. I admire the furniture, especially the grandfather clock, although the room is far too noisy to hear it ticking. From my past, a memory surfaces, washing me in a wave of nostalgia. In our house—the house where I was born—the centerpiece of the living room mantle had been a clock with a miniature pendulum. I watched it for hours as a child, fascinated by its eternal swing.

We intrude into a knot of people. "Jason, I have someone I know you will want to meet," Stephanie says.

I draw a breath as a man turns to us. The stranger from the bookstore! His presence scrambles my thoughts. Was that a coincidence or was he following me that day? This time, when his blue ice eyes meet mine, I see a depth that makes it impossible for him to be young. This man has seen a great deal and … is capable of a great deal. If I am in the lions den, is this the lion?

I make my hand reach out to meet his.

"Jason Blackwell," he says, actually bending and brushing his lips across the back of my hand, sending an electric jolt down my spine. "It is a pleasure to see you again."

All my instincts shout to turn around and run, but I'm not the running type. I don't know who is trying to kill me, and I'm not sitting on my butt just waiting for the next attempt.

"Thank you for the invitation," I manage.

"Thank you for honoring us with your presence," he counters smoothly. "It is good to have a 'rose' in our home again." He turns to Paul and offers his hand. "My pleasure?"

"Paul Nix," Paul responds guardedly.

Jason wears no jewelry except for an ornate silver ring encasing a black stone. Paul seems to have picked up on the tensions spiking through the room, and there is no telling what he might say. I'm already pretty tense myself given that I may be at enemy ground zero.

A rotund man in a bow tie offers a well-padded hand. "Ah, so happy to meet you, Rose. We thought all this time … well, it is a pleasure. I am Samuel Blackwell. Everyone calls me Uncle Sam, like the government." He chuckles.

"And I'm Tina." A diminutive older woman with tawny hazel eyes looks up at me. She wears a great deal of gold, but her gaze is drawn like a magnet to my pendant. I imagine they think I am flaunting it. I am. But if I hoped to identify who is obsessed with the stone, it is a wasted effort. They all are.

"It's crowded in here," Jason says and indicates an open door. "The library is just there." His hand on my back sends another jolt through my body and guides us to an adjacent room. If there are books here, they are inside the dark wooden cabinets. The stained glass windows look familiar.

"Scenes from Chaucer's *Canterbury Tales*," he says, seeing me eyeing them.

My dress is low in the back, and when he removes his hand, I can feel the imprint of his touch on my skin. I feel branded, my senses attuned to his nearness and touch. What is going on here? *This is the villain*, I remind myself. *Possibly the man who tried to have me, and/or my family, killed.*

Paul steps to the windows, examining the intricate details.

"So, you have walked into the lion's den," Jason whispers close to my ear. Goosebumps ripple my spine, both from his intimate breath on my neck and his choice of metaphor.

I lift my chin to meet his gaze. "Have I?"

"You have." His tone is light. He looks down at my foot. "And wounded to boot. No pun intended."

"Are there beasts I should fear here?" I sense he likes to walk the edge. He might reveal something, just for the game of it.

Responding to my challenge, his finger lightly strokes the line of my chin, and I can't even try to describe what that does to me. "There are," he says, "definitely beasts here who would like to devour you. I among them."

Paul turns, his jaw tightening. Maybe he heard Jason's comment, or maybe he can feel whatever is zapping between us.

Jason looks annoyed. Their eyes lock just over my head—Jason having a couple of inches of height on Paul—and suddenly I am afraid for Paul. What have I brought him into?

"So," Paul says coldly, "what's your line of work, Jason?"

Somehow there is a challenge in the casual question.

In response, Jason blinks slowly. "Investments, I suppose," he says. "It's hardly the kind of work you do."

Unsure if he is being arrogant or acknowledging Paul's profession in some way, I hook my arm into Paul's and announce, "I'd like a drink." Without waiting for a response, I steer Paul out of the library.

Stephanie, she-of-the-long-legs-and-impossible-heels, intercepts us. "There you are."

"I'll get you something," Paul offers, turning to me. I've never seen him drink anything but water or milk. His father—author of the handkerchief and extra handcuffs advice—had been an alcoholic, and Paul never touched liquor.

"Wine," I say. "Anything red."

He glances a question at Stephanie, who shakes her head and holds up her glass. "I'm good, thank you."

When Paul has disappeared, she turns back to me, one brow arching. "Leaving Jason's company so soon?" Her words are cool, but I sense annoyance or even anger beneath the surface. I don't blame her. I would not care to have a husband who is a bee to every flower he encounters.

"Is that unusual?" I smile, trying to feel more composed than I do, aware that my cheeks and earlobes are still burning from the encounter with Jason.

"When he turns on the charm, he is difficult to resist. And he always gets the object of his desire."

Oh really? "Well, we'll see," I say.

Uncle Sam swoops by, taking my arm. "Let me show you some of this house. It's truly unusual."

"I'd like that, thank you. I'm sure Paul would love to see it, as well." I am not about to go wandering off with a member of the House of Iron by myself, but I need a break from Jason's intensity to get my thoughts together.

Capturing Paul, we do a quick run through the first floor and the two levels below, neither of which had been visible from the front. Both open onto terraces in the back overlooking the miles-wide basin that the first settlers called Jones Valley. It must once have been a wild, green valley of trees and creeks, but now it cups the sprawling city of Birmingham.

"The real treasures are downstairs," Uncle Sam says, pulling us from the stunning view and leading us back to the central foyer where two dark-stained hardwood stairways meet, one leading up and the other down. Sam heads toward the descending one, but before I take the first step, I look up in time to see a man in a wheelchair gazing down at us.

"Who is that?" I ask.

"What?" He follows my gaze. "Oh, it's my older brother, Theophalus. He'll want to meet you, I'm sure."

Theophalus grasps the edges of his wheelchair and hoists himself into a lift attached to the banister, riding it down until he is level with us. Eyes the color of Jason's are the only thing alive about his lined face, and I wonder how many years separate him from Sam. It appears quite a few.

"Do you want your downstairs chair?" Sam asks him.

"No." His gaze on me is as intense as Jason's and like everyone else, he does not miss the pendant.

"So, you came."

"I did."

"That took some guts, girl." His mouth thins. "You look like your grandmother."

The world seems to wobble under my feet. People who had the substance of fairies in my mind lived real lives; other people knew them. It feels as unreal as the shadow world.

"Don't upset our guest," Uncle Sam says. "I was about to show her the downstairs."

Gripping my arm, he leads me a few feet to the top of a circular stairway, this one heading down. Paul is right behind us.

"Don't mind Theophalus," Sam says. Then with a chuckle, "Or the dark. It's more fun without the lights." Flipping off a wall switch, he fishes in his pocket. "I had a flashlight somewhere."

I produce mine, a tiny thing with a strong light and slip my other hand unobtrusively between the Velcro in my purse to grasp my gun butt. It's hard to imagine jovial "Uncle Sam" as a threat, but I am not taking chances. About halfway down, he directs me to shine it into an arched opening on the curving wall. I almost drop the light in surprise.

Inside, my beam reveals a life-sized tableau from medieval days—a thick wooden table set with goblets and food. Tapestries, arms, and shields adorn the walls. A full knight's armor stands guard in a corner. Men, perhaps just back from a hunt, are frozen in the act of sitting down for a meal. Under the table, stuffed hounds wait, mouths open for a bone. With all the weirdness of the last few weeks, I expect the scene to come to life.

"Paul, you have to see this." I hand the flashlight to him.

"Wow!"

"It's a replica of a hall in 9th Century England," Uncle Sam says, obviously pleased to impress us. "Just the beginning!"

"Did your family do this?" I ask.

"Oh no, it was the original owner. He had a passion for the past. Some say he was paranoid and had secret rooms built and an escape tunnel dug into the mountain, but no one has ever found it or where it comes out."

"Escape from what?"

"Who knows? It was 1920s, the Prohibition era. To escape from the law, the mob?"

At the bottom of the stairs are three huge, thick wooden doors with iron trimmings that look more on the scale of giants. Door number one leads down a long hall with rooms replicating different periods from history. I'm fascinated, but Uncle Sam consults his watch. "Whoops, have to get you back for the big toast."

Back upstairs, everyone lifts a glass to a new year. The Houses, it seems, start their year on Hallows' Eve. Paul gives me a quizzical look, and I shrug and lift my glass.

Afterward, the chatter resumes. An elderly woman snags Paul and demands his attention. I find myself next to Stephanie again with a gap between us and the other guests that allows a few moments of private conversation.

"Tell me about your family," I ask.

She gives me an appraising look and glances over to Paul, to make sure, I assume, that he is too far away to hear us. "How much do you know?"

"I know that I am House of Rose, and you are House of Iron, and apparently"—I take a deep breath and plunge in, keeping my tone light—"we are supposed to be enemies."

She tilts back her head and laughs. "I like you, Rose." Then her mouth tightens. "But you're a fool to come here."

"I was invited."

"I know, but—" She seems about to say something and changes her mind, apparently deciding to answer my original question. "The Houses have celebrated Hallows' Eve together from the beginning of memory. We are not enemies. There has just been a little 'disagreement.'"

I want to ask if disagreement includes murder, but I bite back the question.

She gives me a frank woman-to-woman look. "The women of Iron live a 'normal' lifespan, so I don't have personal memories, but I'm told House of Rose actually began the feuding."

"Why?"

"Some slight." Her brow creases. "A claim of 'rape and dishonor,' I think, and I've heard rumors about murder, but no one shares much with me." She takes a long swallow of her wine. "I'm just a woman."

This throws me, something I will have to check with Alice. There is so much I don't know....

"Someone murdered my parents and sister," I say.

"Surely not someone of the Houses," she says. "Children are so rare."

"My family—" I choke around a sudden knot in my throat.

Stephanie's face softens. "All in that one little house. What a terrible accident."

"It wasn't an accident," I say, but her sympathy, real or not, and just being here, has grown the knot in my throat, and I can't seem to swallow it down. I blink hard and excuse myself to the bathroom to try and get it together. I don't cry, but my nose is running and my eyeliner is smudged. So much for the ace detective forcing a confession from the murderers. A tiny folded bit of toilet paper salvages the eyeliner. I take a deep breath and am about to walk back into the fray when the door swings open. In my distress, I forgot to lock it.

"You'd better hurry," Stephanie says. "She's asking for you."

"Who?"

But Stephanie has already stepped out. I follow her clicking heels to what I think is called a breakfast room, where a cluster of people part to reveal a woman lying on the black-and-white checkered marble floor. My knees buckle beside her. "Alice!"

Her eyes open and blink.

"What's wrong?" I demand. "Has anyone called 911?"

"I have."

—That came from Paul. Thank God. I wouldn't trust anyone else's answer. I grasp Alice's hand. It's cold and clammy.

"Her pulse is rapid and erratic," Stephanie says with clinical detachment, "and her feet are swollen. Has she had heart trouble?"

"What are you doing here, Alice?" I ask.

Her lips move, but I have to lean down to hear her scratchy whisper, "Don't let them—" she wheezes.

"Let them what?" Then, seeing the pain in her eyes, I hastily amend, "Don't talk. Help will be here soon." I'm trying to be calm, but hysteria is pushing on my chest. *Don't go Alice! Don't leave me!* I grasp her hand.

My panic shocks me, and I suddenly realize how alone I felt until I found I had family after all … and now I might lose her.

Her eyes close and the temperature of her body drops, her hand cold and still in mine. It seems to take forever for the paramedics to arrive, and we all step back to let them do their job, but I have seen my share of dead people in my three months of Patrol, and my Aunt Alice is one of them.

Chapter Eighteen

I limp back and forth across the floor of my living room, only peripherally aware that a storm rages outside. For the past two hours, I've alternated between pacing and the bottle of wine on my coffee table. I wish I could cry and loosen my knotted up insides.

I keep seeing Alice sitting in her rocker, smiling and offering me tea. *What am I going to do about her cats?* That makes me think of Angel, who has been hiding under the couch while I ranted and guzzled wine.

I fall into my chair. *Damn it!* Alice said she didn't go to those parties. There is only one reason she was there. She knew I would go, despite her warnings, and she went to protect me. That makes her death my fault. If I hadn't been so stubborn—

Was it a heart attack … or something more sinister? The paramedics said it was probably her heart, but it is quite a coincidence to think she just keeled over in the House of Iron. The medical examiner investigator said there was no evidence of foul play and declined to take custody of the body, so I hired the private doctor who does autopsies, as Alice had requested. My gut insists it was not a natural death, or maybe I just want to think that because it's all I can do … and I have to do something.

I try to remember who was in the kitchen. It seemed as though everyone I had personally met except Theophalus was there—"Uncle Sam," Tina, Jason, "Legs" Stephanie. And, of course, Paul, though he came in after I did. In the academy, we were taught to pay attention to the faces at the scene of an arson, because arsonists often return to watch the fire and people's reactions. Was it the same with a murderer?

And what did Alice's last words mean? *Don't let them—*Do what? Kill me?

Take the rose-stone? My fingers find the pendant hanging from my neck. Is that what she meant?

Stop. Take it one thing at a time.

Instead of railing at my inner voice, I actually listen to it. *Take it one thing at a time.* Okay, first thing: Why kill Aunt Alice? It's hard to imagine her as a threat to anyone. Was it just that she is House of Rose and that some maniac is out to wipe us out?

I can't think. Rain beats onto the porch roof. The wind has blown itself out for now, but there is the "calm before the storm" thing. We are in tornado season, but I'm too distracted to even check. If the house crashes down around me, it couldn't be any more disturbing.

I go back to pacing.

THE KNOCKING CONFUSES ME. I roll over ... and hit the floor with a *thud*. The knocking persists. It takes a moment to realize I must have fallen asleep on the couch, and the sound is coming from my front door. My mouth tastes wicked. My head hurts. "What time is it?" I mutter, squinting at my phone. *Noon!*

"Crap." I eye the empty bottle of Cabernet Sauvignon. No wonder my head feels like an elephant stomped on it. "I'm coming!" I yell at the door.

More to stop the noise than with any clear goal in mind, I yank the door open, expecting Becca or the mailman, who sometimes knocks if he thinks I'm at home and puts the mail in my hand. He likes to chat. I don't feel like chatting.

It's not the postman or Becca who stands on my porch. It's Paul in jeans and a short-sleeved shirt. My mind struggles with the day and comes up with Sunday. The party was Saturday, just last night. I run my fingers through my hair, which has mostly fallen, though my fingers encounter the clip that held it last night.

Paul's red brows lift.

I look down and realize I am still in the little black dress. My hands fly to my ears to make sure I haven't lost Becca's gift earrings.

"You've had a bad night," Paul says with his gift for understatement.

I just nod, not sure I trust myself to try and speak.

"I thought I'd drop by. I'm sorry about your aunt, Rose, and the guys at Homicide send their condolences too."

I imagine everyone knows by now. Rumor moves faster than a speeding bullet in the Birmingham Police Department.

"Can I come in?" Paul asks.

I hesitate, thinking of the empty bottle of wine on the coffee table, shake my head. Bad enough I look like I was in a tornado. I squint at the painfully blue sky. Fall in Alabama is as unpredictable as a roll of dice.

"We can sit out here." I point to the solid balloon on my foot. "I've not been the best housekeeper."

He grins and shakes his head. "And that's supposed to be a new development? Is that why you never let anyone inside?"

He knows the foot excuse is merely that, but he doesn't protest. We sit on the front porch, and he looks at me seriously. "I didn't know you had an aunt in Birmingham. You never mentioned her."

I tighten my lower lip, which wants to quiver. "I didn't know I had one until a few weeks ago."

"You wanna talk about it?"

I look at his broad chest and realize that I would like nothing more than to rest my head there and let him hold me. Maybe I crave a father figure or maybe Jason woke something else in me. Confused, I can't remember what we were talking about.

"What were we talking about?" I ask.

"Your aunt."

I look down at my hands, which have returned to my lap, fingers intertwined, as if keeping me together.

The appearance of a small person on my porch steps distracts me from whatever I might have said next. It's a child, the little boy from down the street who found my rose-stone.

"Hi, Daniel," I say.

"Hi," he replies with a shy wave of his hand.

His face is cleaner than the last time I saw him. When his eyes find the pendant at my neck, he smiles. "Pretty on you."

With that, my heart melts. "Come here."

Obediently, he comes close.

"What are you doing over here?"

He shrugs. The fist plunging into his mouth.

"Are you just visiting?"

"Uh huh."

"Where's your mother?"

"She's sleep."

"Hmm. Would you like a cookie?"

An enthusiastic nod. Then, as a remembered afterthought, "Yeth, please."

I look at Paul. "You want one, too?"

Paul smiles at Daniel. "A cookie sounds good."

In addition to handkerchiefs, Paul always kept candy in his pocket for children. He'd lost a son and his wife years ago in a car accident, and I think he saw his son in every child. I'd never seen him angry until the night we answered a domestic violence call and found a baby covered in fleabites in the crib. For a moment, I thought he might shoot the parents right there. Instead, he snatched the infant and shoved it into my arms. "We ain't leaving him in this," he had growled. I don't know whether the Department of Human Resources ever put the baby in foster care or returned her to the parents, but I was glad to be able to get the infant out of that house. Foster care is not always the evil some people make it out to be. I know.

On my way to the kitchen, I snatch the wine bottle off the coffee table and kick aside a pile of dirty clothes in the hall waiting to get high enough to put them in the washing machine. Purposefully ignoring the dishes in the sink, I dig some chocolate chip cookies out of a cupboard. I can't remember when I bought them, but the bag is unopened, so they're fresh, right? Thinking Daniel might get thirsty eating cookies, I pour him and Paul a glass of milk and get a Coke for myself. I need the caffeine and don't want to bother with tea or coffee.

With three glasses and a bag of cookies to carry, I find a tray and carefully return to the porch to find the men discussing the subject of primary interest to every Alabama male and some rabid females—football. Daniel is apparently a University of Alabama fan, and I can quickly tell this five-year-old knows more about the team than I do, despite the fact that it is my alma mater.

Daniel ignores the milk and takes a cookie in each hand.

Paul drains his glass, leaving a rim of white in his mustache. "Uh, mind if I use your facilities?"

"Sure," I say, giving up on keeping him out of the house. At least my bathroom is clean. What had Alice thought of my sloppy housekeeping? The thought of her closes my throat, so I focus on Daniel. We consider each other. I have never known how to talk to kids.

"You don't look like a policeman," he says, solving the problem. "My mommy says you are."

"She's right. I am."

"Okay." He is intent on the remaining cookies.

"Don't you remember I came to your house before?"

He shakes his head. Apparently I was just a uniform that night.

"So ... what do *you* want to be when you get big?" I ask after a moment of silence, bereft of any better question to ask.

"A doctor."

"What kind of doctor?"

He scrunches his face in confusion.

"A doctor for grown-ups or for children?" I ask.

"Not children."

"How come?"

"They cry."

"I see. That's true. So, a doctor for grown-ups. And where do you want to work?"

"UAB."

The University of Alabama at Birmingham is a mouthful for anyone. "Do you want to work a day shift or a night shift?"

"Day."

"I see you have this all planned out." I tilt my head. "Doctors don't eat too many cookies or they get a tummy ache. Besides, your mother might not like me spoiling your lunch."

"She not mind," Daniel says.

I sniff. This is the second time Daniel has been out of the house on his own, or the second time I know of. Maybe there have been other times. She seems like a nice enough person, but maybe I ought to make a call to DHR—

Paul rejoins us, and I stand, brushing crumbs off my lap, preparing to walk Daniel home. A cool draft on my legs draws my gaze down to my somewhat skimpy "little black dress" and bare foot. "I can't go like this. I need a shower and … um …different clothes."

Paul rises. "I'll take him home."

Relieved, I turn to Daniel. "Mr. Paul is a policeman, too. It's okay to go with him."

Daniel nods.

"The house on the corner, right?" Paul asks, reaching out for Daniel's hand.

I point to confirm it. "The one right beside the alley."

He glances at me, and I know he realizes I am thinking what he is thinking—that is the spot where I shot Zachary and where Paul almost died. It is, I realize, a place and moment in time that will always bind us.

Chapter Nineteen

The funeral is a graveside service at Elmwood Cemetery. With the calendar flip to November, the weather has decided to gear up for winter, and the wind's bite carries an edge. Graphite skies gray the world. I stand near the spot that is to hold Alice's body, the hole genteelly covered with artificial green turf.

This is my first visit to the family plots. While we wait for her body to arrive, I wander among them, trying to connect with the people whose names are engraved on the headstones. My family lies here—my birth parents, my sister, and my grandmother. When I first see the inscription on my sister's stone, I suck in air. My name is there as well, with dates of birth and death. Alice "buried me" to protect me, to reinforce the belief that I died in the fire. How had she pulled that off? So many questions, and the only person who could answer them is dead.

I return to the site where she is to be interred and sit on one of the hard black-draped chairs beside Becca. Paul stands behind me in full uniform with a lifesaving medal I have never seen pinned to his chest, his sleeves rippled in gold stripes for the years he has served on the force. I am touched by this formality. Tracey has also come, though wearing a suit and tie.

Why has Alice's death affected me so strongly? I haven't known her but a few weeks. Am I grieving for her or for myself? I thought I came to terms with being orphaned long ago. Maybe that is the problem—I was resigned to being alone, found I was not, and now I am again ... and that hurts.

I am glad I got to see you again, Aunt Alice, I tell her silently, as a fine rain, more a mist, begins to fall. *I don't regret that.* Then I add, *I am feeding your cats every day.*

A man approaches and introduces himself as a retired colleague of Alice's at UAB.

"Colleague?" I ask stupidly.

"She was a brilliant professor."

"Umm ... were you in the same field?"

"No, I was microbiology and she was physics, but we had tea occasionally." He smiled. "She did love her tea."

"Yes," I say around the knot in my throat. "She did."

A physics professor? That explains her fascination with quantum theory. The feeling of loss envelops me again. This woman who was a doctor, a pharmacist, a physics professor, and my great aunt was so much more than the eccentric old woman I thought she was. And now she is gone. Anger churns with the grief. If someone is responsible for taking such a person from the world ... from me, *I will find him.*

A black Buick pulls up, and my heart does a flutter dance, remembering the black Buick that ran me down. Is it the same one? Maybe I didn't have to find my aunt's murderer; maybe he would find me. My hand slips to the hidden opening in the side of my purse, ready for someone to jump out of the car and start spraying bullets.

When the car door opens, members of the House of Iron step out into the drizzle—Jason, Sam, Tina, and Stephanie, the door guard, and two others I don't recognize, a thin man with a hat pulled down deep and an elderly woman. Everyone wears black. Another car pulls in behind them with more people I do not know. They all join us under the canopy, each carrying a single long-stemmed red rose. I feel as if I am in the middle of a scene from *The Godfather.*

Feeling me stiffen as they approach, Becca leans over to whisper in my ear. "Who are they?"

I can't answer her. My mouth is dry. My breath erupts in short bursts. Becca grabs my arm. "Rose? Are you okay?"

With a shake of my head, I try to pull myself together, to calm my fight/ flight reaction. Paul puts a steadying hand on my shoulder. Tracey looks from me to the procession and slips his hand under his jacket where he wears his gun in a shoulder harness.

Jason, impeccably dressed in a starched white-collared shirt and tie with a black wool overcoat, notices the gesture, and his cheek twitches, a flicker of movement in the chiseled face. His impossibly blue eyes catch mine. On his arm, Stephanie frowns, her body language proclaiming her irritation at having to negotiate the muddy ground in heels.

"Uncle Sam" gives me a kindly, sympathetic nod. The diminutive Tina touches a hanky to her eye. *Drama or remorse?* I appraise each one. My analysis morphs into anger at their intrusion on a family service. I didn't invite them and don't want them here. I don't know if they had anything to do with Alice's death or my family's or the attempts on my life, but my choices are limited at the moment; I can either make a scene or ignore them.

I decide to ignore them.

The service is short and generalized. I'd found the Episcopalian minister in the phone book. My adoptive family was Episcopalian, though we rarely attended services. There wasn't much I could tell the priest about Alice, except that she was bright and always cheerful and would step in front of a truck to save someone she loved. That was as close as I could get to saying she attended a party at a risk to her life in order to protect her stupid great niece who thought she could face her enemy and her fears.

When it is over, Becca, Paul, Tracey and I shovel a bit of dirt onto the casket. Fortunately, the members of House of Iron don't try to speak to me. They simply walk by, dropping their roses, one by one, onto the casket.

THE NEXT MORNING, I GET a call from Alice's attorney, Mr. Ed Ward, and set up an appointment for that afternoon. He has an office downtown. I consider whether to put on my detective outfit and decide not to. I go in blue jeans and throw a jacket over a tee shirt that reads, "I am a police officer. To save time, let's just decide I am never wrong."

First, I take a side trip to the pet store where I buy Angel a scratching post, dry cat food, a litter box, although she asks to go out, a red collar, and miscellaneous toys I hope will distract her from destroying my furniture and toothpaste. Then I drive downtown, along Birmingham's beautifully landscaped 20th Street, and find Mr. Ward's building in the high-rise Harbert Plaza. The building's black and gold granite patterns, topped by a dark pyramid make me think of Egypt. On the fifteenth floor, I wait in the pristine, white-marbled lobby until he comes out to meet me. We shake hands. He has gray sideburns and an otherwise baby face.

"I am sorry about your aunt's death," he says.

I don't know what to say in reply, except thank you, and besides, there is the constant threat of a knot in my throat, so I nod and follow him to his office, a surprisingly small space full of stacks of folders and pictures of his family stuck in every nook.

Taking out a folder, he opens it. "I have a will from Alice Rhodon, and I can read it for you or just give you the high points. It's pretty simple."

"Just tell me."

"You are the only heir. Apparently, she was the executor of your grandfather and your parents' estates and made regular deposits in a bank account in your name."

Child-like, I'd just accepted without question that my adoptive parents had saved the money that put me through college. I was so wrong.

"But there is an additional amount you will inherit. It comes with the requirement that you take care of her house and cats in perpetuity."

"How long is that?"

With an indulgent smile, he says, "At least as long as you are alive."

I sniff. What he doesn't know is that might be longer than the house, which is already approaching the century mark.

In spite of my sadness at having to be here, I am curious. "How much money?"

He gives me the figure, which seems a lot, but Alice would know that I would be around for a while. That is, if I survive House of Iron's attempts to kill me.

"You understand the stipulation that you must keep the house and never sell it."

"I understand. Do I actually own the house?"

"You do and the cats."

I take a deep breath. That makes four cats. I am a cat person, willing or not. Of course, I would have made sure they were okay without the will, but I was thinking of trying to find homes for them. Now that is not an option.

"There is also mention of a family heirloom, a red diamond that is—"

I touch my chest where the pendant hangs under my tee shirt. He can probably see its outline. "I already have it."

"Excellent."

He gives me the keys to Alice's house, along with a key to a safe deposit box and information on my accounts. Most of the money, it seems, is invested.

"I own a house and four cats," I say to the reflection in the polished surface of the elevator doors as it plunges back to the ground. My image seems unaffected, but I keep running over it in my mind like a tongue exploring a lost tooth.

There is a lot I have to sort out about who I am, but my next stop is a checkup with the doctor. He has my leg x-rayed to monitor the healing. I wait, trying to achieve a state of restfulness on a table that seems designed to be as uncomfortable as possible, thinking about Alice and history and how complicated life is.

The doctor returns, frowning. "Ms. Brighton, I don't know how to explain this, but your leg is healed."

"I thought I had two more weeks."

"You did, but it's completely mended. I've never seen anything like it in thirty years of practice."

Is that something I've inherited as a child of the House of Rose? A fast-healing gene? "Well … great. Does that mean I get this thing off my leg?"

"Yep. No need for it, but I do want you to be careful. I'm putting you on light duty for another week, just to be sure."

MY NEXT STOP IS REGIONS Bank. The signature cherry tree on the plaza is still draped in autumn crimson, but the season has definitely turned, especially at the corner of 5th Avenue North and 20th Street, where the tall buildings create a wind tunnel. I hug my coat close and tuck my chin, pushing my way through the revolving door.

The vault is downstairs, I am told. I ride the escalator down and present my key, the letter from my attorney, and a copy of Alice's death certificate to the attendant. She confers with someone and has me sign a form before taking my key and hers to unlock one of hundreds of boxes in a room behind heavy bars. She pulls it out and leaves me alone with the long rectangular metal box.

Inside, I find a man's wedding ring and two sealed envelopes. I lay the ring aside and open the first envelope, which contains a typed letter:

> Dear Rose,
>
> I have not felt well for several weeks, and I'm afraid something will happen to me in the near future. What I most want to say is that having you grow up without being able to be with you has been the most difficult task of my life. You will probably never forgive me for that, but I did what I thought was best. I hope I had a chance to explain it to you, but if not, you will just have to trust me.
>
> Your mother left a sealed letter to you. It is in the box.
>
> Remember Family is the most important thing.
> Love,
> Your Great Aunt Alice

I have to dig in my purse for some tissue and blow my nose. Then I open the second letter which is handwritten in a lilting script:

> Dear April Rose and Amber,
>
> If you are opening this, it will mean I am dead. I have given this sealed letter along with the family heirloom to your Great Aunt Alice for safe keeping and to give to you when she deems you are ready. I have seen a future where a grown April Rose appeared

to "find" the heirloom on the street and another where she was sitting with Alice and showing it to her. There were many questions on April's beautiful face. I have not seen what will happen to me, but I must assume I will not be there to answer them or to give you the stone. You are both too young, as I pen this note, to give you such a burden. I will try to do so in this letter, but I must be somewhat cryptic in case it falls into the wrong hands.

The heirloom has a very long history in our "Families." It possesses the ability to contain the "talents" of all the Houses without the disasters that can occur if those are otherwise mixed. The rightful possessor of the heirloom is the Y Tair, who has the blood of all three Houses and can call upon those talents as needed wherever she is, or—the Universe forbid the need—combine them. This ability ultimately protects everyone from the horrors that can unfold, both from fear of those different or from those who need restraint in using their power over others. Until the last century, the Y Tair was considered head of all the Families, and her word was law.

One of the Family Houses protested this arrangement and formed a secret cabal to eradicate our branch. I am convinced that not everyone, even inside that House, knows about the cabal and their intentions, but it is powerful. They have put forth misinformation and exaggeration of the dangers of mixing our families', all with the ulterior purpose of eradicating our line and thus preventing the rightful heir, the Y Tair, to carry out her duties and responsibilities to guide the Families. I fear that some cabal members are more radical and may have been behind actual deaths, but I cannot prove it. Use care in dealing with them.

The only other thing of import in Family matters is that April may find she has talents not normally associated with our House. I do not wish to break my mother's confidence, but her genetic father may be Family. If true, April, you must take especial care, because you will surely be a target for the cabal

*should they discover this. In any case, you must pass
the heirloom to your first daughter and tell her of its
ability.*

*Take care of each other. I love you both more than
I can say, and I am so glad dear Alice will be there for
you. I am so sorry to have failed you both in that.*

Love Always,

Mom

THIS TIME, WHEN I TURN the key in the lock to Alice's front door, it feels as if the world has turned itself upside down. Only a few weeks ago, I walked through this door to meet a total stranger. Now the house is mine.

The cats have a "cat door" in the back, so even though I skipped checking on them this morning to do my business downtown, I'm not afraid of encountering a horror show there, but their bowls are empty. Getting their food and rinsing out the water dish takes far too little time, and now I have to face the house, *my* house. It's been hard enough to come here every morning since she died, now it feels unbearably strange to think of myself living here.

My mother surely visited Alice many times. They were just next door. She may have sat in these chairs or surely at the kitchen table having tea with her aunt. I would give anything to have her to talk to, to lean on. She said she failed Amber and me. If so, I failed my little sister. I couldn't protect her any more than my mother could protect me. Her letter was addressed to us both, so my mother didn't know Amber and all the rest of our family would be killed.

Wood floors creak at my step as if identifying me as an intruder. How can Alice be *gone* when she animates all these plants that occupy every window sill; the slope of a carved giraffe's neck on the fireplace mantle; the worn cover of a bedside book; the scent of lavender in the bathroom? Childhood memories, as ethereal as the taste of fog, brush the back of my thoughts, but there is no tin of candy in the closet, no cookie jar on the kitchen table. The cats swirl around my legs and make plaintive protests, echoing the squeaky floor's complaint that I am not the person who belongs to this house.

The cats are right. I am a stranger and I can't stay here, at least not yet. I fill the bowls with dried food and fresh water, check the windows, water the plants, lock the doors, and return to my own house just in time to intercept the mailman on my porch.

Inside, as soon as I drop onto the sofa, Angel jumps into my lap and circles, finding the right spot to drape across my thighs. She doesn't care whether her human-person is a witch or not. A lap is a lap.

Shuffling through the junk mail, my heart pounds at the return address on a manila-sized envelope. It's the private physician Alice requested I use for an autopsy. I tear it open and scan it and then sit on the couch in the living room and read through it again slowly. The conclusion is the same the second time around—heart failure. They list her age as seventy-three. I can't help smiling. Alice would have liked that.

My smile is fleeting. Dark and jumbled thoughts ricochet. Desperate to distract myself, I pick up the small diary and translation dictionary I purchased at the bookstore. There are only three pages. Glad to have something to focus on beside feeling sorry for myself, I get to work.

To my surprise, the diarist's House was neither Rose nor Iron, but Stone, though he never says how his magic manifested, perhaps worried about being caught writing down House secrets. Mostly he seems angry and isolated, in love with someone forbidden from another House. That's an old tale! Capulet and Montague, the two feuding houses of Romeo and Juliet, spring to mind. I can't remember what grade my class was made to read the play and assigned roles. I was the introducer and had to memorize the first stanza. I can still quote it:

Two households, both alike in dignity....

I close the diary, which cut off abruptly. "Wonder what happened to him, Angel," I say aloud. "You suppose he and his lady ever got together? My mother hinted that her mother—my Grandmother Lilith—may have had an affair with another House as well. Our Aunt Alice never said anything about that, but I believe she kept more secrets than she told."

Chapter Twenty

The following morning, a Saturday, I walk to Alice's house earlier than I am accustomed to. Monday, I return to work. I'll be on light-duty, even without the bootie, which translates to stuck in the office, but I need to get used to getting up and taking care of the cats on an earlier schedule.

When I return home, I open the door to my study for the first time since the shooting, determined to go in. I chose this room because of the light. I think it was originally a sunroom. Windows cover both the eastern and southern walls. The south windows look out onto my small, leaf-strewn backyard with the two faded chairs and beyond that, the wooded slope of Red Mountain. A few brown leaves still cling to gray-brown tree trunks and limbs, but the dark green of the loblolly pines dominate the color palette.

Sunbeams filter through the room's eastern window, catching dust like a nebula incubating tiny stars. When we were little, Amber and I would sit for hours beneath the window in our room, trying to catch magic fairies in a beam of sunlight.

"What do we do if we catch one?" I remember my younger sister asking.

"Put it in a jar," I said, "like a firefly."

We tried, but as soon as we moved the jar of "fairies" out of the light beam, they disappeared.

A half-finished canvas waits for me, acrylic over watercolor, an abstract in yellows, oranges, and reds against a blue haze. My brushes also wait; everything waits. I'm not sure what I was trying to express—a need wells up in me on occasion, and when I can't stand it anymore, I come into this room to paint it away.

IT'S A RELIEF TO RETURN to work two days later, even confined to my desk. I thought being at the office would help take my mind off Alice, but after I make all my calls to victims and return the cases that require field work to my lieutenant, boredom sets in, and that means my mind races in circles, trying to figure out all the questions that Alice can no longer answer.

I try to put them in some sort of order:

Who killed Alice, torched my family, and wants me dead? Okay, that's three questions. Despite the autopsy report, my gut still insists they are all connected. Alice was certain that the House of Iron wants to wipe House of Rose off the map. So was my mother. I wonder if any of this has to do with the *Y Tair* person she said traditionally "guided" the Families. Alice also tried to tell me about that, but I was so overwhelmed with the whole magic-and-witches thing, it didn't sink in. And Alice is not here anymore to ask.

The important question now is: What am I going to do about it?

PAUL APPEARS AT MY DESK. "Wanna grab some lunch?"

At this point, I would grab anything to get out of the office. I loop my purse over my shoulder and stand. As we walk out, the lieutenant hollers. "She's on light duty, Nix. Don't get her hurt!"

This would be the one day when the office is almost full. Everyone looks up. Paul frowns. Sourface snickers. My ears burn.

"Let's take my car," Paul says as soon as we're out the door.

"Fine with me."

When we are ensconced in his car, which is as neat as mine is not, Paul pulls out of the lot. "Where would you like to go?"

"To be honest, I'm not hungry, which is a first. What I want is to see some water."

To his credit, Paul doesn't blink at this odd request. "Well, there's the Cahaba River and Village Creek, or do you need a lake?"

Actually, what I want is the sea. I want to go south, all the way to the Gulf, to get away from the reminder of my losses and the threat that hangs over me like a brooding shadow. I have this desire to throw my sadness out into the water, to breathe the brine and hear waves thudding the shore like the earth's heartbeat. It's a pull most every Southerner I know understands.

"At this point, a fountain would do," I say.

"Know just the place, and if you get hungry, we can go from there."

The round Storyteller Fountain in Five Points South sits in front of a large, ornate Methodist church in the heart of the city's entertainment district. In older times, trolley tracks grooved the five roads that spike from the fountain. Now the streets are paved over and in some places the sidewalk is buckled from the earth's silent shifting. But Paul is right about food being within easy reach.

The area hosts a cluster of restaurants, from chain fare to unique eateries that have brought home the national-awards bacon. They are normally beyond my budget for lunch, but I guess I could use some of my inheritance to eat at someplace fancy like Highlands Bar and Grill, Hot and Hot Fish Club, or Chez Fonfon, if I wanted to.

It's a crisp December day; the trees have lost their late-autumn dress, but the sky is a perfect blue. Unlike the well-groomed central downtown that lies a dozen or so blocks to the north, Five Points South is an eclectic blend of commerce and people. A bearded guitarist with sad eyes sits on the fountain's ledge, his fingers plucking a scattered melody. Standing nearby, a black man with multicolored, beaded dreadlocks fiddles with the feathers and ribbons on his spirit stick. Medical employees in blue scrubs from the nearby UAB Hospital cross the street in a flock to the Pancake House or Starbucks. The weather is perfect, and the outside seating is full.

What all these people have that I don't have is that they are doing what they are supposed to be doing, a feeling I have lost ever since I walked through the Burglary Unit doors. I don't feel like a police officer anymore, just a paper pusher.

Paul is watching me with his arms crossed and one thick, red brow lifted, I guess to see if this fountain salves my desire for water. I've driven by dozens of times, but never stopped to look at it. Fairytale animals gather around the storyteller, a creature with a man's body, a ram's head, and cloven hooves.

"The homeless folks call him 'Bob,' " Paul says.

Bob is reading a book, and his animal audience sits on lily pads or on the backs of a large dog and a turtle that, in turn, sit on lily pads. They all listen with rapt attention.

"You know," Paul says, "at one time there was a hue and cry for the fountain's demise."

"What? Why?"

"Some religious job decided Bob was a satanic figure."

I squint up into the sun. "To me, Bob seems a peaceful, intelligent fellow." If those same folks who demonized Bob knew I was a witch, no doubt there would be calls for my demise, as well. As soon as I complete that thought, I realize I've accepted who I am, as strange as it all still seems.

Across the street, the kneeling sculptured figure of Brother Bryan seems to balance out the spiritual battleground, and I suddenly see Bob as the keeper of ancient knowledge and old ways, forgotten by the people who pass by every day, but remembered by the other creatures and even the plants. Alice tried to teach me a little bit of it, about the connectedness of the world, but now she is gone.

Why can't I cry? What is wrong with me? Water gushes from the fountain, but my damned eyes are dry as a desert.

At a sudden shout, I turn to see an elderly woman sprawled in the crosswalk. Paul is at her side before I can react, lost as I am in deep thoughts and melodramatic self-pity. Chiding myself, I join him.

"Are you alright?" I ask her, taking her other arm and helping her to unsteady feet.

"He took my purse!" Her voice catches. "Pictures … my grandchildren—"

"Which way did he go?" Paul asks the people now gathering around us.

"That way." The black man with beads in his dreadlocks points east down Magnolia Avenue. "Black shirt and a white cap. Shouldn't be hurting no old woman," he adds with a disdainful shake of his head.

"Stay here and call it in," Paul snaps at me and sprints down Magnolia Avenue.

I call 911 on my cell and give them the info. I know someone is supposed to stay with the victim, but I turn to a man who took Paul's place beside the woman and is helping her to the fountain's edge.

"Keep her here," I order, forgetting that I'm not in uniform, and he doesn't know me from Adam, and I start jogging down 11th Avenue. Magnolia and 11th come together in a "V" at the fountain. If the suspect realizes Paul is after him, he may decide to cut behind the church. This is part of our old beat, and I know he can get into the church parking lot and around an imposing iron fence that has a gap where it meets the wall. If he does that, he'll come out on 11th Avenue, right in front of me.

This is the first time I have tried any gait faster than a walk on my newly released from boot-prison foot, but it behaves itself, and I increase my speed. As I run, I work my right hand into the Velcro on my purse and onto the butt of my gun, pressing it and my purse tight against my hip and congratulating myself for not listening to Becca and trying to wear heels.

The avenue is sandwiched between the imposing Methodist church on the left and the Old World stucco and red clay roofs of Chez Fonfon and Highlands Bar and Grill. I am just across from Highland's when a young man in a black shirt and cream-colored cap dashes across the street in front of me. If I were a witch worth her salt, I'd send a spell to trip him, but that is not in my skill set … that I know of. This calls for old-fashioned policing—I run after him.

He darts through Highland's parking lot, and I think he's headed for the Chick-fil-A behind the restaurant, but instead, he jags back to the left and jumps onto a wrought-iron gazebo in the back yard of the three-story Hassinger Daniels Mansion, one of only two homes left from the turn-of-the-century Silk Stocking Row. For a moment, it flashes through my brain that the house's original owner had ties to the iron and steel industry, and I wonder if I am just chasing a common thief or someone more sinister. *Is this a setup?*

The suspect's sudden change in direction cost him some of his lead, giving me a chance to close in. He hasn't looked over his shoulder, no doubt thinking he has cleverly lost his pursuer by going through the church parking lot. To my dismay, I am breathing hard up the small incline. I've gone too long without working out since that car tried to run over me, but I manage to get a hand on his shoulder and whirl him around. Surprised, he stumbles, and I stick a foot behind his heel and help him to the ground at the feet of a torch-carrying angel that stands watch in the gazebo's center.

Paul appears at that point, which is a good thing, because I don't carry handcuffs in my purse; it's heavy enough. With neat expertise, Paul rolls him onto his stomach and cuffs him.

Despite the tightness in my chest, I am light, exhilarated, and I can feel the big grin on my face. For the first time since the shooting in the alley, I am doing what I am supposed to be doing. This is who I am.

A movement in the corner of my eye snags my attention, and I turn, just catching sight of a young black man with spiky red hair duck behind the trellis outside the Chick-fil-A on 20th Street. I'd know that hair anywhere. I plop onto a bench in the gazebo and try to catch my breath, but my mind is whirring. What is Carrot Man doing here? Is he following me? Am I in danger?

Awkwardly, I reach into the ground for the living-green. To my surprise, it's not difficult, now that I have done it consciously. The golden magic comes willingly, filling me with charged warmth. Now what? How do I access the black and gray world of the future? For a few minutes I wait, but nothing happens.

Paul puts a hand on my shoulder. I blink and realize a patrol car has pulled up, and a uniformed officer is helping our captive into the back seat.

"You did good," Paul said, "but I am in deep shit with your lieutenant for letting you run after a purse snatcher. You heard him. I'm not supposed to let you get broken again." He hesitates. "Are you okay? You didn't hurt anything, did you?"

I shake my head. "I'm fine."

He drops a woman's purse into my lap. "Good. Then let's go find the little old lady this belongs to."

Chapter Twenty-One

Over the past several weeks, I've thought hard about taking someone into my confidence, at least partially. Consulting my list of friends doesn't take long, as I have exactly three: Becca, Paul and Tracey. Becca would be my choice of a confidante, but I don't want to expose her to danger, and I can't see that she would be much help if "shit hit the fan." Lohan seems like a good guy, but I just don't know him that well.

That leaves Paul. I'm not good at reading men, but I believe he has an interest in me beyond friendship. In addition, the unwritten "code of blue" means I could probably trust him not to rat on me. But no matter how many times I practice what to say, it is impossible to imagine Paul coming to any conclusion other than that I am completely psycho.

I end up calling him anyway, just because I'd like his company. It's Saturday, so he's not working, but he doesn't answer his cell, and I have to leave a message. I'm sure I sounded like a half-wit, mumbling about hiking the woods below Vulcan and trying to invite him without making it sound like a date.

Vulcan was the Roman god of fire, metalworking, and the forge, but in Birmingham he is the city's icon. As the world's largest cast iron statue, he's a source of pride and a reminder of the Magic City's roots in the iron and steel industry. Standing on a pedestal atop Red Mountain, Vulcan overlooks the city's heart, while his exposed rear end moons the neighboring suburb of Homewood.

Rather than risk a repeat idiot-phone performance with Paul, I decide to go for a hike alone. I've climbed the side of Red Mountain many times. Access to the trail is only a few blocks from my house. With my overlarge plastic bootie on my foot, I've been stuck indoors for the most part, and I ache to get out in the woods. Not wanting to lug a purse on the trail, I thread a holster into the belt on my jeans. In case Paul calls back, I stick my phone in my back pocket and a Bluetooth in my ear to keep my hands free.

Angel weaves loops through my ankles at the door, and I reach down to her. She lifts her head to touch her nose to my index finger, a ritual we appear to have developed that seems to function as "hello, person-who-feeds-me-tuna fish" or "goodbye, person-who-feeds-me-tuna fish." Afraid she might follow me, I maneuver her back with my foot. Normally, if she wants out, she yowls, but when I open the door, she stops dead and considers the whole idea of going out as if it had never occurred to her. I've learned the best response is just to play along, holding the door open until she decides to sashay out. All this occurs in reverse if I want her to stay inside; then she is a lightning bolt out the door.

The day is a little chilly but the climb warms me quickly, and I am soon too hot in my jacket, removing it and tying the arms around my waist. If someone happens by and sees my gun, they can just deal with it.

As always, the woods settle me in a way I can't explain—the crunch of leaves and pungent smell of earth, the patterned play of light through the mostly bare branches, tightly budded in readiness for spring. I've always felt part of the earth, connected to it. Now I understand why. My House, my family, are bound to it in a unique way. Maybe it's not such a coincidence that I returned here, to the place of my birth. Maybe it was the call of the woods and hills and the rich seams of coal as much as the rose-stone that brought me home.

I take the old road and after a while I veer off the path and angle up the side of the mountain, not sure where I am going or why, just following a vague pull. Somewhere above, Vulcan looks out over the spear he has forged, but I can't see him for the tangle of tree branches, even without their leaves.

My mind occupied with avoiding brambles, I move brush aside to reveal a hidden stack of stones. Part of a mine entrance? Mines riddle this last ripple of the Appalachians in northern and central Alabama. Some show up on old maps, but many don't.

What was it like when the mines bustled with men, risking their lives to go into the earth's belly? In earlier days, police arrested black men off the street for vagrancy and other vaguely defined petty crimes. As punishment, they toiled in the mines for the "Big Mules," the wealthy, powerful men who owned the land, the mines and the factories. Poor whites worked the mines, too, and lived on company land, shopped at company stores, and built up debt they could never repay. There's a lot of ugly in this city's past.

Abandoned for decades, the entrance to this mine has partially caved in. The living-green, making up for its banishment, grew over the opening, concealing it. Pulling a cluster of brown-leafed vines aside, I take a step inside, and fish my little flashlight from my jacket pocket. While I'm at it, I put the jacket back on, chilled in the damp twilight of the cave.

My light illuminates an area no bigger than my kitchen, supported by thick, rotting wooden beams. It doesn't look terribly stable; in fact, one large stone has apparently fallen from the ceiling. The back wall caved in long ago, as evidenced by a partially exposed rusted iron beam among the rocks.

From inside, I can see out through the tangled shrubbery and realize the opening is larger than it appeared. In summer, I would never have found this place.

When I sit on the ground, a tingle runs through my body, like the first sensation when blood starts to return to a foot that has gone to sleep. Is the living-green trying to tell me something? After my clumsy and failed attempt to scry in Five Points South after chasing the purse snatcher, I'm not very confident in my ability to make it work. So far, the future-seeing thing has seemed random and not controlled by me, at least not consciously. But I lean against the large stone, facing the mine opening and lift the pendant over my head, cupping it in my hands. The worst that can happen is nothing.

Watch the rock grow.

At first I can't see the facets, but as my eyes grow accustomed to the dim light, the diamond heart unfolds … and gives way to another layer … and another. The living-green flows up into me, cupping me in the same way the pendant is cupped in my hand.

In a world of softly rippling black and gray, I see a shadow of myself sitting cross-legged in the exact same spot and position I am sitting. *Is this a future-vision like the one of Zachary shooting Paul?*

In slow motion, the shadow-me starts to lift the pendant back around her neck. Through the curtain of brown vines that covers the mine entrance, a small silver casing with a copper top slices slowly through the molasses air. Six months ago, I'd never seen one up close, but now I've seen and handled hundreds of them.

It's a bullet. And it's headed for my chest

Chapter Twenty-Two

A burst of adrenalin breaks my connection to the shadow world where I have just seen the future—a future that includes a bullet with my name on it. I tuck and roll. A sharp ping sounds just behind me. Spitting dirt from my mouth, I belly-crawl behind the big stone and draw my own gun, wondering if I dare peek around the edge. I never heard the shot, just the sound of the bullet hitting the rock, which means someone is using a silencer. The bullet I saw up close and personal was not one I was familiar with, but the uncanny aim indicates a scope on a rifle. There's no telling how far away my shooter is.

My heart is thudding like a herd of buffalo. I risk a quick glance around the stone's edge, and another *ping* rewards my idiocy, followed by a puff of pulverized stone. Not going to do that again, or risk a wild shot down the mountain that might find its way into the residential neighborhood below.

I reach for my cell to call 911 just as it signals an incoming call—Paul's number. I hit the green, "Answer call."

"Paul?"

"Hi. Got your message. Where are you?

"I'm in an old mine above the Vulcan trail, but don't come near. Somebody with a rifle, scope, and silencer is taking pot shots at me."

"Somebody's *shooting* at you?"

"That's 10-4, but I've got cover now."

"I'm already part way up the trail. Hang on!"

"No! Don't be stupid, Paul. I can't see him, and he's really accurate. Can you stay where you are and get help?"

A hesitation. "10-4."

When he breaks the connection, I check the GPS on my cell for my location.

When Paul calls back, I give him the coordinates and hear sirens at the same time. He must have put it out on a police radio. God, they sound good!

Still, it seems forever before I hear anyone. Can't blame them. I wouldn't want to walk into a shooter's line of fire either, a lesson hammered home in the Academy when we were presented with an "officer down" training situation inside a house. Using the protocols we'd been taught to clear each room, my "partner" and I found the downed officer lying in a hallway. I thought I'd cleared the bathroom that opened out onto the hall, so I knelt to check on the victim. That's when the suspect popped up out of the bathtub and "shot" me.

Of all people, I should have known better. The bathtub was my shelter as a terrified child, hiding from the man who had murdered my family, maybe the same man who is focusing right now on this rock through the crosshairs of rifle sights.

But surely the sound of sirens has driven him away.

Paul is with the officers who scour the woods and find me after a few shouted exchanges.

"Rose!" he calls before getting in my line of fire. "It's me, don't shoot!"

I've rolled onto my back with my head against the stone, not even daring quick looks to make sure no one creeps up on me, trying to use my ears, but no more shots have been fired since Paul's call.

"I'm in here!" I shout, dropping my hand and gun onto my thigh in relief. Only then am I aware of the pounding in my head.

Paul charges in and kneels beside me, his own gun in his hands. "Are you hurt?"

My head feels like the stampeding buffalo from my heart took a detour into my temples. "I'm okay."

"You are a magnet for trouble."

I exhale. "You say the sweetest things, Nix."

He holds my gaze for a moment, his usually ruddy face pale, and breaks into a laugh. He grasps my shoulder. "What happened and who was shooting at you?"

"I was just exploring this mine entrance when someone took a pot shot at me, a couple of shots actually, and I dropped behind this stone."

"Good thing he was a rotten shot."

"Ah … yeah." *More like, good thing I saw a bullet headed my way before it was actually fired.*

Two patrol officers stand at the entrance. "Everything okay, Sergeant?"

"Yeah, we're 10-24 in here," Paul says. "Everything's okay."

Everything is not "okay," but it could have been a lot worse. I insist on hanging around while an evidence technician searches for the bullets inside the mine entrance. He finds two embedded in the back wall.

Paul insists on escorting me home.

All I want is a hot shower, hoping the steam will ease my pounding head. "I'll wait for you," he says, plopping himself down on my couch. I frown at Angel, who apparently never saw a lap she didn't want to occupy and has jumped into his. "We'll be fine," Paul smiles, stroking her. "Go wash up."

Despite his presence in the next room, I lock the bathroom door and lay my gun and phone on the top of the toilet.

I think better in a hot shower … and I need to think. *How could anyone have known I was going up that trail?* I didn't tell anyone I was going, except Paul. But it was no random shot that found its way through the narrow opening leading into the mine. Someone has to be following me. I flash to the fountain at Five Points South where we chased the purse snatcher to the gazebo behind the Hassinger Daniels Mansion. I had looked up and seen a black man with spiky red hair duck behind the trellis half a block away—Carrot Man. I lift my face to the hot stream of water, reviewing what I know about him: He knew Zachary, the boy I shot, and some man with "stony eyes" who hired him and Zachary for "jobs." Had that man hired Carrot Man to watch me … to run over me … to shoot me?

Nowhere is safe.

I make myself get out of the shower, which strangely feels like a more secure place than outside it—maybe precisely because it was my childhood hiding place. Why didn't I bring clothes into the bathroom? And while I am worrying, what would stop someone with a rifle scope from shooting into my living room window? I can't remember if I left the blinds open or closed. Tying my bathrobe securely, I drop my gun into the pocket and step out into the hall, still wet under my robe, my hand deep in the furry pocket.

Paul is waiting for me; or rather I almost run into him and have to step back. A thin white line marks his mustached upper lip. He grins sheepishly, and I realize he is holding a glass of milk in one hand and a chocolate chip cookie in the other.

"I was hungry," he says.

I will never be able to explain why I step between his hands and kiss him.

Chapter Twenty-Three

The kiss I give Detective Sergeant Paul Nix is not a wimpy one. He drops the filched cookie and the milk, which fortunately was in a plastic cup. To give him credit, after a moment of shock, he reacts, both hands lifting to cradle my face. Tenderly at first, and then, as fire kindles between us, his hands move down my neck and under my robe onto my bare shoulders. His mouth leaves mine and follows the path his hands took, down the pulsing vein of my neck, lingering in the hollow of my throat.

With a soft groan, I let my head fall back and reach down to untie my sash. Slowly, he pushes the robe off my shoulders, and it crumples to the floor with a *thunk*.

Fortunately, my gun doesn't go off.

"God!" Paul breathes and picks me up, cradling me in his arms. My bedroom is only a few steps away. He lays me down. I note that the blinds are shut, and then we are lost in each other.

Two hours later, we lie quietly, and, for the first time in my life, my head is cradled on a man's chest. Light copper hairs tickle my nose, but I don't want to move. His hand strokes up and down my spine.

I may have made the stupidest mistake of my life, but I don't regret listening to my heart instead of my head.

"Rose?"

"Umm?"

"I didn't realize you were … that you had never—"

"Spit it out, Nix."

"Was I too rough?"

I nip his nipple.

"Ouch!"

"No, you were not too rough."

His hand moves up into the mass of my hair. "I want to stay here."

I smile.

"Seriously. Someone's tried to kill you twice. I'm not leaving you alone."

"Is that an order, Sergeant?" I ask, climbing astride him.

"God, you are beautiful," he sighs.

"That's not an answer."

He groans. "Am I supposed to have an intelligent conversation in this position?"

"I just want you to realize that you don't have any rank in my bed."

"Yes, ma'am."

I WAKE TO A DELICIOUS smell and roll out of bed, grabbing Paul's shirt and stumbling to the aroma's source, which turns out to be the kitchen. All the dishes that had been piled in the sink have disappeared, and my kitchen has never smelled so good, except when it had Alice's chicken and dumplings in it.

"What wonderful thing are you making?" I ask.

He turns and smiles.

How did one milk mustache and a chocolate chip cookie change everything?

"Good morning, beautiful. Scrambled eggs with onion, and a little cheese. Nothing fancy. I'd make bacon, but you don't have any."

I snort. "You're trying to bribe me."

"Is it working?"

I move behind him and look around his arm at what's on the stove. "It might. What else do you do?"

"I'm pretty good at laundry."

Angel chooses that moment to give a plaintive meow and rub my calves, her tail held in the horizontal crook that means she wants attention.

"Do you have cat food, or does she want eggs?" Paul asks.

"Tuna fish." Reluctantly, I worm out of his arms and open a cabinet door to reveal stacks of one-serving canned tuna.

"Wow."

"Becca says I ruined her the first time I gave her a can, and it's true. She won't eat anything else."

I feed Angel while Paul finishes making breakfast. As usual, Angel attacks the tuna fish as if she is starving, tail now vertical. I'm beginning to understand what Alice meant when she said her cats talked, just not in words.

Paul raises his brows. "I didn't think she'd be hungry after lapping up all that milk I spilled last night."

"The milk! I forgot all about it."

"I did, too, until I got up this morning and almost stepped on the cup. There wasn't a drop of milk anywhere. I put your gun on the coffee table."

With a flourish, he lays a plate of golden eggs, glistening with melted cheese, along with a cup of milk and steaming coffee on the table. I am in awe at how he managed to produce coffee from a can of grounds. We sit and eat.

"It's a good thing I like a girl with an appetite," he says, not long after, nodding at my empty plate.

"I bet you say that to all the hungry girls you cook for."

He takes my hand, making me look him in the eyes. His are gray-green hazel with specks of amber. "There aren't other girls."

"Why not?" I am genuinely surprised.

"I swore off relationships after my wife died. I'm out of practice."

I tilt my head. "Are you fishing for a compliment?"

"No." He gives me a wicked grin. "Although you haven't exactly had enough experience to offer a fair comparison."

"Maybe not, but I am a happy girl."

He tightens his grip on my hand. "I want you to be happy. Rose, I don't want to scare you off. I know how private you are, but I want to be in your life, not just your bed."

I blink in surprise. "Is this the same man who snapped at me when I didn't write a report fast enough?"

He frowns. "I did do that, didn't I? I told you I wasn't good with women."

"You did, but I forgive you."

He sits back. "Last night, before—"

"I attacked you?" I finish, setting the cup back on the table.

"Yeah, before that, I was trying to figure out how to convince you to let me sleep on your couch."

"Why would you want to do that?"

"Rose, you keep forgetting that someone has tried to kill you twice in the last couple of months."

I have, which is pretty amazing.

"I'm still willing to sleep on the couch, if you want. I don't want to rush you into anything, but I want to be here."

I clench my teeth. "To protect me?"

"Yes, damn it. Is that so awful?"

"What are you going to do when I have to go work my cases? You can't just tag along, you know. And you might have a homicide or two to deal with."

"I know I can't be with you all the time, but at least whoever it is will know you're not alone at night."

My gaze drifts to the kitchen window, unconsciously looking for a glimpse of red spiky hair. Maybe it would be good to have someone here besides a cat. But the thought of giving up my privacy sends a bolt of panic through me. This is my house; I have things the way I want them. Okay, maybe I'm not the best housekeeper in the world, but living with someone is a big commitment with compromises and … I'm not ready. I hardly know who I am at this point. Not only that, but whatever this is that has happened between us is a fragile thing, just born. I don't want to smother it. All of this floods into my mind at once and gets stalled trying to come out my mouth.

"I—"

"Stop," Paul says. "You don't have to explain. I understand. It's too much to ask after one night. It's just, I've felt this way since I first met you, so it's a no-brainer for me."

"You have?"

"You had me at 'hello.' That's probably why I was tough on you."

I have to laugh, and that breaks the discomfort and tension that was building inside me. Angel, who has finished her tuna breakfast, lightly jumps onto a chair and from there, the table, checking out what little remains of our breakfast. "Angel!" I grab her and dump her onto the floor. She stalks to a corner and lifts a paw, licking it and dabbing at her ears to regain her dignity.

I sip my coffee. "So now what?"

"Well, it's Sunday." He grabs a handful of my wild curls and pulls me toward him. "I promise I'll be out of your hair by midnight."

Chapter Twenty-Four

Monday morning, my phone *pings* while I am opening a can for Angel. Her meows are more insistent than the phone, so she gets her breakfast before I check it. But when I do pick up my cell, my heart skips. It's a news alert. "Officer Hoffman's Appeal—Guilty Verdict Upheld."

Paul's words come back to me. *There was that pesky bullet in the guy's back. Hoffman never had a chance of winning that one.*

It's been ten weeks since I shot and killed Zachary. The state has sent their findings to the D.A. He's dragging his feet on making a determination on whether to take my shooting to the Grand Jury and press criminal charges against me. Paul says he's a politician and waiting for the incident to die down. If that's so, he will probably wait longer now that Hoffman is back in the news. I feel like I'm sitting below a cliff with a boulder balanced above me, tottering on the edge. Meanwhile, nothing is slowing down. Yesterday, someone tried to kill me for the second time in my adult life.

At the threshold of my front door, I hesitate, a vein fluttering in my throat. Will Carrot Man be watching for me through the crosshairs of a gun? I find myself actually considering whether I am going to hunker down inside these walls for the rest of my life or walk through the door.

Angel meows. She would probably be fine with her human slave sticking around to open those annoying tuna fish cans.

"Not going to happen, Angel," I say, taking a deep breath and stepping out into a cold, overcast, windy day. Winter has arrived, at least for today.

At the office, it's difficult to pay attention to the stack of paperwork awaiting me. My mind bounces between the sweet night with Paul, the *ping* of a bullet inches from my head, and visions of living behind prison bars like

Hoffman. By lunch, I am desperate for Paul to call and offer a distraction. Finally, he does, but just to say he's tied up on a case.

Annoyed and hungry, I reach down to grab my purse under the desk. When I look up, Tracey has appeared.

"Want to go to lunch?" he asks.

"Sure, where did you have in mind?"

"You don't happen to like Indian food, do you?"

"I happen to love it."

"The girl of my dreams. You know the little place off Highland Avenue?"

"I think I've seen it on patrol, but Paul wasn't big on non-American food."

Taj is a hole in the wall inside a strip shopping mall on Highland Avenue at the edge of Five Points South business district. Snagging a parking place in the small parking lot requires knowing the rules of the dance. Because the strip harbors a small Western Supermarket, turnover of spaces is high, so parking is a game where one has to track which space "belongs" to which waiting vehicle.

Inside, the place is larger than it seems with another quiet, darker room in the back. In Indian fashion, it is festooned with colorful decor. A canopy in deep red, yellow and green hangs over the bar. Paintings of India fill the walls. The god Shiva sits on a counter top with a stringed musical instrument. He also occupies a place in a display case with other cultural paraphernalia near the buffet line. The steaming dishes look wonderful. I take some of everything.

Over butter chicken and *sarson da saag*, Tracey gives me a strange look.

"What?" I say around a mouthful. Tracey usually catches me up on department gossip. Has the word leaked out about Paul and me? Already?

"I can't help but notice that you seem to be a magnet for bullets and speeding cars," he says.

"The *sarson* is spicy," I say, "but I can't stop eating it."

"Rose, I've figured out you don't like big noses in your business, but I just want to let you know that I'm here if you ever want to talk about anything or need back up."

I don't respond for a moment. When I first walked into the Burglary Unit completely clueless, it was Tracey who offered his assistance. He showed up at the hospital though he hardly knew me. At Alice's funeral, reading the panic stricken look on my face when the carload of House of Iron arrived, he'd put his hand on his gun, ready to do whatever was called for. I believe this is an official offer of friendship. I suck at that, but I'm trying to learn how to do it.

"Thanks."

THE DAYS PASS SLOWLY, EVEN though, in addition to Paul Nix, I have lots to think about—the same tangle that has been plaguing me since I stepped foot in this town. To be honest with myself, maybe it has always shadowed me—the how-to-figure-out-who-killed-my-family that now includes a who-is-trying-to-kill-*me* part.

I keep coming back to Alice's death. I looked up the symptoms Stephanie noted while Alice was dying on her kitchen floor, and they do match the doctor's report of heart failure. Still, I can't shake the feeling that something is wrong. Deep down, I just don't believe she had a "normal" heart failure, despite her age. Something about her death doesn't seem right. I have begun to respect my gut feelings, even when they collide with reality.

The hell with it. I grab my coat and leave. Lieutenant Fish, deep in discussion on the phone, never looks up.

At Alice's house, I examine each room, especially the kitchen and bathroom, but I can't find any indication of poisoning. Not that I have a great idea what to look for that might give someone a delayed heart failure, especially as they haven't even sent me to detective school yet. There are no medications anywhere, just her plants, which I guiltily water. Sometimes I forget the plants.

She didn't seem to use any makeup or even lotion, but I pick up a bottle of cologne in the bedroom and sniff. Honeysuckle. It smells like Alice. That would be an ingenious way to hide some kind of toxin or poison. She would have put it on her skin every day. I know there are substances that can carry through the skin. Ingenious. I pop it in a plastic bag and stick it in my purse.

In the bathroom I stare at the sink. Poisoning her water would be difficult, and the plants seem fine, despite my abuse, but I check under both the bathroom and kitchen sinks, and go outside to check the line where it comes into the house. Nothing. It couldn't be something in the air or anywhere the cats go, as they appear quite healthy. And if Angel is any guide, cats go everywhere.

I sit in Alice's chair to think. Instantly, Charlie, the Siamese, claims my lap, kneading my stomach. Absently, I stroke her, as Angel has trained me to do. If there was no poison in the house, how could Alice have been exposed? Maybe she ate or drank something at the House of Iron, some snack meant for me. That seems a bit cumbersome. I am being paranoid. Maybe I am just being paranoid, and it all just feels wrong to lose her because I had only begun to know her.

Running out of ideas, I put Charlie down. Curled on a pillow on another chair, Alexander, coat black as midnight, watches me, while Boo, stretched along the back of the sofa licks his spiffy white paw, the tip of his tail twitching.

"Guess it's just us now, guys."

Chapter Twenty-Five

When my cell rings the next morning, I'm disappointed the caller isn't Paul. Guilt replaces regret at the obvious distress in Becca's voice. "Becca, what is it? What's wrong?"

"Everything," she wails.

"Meet me at the Pita Stop," I say.

"I can't afford to eat."

"The Pita Stop, Becca," I order. "In fifteen minutes."

Sniffling, she hangs up.

"I'm going out," I announce to the empty office.

"Are you going to tell me what's happened?" I demand when we are seated.

Becca blows her nose. It is already red, as are her eyes, her eyeliner smeared. Becca's eyeliner is never smeared. This is serious.

She takes a long swallow of sweet ice tea and one more sniff. "I lost my job."

"What? Oh no, what happened?"

"My boss tried to cop a feel." She hiccups.

My hands clench. "That jerk! And he fired you because you wouldn't let him?"

"Not exactly."

"Well, what exactly did he fire you for? There are sexual harassment laws, you know."

"Umm, well, probably he fired me for hitting him with his golf club."

I almost choke. "What?"

She hiccups again. "I know. They had to take him to the hospital for stitches. Don't laugh, Rose. I'm blackballed. I'll never find another job in a law firm. You know how everyone talks to everyone."

It takes a hard bite on my upper lip to keep from laughing. "Okay," I say finally. "We can think our way through this."

Becca's lower lip quivers. "I can't go to my aunt, Rose. I am not going back there. I never told you about it, but my uncle … hurt me when I was young."

This quenches any remaining desire to laugh. "I didn't know. I'm sorry."

The waiter returns to take our order.

"The usual," I say firmly, and to Becca, "I'm paying."

"But—"

"No 'buts.' You can pay me back when you get another job."

"Maybe I can flip hamburgers or something. At least I still have the waitress job."

"What are you talking about? You're a highly skilled receptionist."

Tears fill her eyes. "I was saving to go to law school. They have classes downtown at night, but I'm already a month behind on my rent. Crap, I am such a mess. I don't mean to dump all this on you. I don't expect anything; I just needed to tell somebody."

I take a breath. "Well, the first thing we have to do is find a—Becca, I just had a brilliant thought."

She looks up. "What?"

"My Aunt Alice left me her house. You can live in it!"

Her eyes widen. "Don't you want to live in it?"

"No, I don't. I can't handle the cats and the plants … and being in her home."

"But it's too much. I can't afford a house—"

"Who said anything about money?"

"That's not right. I would never ask that of you."

"You don't understand, Becca. Alice left me money to take care of the house. And it would be a great favor to me. You know I hate cleaning my own house."

Becca's eyebrows rise.

"Okay," I amend, "when I get around to it, I hate it, and I'm not an early riser. Since Alice died, I have to get up early every day and go feed her cats and water her plants, and God knows, that place could use a vacuum cleaner."

Hope replaces the devastation in her face.

"Are you sure?"

"Positive. Are you willing to do that? There are three cats. Two live mostly outdoors though."

"I love cats."

"And lots of plants. I haven't the faintest clue what they are, but I feel responsible for them."

"Oh, Rose, you are the *best* friend! How can I thank you?"

"By not letting that jerk stop you from getting out there and finding another job in your profession. A better job."

She sniffs, hiccups, and lifts her glass. "To getting back out there."

I clink her iced tea with my lemon water.

THE HOMICIDE OFFICE IS JUST down the hall from the Burglary unit. I get stares and a low whistle when I walk through the door and ask for Paul. I'm sort of used to that, but I know the tongues will be wagging. I'm the rookie who shot a burglar and caused a lot of stir. I regret my decision to enter the hallowed Homicide office and turn on my heel, or what little heel I wear.

"Rose!"

I turn back. "Detective Nix. May I speak to you a moment ... about a case," I add loudly.

He follows me back into the hallway.

"I'm sorry, Paul. I wasn't thinking."

"Sorry for what?"

"You're going to get harassed; I should have just met you somewhere."

He grins. "They're just jealous. Feel like getting out tonight? Can I take you to dinner?"

"I have a favor to ask you."

"Anything."

"This is serious."

"Okay, what?"

I pull the cologne bottle from my purse. "I need this analyzed."

"What is it?"

"Cologne."

He starts to open it and lifts it to his nose.

"Don't," I say, grabbing his arm.

He freezes. "What the hell is it?"

"That's what I want to know. Can you get the lab to check it out?"

"Not unless I hook it to a case. You know how backed up forensics is."

I swallow. "It's from my great aunt's house."

He looks at me. "You think she was poisoned by her perfume?"

I don't say anything, but my earlobes burn.

"Rose?"

"What?"

"What is this about?"

"You said you would do anything for me."

"Rose, I was there when your aunt collapsed." He lifts the bottle. "This doesn't make any sense. A doctor signed the death certificate and did an autopsy. He found no evidence of foul play."

"Well, maybe he was wrong."

"I'm pretty new in this unit. I don't want to screw it up."

"Paul, I can't explain right now, but I think it's related to who's trying to kill me."

For a long moment, he looks into my eyes, and then he brushes my cheek with a finger. "I'll try."

"Thank you." I start to turn away and turn back. "Pick me up at six?"

Chapter Twenty-Six

I am a tree, ignorant in winter's slumber, barely aware of roots dug deep into the earth or the thirst that compels them. The fire begins at my outer branches, bright orange against the dark night, wiping out the stars, eating its way toward the trunk, burning me to wakefulness and a sweaty tangle of sheets.

Confused, I blink at the clock, which says it's 3 a.m. That means I've had exactly two hours of sleep. I roll over, expecting to encounter Paul, but the bed is empty except for Angel, stretched out, her head on a pillow. It's amazing how much room this small cat can claim.

My cell phone rings.

"Hello?" I say, groggily.

"Rose? Are you awake?" Paul says.

"That's a stupid question. If I weren't awake, I would be after answering the phone." I yawn. "Yes, I'm awake. Why did you leave?"

"I thought you didn't want me to stay."

I don't know what I want, but I don't have to explain my way out of my contradictory feelings, because his next words shake me.

"I've got my first homicide call, and I think you should come out here."

"What? Why? Where are you?"

"I'm near that cave on Red Mountain."

As Paul had promised, a patrol car waits for me at the trail's entrance. Two patrolmen escort me up, guns drawn, which means they haven't located the suspect. I pull my jacket closer, hearing again the *ping* of shots on the rock, shots that chipped out stone precisely an inch from where my head had just been. If that sharpshooter has me in his sights, the presence of these patrolmen isn't going to amount to a hill of beans.

There's another reason to pull my jacket close. It's snowing. Reflexively, I do a mental check on my stock of bread and milk. Any amount of snow sends everyone in the South rushing to the grocery store, sure the end of the world is nigh, and bread and milk will be impossible to find. But since that first night with Paul, I keep an extra carton of milk in my fridge anyway.

A circle of flashlights marks the crime scene, and Paul steps forward to meet me. He grabs me by the shoulders. "I thought—"

He doesn't finish what he was about to say, but I figure he means he thought at first that it might be me up here, even though he left me sprawled in my bed.

"Rose, look at the body and see if you recognize him. There's got to be a connection."

I follow him to the body. It's a man with rugged, handsome features, dressed as one would expect for the time and season. I lean closer and see the small bullet hole drilled precisely into the center of his forehead. The snow at the back of his head is stained with blood and bits of tissue. I shudder.

"Did you know him?" Paul asks.

"No. I've never seen him before." This has to be connected with my shooting, and that means House of Rose/House of Iron business.

Paul shakes his head. "Nothing. Not even an ID. Looks like a robbery … or somebody wanted it to look like a robbery."

"When did it happen?"

"Not sure, but probably not tonight."

The snow is falling, coating the bare tree limbs in sleeves of white and covering the body like a shroud.

"What about footprints?" I ask.

"We've got one; the snow's covered everything else."

"Can I see it?"

"Sure."

About fifty yards southeast down the slope, a patrolman is stationed under a hardwood tree with a low branch accessible to a person, if he were in good shape. Above us, two branches up, is a flat platform like a hunter's stand.

"I think he was up there," Paul says. "He left an impression in the ground when he jumped down. We've just got this one print that was protected from the snow by that evergreen branch." He points to a heavy sweep of pine. Below it is most of a large print.

I drop to one knee, careful not to disturb the snow around it, though I was sure they had already photographed it.

"Have you got a quarter?" I ask.

Paul fumbles in his pocket and hands it to me. I put it down beside the print, pull out my cell phone and make my own photo.

"Nice work, detective."

"Maybe I'll make Homicide someday," I mumble, my head bent over my phone trying to hold it steady in the cold.

I find the older photo I'm looking for in my phone's files and hold it for Paul to see. He examines it for a minute, comparing it to the one on the ground. "Could be the same shoe. Same size. Tread is identical." He looks up at me, his eyes hard. "That's the footprint from outside your window, isn't it?"

I nod.

"So the man who shot my victim by the mine entrance is possibly the man who shot at you last week and the same man who was prowling around your house in the middle of the night, and … maybe the same man who tried to run over you."

A lot of maybes to put on a footprint, but I am thinking the same thing.

Again, he takes me by the shoulders. "Rose, there was nothing but perfume in that bottle."

I tighten my lip stubbornly.

Paul's fingers tighten on my shoulders. "What is going on here?"

I don't answer.

"You know more about this than you're telling me. Don't you trust me?" There is disappointment behind the fixed gaze he holds on me, and I know he is hurt that I am keeping things from him.

All kinds of emotions are chasing their tails in my head. But he doesn't own me, and I don't owe him anything, and I shake off his hands. "Back off, Nix."

"I'm not going to back off. This is my case and your life is in danger."

"It's my life."

He gives me a shake and that is the last thing I need. I step back and wrench away from him, turn and head back down the hill wrapping my arms around myself. I'm angry at him for putting his hands on me like that, but deeper down I realize I am an idiot. Paul wants more from this relationship than I'm willing or able to give him. This isn't a movie where a secret as basic as who—or what—I am doesn't matter. *It matters.* But I can't risk telling him. He'll insist I see a shrink … or worse, and I can't keep lying to him. And more importantly, I can't put him in danger. This has to stop. I have to stop it.

It's hard to ignore the tightness in my chest, but I remind myself that I have worse problems on my hands than Paul's disenchantment. Someone is trying to kill me. And I have to figure out what to do about it.

Chapter Twenty-Seven

I walk home in the crusty snow to find the last thing I expected—an invitation to dinner from Jason Blackwell of the House of Iron who possibly wants me dead, although a dinner invitation seems a strange choice of weapon. Maybe now he just wants me. I don't particularly like the fact that my heart rate shot up when I saw the signature. But I am not dead … yet.

Yesterday morning's coffee, made for me by Paul, is ugly in my mouth, but I need the caffeine and all I have in the cabinet is herbal tea. The envelope had been slipped into the mailbox on my porch, no stamp, and I open it at the kitchen table. The gold-inked invitation is a formal invite to dinner. *What century are we in?* For a moment, I wonder if I have somehow slipped into the shadow world but the opposite way, into the past.

Angel, seeing an unoccupied piece of paper, jumps up and lies on it, reaching out her paw to touch my hand. I sigh, assured I am in the "right" world. Why worry about her being on the kitchen table, when I know she walks all over it and every other reachable surface when I'm not here? I have a perforated toothpaste tube, salt on the floor, and underwear scooped out of the drawer when I leave it open. Okay, maybe it's hard to tell if she does that or I do, but I'm pretty sure the pair I found hanging on the lamp was her doing.

I stare into the black, scummy void inside my cup. Angel, still claiming the invitation from Jason as her personal space, rolls onto her back and looks up at me coquettishly. Maybe she is showing off the little red collar I bought her to go with her shiny red rabies tag.

I paw through the other pile of papers, Alice's bank records that I asked for going back to when she opened the account. They charged me for them, but I had insisted, armed with the lawyer's instructions and "letters of testamentary" document that states I am the executor of her will and estate. It's now 5 a.m., too early to get ready for work, but an hour of sleep is just going to make me worse. I spread out the papers and go over them entry by entry, looking for payments to the adoption agency. Then, one flip of the page, and something unexpected jumps out at me.

"I think I see how the House of Iron caught on to Alice," I say aloud.

Angel seems unimpressed.

I tap at an entry. "She messed up and sent a check directly to the University of Alabama with my name on it, instead of funneling it through the adoption agency's post office box. Angel, do you think that Iron has tendrils into the bank here? It wouldn't be that hard, with all their money." It's the best theory I've come up with so far. I test my logic: So, they had an inside to Alice's bank records and discovered I was alive and at the University of Alabama. Then all they had to do was keep an eye on me. They knew the rose-stone would sing its siren song sooner or later, and I would be returning to Birmingham.

I am pacing now, but stop to put the coffee dregs in the microwave. Maybe heating it up will make it palatable. While I wait, I inform Angel about the dinner date invitation. "What now? Should I ignore it? Go?"

The microwave *dings*. I retrieve the coffee, which is worse than it had been cold, make some herbal tea instead, and plop back down in my chair to rub Angel's proffered belly. She immediately sinks her claws lightly into my hand. She wants it, but she doesn't. Fickle girl. Just like her human. She rakes her back paws into my hand, claws carefully sheathed, playing at disemboweling me I suppose.

"I know," I tell her. "Going to dinner with Jason Blackwell would be an extremely stupid thing to do."

Chapter Twenty-Eight

The Club (pronounced with emphasis on "The") is a private dinner club atop Red Mountain overlooking the city. Very posh. I wear my black dress and a pair of heels I bought, which are killing me. How do women walk in these things? I let the valet park the car, because I don't think I could make it all the way across the parking lot.

In spite of the fact that she is dead, I can hear Alice in my head protesting how dangerous it is to meet Jason Blackwell anywhere. I wonder if any of my family members were prone to do dangerous or impulsive things. If so, I inherited it, and it's not my fault, right? Besides, I've got to have info, and I'm not going to get any sitting on my butt.

Also, I'm not being disloyal to Paul because a) I'm just meeting Jason to get data, and b) I broke up with Paul. We argued for almost an hour on the phone. He wasn't happy about it. I'm not happy either, but his need to dig is something that he won't and can't stop doing, any more than I could if I were in his shoes. And it's not just that, but what he will find out if he digs deep enough—what I really am. And then what? It's better to leave it this way.

Hence, I am, for the sake of gaining intelligence about House of Iron, practically standing on my toes trying not to fall on my face. My sympathies to the Chinese girls whose feet were bound in ancient times to keep them small for the aesthetic taste of Chinese men. Thinking about that horrid practice makes me angry. *Why am I torturing myself on these stilts for the pleasure of men?*

By the time I make it to the private dining room, I'm scowling.

"*Ciao*, Rose!" Jason greets me, rising from his chair at a table by the expansive window. "You are beautiful even when you look ready to eat the first person in your path."

"I look like that?"

"Indeed."

"It's the shoes."

"Ah." He pulls out my chair, and I sit … gratefully.

A bottle of wine chills in a bowl on a small stand by the table. I've seen setups like this in movies, but this is way out of my comfort zone. Jason gestures at the wine. "I took the liberty of ordering. It's a fine year. Would you like to try it?"

"Yes."

He lifts a finger and a waiter I didn't even see glides to our table and opens the bottle, pouring a small amount in Jason's glass. It would be nice to have a touch of James Bond sophistication with wine at this point, but I can see it's a French white from the label, and that's about the extent of my wine knowledge. Fortunately, Jason seems at home with the requirements and takes a sip, savoring it on his tongue for a moment before nodding assent at the waiter, who pours my glass first, then his. I watch all this with fascination, and because I am afraid to look at my date. He almost hurts the eyes. Suddenly Becca's voice is in my head: *Oh my God, Rose. Does he have a brother?*

That breaks the spell and I smile. *Thank you, Becca.*

"So, has anyone tried to kill you lately?" Jason asks, turning his attention to me.

I laugh and chastise myself for being so easily charmed. This man, I remind myself, may have lived a lot longer than I, despite his youthful looks. "Actually, I have managed to outwit a sniper since we last saw each other."

His face, which I am watching carefully, hardens. "I didn't know that. He missed, I assume."

"How do you know it was a 'he'?"

Now it is his turn to laugh. "Be easy, detective. I do not know that. It was a chauvinistic guess."

The waiter sets down a basket that smells heavenly. Jason folds back the white linen to reveal the warm breads inside. "You must try an orange roll, house specialty."

I bite into it and close my eyes. After I swallow, my tongue finds the bits of crystalized sugar on my lips.

Jason clears his throat. "I'm not sure if I wish to eat or simply watch you eat."

I open my eyes, my earlobes burning, and snatch at the menu.

I order fish, and he orders lamb. Appropriate. I feel like a lamb stalked by a wolf and wonder if I used enough deodorant to last through dinner.

"Umm, would your wife approve of us being here?" I ask.

"My wife?"

"Stephanie."

He leans back. "Stephanie is my step-aunt, though she is younger than I, but to answer your question, she definitely would not approve."

Aunt? So much for my assumptions. But Stephanie mentioned that women of House of Iron don't live extended lives. That would make sense, if anything in this can be said to make sense. They are the "normals" in that House.

Jason's gaze drifts to the huge window that looks down into the valley. "It is a beautiful view, isn't it?" Below us, the lights gleam like multicolored gems.

"It is." But I look away because the view reminds me of Paul and "our" place overlooking the city

"Sometimes," Jason says, "when I cannot sleep, I look down on this from my bedroom window."

Warning bells ding in my head. This personal revelation is a bit of intimacy meant to make himself appear more human, a little bait thrown out to gain my sympathy.

I can play the game as long as I know there is a hook beneath the bait … right?

"You have trouble sleeping?" I ask.

"More often than I'd like."

I wonder what *his* nightmares are about.

I take another swallow of wine and decide it is time to stop flitting around. "I have a question."

He arches a brow.

"Who is trying to kill me?" I ask.

For a swiftly passing moment, his face tightens. Anger? Then the lines smooth and he considers me.

"I do not know."

"You have no idea?"

"No."

Was there the slightest hesitation before that answer? He takes my hand and lightly rubs a thumb down the inside of my wrist. My pulse jumps. "Jump" is the wrong word, more like "catapults."

"Are you certain someone tried to kill you? Perhaps the man in the car was intoxicated."

"If I wasn't sure, the bullet fired at me a week ago fixed that. A man was killed later in the same exact place." *Not exact, he'd been outside the mine entrance, but close enough.*

His lips part in surprise, and he hesitates. "Are you speaking of the man found in the woods on Red Mountain?"

"Yes."

"I did know … or I read about it, but I had no idea you were connected."

I don't tell him I lost Paul over it, and I try not to look at those sensuous lips and imagine how they might feel against mine, a truly difficult task. What *is* it about this guy?

I take a deep swallow of wine and feel it burning into my chest. "Are we going to have an honest discussion?"

His mouth crooks again. "That would be novel."

"Answer the question," I demand.

"Yes. Yes, we are going to have an honest discussion." He is amused again, which is irritating.

"You know more about who might have tried to kill me than you are telling me."

"What makes you say that?"

"I'm a detective, remember?"

"I think you are prejudiced against the House of Iron."

"Maybe."

He leans back. "I honestly don't know. At times I've thought it could be someone in my House, but I've no proof of any kind. Most of my youth was spent in Italy where my father had a villa and a mistress. After his death, I remained there. It is still my primary residence."

"So who comes to mind when you think that?"

"Let us not play this game. I have no knowledge that my family is involved. If I ever have, I will tell you. I find I have a desire to keep you alive. *Frutti proibiti sono i più dolci.*"

"Which means?"

"Forbidden fruit is the sweetest."

My ears burn again. "Is that a promise, Mr. Blackwell?"

"It is a promise." He smiles. "Enough of that. Now, let's talk about you."

My defenses rear up. "What about me?"

"I take it you are not a social butterfly."

"Was it the shoes thing?"

He laughs. "In part. You are intriguing, Miss Brighton, though forbidden fruit."

I sip my own wine. "Forbidden? In what way?"

"House of Iron and House of Rose never … intermingle."

"Really? Why is that?"

"Let us call it a strong cultural tradition. Both Houses must marry outsiders."

His reaction makes me suspect this prohibition is more along the lines of prejudice, and my jaw tightens. "Them" and "us" exist even among the witches and warlocks.

"Since we are being honest and everything," I say, "tell me why you think the fire that killed my family was an accident."

"That is how it was reported by the police and fire department at the time."

I'm caught off guard. "Are you telling me it was ruled accidental?"

"Yes, of course."

I take a deep breath. "It was not accidental, Jason."

"And why are you so certain of that?"

I take a deep breath, watching him. "I was there."

A small intake of breath. He is genuinely surprised.

"Did you not know I was listed among the dead?" I ask.

"I was not in this country at the time. Of course, I heard about it and that it was blamed on an electrical fire. You must have been a small child. How did you survive?"

"I climbed out a window."

"Did you see anyone?"

"Yes, but not clearly."

He waits.

"He was slender. He seemed tall, but that's from a child's perspective, and he was wearing black."

"That description could fit a lot of people." Jason's mouth is a grim line.

"I know. I've always called him Mr. Black in my mind."

A thin man dressed in black stands in front of the open window, a match in his hand. I shiver.

"Are you cold?" Jason starts to remove his dinner jacket.

I lift my hand to stop him. "No, I'm fine."

"Did you tell the police?"

I take a sip of wine. "No. I was five years old. My aunt—"

"Who died in our house?"

"Yes. My great aunt shipped me off to a foster home to hide me."

"From the murderer … 'Mr. Black'?"

I know he has not missed the irony of his last name being Blackwell. "Alice believed it was someone from the House of Iron."

He bends forward slightly. "What matters to me is what *you* believe."

"Why?" I ask, slightly breathless at his proximity and alarmed at how easy it would be to believe him.

With a smile, he leans back in his chair. "I would think it is pretty obvious."

"I thought Rose and Iron never *intermingle.*"

"I did not say I want to have a child with you."

"Right." My ears burn hotter, both from embarrassment and a sudden surge of anger. "What is the problem? Would it dilute the bloodline?"

"It is not that simple. There is apparently a risk of offspring that are … abominations."

"What kind of abomination? What does that mean?"

"To be honest, I do not know. It is lore passed down for thousands of years."

I swallow. "Thousands?"

He smiles indulgently. "Our kind has been around quite a while. The reasons for some things are lost to time, and we must rely on traditions. The first tenet hammered into our psyches is the necessity for secrecy. We cut our teeth on the tales of burning and torture."

"I wasn't raised that way."

"This really is all new to you, is it not? It's hard to grasp the concept that you were not indoctrinated with tales of warnings and our days of glory."

"Days of glory?"

"Mostly in western civilization, although our kind are scattered across the world. In what is now Europe and the Middle East, it is claimed we go back— some say as far as the days of Noah." He has the grace to accompany this pronouncement with a brief smile of indulgence—"but at least as far as the Stonehenge scientist-priests and the early Greek philosophers. The history gets a little more solid into the Middle Ages. Your House has particular links with the Knights Hospitaller."

I arch my brows. "And I suppose the Masons 'get in there' as well?"

"Actually yes, some of the secret orders," he says without a blink. "We played roles in history behind the scenes—all the dramas of England's monarchies and wars, at least according to our own accounts. We have the advantage of time. Perhaps we have not always used it wisely."

At the look on my face, he smiles wryly. "This all must be … unsettling at the least."

That is an understatement. I imagine I seem a terribly young, impulsive and ignorant member of his rival House. My entire twenty-two years I never knew who I really was, and the more I'm learning, it seems the more distant I am from my own assumptions.

Our food comes at that moment. It is beautifully presented, with a small sprig of cilantro and a lemon wedge cut artfully in a spiral design, and I realize I'm starving. While he talks, I eat, feeling his eyes on me again. I want to believe he had nothing to do with my family's murder. I can't explain why. I just do. Maybe because his eyes are so blue.

When our plates are whisked away, I excuse myself from the table to powder my nose and wobble my way down the hall. "If I ever try to wear heels again, just shoot me," I mumble aloud.

A platinum-haired lady exiting the women's restroom gives me an odd glance. I smile and point to my ear. She sniffs in disapproval of the concept of people talking on invisible phones in public and walks on with her nose in the air.

Once inside, the first thing I do is kick off the shoes, sit on the toilet seat and rub my arches. I linger just long enough to give my feet a reprieve, wash my hands, and reapply lip gloss. Lipstick requires far too much aim and control. My hair is curling wildly from the moisture outside, but there's not much I can do about that. I wash my hands and dry them in the curls, a temporary taming technique. Reluctantly, I slip the heels back on.

In the hall, a girl with freckled skin and bony elbows steps carefully around the corner, balancing a tray of glasses. Unbeckoned, a surge of living-green sweeps into me. The girl freezes, and a shadow girl steps ahead of her, slightly out of focus, moving in my direction.

A portly shadow man exits the men's room, which is next to the women's room where I stand, and bumps into the girl, spilling her tray. He turns on her, angry and wobbly, probably drunk. I can't hear anything he says to her, but it isn't necessary. The slump of her shoulders reflects his abuse. The whole thing fades, and the girl in my universe or timeline resumes walking toward me.

Without thinking about it, I step to the men's room and lean against the door. Someone on the other side pushes to get out, but I set my weight into it.

"What the hell?" he slurs from inside.

When the waitress is safely past, I move away from the door, and it bursts open. The man staggers out like carbonated foam pent up in a can. At that moment, the headache that seems associated with seeing into the future hits me, and I just happen to step on his foot with my heel. "Oh, I am so sorry," I say and leave him cursing and limping in a circle.

These shoes might be good for something, after all.

After dinner, I fend off Jason's offer to take me dancing. It's difficult enough to keep my dignity from across the table. If he put his arms around me, I think I would melt right there into a puddle at his feet. Not happening. I thank him and call it a night. He's obviously not happy and neither am I, but I'm safe.

Chapter Twenty-Nine

The next day, despite a restless night, I am back at work. My period of light duty is officially over, and as soon as possible, I'm out of the office, interviewing my victims and paying a visit to the public library, where I search back through old copies of the *Birmingham News*. I'm not sure of the exact date, but it was spring. I remember the blooming azalea bushes. I go on the assumption that I was five years old, as Aunt Alice had mentioned. Still, it takes two hours of hunting before I find it on the second page:

"Family Dies in Night Fire."

I am listed as one of the dead. "…two children, April, 5, and Amber, 4, were among the casualties." *April.* My name was April Rose Hawkins. My adoptive family had given me their surname and the hated, "Veronica," but had honored Alice's request through the agency to give me the middle name of "Rose."

Carefully, I scan the stories for the next several days. Nothing. Then I stumble on a tiny article on the back page that says, "Fire and police investigators have ruled last week's tragic fire on Southside accidental."

I write down the names of the investigators.

With a phone call to the fire department, I learn that their investigator died of heart failure shortly after the fire. Police Personnel confirms the arson detective died in a car accident one week later. And a call to the medical examiner's office that the examiner had a massive stroke a month after that. They were loose ends. Did the man I am calling Mr. Black bribe them? Threaten their families? And then kill them? It's hard to imagine how he might have covered up an arson-homicide. The bullets would not have just disappeared from the bodies; gasoline would have made the fire more intense in particular areas. And there was a body missing—me.

And there was the bank. If Alice's slipup paying the university directly that one time was the clue Black had been waiting for, it meant that somehow he had gotten access to Aunt Alice's account. Whoever he was, he had fingers in the fire and police departments and a major bank. That took money or political power or both.

Shaken by the article on my family's death, I drop in on Becca at my dead aunt's house.

"The place looks great, Becca," I tell her. "Even the plants look happy."

I'm not just saying that. They do—the leaves are the right shade of glossy green, not the dejected yellow that plants under my care inevitably turn. So much for my heritage of drawing power from the "living-green," or maybe that's the problem. Maybe I suck the life right out of them. I'm just not good with living things, including, it seems, boyfriends and probably pets. Fortunately, Angel is a survivor.

"I love this house, but I feel like a visitor," Becca says, glancing down at the cats winding around her ankles. "Would you like a cup of coffee?"

Somehow, coffee doesn't feel right here, even if I liked it. "How about some tea?"

"Iced tea?"

"No, hot tea. There's some in the kitchen. You want me to make it?"

"God, no. You'd burn the water."

I join her in the kitchen but let her make the tea. Charlie now weaves around my ankles. It feels sad to be in Alice's house without her.

"So, are you going to tell me about the date with Mr. Handsome?"

I shrug. "It went fine. A nice dinner."

"And afterwards?" she prods.

"I just went home, Becca. He was a gentleman."

Her face fell. "Oh well."

"I'm not going to lie. He makes me wobbly."

"Does he have a brother?"

"That's the second time you've asked that!" I laugh.

"It is not."

"You weren't actually there the first time. Oh, never mind. It's a joke. How's the job hunt going?"

"I've got resumes in at a few law firms and one interview scheduled. Meanwhile, they're letting me work more hours at the convenience store, and that pays groceries and utilities."

"Great."

"I'd be homeless, though, without you."

"You're doing me a favor, remember? I couldn't keep all this going." I wave at the cats and plants. "The house would just sit here, and I'd be paying all the bills. Now you're taking care of it all. We just have to find you a job that will appreciate you."

She frowns. "What do I say if they ask me why I left my last place of employment?"

"Tell them the truth. You didn't do anything wrong."

"Rose, I can't tell them I hit my boss with his golf club!"

"Why not? He deserved it."

"It'd sound like I'm a … troublemaker."

"You're right. Just tell them they downsized or that you wanted a better opportunity. Believe me, your ex-boss isn't going to want that story to come out."

She sighs. "Maybe they won't ask."

I don't have anything useful to add, so I just reach down and stroke the cat.

"Okay," Becca says, setting the tea and a clear bear-shaped honey dispenser on the kitchen table. "Give me the scoop."

"About what?"

"About whatever's got you tied up in a knot."

I look at her in amazement. "It shows?"

She gives me a grim smile of satisfaction. "This is *me*—best friend— remember? I cried on your shoulder; now it's your turn." She pours honey into a spoon, and I watch it dribble and curl into a golden pool in her cup. What has me tied in a knot is not anything as simple as losing my job or my boyfriend or my newly found aunt.

"Is it a work thing?" she asks.

"Umm … sort of."

"Does it involve murder?" She leans forward.

"Becca, you know I work in the Burglary Unit."

"I know, but burglary could include murder."

My fingers drum the table, remembering a long-ago burglary that had turned into murder and arson. "It started there," I say quietly, my steady voice a counterpoint to the churning chaos that memory always evokes.

"Where? What started where?"

To my surprise, I take a deep breath and a terrible risk and tell her everything, even about the Houses and my sometimes ability to see the future, and the possibly real Mr. Black. I never thought I would tell anyone, or that she would believe me. How could she? But she listens through it all, and when I'm finished, she says, "That's the most unbelievable thing I've ever heard."

"You think I'm cracking up, don't you?"

She meets my gaze without hesitation. "I believe you, Rose. I always thought aliens have been here before."

I don't cry, but I want to cry and laugh at the same time. "I'm not an alien."

"Well, whatever."

It is the kindest thing anyone has ever said to me. I have been so afraid to tell her, thinking she would run as far away as she could, but here she is—believing me—when she should be scoffing at the outlandish story. I can never repay her for that.

She eyes the pendant at my neck or, more precisely, where it lies tucked under my shirt. "Does it help you see the future?"

I sniff, blow my nose on a napkin, and nod. "I think so, but it's more that it helps me focus, I think. But I can't control seeing the future or predict when it's going to happen." I wonder if I should tell her about seeing her in a prison cell, but I don't want to scare her.

"Rats, I was going to take you to the dog track."

"Becca, you are a most amazing person."

"Look who's talking!"

"Are you going to be able to keep this secret? They'd lock me up, you know."

"Oh, I dunno, there are a lot crazier people roaming the streets. I met one the other day who was talking to the stop light."

"I don't talk to stop lights," I say. Her humor worms its way into the tightness in my chest and loosens something there, an aloneness I have carried all my life.

"See, there's hardly anything *really* unusual about you," she says.

I snort. "All this feels as if I've stepped into a movie, but I'm in Birmingham, Alabama. Why here? That's one of the mysteries." I take a sip of tea, wishing I knew which plant leaves Alice had used. None of the commercial bags taste as good as her tea.

"You mean why did the Houses come here?" she asks.

"Yes. Alice said it had something to do with the ores in the earth, but there's iron and coal everywhere, isn't there?"

"I don't know, but Birmingham is unique. You didn't grow up here, but that's something I've heard since fourth grade. Birmingham is the only place in the world where all the ingredients to make useable iron and steel exist together—iron ore, coal, and limestone. That's why the city grew so fast in the late 1800s and why it was called 'The Magic City.' "

I stare at her. *Magic City*. Iron and coal together. I can't help but wonder if there is some synergy to that; otherwise, why didn't the House of Rose go one way and the House of Iron the other? Why did they want to be together? Especially with—what had Stephanie called it?—a feud going on between them.

"Maybe that's it. Maybe that's why both the Houses came here." I muse aloud.

Becca leans forward, "Well, all I have to say is if anyone is trying to hurt you, they better just watch their britches!"

"What?"

"That's what my Granny threatened when we got into mischief—'I'll get my switch. You better watch your britches!' " She grins. "All the kids and the chickens would scatter like the devil was after us."

"Chickens? *You* lived on a farm?"

"Heavens no, just visited. She died when I was eight, anyway."

Recalling what she said about her uncle, I imagine Becca's time on the farm was one of the few happy memories of her childhood.

She straightens, as if pulling back from the past. "Well, what are we going to do?"

I frown at her. "We?"

"You don't think I'm just going to sit around and let some skinny man with no fashion sense kill you, do you? He's probably doing other bad things, as well. Besides, I don't have a job at the moment, at least not in the daytime."

"I can't put you at risk, Becca. These people are extremely dangerous."

"Jason doesn't sound dangerous." She tilts her head at me as if evaluating my reaction.

"Maybe. Maybe not. But someone killed my family and is trying to kill me. I don't want to involve you or bring you to anyone's attention."

She sips her tea and settles it back on the table precisely inside the ring the cup had left. "Rose, you can't do this all by yourself."

Again, I blink in wonder at her. I have always done everything by myself.

THAT EVENING I FIND THE studio door ajar and paint splashed over the floor. My first instinct is to reach for my gun, thinking someone has broken in, but I notice the little paw prints in primary colors that lead across the hardwood floor and realize Angel is responsible for the destruction. The prints fade out by the time they reach the door. This explains why I didn't see her when I came in—she's hiding. One thing I've learned about cats—when they hide, forget finding them. It's as if your own house grows places you've never seen to swallow them.

I must have left the studio door open when I went in this room looking for a sweater in the closet. With care, I step over the paw prints and spilled paint and kneel at the far wall where I have older paintings stacked, arranged by subject matter. I pull out the abstracts, spreading them across a section of floor. In almost every one I have painted a thick line of vertical black through it.

For a long time, I stare at that slash of shadow that is almost obscured in the overlapping yellows, orange-reds and smoky gray edges. It makes sense now, this painting of my subconscious memory. Over and over I'd rendered it, not understanding that I was painting fear, anger, and agony, painting what had been done to me, the theft that had left me so alone.

With a light finger, I stroke the dark vertical line. I *will find you, Mr. Black.*

Touching him, even in such a vicarious way, makes me feel … polluted. As soon as I finish cleaning up the spilled paint, I'm in the shower, letting the hot water wash the sensation from me. It warms me up enough that I don't bother with a bathrobe to finish getting ready for bed.

Without thinking, I reach for the perforated tube of toothpaste that has been sitting on my bathroom counter since I discovered Angel had thought it interesting to dig a claw into it. Of course, I bought a new tube—thinking about all the places her paws took her—but hadn't bothered to throw this one away.

Feeling a desire to tidy my surroundings I start to toss it into the trash, but freeze before releasing it to fall to the basket. My fingers hunt for the perforation that Angel had left but don't find it. Curious, I turn it over, confirming that it is perfectly smooth, like a new tube, except it is partially squeezed and the end is neatly folded, a habit my adoptive mother drummed into me, even though it is at odds with my usual housekeeping habits, or lack thereof. I stare at it—longer than I had stared at the paintings—trying to wrap my mind around what has happened.

There is no claw puncture in this toothpaste tube. But there has to be. I check the medicine cabinet for the new tube, thinking perhaps I switched them, but no, that one has more toothpaste and no puncture either. Have I inadvertently stepped into another universe or timeline where Angel didn't claw my toothpaste? The fact that this is my first thought is a testimony to the weirdness I have been living with since I shot Zachary in the alley.

I check the medicine cabinet again, just to confirm the new tube is there and pick up the tube that is supposed to have a small hole in it, taking it closer to the light and examining it methodically, as if it were a crime scene. *No hole.*

My brain is stuck. I can't seem to get past the state of staring at the tube and convincing myself that I'm not imagining things. There *was* a hole in it before; I'm sure. Deliberately, I fill my lungs with air and slow down my breathing, which has escalated into shallow pants. After everything that has happened to me, I can't freak over a tube of toothpaste. There is a logical explanation.

I have no one I can ask to determine if such a thing is possible, so I use the principle of Occam's Razor, something they might have taught me in detective school—had they sent me—but that I picked up from reading books. When there are competing theories, the simplest explanation should be pursued. Forget timelines. If I am not in a different universe, someone has replaced my toothpaste with this one. Why would anyone do such a thing … and how?

Start with the first question, I tell myself. Why? Maybe someone wanted my old tube? That makes no kind of sense. But whoever put it on my bathroom counter planted it to look just like the one that was replaced. He or she must have squeezed out enough to match what I'd already used and folded up the bottom just like I did, and most likely wouldn't have noticed the small hole midway down. As I'm staring at the toothpaste, my hands begin to shake, and I grab my cell phone.

Becca is on my speed dial. *Please answer*, I beg as the phone rings.

"Hey!" The sound of her voice loosens the band around my chest.

"Becca, this is Rose."

"I know; your name pops up on my phone, silly. What's up?"

"I have to ask you something that's going to sound weird—"

She laughs. "Oh my God, girl! After everything you're in the middle of, nothing could sound strange!"

"Okay, don't say I didn't warn you." I take a breath. "Have you used any of Alice's toothpaste?"

"What? Use a dead woman's toothpaste? No way."

"Good; that's good."

"Rose, why are you asking me that?"

I take a deep breath. "Because I think someone has substituted my toothpaste."

"Maybe this *is* getting weirder. Why? And who would do that?"

"Probably the same person who tried to run over me and shoot me."

Becca clears her throat. "I don't mean to be dense, but substituting your toothpaste doesn't seem to be in the same league with those things."

"It is if there's a toxin or poison in the toothpaste."

She gasps.

"Becca, I don't believe Aunt Alice died of natural causes."

After a long hesitation, Becca says, "I'm afraid I threw her toothpaste out. Can you get a lab to analyze yours?"

"You mean, will they think I've lost it?"

"Uh, yeah."

"Most likely. As you know, I've kind of messed things up with Paul, and I already pushed to get him to have a bottle of Alice's cologne analyzed, which turned out to be ... a bottle of cologne."

"You still haven't spoken to Paul since that dead person he found?"

"No."

"Rose."

"Becca, it's more complicated than that."

"Love is always complicated."

I take a moment to digest that. My life has been a concerted effort to keep love uncomplicated by rejecting it in all forms. Was I pushing Paul away for the same reason? Or was it because of the pull I felt toward Jason? That was definitely sexual attraction, not love, right? Or was love like a magnet that keeps switching poles?

"Look," I say, "assuming I'm right about the toothpaste being poisoned, three people have had access to my house since I got Angel. And one of them is dead."

"What's Angel got to do with it?"

"She punctured my tube, remember? I'm sure I mentioned it to you, along with her other antics."

"I forgot."

"That's how I know it's a different one. This tube is perfectly smooth. No hole."

"It's just so weird."

"We're looping here. There's nothing about any of this that is not weird."

"But how would brushing your teeth with poison hurt you? I mean, people don't swallow their toothpaste."

"I'm not an expert on that, but there are some substances that can carry stuff through your skin. Maybe they mixed it with that." I'm sounding paranoid even to myself.

"How old was Alice?

"She said she was over a hundred."

"Uh, that's pretty old. Rose, old people have heart failure."

"Yes," I admit, "I know."

"I know it's been hard to lose the only real family you had," she says.

"Damn it, there *was* a hole in my toothpaste!"

Her voice is hesitant. "I'm sure there was. I wasn't questioning that."

But all of a sudden *I* am questioning that. Am I losing my mind?

Chapter Thirty

I jump at the knock on my door and grab my purse, snatching apart the Velcro and drawing my gun. The solid weight in my hand is a familiar comfort, especially since I'm in my pajamas watching *Men in Black* and eating popcorn as a late dinner.

My door is solid. No peephole. Glock pinned against my side, I flip on the porch light and lift the edge of the curtain to see who it is. A woman and child stand in the yellow pool of light on my front porch. Daniel and his mother. Something's wrong. Daniel should have long been in bed.

I stuff the gun back in my purse but keep the purse on my shoulder and open the door. Angel darts out.

"Hi, Ms. Pate," I say and look down. "Hello, Daniel."

"He-llo," Daniel says, looking up at me with dark, sleepy eyes. It should be illegal for a boy to have lashes like that.

"Is anything wrong?" I ask.

"Well … not exactly." Ms. Pate tucks a lank lock of brown hair behind her ear, and it promptly falls back against her angular cheek.

I hesitate. A faint odor that I associate with alcohol sweating from pores emanates from her skin, but it's chilly outside, and Daniel's cheeks are red. "Would you like to come in?" I ask.

She shakes her head. "No, thank you. Just thought you ought to know."

"Know what?"

"About the car." She jerks her head to the side and slightly over her shoulder. "Don't look. He'll know I'm talking about him."

"Who?"

"Whoever's been sitting in that car for the last couple of weeks."

A chill jolts down my spine. "I don't see a car."

"He just pulled up a little while ago. In the alley beside my house, you know, where you—" She hesitates. "Where that man was shot. The last streetlight's out; the car's back in the shadows."

"Thanks. Do you know what kind of car it is?"

She shrugs. "I can't tell the color in the dark."

I have to smile at this. Ask a man about a car and he will give you the make and model; a woman sees the color. Even after three months in the training car, I had a hard time telling anything about a car other than its color. My job was to call in the make, model, and tag number when we were about to stop a vehicle, and I had to rely on Paul for that info. It always seemed kind of magical to me that he could tell before we got close enough to see an insignia.

She thrusts a foil-covered plate toward me. "I brought you these." She straightens and gives me a wink. "Thought it was a good idea to look like I was bringing something to you."

"Very clever. Thank you, Ms. Pate."

"Can I have a cookie?" Daniel asks, his gaze pulled to the TV where a monster chases a cat for the tiny jewel galaxy it wears on the collar around its neck.

His mother takes his hand. "You've already had too many, and it's past bedtime. Say goodnight."

"Night," Daniel says with disappointment.

I wait until she is safely inside her house before turning off the TV and living room light and flipping on the bedroom light. But I am not going to bed, not with someone watching my house. *How long has he been there? Who is it?*

Hastily, I pull on my jeans and a tee shirt and thread my holster and handcuff holder onto the belt. It's late December, but I have a high tolerance for cold and just throw on my blue jean jacket to cover the gun, wanting to be able to move my arm freely if I have to. My cell phone and badge case go into back pockets and the tiny flashlight into a front one. Feeling my way along the kitchen wall, I slip out my back door and into the tiny yard, my heart hammering.

With a growing sense of dread, I circle around the block to stay out of view, unable to make my feet move faster than a walk. Am I hoping he will be gone when I turn that last corner? I have waited almost all of my life for this. Do I have the nerve to shoot him? I want revenge for what he did to my sister, mother, father ... and for what he did to me. I will kill him if I have to. *And what if I don't have to? What if he gives up?*

I stop in my tracks with that thought. What do I do? Arrest him? I have no proof of anything other than a vague childhood memory, the dark vertical slash in my paintings. I can also throw in that I think my toothpaste has been poisoned. The absurdity of the whole thing roots me to the ground. If I'm not immediately fired, I will spend a lot of time in Counselor Faulkner's office.

But I don't stay stopped. It doesn't matter that I don't know what I'm going to do. It doesn't matter that I am sick with fear and anger. *Enough. You've caused me enough grief, Mr. Black. It ends here.*

My elaborate circling to get behind the car brings me to the same place where Paul dropped me off to chase Zachary. The car is parked at the alley's far end, where Zachary stood when I shot him. Above, the one working streetlight is now out, and I can't tell much about the car either, not even the color.

Not much choice how to approach. I hug the shadows cast by the thick brush on the right, gun in my clammy hands, retracing the steps I'd taken the last time I had come down this alley. At any moment, I expect the door to open and Mr. Black to glide out and—I don't know what. I try to pull living-green, hoping my extra "spidey" sense will click in, and I will see what happens before it happens, but I am so intensely focused on the car door, I can't pull it. I am close now, only twenty yards separate us and—

The driver's door opens. I stop, tightening my grip, and aim at the door. My heart stammers. *If he's armed, he's a dead man—*

A dark figure unfolds and faces me, not as tall as Black ... more solid.

"Paul!" I almost choke on his name, nauseated by the adrenalin that shot into my bloodstream and now has to be reabsorbed.

His arm drops. "What are you doing out here?"

I take a breath, trying to calm down, but my emotions are jagging like a lightning storm, and I can't tell what I'm feeling. I settle on mad.

"Why are you spying on me?"

"I'm not spying."

"Really? What do you call it when you sit and watch my house every night? *Surveillance?*"

It's his turn to bristle. "I—"

But I have no intention of letting him say anything, not until I'm finished. "You climb in my bed and then treat me like a suspect."

A movement in the window of Ms. Pate's house makes me regret my shouted accusation in the middle of the road, but I'm not backing down.

"Can I say something now?" Paul asks.

"No."

His obedient silence makes me angrier. I want a fight. I want to hit him for ... for *hurting* me. I've worked so hard all my life to keep people "out" so they couldn't hurt me, so I wouldn't—*damn it!*—lose them. I just want to hit something, preferably Paul.

We stand in the alley facing each other, the air crackling with tension. I wouldn't be surprised if it creates a power surge and opens a timeline where I shot Paul when he stepped out of the car or he shot me, or God knows what else might have happened and probably did ... somewhere.

He takes a deep breath. "We need to talk, but not out here."

I glance at the curtain in the window, pretty sure Ms. Pate is listening to every word.

"Maybe in your house?" he ventures.

"No."

"My car?"

It seems an acceptable compromise.

He gestures to the passenger door, and I get in. Before I can close the door, a small gray animal launches off the ground into my lap. Angel places two paws on my chest and lifts her head up to touch my nose in greeting.

"Hello, Angel," Paul says quietly and reaches over to stroke her. She arches her back under his hand. It seems such a normal moment that I realize how scared I was when his car door opened. I was certain I was about to face the man who has been trying to kill me since I was a child.

Chapter Thirty-One

Some of my anger at Paul has dissipated or at least cooled. We sit in his car in the shadows. "Can we go somewhere?" I ask.

He starts the engine. "Sure. Where do you want to go?"

"Just away from here." I lower my window partially, wanting to breathe fresh air, but not wanting to risk Angel jumping out. It doesn't seem to have entered her mind; she is curled happily on my lap.

"Is it okay for me to say something now?" Paul asks.

I feel a bit stupid for demanding that he not talk earlier, but I'm not about to let him know that. "Depends on what you say."

"You know I'm not good at talking."

I have to smile a bit at that. He is not the smooth-talking Jason Blackwell. "Well, I think you'd better try."

With a deep breath, he says, "Rose, I was just worried about you. I know you're up to your eyeballs in something—" He glances at me and back to the road. "And you don't have to tell me anything if you don't want to."

"I'm glad we have that settled."

"But I do have a job to do, you know."

I bite my tongue. "I know."

"Then why can't you tell me?"

"I just can't. You will have to accept that, at least for right now." I know Paul's practical, just-the-facts mind well enough to know that he would think I was nuts. Unlike Becca, who has believed in alien visitors and God knows what, Paul is a policeman through and through. He only believes what he can see.

His cell phone rings.

"Damn," he says.

"Aren't you going to answer it?"

"No, I want to talk to you."

"Paul, you're a homicide detective. What if someone's dead?"

With a sigh, he answers the phone. "Nix."

A pause. "Where?" He raises an eyebrow at me, and sighing, I grab the pad of paper and pen on the console to write down the address.

We have not gotten much more accomplished in mending or further ripping apart our relationship when we arrive at a familiar house. Even in the dark, I recognize it from my visit to Zachary's mother. *Oh no.* A sickness settles in my stomach. *Is everyone I touch going to die?*

Paul looks over at me. "You okay?"

"I'm fine."

"You can wait in the car."

"My badge is just as shiny as yours, Nix." I must have been glaring at him, because he holds up a hand to ward me off.

I watch Angel to make sure she doesn't jump out of the car and lock the doors behind us.

Inside, there is no crime scene tape. Zachary's mother is sitting in a chair in a small, but immaculate kitchen, which makes me feel a bit better—at least *she* is not dead—but she's staring off into space.

"Where's the crime scene?" Paul asks a uniformed officer in the living room.

"Back yard." He thumbs over his shoulder.

We go back out the front and around the side of the house. A body lies face up in the small back yard, one foot propped on the bottom step. Three more lead up to a back door.

"Did the paramedics move him?" Paul asks the officer guarding the scene.

"Yeah, they rolled him over. He was facedown when I found him."

"Who called it in?"

"Lady inside made the call. Says she'd been out for a couple of hours, came home and just found him. Nobody pays any attention to gunfire in this part of town."

Paul squats near the victim, examining the neat bullet wound in his forehead and the ground nearby. "Looks like one shot and not much blood for a head wound, so he died quickly."

The officer smirked. "Bullet through the head will do that."

I am looking at the body through a fog. That red hair—"I know him." Paul looks up at me, questioning. I know he wants to say something like, *Strange how you have connections with my homicides,* but he doesn't say anything. At least I don't hear anything, because the world is going gray and black.

This time, the shadow figure that disengages from the body rolls over so it is facing the ground before floating up into an upright position. He takes two steps backwards up the stairs. A dark hole blooms on his forehead, disappears, and the figure takes another backward step into a now open door.

I sink onto the ground.

"You okay, Rose?" Paul asks, suddenly at my side.

I stare at him, my head throbbing with vision-hangover.

"I know him," I hear myself say.

"Who is he, Rose? How do you know him?"

I swallow in a dry throat. "They call him 'Carrot Man.' He was one of my suspects in a stolen gun case."

"Got any idea who killed him?"

"I think … I think whoever shot that man on Red Mountain."

"The same man who shot at you?"

"I can't prove it, but I will be surprised if the bullets don't match up as coming from the same rifle."

"Why this 'Carrot Man'? You and the victim on Red Mountain were in the same area, but this is miles away."

"I don't know, but there's a connection between him and Zachary, the man I killed in the alley." I'm walking a fine line here, I know, but another man is dead, and I have to tell Paul what I know without telling him so much he disregards everything and labels me a nut case.

Paul's brow is wrinkled. "What connection?"

"They both worked at the same car wash, and the woman inside is Zachary's mother."

Paul frowns and turns to reply to something the uniformed officer at his elbow has asked. I slip back around to the front and into the living room, where Zachary's mother now sits alone, staring out the front door. The heating system must be going at full blast. It's an oven in here. I sit in a chair opposite her.

"Do you remember me, Mrs. Jones?"

She nods. "You came after Zachary was killed."

"You know that Zachary was shot because he was about to shoot a policeman?" I ask, defensively.

"That's what they say."

I bite my lip. I hadn't meant to say that. If my head wasn't hurting so bad, I could think clearer. "You know the man in your back yard, don't you?"

"I know him. He was a friend of Zachary's."

"He's the one who called you to the scene that night?"

She nods.

"Do you know who shot him?"

A headshake.

"Do you know why he was killed?"

Her mouth moves silently.

"I'm sorry; I didn't hear that."

For the first time, she looks at me. "I wasn't here when he came this time, but he's been here before. Said he had to tell me that it should have been him, not Zachary, and he was sorry."

"That's all he said?"

"He said it was that policeman's fault."

"Policeman? What policeman?"

"That's all he'd say. He's been coming over since then, bringing things. A sweater one time and twenty dollars the next."

"I'm sorry," I say. It sounds lame, but I mean I am sorry about her son and about the dead man in her backyard, about the bleakness of her life, and that I was helpless to make any of it better.

She tightens her lower lip and gives the barest of nods.

I leave out the front door to be out of the way of the investigation, grateful for the sharp bite of cold air, and sit on the top step of the front porch, waiting for Paul. My mind is churning, or trying to churn, given that my headache has gotten worse, and my stomach is sick with what is starting to be a very unwelcome theory.

Chapter Thirty-Two

Road trip. One perk of being a detective is I get the Christmas holidays off. Becca is taking care of Angel. White beach, waves, and a piña colada are calling my name. I need to be alone, especially away from Paul. There are coincidences and red flags bouncing around in my head. The unbridled horizon has always calmed my spirit and given me perspective. That's what I want—perspective. And a piña colada wouldn't hurt either.

The five-hour drive is boring and uneventful. Just what I want. I switch off my cell phone and don't even turn on the radio, just let the thoughts churn.

I assumed Jason or Alice would be on my mind, but it is Paul who occupies my thoughts. I can't drive anywhere on Southside without remembering a call that brought us here or there. Every street seems to contain a shadow of memory associated with my three short months of working Patrol with him—a house where we arrested a drunk man for hitting his wife; a yard where Paul stopped to talk to a child on a tricycle about not venturing into the street; a corner where he crawled into a smoking car with a woman wedged behind a crumpled dashboard and steering wheel, talking to her until the firemen arrived to cut her out. And of course there is the corner a half block from my house where we stopped the young man who had broken into my great aunt's house, stolen a pendant, and paid for it with his life.

Maybe that is one of the reasons I have to get away, away from those memories, somewhere to wash the tangled cobwebs out of my system. It would be helpful if my case were resolved. The state investigator finally sent in a recommendation of justifiable homicide, but given the political pressure, the D.A. is sending it to the county Grand Jury. Tracey told me that could take anywhere from a week to more months.

I take a left off Highway 59, onto the Foley Beach Parkway that will take me right into Orange Beach, the last stop before the Florida line. It's a toll road that bypasses the traffic on 59. Crossing the Intracoastal Waterway, I glance to my left at the yachts parked at The Wharf and consider finding a restaurant and bar in the upscale complex, but I decide I prefer something more hole-in-the-wall on the beach.

I find a weekend rental across the street from the beach. First on my to-do list, after dumping my bag in the room, is to find a bar, order a piña colada, and drink it. And I do, sitting on a stool at the bar. Fish net, ropes, and a huge anchor decorate the walls. A hefty, unshaved man hasn't taken his eyes off me since I walked in the door.

He leaves his dark corner, sidles over, and tries a pick-up line on me.

"Not interested," I say when he appears unaffected by my glower.

"Come on, a girl like you at a bar like this? How much?"

I stand and throw the drink in his face. Melodramatic, I know, but it just seemed like the script called for it.

He takes a wild swing with his right. Fortunately, he's been drinking a lot longer than I have. I block it with my left forearm, step into him and bring my knee up into his crotch, hard.

"Refill's on the house," the bartender says, as the man staggers away, bent over.

"Put it in a go-cup, please." I'm not sure what the local law is here, but the bartender doesn't say anything.

It's December and the beach is deserted. Salt air fills my nostrils. Without thinking about it, I reach for the living-green. The sea should cradle it everywhere, in the plankton, the seaweed, and the fish. All life on our planet is carbon-based, but the richest sources of energy lie beneath the waves, deep underground in dark pools of compressed oil. Strange that I can't reach through the sea water. But there is plenty under the shore. Millions of years ago, all of the state was ocean and all that life ended up encased in rock. I pull just enough to complement the high from the piña colada, flooding myself with golden energy. Maybe it works like lightning, seeking the path of least resistance. If I could bottle this, I'd be a billionaire.

Eventually I let it drain away and feel emptier than before. The wind blows hard off the water. I've never been bothered much by cold, but I zip my jacket up to my chin.

Clouds sit low and gray all the way to the horizon. No spectacular sunset for me, but it suits my mood. I walk along the beach for a while, trying to clear my mind. Not working. I walk back and sit in the pearl-white sand, breathing in the brine with the past that haunts me.

Vague memories swirl, not the gray-black of magic, just childhood memories—watching my mother, my real mother, build drip castles from watery sand and delight me by packing wet sand around my bare foot. When the sand dried, I withdrew my foot, leaving a miniature cave she called a "frog house." I made endless frog houses, thinking I was building a city for frogs that would take up residence when we left.

A wedge of pineapple in my drink has captured my attention. My free hand traces the diamond pendant beneath my jacket and shirt, toying with the idea of trying to scry into the past instead of the future. It is possible. I did it with Carrot Man, backing up time to see him take that fatal step down from the back stoop, the bullet piercing his forehead, and his fall. Right now, I want very badly to be able to see my dead parents and ask them a few questions.

As a young girl growing up in my adoptive family, I believed I was secretly a princess, and my real royal family would come find me one day. Instead, I learn I am a witch, and my royal family was a handful of hunted women, now down to one: me.

"Well, that 'one' is going to be a hard bitch to kill," I promise my drink.

"I agree," says a familiar voice behind me.

With a start, I twist around, the wind blowing my hair into my eyes. "Paul! What the hell are you doing here?"

He sits beside me on the damp white sand.

"Well?" I demand, with only a very slight slur to my voice. I feel violated. This was my private escape, and damn it, he is one of the things I am running from.

"I'm sorry. I know you want privacy, but I—I'm worried about your safety."

Or wanting to know how I am connected to your cases. It occurs to me that everything about relationships revolves around trust. I destroyed Paul's trust when I wouldn't tell him why I wanted him to test a bottle of perfume or how I thought my stalker was connected to his homicide. And he hurt me when he wouldn't trust me without me telling him those things.

And here we both are.

"How did you find me?" I ask.

"I followed you down here."

"Well, you did an awfully smooth job. I checked my rear view more than once, and I could have sworn nobody was following me."

"I'm good." He sits beside me.

"Paul, you are not *that* good."

He looks away.

I narrow my eyes at the back of his head. "You put a GPS tracker on my car."

His shoulders drop, and he looks back at me. "You're a damn good detective. You should be working Homicide instead of me."

To my surprise, I'm not angry. Maybe it's the alcohol or the self-pity I've been drinking.

"I didn't realize that was a piece of equipment available to detectives," I say with just an edge of sarcasm.

"I … er … borrowed one from Narcotics. Have an old buddy there."

Waves boom against the shore. The wind tangles my hair, even when I face the sea.

"The thing about the sea," I say, "is that it makes your problems look small."

He reaches for my hand, but I pull it away. "We don't trust each other, Paul," I say. "I'm not good with that. You shouldn't have come."

Chapter Thirty-Three

My retreat to the ocean is complicated by Paul's presence. I don't know if he had ideas about sharing a bed, but I make him get his own room. Before dawn, I check to be sure his car is still in the lot and head back to Birmingham. I know he can follow me, but I have mixed feelings about him going to the trouble to scrounge a GPS tracker and put on my car. On the one hand, my life *is* in danger, and it's sweet that he cares that much. On the other, it feels like I'm being investigated … or stalked.

BACK HOME, I LOCATE THE device and pull it off the car, switching it off. I consider throwing it into the woods but relent. I'll deposit it on his desk as a Christmas present.

Christmas. This is a pretty shitty way to spend the holiday. What seemed like a perk as I headed to the Gulf now dumps a bucket of depression on my head. As a rookie in Patrol, I wouldn't have had to worry about how to spend the holidays. Having no seniority, I was sure to have to work. Now that I am a detective, I get all the holidays to spend … with myself.

Just stop it! I order my mind. Way too much self-pity going on here.

I'm just opening my trunk to get out my bag when a familiar voice calls out from across the street.

"Well, there you are!"

I look around to see Becca, in a long wool skirt and two-inch-heeled red boots, exiting her car.

"Hey," I respond grumpily.

"I was just coming over to feed Angel," she says. "You're back earlier than you said you'd be. Where did you go anyway?"

"Orange Beach."

"What? And didn't take your best friend?"

"I thought you didn't like the beach."

"I adore it; it's just my skin that doesn't. But this is winter, best time to be there."

Becca is very fair-skinned. I rarely get sunburn, perhaps courtesy of my heritage as a fast-healing witch of House of Rose.

"Come on inside," I say, swinging my gym bag over my shoulder.

We ascend the steps together, and I toss the bag onto the couch.

"How can you possibly pack enough clothes in that little thing?" she says, eying the bag.

"What can I get you?" I ask, ignoring her question. "Water, tea, a coke?"

"I'm kind of hooked on hot tea, thanks to you. What have you got?"

"Not sure. I bought a variety pack at the store. It's not the same as Alice's tea. She picked leaves right off her plants. Maybe we … er … you can figure out which ones, but be careful. Some of them are pretty exotic."

"She seemed like really a nice person, Rose, from what you told me. I know you miss her."

At the moment, I don't want to talk about Alice, so I reach down and scoop up Angel, who has not stopped weaving between my legs since I walked in the door.

Becca looks around with a frown. "Maybe I could pay you back for Alice's house by coming over here and tidying every now and then."

"I told you, you're doing me a favor taking care of things there." I follow the path of the gym bag and collapse on the couch. "Why does driving feel like a five hour workout?"

"Poor baby. You just sit right there and I'll make the tea."

When she brings the steaming cups, I nudge Angel from my lap, afraid I might spill it on her.

Becca sits in the chair opposite.

"How's the job hunt going?" I ask.

"Like I thought it would. Nowhere."

"Don't give up. That's the only way to ensure you never succeed."

"What are you now, the Wisdom Witch?"

I laugh.

"Good to hear that," Becca says, reminding me of Alice.

"Tell me something," I say, resting the steaming cup on the coffee table.

She frowns. "That's going to make a ring. Don't you have a coaster around here somewhere?"

"I'm serious."

She sips her tea. "Okay."

"Why on planet Earth, did you pick *me* to be your best friend?"

"What makes you think it was all my decision?"

"Come on, Becca. You know I had nothing to do with it. You barged into my life."

She stiffens. "I can barge right out, if you want."

"No," I say quickly. "That's not what I mean. See, I can't even—"

"You're not anti—"

I hold up my hand, interrupting her. "Let me finish. Really, I haven't the slightest idea how to be a friend … or a lover, for that matter. I've spent my whole life running from people, afraid I might have to have a relationship."

"Well, you've had to deal with a lot of stuff."

"You, on the other hand, being a 'normal' person, could have had lots of friends."

" 'Lots' is not the same as a best friend," she says. "And besides"—she hesitates—"I'm not normal, either."

That stops me. "What do you mean? Are you talking about what your uncle did to you? Because that's not—"

"No. I'm not talking about that."

I wait.

She picks up her tea again and blows on it, sets it down, sighs, and reaches up to her right eye, pulling down on it with her forefinger and pinching her contact lens off her eye, which glows … pink … in the light, and, when she tilts her head, the lightest blue I have ever seen.

"Well," I say, after a moment's silence. "That is unusual."

"I'm an albino."

An albino. A person born without color pigment. "I'm relieved. I thought you were going to say you were an alien."

She cups the contact lens in her palm and gives me a wan smile. "Be serious."

"I am."

We look at each other for a moment and burst out laughing together.

"So, I'm a witch, and you're an albino," I say finally. "What's that got to do with why you picked me for a friend?"

"In the right light, my eyes seem pink or even red, even though they aren't really. It freaked out all the kids, even some adults. My parents wouldn't let me wear contacts until I was fifteen. So, no friends. Who wants to be friends with a demon-girl? I always wanted them, but I … try too hard. You came along, and it didn't make you freak that I jumped into your life."

"That's it?"

"Yeah. Pretty pitiful, huh?"

"Pretty lucky for me," I say.

She blinks back tears. "You mean that?"

"Of course."

With a sniff, she says, "Fine," and bounces up, snatching both our cups, though mine is still full. "I want another cup."

Chapter Thirty-Four

The desk officer at the precinct waves me inside. I've been back here a few times to talk to the arresting officers on my cases, but this trip is for my own purposes. Timing is everything. It's 10:30 p.m., fifteen minutes before roll call starts for the morning shift, which is really the late-night-and-into-the-wee-hours-of-morning shift. And it's Friday, which means Sergeant Thompson, lovingly referred to as "Sarge," is at the precinct doing "the books," i.e., the leave and attendance records, a job he hates and puts off until the end of the shift. I'm counting on him being tired and not wanting to chat too much.

He is exactly where I thought he'd be, with the scowl I remember, slowly typing in data with his two forefingers.

"Morning, Sarge."

He looks up. "What are you doing here, Rose? We don't get many visits from detectives."

Yep, tired and grumpy. I slip into the seat across from his desk, a place I dreaded to occupy as a Patrol rookie. A lot has happened since then: I have killed a man; lived through a couple of murder attempts; learned I was a witch; gained a best friend; and lost my last living relative ... oh, and my virginity. That will change a girl.

"You waiting to catch somebody coming off the shift?" Sarge asks.

"Actually, I'm trying to figure out who I need to catch, maybe a couple of people."

He glances at his watch. "Well, how can I be of service?"

"Can you print out worksheets for me for last Friday night? I'd like to see who was working." A lie. I'm not interested in the time sheets.

Sarge gives me a put-upon frown and stares at the computer screen. "Give me a minute."

He punches a couple of keys, swears, and punches another one. "There. Unless this damn thing is broken again, it should be printing out."

"I'll get it. I know you're busy."

A minute later, paper in hand, I stick my head back in the doorway. "Thanks, Sarge. Um, you got a minute?"

He scowls again, as I knew he would. "A couple. Sit your butt down."

I comply.

"How are you, Rose?"

I smile. Underneath that bear face is a golden heart. "I'm fine, Sarge, really."

"I know it's gotta be tough being singled out like that. I've asked to have you back."

"You have?" I'm surprised.

"You need some more time in Patrol."

"I know. I would like that. I asked to come back."

"That was a mistake. Didn't Paul teach you never to ask for an assignment? It'll be the last place you'll ever go. The trick is to ask to be asked for."

"I'll remember that." I take a little breath. Sarge and Paul were good friends. "Paul was a great training officer," I venture.

"The best. Got that from the military."

"The military?" My heart skips a beat.

"Yep. Navy SEAL. Sniper. Don't come any better."

Ice slides down my spine.

"He's a hero. Came home from Afghanistan with a purple heart, chest full of medals."

"I didn't know that," I manage. "He never talked much about himself."

"He don't believe much in words. I saw him in his dress uniform at a military funeral."

I remember him in his dress police uniform at Alice's funeral. He wore a medal then too and had never mentioned it. My throat is suddenly dry and I stand. "I'll let you get back to work."

"Don't worry about it, Rose. Do your time where you are. Soon as you get to liking it, they'll move you."

"I hope it's back here."

"That shooting was a damn shame, but it wasn't your fault."

"Thanks, Sarge. That means a lot to me coming from you." I mean it.

On my way out the door, I almost bump into Paul.

"Hey," he says, "what are you doing here?"

"I could ask the same," I say, my heart stammering. I wave the worksheet I got from Sarge under his nose. "Checking on something," I say lightly. "A case."

His eyes narrow at me. "You okay?"

"Yes, sure. Why?"

"You're acting funny."

Does he know why I'm here? "Gotta run."

He grabs my arm as I turn.

"Wait, Rose. There's something I want to tell you."

"Yeah?"

"Listen, I miss you. I need … to talk to you." He glances over my shoulder at the chaos of the changing shift going on behind me. "In private." His eyes lock onto mine.

"I don't have time right now," I stammer. "I'm sorry."

His fingers bite into my arm.

"That hurts, Paul."

He looks down at his hand in surprise. "Sorry."

"We can talk later," I say, my pulse filling my ears like the rush of surf, and wrench myself free.

Chapter Thirty-Five

"So, what have we got?" Becca asks, tapping a freshly painted bronze fingernail against Alice's kitchen table. "Bounce your thoughts off me, detective. It always helped Sherlock Holmes to verbalize."

"What we've got is a mess."

"I mean about the murders." She has removed her red boots and runs her toes over Boo, who lies curled around her chair leg. Alexander and Charlie writhe in contorted play with a toy catnip-stuffed mouse in the corner.

"Well, we have two men dead," I say, "one found on the mountainside in the same area I was shot at—"

"Do you think the shooter thought he was you?" Becca interrupts.

"Possibly. Paul said the time of death was estimated at dusk the previous day, so the shooter could have assumed it was me."

"But how did he know you would go up there that first time when he or she shot at you?"

My chest tightens. "A good question." I take a breath. "Unless they were following me, nobody knew, except … Paul."

"Paul?"

"I called him before I went hiking." I can feel my brow furrow, and I meet her eyes. "Becca, as much as I hate it, what do I really know about him?"

"He's a police detective!"

"Yeah, so am I. I'm also a witch."

"I'm still getting used to that. It's just so … cool. My best friend is a witch."

"I meant that you just think you know about a person."

"Let's look at the other victim," she says, making me smile at the quick change to a sleuth-solving expression. "The dead man from last Friday night.

What's his connection?"

"Carrot Man? He worked at the car wash with Zachary, the man I shot. I interviewed Carrot Man on a stolen gun case, and I think he might have been following me. I saw him in Five Points South one day, but he ducked and disappeared. He was my chief suspect, until he became dead."

"Hmm. Did he say anything interesting when you interviewed him?"

"He admitted that a white man occasionally got him and Zachary to do 'jobs' and implied that's what happened with Zachary. If that is true, somebody hired Zachary to break into this house and steal the pendant." I swallow, "But here's the thing, Becca. Zachary's mother said Carrot Man told her that it was all 'a policeman's fault.' That was right before Carrot Man got nailed in the head, just like the man in the woods."

"Wow."

"They were both sniper shots," I say, watching her to see if she gets the significance. "Right in the middle of the forehead."

Her eyes widen and the golden arches rise. "You think a *policeman* did it?"

"Not just any policeman. We're trained to shoot to stop."

"I'd think a bullet to the head would stop somebody."

"No, you never aim for the head. It's too small, relatively speaking. You aim for the greatest possibility of hitting your target, which is likely to be moving. That means center mass, not the head."

She frowns. "So it *wasn't* a policeman."

"It could be, if it was one with special training." The title of an old movie I've seen rerun on TV plays in my spinning head—*Sleeping With The Enemy*.

I have to be wrong. Have to be. Lots of policemen served in the military.

"But why steal the diamond now?" Becca asks. "We need a motivation. If those Iron people knew Alice had the diamond all this time, why wait to get it? How did they even know who you were or that you were here?"

"Alice said she had a 'feeling' I was coming back, and that's why she pulled the rose-stone out of its hiding place to polish it. I don't know. Maybe House of Iron knew too. Alice messed up one time and sent a check for my tuition directly to the university. If they caught that somehow, they would know where I was and when I graduated, and if they have fingers that deep into everything, like Alice said they did, they would have known I moved here and even that I applied for the PD."

"Maybe they were ready to make their move and didn't want you to get your hands on it. It makes you more powerful, doesn't it?"

"Not sure what it does. My mother said something about it holding all the powers of the Houses in her letter. But why wait until I was so close? Like you said, if they were worried about me getting the rose-stone, why not take it sooner?"

"Uh … they didn't want to tip their hand with Alice? Let her think she had been successful in covering up your existence so she wouldn't warn you off? Maybe you're the priority, and the stone was just bait."

That is possible. "Good thinking, Becca."

She beams.

Then I frown.

"What?"

I can't answer right away. Until I started suspecting Paul, it never occurred to me before but, now—how was it that Paul and I happened to be in the neighborhood right when Zachary stole the rose-stone? I try to remember. Something nags me, something—

"Becca," I say aloud, "what if that whole incident in the alley wasn't just coincidental?"

"What do you mean?"

The images from that night flash again through my mind: *I jump out of the car and chase the suspect down the alley. Suspect turns my way. Patrol car screeches up behind him. Everything stops. In the gray and black shadow world, man jerks back to the patrol car. Man shoots Paul.*

Back to real time—I shoot suspect before he shoots Paul.

Wait. Replay that. *I jump out of the car and chase suspect down the alley. Suspect turns.* Why did he turn? I had stopped before that. If he'd heard me, wouldn't he have turned sooner? It was as if he knew I was supposed to be there, but I was in deep shadow next to the house. I don't think he saw me.

"What if," I say slowly, "the man I shot in the alley was supposed to shoot me, but got distracted and frightened by the arrival of the patrol car? What if he was hired to steal the rose-stone and shoot me?"

She blinks at me.

"I would be dead and 'they' would have the rose-stone. Two birds with the same stone. No pun intended."

"I never thought of that. It sounds complicated."

"If he hadn't found the stone, I would still be dead. Logically, you are right. I would be the priority, as they could have gone for the stone any time. It *was* bait all along. They left it alone, waiting for the House of Rose biology switch—maybe something like a very late puberty?—to turn on and bring me to it."

"Wow," she says.

"Paul ironically saved my life by his arrival at the alley, but what if that was an error or if he disobeyed orders? What if he was supposed to arrive just *after* I was killed?"

Becca's toe nudges Charlie, who has jumped down and stolen the toy from the other two cats.

"And what if," I continue, "as Carrot Man's last words to Zachary's mother implied—the person who was supposed to have taken that burglary job was the older, more experienced Carrot Man, and he chickened out and got Zachary to take it on?"

"Why do you think that?" Becca asks.

"I think Zachary broke into a house a few doors down from Alice by mistake. The woman there said he seemed surprised to see her, and he didn't threaten her. He just ran away. Shortly afterward, Alice's house gets hit. That would explain Carrot Man's presence, maybe as the getaway driver. And it would explain his call to Zachary's mother after I shot Zachary, and why Carrot Man ended up lying on her back steps with a bullet in his head. He was a loose end who knew too much."

The burglary was reported very quickly. *By whom?* Alice had not been home, so she didn't make the call. I checked the dispatch logs that first day in the Burglary Unit, and the call reporting the burglary came from an unknown cell phone. I assumed it was from a neighbor, but maybe Carrot Man made the call on a throwaway phone.

I am sick to my stomach with the implications of a set up. Paul would have to be involved. He was driving. He'd asked for the keys when we left the diner. If we hadn't gotten that first domestic call, he could still have had us nearby at precisely the right time. Maybe he even got a signal. I can't remember whether his cell phone chimed, but we both heard the call go out from the dispatcher when we were in Daniel's mother's house. The something niggling my subconscious gives another tug. Something about Paul's reaction. I search my memory, trying to remember what it was, but it eludes me.

"And this, Becca," I say aloud, "I went to talk to my patrol sergeant on a wild goose hunt, just to see if I could learn something more about Paul. I was hoping to find out my suspicions were stupid, but … Sarge told me that Paul was a Navy SEAL sharpshooter."

Becca gasps. "That's why you were talking about the forehead shot. A sharpshooter has that target thing on his gun."

"A scope, yes. Their job is to kill immediately and that's where they aim."

"But didn't you tell me you were with Paul when you went to the homicide scene where Carrot Man was killed?"

"That's right."

Becca curls her lips over her teeth in distress. "How could Paul have shot him if you were with him?"

I've thought about this too. "Carrot Man was shot a couple of hours before I met Paul. When my neighbor came to tell me Paul was watching me, she said the car in the alley had 'just pulled up.' So he had time to shoot Carrot Man that night and then come to check on me."

"Hmm, what about at the beach? He could have doffed you there."

"No, not really, we were in public view the whole time. And I made him get a separate room and left before dawn."

"It's all kind of far-fetched," she says reluctantly, "except—"

"What?"

"If Carrot Man called in the burglary and expected Paul to be at a certain place, it would have to be timed so Paul would know when to be close to Alice's house, right?"

"Right."

"So how could that have happened?

"Alice said she went to a Yoga class on Tuesday nights. If that was a regular pattern, someone watching her would have known she wouldn't be there."

"Oh." Her face falls.

"But you're right about timing. It had to be more precise than that. There's something I'm missing—"

I have it.

"Paul did something strange when the call went out for the burglary in progress at Alice's."

"What did he do?"

"He looked at his watch."

A puzzled wrinkle appears between her brows. "What's strange about that?"

"It just is. There was no reason for him to want to know what time it was at that moment. The dispatcher would have given us the time of the call later, and it's just not a normal thing to do with a priority call being given out so close to us. What if he knew the burglary was supposed to happen at a certain time?"

"Still seems like it's all circumstantial. I've always liked him."

My stomach twists again. "There's another thing."

"What?"

"My toothpaste."

She rolls her eyes. "That again."

"Becca, someone substituted it. I *know* it had a hole in it, and it didn't miraculously heal itself."

"Okay, sorry." She puts a hand up to ward me off, and I realize I must have been glowering again.

"Let's keep this logical," she says. "Who had access to your bathroom during the time between the toothpaste *cum* hole and the toothpaste *sans* hole?" she asks.

I've been over this countless times in my mind. "Paul, Alice … and you."

"Me?"

"You asked."

"Well!" She crossed her arms over her chest. "Now I'm a suspect! Rose, please tell me you don't think it was me."

"I don't."

She sniffs, reminding me of Alice. "And when did Alice have access to your bathroom?"

"She came over one day after I got out of the hospital. She brought chicken and dumplings—"

"Oh man, I am always in the wrong place at the wrong time."

"It was good," I say wistfully.

"She used your bathroom?"

"Actually, I don't know if she did or not. She went to the kitchen to heat up the dish, so I didn't have eyes on her the whole time. She was gone long enough to have slipped into my bathroom and swapped the toothpaste." I press my lips together and take a breath. "She knows an awful lot about plants. She was a pharmacist in England and a doctor."

Becca's arches lift. "A pharmacist *and* a doctor?"

"Yes, and she has plants from around the world here, some quite valuable, she said."

"You really think Alice would have poisoned you?"

"This whole thing is so wild. I don't think she would, but she had the means and the know-how. I'll be damned if I know what her motivation would be. She left me her money."

"Doesn't make sense. What about Paul? Would he have had the opportunity for a switch?"

"Yeah."

"When?"

My earlobes burn. "Well, he came over right after Aunt Alice died and, uh, he spent the night once."

Becca grins. "I knew it!" She props both elbows on the table, cupping her chin. "Well—?"

"That's too much detail. Drop it."

She heaves a dramatic sigh. "Okay …. Oh man, I just thought of something."

"What?"

"You know that movie, *Sleeping With The Enemy*?"

"Yeah."

We are both silent for a while. Our tea has gone cold.

"Could the toothpaste switch have been anyone else?" she asks finally. "Maybe someone broke into your house?"

I recall the footprints outside my window and Angel's aggressive reaction in the middle of the night.

"No, I check my windows and doors obsessively. No one broke in."

"Okay," Becca says, "Paul had access. What about motivation?"

"I have no idea. And I've never had the opportunity to check the soles of his boots to see if the pattern matched the ones outside my window. Actually, I did that time he was … there, but it didn't occur to me. That was before we found the print in the woods. His feet are about the right size, though."

"And Alice?"

"Why would she hide me after my family house burned, send me college money, and keep the rose-stone for me, and then try to kill me? That just makes no kind of sense."

Another dark thought occurs to me. "All the while I was in the hospital, and Paul was sitting in my room, supposedly guarding me—"

Becca's eyes widen. "He could have been waiting to kill you!"

I feel sick. "If you hadn't been there, he might have had the chance. The PD probably would have let him fill in for the guard on my door. He could have smothered me or something while I was unconscious."

"But he certainly had the opportunity the night he was … um … at your house."

"Too many clues would be left. He would know better. Or—"

"Or what?" she asks.

"I don't know 'or what,' " I confess. "It just feels wrong."

"It's gotta be hard to believe something like that about someone you thought was your friend, especially your lover." Becca's gaze drops to the cold tea. "On the other hand, they always say what a 'nice, quiet person' the neighbor was who brutally murdered six people next door."

I don't have an answer, and we both stare morosely at Charlie who has not caught our mood at all and is, in fact, playing wildly with the mouse toy, throwing it in the air, batting it across the room, and scampering after it. Alexander and Boo join in, and, for a moment, it's a free-for-all. Then they all run inexplicably from the room, leaving the mouse.

Cats are strange creatures.

Becca bends over to straighten the kitchen rug. "What's this?"

Lost in my mental tangles of what-ifs, I don't pay much attention.

"Rose, look," Becca insists.

I lean over. The cats' play has flipped over the edge of the basket-weave area rug that covers Alice's old hardwood floor beneath the kitchen table. A thin line on the floor runs counter to the wood.

"Looks too straight to be a crack in the wood," I say. "How far does it go?"

"I don't know," she says. "The table leg is sitting on top of the rug."

Ready for a distraction from the unwanted path of my logic about Paul, I assist her with moving the table to the corner of the room. Dramatically, she swipes the rug aside.

We are quiet for a moment, absorbing the fact that there appears to be a trap door in Alice's kitchen.

"I didn't know this house had a basement," Becca says. "There's not a door anywhere."

"Not necessarily a basement," I say. "It could just be a small area where she kept something. If she even knew it was here. This house is pretty old."

"You think she never moved the rug?" Becca asks with a bit of incredulousness.

I forget not everyone's idea of housekeeping is as fuzzy as mine.

"How do we get it open?" Becca asks. "It looks pretty tight."

We try different things. A butter knife works the best, and I am able to pry it up enough for Becca, who, being careful not to break a nail, gets a serving spoon under it.

Once we get it started, it isn't that hard to lift it up. In fact, it's hinged with a handle on the inside. A set of stairs descends below.

"It's dark down there," Becca observes over my shoulder.

"I'll go first. I mean, what could be down there?"

"Spiders. Snakes."

I don't care for snakes and spiders, but my personal phobia is small, cramped spaces ... and fire. But even the most macho policeman is susceptible to an unexpected creepy crawler. A well-worn rubber tarantula made the rounds on patrol car seats, and I was not immune to a reaction. Then again, I didn't feel too bad after I learned one officer had to buy a car seat cover to hide a bullet hole.

I tell myself the space below is surely roomy and pull out my pocket flashlight. It lights up the stairs, but because of the steep angle, not much else. "Guess we'll have to go down and see what's there." I say.

"We?"

I lead the way, fanning my flashlight, but there's not much to see except the stairs between two walls. There's an opening at the end of the wall to the right, and I make sure to scan the flashlight over our heads so nothing falls on us from above and gives us heart attacks.

"What does a witch keep in the basement?" Becca whispers from behind me.

My hand itches for my gun at that question, but I left my purse on the kitchen table. I think about going back for it, but resist the idea. I'm more likely to stumble in the dark and shoot my foot off than need it. After all, what could be down here?

Once we are around the wall's edge, my light finds a set of switches. Super. I flick them all on. The place lights up like a hospital surgical room. I imagine

Becca's mouth has dropped, because mine certainly has.

The area is about half the footprint of the house. It has a linoleum floor and finished walls. Shelves of exotic plants line the walls, thriving beneath the grow lights that have come on simultaneously with the overhead lights. An array of glass beakers and small burners worthy of a chemistry lab crowd a large table.

In the back of the windowless room, a bookshelf lines the wall, along with a refrigerator, washstand, toilet, and bed. And on that bed, snoring lightly, is a petite woman with silver hair.

"Oh my God," Becca says. "Who is it?"

"That," I say, playing the flashlight over her face, though it is plainly visible in the stark light, "is my great Aunt Alice."

"But she's dead!" If it is possible, Becca's fair skin has paled.

"Apparently not," I say dryly.

At our voices, Alice opens her eyes, blinks in confusion, and turns her head, catching sight of us.

"Oh," she says and sits up. "Well, it is about time you found me. I have read every single book down here twice, and I am dying for a decent cup of tea."

Chapter Thirty-Six

Alice refuses to talk until she is sitting at her own kitchen table with her tea. At her insistence, I closed the window curtains before she came upstairs. All three cats are in the kitchen, meowing and weaving about her legs. My shock is wearing off, replaced by a growing anger.

"I'm very confused," Becca begins. "I was at your funeral."

"I am sorry about that. It was necessary."

"Necessary?" I almost spit the word. "Do you know what you put me through?"

Her green eyes immediately fill with tears. "Oh dear, I didn't think it would be so much. You hardly knew me."

"You are the only real family—and you *left* me." I don't have control of myself. I'm not sure if I'm going to break into sobs or hit her.

"I am truly sorry, Rose." She doesn't try to say anything else, waiting for me.

"How did you do it?" Becca asks, not waiting for anybody.

"I don't know if you want to hear all that right now," Alice says, putting a hand on Becca's and casting a worried glance at me.

"No, tell it," I say, needing the time to get myself together.

Alice looks from me to Becca and back to me. "How much does she know, Rose?"

"Everything."

Alice frowns. "That is dangerous."

"I would never do anything to hurt Rose," Becca says.

"I trust Becca." I say. "And I needed someone to talk to, since you left me alone."

She pulls back a bit and sniffs. "Well, I suppose the cat is out of that bag."

"Why did you fake your death?" I ask.

"I did it to save my life. I had planned an exit for years as an option. I wanted to be here for you and guide you as much as I could. But I was suddenly enveloped with the premonition that I was going to be targeted. They probably left me alone these past years as a beacon for you, and once you appeared, they decided enough was enough."

"Why didn't you warn me what you were going to do?"

"I thought it important that your reaction be genuine, and I didn't think acting was a talent in your repertoire."

"But right under their noses! Alice, that was so risky."

"Perhaps a bit bold," she says and smiles. "I wanted to make sure there were no questions about it."

"Well, you fooled everyone, even the paramedics."

"That's just amazing," Becca says.

"Alice, what were you trying to say to me when you were 'dying' on the kitchen floor?"

"I'm not sure."

"You said, 'Don't let them—' "

"Oh yes, 'Don't let them hurt you.' I couldn't seem to get it all out."

"I think they have known I was alive for a while," I say, "and they knew exactly when I appeared back in Birmingham."

"But how did they know?" Alice asks. "I was so careful."

"You sent a check directly to the university," I say. "I found the notation of it in your bank papers."

She puts a hand in front of her mouth. "Oh my, I did write a check from my account, but only once. They kept sending the adoption agency notices about how the money was overdue, and I didn't want you to have any trouble." She sighs. "I never paid any attention to those bank statements."

I note Becca's eyebrows rise into the familiar golden arches. It's not easy for someone who counts pennies to understand how balancing your checkbook isn't a priority.

"My mistake," Alice says. "I suppose I made a dog's dinner out of the whole thing. It's easy to forget how much power Iron wields."

"Magical power?" I narrow my eyes at her. There is so much I don't know.

"A good part of it, but money can buy power and influence, as well. You mustn't trust anyone who is not House of Rose. No offense, dear," she adds, patting Becca's hand.

Becca's mouth is a grim line, and I imagine she's not protesting her implied untrustworthiness only out of respect for Alice's age and her status of recently rising from the dead.

"Speaking of money," I say, "I haven't touched what you 'left' me, other than paying utilities on your house. We'll have to figure out how to get it back to you without arousing suspicion."

"Oh no, dear. That was your money, anyway. It was your inheritance from your parents. Not to worry, I have my own stash."

"But what about how you faked your death to save your life?" Becca prompts, her curiosity greater than her indignation at being included in the not-to-be-trusted category.

"House of Iron has been destroying House of Rose for years," Alice says. "Rose and I are the last. Aside from the premonition, I've always known it was only a matter of time before they snuffed me. Rose had the stone, but I only had my wits."

"No magic?" Becca asks.

"Well, perhaps a tiny bit."

Becca's eyes widen. "You faked your death with magic?"

"It's not that complicated, actually. An extract from a particular South American plant has the ability to slow down heart rate and breathing; it's almost like being frozen."

"That was on a Sherlock Holmes episode," Becca says, disappointment tingeing her voice. "So, it wasn't magic."

Alice smiles. "Well, I did give it a little 'push' to make it stronger. Had to fool the paramedics, you know."

"Wow."

"What about the autopsy report?" I can't help asking. "I have a copy that said you died of heart failure."

"Oh, quite. That was actually a somewhat made-up document."

I feel my eyebrows lift.

"Perhaps it's better you don't know all the details. Let's just say, I've known the doctor and the undertaker for a very long time, and they both owe me a lot of favors. How do you suppose I faked *your* death, Rose?"

I suddenly remember the paper Alice had given me with her preferences for interment. I had referred to it when the police asked who I wanted to come collect the body. Of course, she had wanted a closed casket, too … and no cut flowers or plants. She had even supplied the name of a doctor who did private autopsies, which, of course, never happened.

"Well, what are you going to do? How are you going to live?" Becca, my practical friend, asks.

"I'm not daft, dear, and I'm not a stranger to changing my identity, but until the air clears, so to speak, I've prepared my little nest downstairs. I was hoping Rose would move into the house, so I wouldn't have to stay in the dark so long."

"Becca is living here," I say.

Alice smiles. "Well, that is very nice. So, you've been taking care of my pussies?"

To her credit, Becca only hesitates a moment. "Yes."

"And a lovely job. They all look extraordinarily well."

"I imagine they knew you weren't far away."

"And how would they know that?" I ask cynically.

"Smell, silly," Becca says. "Cats are animals; their sense of smell is way better than ours. Besides," she stoops over and strokes Charlie, "these are a witch's cats."

Chapter Thirty-Seven

My assault team consists of a slender, fashionable ash-blonde and an elderly herb witch. Equipment list includes gun, police radio, pocketknife, flashlight, a small bottle of aspirins, compass, a pair of binoculars I purchased at a hunting goods store, two cheap phones with Wal-Mart phone cards, and a black sweatshirt with a thin horizontal blue line that I rarely wear. It says, "And maybe remind the few, if ill of us they speak, that we are all that stands between the monsters and the weak." Alice has one of the phones and Becca has the other. Alice is staying in her basement hideaway with her phone. Becca's job is to keep behind me and call for help if necessary.

My preparations might be excessively paranoid, but after Alice's warning about the power of Iron to influence or buy their way past privacy laws into any institution, I'm not taking any chances. Did Iron somehow listen in on my phone call to Paul the day my hike turned deadly on Red Mountain? *Are they tracking me via my phone GPS signal?* I've not forgotten Paul's trick with a tracking device on my beach jaunt. On the assumption someone might be watching my house and see me leave, my smart phone is sitting in my car, which is parked at Becca's old apartment, and we are using Becca's car. Of course, they could be watching that, too, but paranoia can go on *ad infinitum*, and at some point, I have to actually do something.

I haven't told Paul anything. He is still a suspect, although my heart has never believed that. I'm hoping to vindicate him. My heart could be an idiot.

My stalker might have just followed me into the woods that day and decided to take a shot. If so, it leaves the puzzle as to why a supposedly innocent hiker was killed. True, he could have been mistaken in the dusk for me, but it wasn't me. That means no one followed me, at least on that occasion—it means someone was waiting, watching *that location*. And that means he thought I would return.

Why?

The only thing that makes sense is that there is something in those woods, to protect ... from me. It can't be something so vulnerable that anyone could find it, or there would be a string of bodies of innocent hikers, and that hasn't happened. I think only I can find it, and that's exactly what I'm going to do. Or give it my best shot.

Before we leave, I talk with Alice.

"What exactly is the power of the House of Iron?" I ask.

"Oh, I think on the quantum level—"

"Stop," I interrupt. "I'd like to hear your theories, but another time. What I want to know is what can they do and what can I do?"

She gives me a long look. "The Houses keep their secrets. Iron is a master of manipulation. It is believed they must touch their victims to use their power. You should be immune to that, but Becca is not."

I take her warning to heart, but trying to convince Becca to stay behind is a wasted effort.

"Don't even think about it," she says. "I will follow you whether you want me to or not."

I believe her and, short of tying her up somewhere, I think she's safer being close to me than wandering around Red Mountain on her own.

Alice taps her finger to her lips. "As to your abilities, no one knows the answer to that. The traditional powers of our House are those of healing and an occasional scryer, but you are unique, and there is no way to know how your abilities will manifest themselves. How much power you can draw and how long you can hold it varies from person to person. With my premonitions, it is more a feeling than seeing, but I don't think seeing the future is a skill wielded like healing. Your mother said when the vision wanted to be seen, it seemed to pull the living-green at the same time. And my limited experience bears this up. I don't seek the feelings about the future that sometimes descend on me. Does this make sense to you?"

I nod. "Sometimes I get a vision after I've pulled the energy up, but sometimes, it just happens." I am thinking about seeing Carrot Man reanimate as time flowed backward. I hadn't drawn the living-green beforehand, at least not consciously.

"Are my abilities dependent on the rose-stone?" I ask.

She looks thoughtful. "I think touching the stone awoke your latent ability to draw the living-green, but your mother never wore the rose-stone, so the power, the real power, must come from the living-green. You, yourself, are the conduit. Perhaps the rose-stone was used in some way in the past, but I don't know how."

"My mother wrote that it had something to do with using all three powers at once."

"What it does and how has been a closely guarded secret passed from mother to daughter. I'm so glad she wrote you that letter or the knowledge would have been lost!" She looks poised to say something else.

"What?"

"I just don't know if this might be helpful or hurtful—"

"Alice, I'm going to war, and I need to know everything you can think of to tell me. I have no idea what I am walking into."

"Well …." Her forehead wrinkles, giving her a rare troubled expression. "There were rumors that your grandmother and—" She stops and starts over. "That your mother might have been the product of an extramarital affair."

"And that might help me how?"

"It is who the man was … or was rumored to be," she says, apparently relieved that I'm taking this shocking news in stride.

"Well, who was he?" Becca bursts in.

Alice meets my eyes. "A man from the House of Iron."

"I know this is disturbing," Alice says, patting my arm and totally misreading my reaction.

"It's not disturbing," I say. "I mean, it is, but not because my grandmother had an affair. My mother implied as much."

"So, you're saying Rose has the blood of a witch *and* a warlock?" Becca says, clearly excited by the idea.

"Yes," Alice says, "apparently."

"What does that mean?" I ask, remembering Jason's allusion to family lore about abominations.

She shrugs. "No idea. According to theory, it shouldn't be possible for the magics to comingle, but there are stories that on occasion they create a strong attraction between people of different Houses and that the offspring—"

"Stories? No facts?"

"Some call them prophecies—especially those about the *Y Tair* who has the blood of all three Houses and will restore us to our days of glory."

Days of glory. Jason used that phrase too. But I suspect House of Iron's idea of glory is more about wielding power and influence than the *Y Tair's* governance.

Never mind the days of glory and the stories. I am in dire need of facts. "What about the 'abomination' part? Is that true or not? In the letter she left me, my mother claimed that was purposeful propaganda designed to keep the Houses apart."

With a troubled look, Alice shakes her head. "I can't give you facts. It is impossible to disentangle history from lore. All I can tell you is that I've heard stories of offspring from mixed blood … going very wrong."

Abominations. Is that what I am?

"What have you observed about your abilities?" Alice asks.

"So far, I've seen glimpses of the very near future and once of the past and once"—I'm thinking of the vision of Becca behind bars, but suddenly realize I have no idea if that was past or future or even in this universe.

"Your mother would be so proud and—" Alice hesitates.

"Relieved?" I say, completing her sentence.

"Yes, relieved—relieved that her mother's misstep didn't deny you your heritage."

A stab of sadness gives me pause. How much would I love to have my mother with me now to guide me through this. But I don't say that aloud. Instead, I ask, "Are there any stories about being able to control the visions?"

"I've never heard any. As I said, for your mother, it was not something she could control. If she could, she would never have been in the house when—" Her voice catches and she trails off.

I am quiet. Alice is right. If my mother had foreseen the arson, she would not have been there or allowed her husband and children to be there to become victims. The visions warned me when I was about to be killed by a sharpshooter's bullets, but not when a car was barreling down on me. I can't depend on it.

With a stern plea to Alice to stay in the basement until she hears from me, we take Becca's car and return to my house. There is one more task I need to see to, as well as making sure Angel has plenty of dry food and water, figuring she will deign to eat the dry stuff if it is her only choice. I open her kitchen window so she can go out at will. When we are back in Becca's car, I drive an erratic path to ensure we lose anyone who might be following. I feel a little silly, but remind myself that this is not a game.

Finally, after I'm certain we have not been followed, we drive around to the far side of the mountain to the parking lot at Vulcan Park and nestle Becca's car near some others. I wait ten minutes.

"We're good," I say with one last check of the parking lot. Nobody has come in behind us. We pile out of the car and climb the steps to the top plateau. The granite patio between the statue and the museum is actually an engraved map of the area with the locations of the historic mines and railroads that fueled the city's beginnings. Over a hundred feet above us towers the cast iron statue of Vulcan. From this angle, I can see his gray hand resting on a massive anvil. His other arm lifts a spear he is forging. He holds it aloft, presumably checking to see if it is smooth and straight.

We travel for a ways along the civilized, level path of the Vulcan trail, which runs along the long defunct mineral railroad bed that served the mines.

Unlike my previous encounter with a gunman when there were still a few autumn leaves on the trees, the trees are now bare. Aside from the scattered loblolly pine and cedar, there aren't many places to hide.

Following some internal pull, I lead us off the path up a sloping incline. A light crust of frost crunches beneath our feet, and our breath fogs. Trees hold their buds for the coming spring tight. Normally the woods calm me, but today I am wound taut, waiting for a bullet to find me, or worse, to find Becca. I should not have brought her into danger like this. But she insisted. Periodically, I stop and use the binoculars to scan for snipers in the woods and the neighborhood below.

Becca has other priorities, wobbling her way on the uneven footing and swinging a long stick over her head to make sure a spider doesn't fall on her. Despite my warning, she has dressed more for shopping than hiking. Her idea of a walking-in-the-woods outfit includes tight jeans, a stylish short leather jacket, and her two-inch-heeled red boots.

Maybe I didn't give Paul enough credit. Maybe, assuming he is not my assassin, he would calmly listen to the fact that I am a witch from a long line of such, perhaps even with a touch of warlock blood. Maybe he would understand that I'm looking for something only I can find in the woods on the north side of Red Mountain, but don't have the slightest clue what that might be. Sure. No problem. *When pigs fly.*

"I think I know why no one tried to follow us," Becca whispers.

"Why?"

"They think you're dying."

"What? Oh, the toothpaste thing. You finally believe me on that?"

Before she can answer, I hear a *crunch* and freeze. Becca grabs my arm. "What?"

I put a finger to my lips.

Another *crunch.*

Without conscious thought, I find my gun has migrated from my holster to my hands, but I'm not sure where the sound is coming from or how I'm going to hear anything with the loud thud of my pulse in my ears.

Another *shuffle.* I whirl, aiming at the sound.

A tiny head lifts from a pile of frosted leaves, and a gray squirrel darts out and up a tree, flipping its tail in agitation. A rush of air escapes my mouth and I holster the gun.

Becca lets out her breath too. "So where are we? Are we close?"

"I think so. I'm pretty sure the mine entrance is over there." I point. Now that I think about it, how do I know that? It is pretty well hidden, but I never doubted I could find it again. *Magic? Is there something about this place that beckons?*

Indeed, in about twenty minutes, I've found it. Carefully, I move brambles from the entrance.

"Whoa," Becca says, hesitating at the shadowed entrance. "You suppose there are spiders?"

"No spiders this time of year."

Her attention shifts to the ground. "What about snakes?"

"Becca, snakes winter below ground in holes." I'm not totally sure of this, but maybe it will ease her mind. "Just don't step in a hole."

"I'll follow you," she says, maneuvering behind me.

Inside, everything is exactly how I remembered it, with the large fallen stone that saved my life roughly in the center. Dripping water has frozen into streaks along the back wall. The other walls are stacked stone and dirt. The air is colder in here, piercing through my jeans with a sharp edge. It would have felt great in midsummer, but I pull my jacket closer and make Becca sit behind the rock, just in case I missed seeing a sniper in the woods. With the binoculars, I take another slow swipe to make sure.

"Now what?" she asks, tucking her gloved hands into her armpits.

For a while, I don't answer, because I don't have a clue what's next. I run the flashlight beam over the stacked rock walls, looking for … I don't know what. "This is the right place. I feel it."

"What do you feel?" She leans forward, excited, I imagine, that magic might finally be in play. I wish I could give her a few Merlin fireworks for her faithfulness and acceptance of me.

"I can't explain it," I say. "It's a vague, tingly sensation, like the first moment you realize your leg is asleep."

"But before it starts hurting?"

"Yeah. I felt the same thing before, and I'm pretty sure that something drew me here that first day. I didn't just stumble on this mine entrance."

"Well, I don't feel anything," Becca says. "So, it *is* about magic."

"Maybe, but just how is that helpful?"

"You're the witch," she says smugly. "I'm just the witch's best friend."

After another check of the walls with my flashlight, I decide we are safe from any immediate cave-in and sit perpendicular to her, at an angle from the entrance, so I'm not an easy target.

"The last time I was here and had a … vision, I used the rose-stone."

"Well, try that," she suggests.

"I can't."

"Why not?"

"I don't have it."

She lifts one golden arch. "Why not?"

I shrug. *Instinct, premonition … idiocy?* I'm not sure. "I just thought it better not to bring it."

"Rose, that doesn't make sense." She is thoughtful for a moment. "But didn't Alice say you were the real conduit, anyway?"

"She did."

"Then try. I'll be quiet."

I take out the aspirin bottle and pop a couple. Experience has taught me that if I'm successful in having a vision, I'll pay for it with a dynamite headache. Maybe taking something beforehand will help. Then I lean back against the cold wall and close my eyes.

The same thing occurs that happened when I spotted Carrot Man in Five Points South and tried to scry—nothing. Maybe I'll never be able to do it again. Do I *want* to see the future or the past? I can forget about all this and go back down the mountain and live like a normal person … except for the little matter of someone stalking me.

I let go of my fluttering thoughts. The times I have seen through time's veil, I hadn't been trying. Maybe I can just bring my thoughts gently to a place of stillness and see what happens. *Watch the rock grow.* I cup my hand, imagining the rose-stone in my palm. How can a diamond, a rock, help find the living-green? *How stupid*, I realize suddenly. Of course, a diamond isn't just a rock; it's pure carbon—the stuff of life, a gift from the stars that formed into the living-green, died, and sank into the earth, hardened by the heat and pressure deep in the earth over millions of years, and crystalized into diamond.

With this thought, I am able to better visualize the rose-stone, the facets within facets, light refracting through the crystal lattices, and mentally I reach down, sensing the dark veins that run like black blood through the earth. All the mining that was done here over the past century has not begun to deplete the coal that is here, not the deep seams, but I have to go around dark rivers of what I assume are iron seams. The iron is far more prevalent than coal here and I have to find my mental way around it. As I reach for a rich coal seam, I can feel that energy surging easily up into me. How can I have been so dead to it all my life? The word "alive" has taken on a whole different dimension. I have been walking through life wrapped in layers like a mummy, and now I am naked, absorbing the sun's gift. I could bask in this forever.

I have no idea how long I do just that. Faintly, I hear Becca's voice. "Rose! Rose, come back!"

When I open my eyes, at first the world has a haloed glaze, but that fades, and I realize Becca is shaking me. "What?" I mumble. "What's wrong?" I'm trying to remember what I am supposed to be doing. *Is Becca in trouble? Where is my gun?*

"You've been like this for over an hour. I got worried."

"I'm okay."

She sits back on her heels and shivers. "What now?"

I realize I have not been fazed by the cold. In fact, warmth still pumps like melted sunlight through me. I take off my jacket and drape it around her shoulders.

"No headache," I say with a smile of relief. "I don't think it was the aspirin either."

"Why then?"

I frown, thinking. "Actually, my head has never hurt when I drink the living-green, only when I scry."

"Oh, so now what?" Becca asks, and I see she is trying to hide that her teeth are chattering.

"I'm sorry, Becca. I know you're cold, but I need a little more time."

"Okay. Can I just lean against you a bit? Maybe some of that magic will warm me up."

"Sure."

Once again I pull the energy into me. Alice said my need would drive my gift. I focus on my need to understand this place, to know its secret—

At first nothing happens, but as I sink deeper into my need—my life is at stake; the line of my House is at stake—the world inside the mine shifts to a wavering black and gray. It's a subtle change, because we are already in shadows, but I recognize it as a scrying.

Minutes pass. This is new. Does it mean time is wrinkling forward or back? I wait, keeping my focus on my need and holding the golden energy. More minutes pass.

Suddenly, a thin shadow-man walks backward from the cave opening. He wears a long overcoat and carries a plastic container, the kind used for gasoline. Passing just in front of where Becca and I sit, he doesn't seem to notice us, continuing to walk backward almost into the far side of the mine wall. I realize a section of the wall is open, revealing a lit passage. The man steps up, heel first, onto a raised floor, pauses and the wall closes, leaving a thin, jagged outline of light around the section of wall. Then the light disappears and the doorway is a seamless wall of stone.

When I emerge from the vision into the real world, I'm trembling.

"What is it?" Becca asks, wrapping her hands around my arm. "What did you see?"

"I think—" I have to stop and swallow. "I think I just saw the man who murdered my parents and sister seventeen years ago."

Chapter Thirty-Eight

Sitting beside me, her arm linked in mine, Becca gasps. "You saw him? The man who set your house on fire?"

"I think so."

My need, I had thought, was to see this mine's secret, but maybe on a deeper level I needed to see who had killed my family and who was trying to kill me, and the magic showed me. But I still don't know enough. The man who stepped through that doorway in the mine's wall looked familiar, though his face was shadowed by the gray world. He was thinner than Jason, but that doesn't mean Jason wasn't involved. It had not been Paul, but again, that doesn't give him a pass either. It just means Mr. Black himself had been the one to actually shoot my family and burn our house to the ground. *Who was he?*

"So," Becca says miserably, "you think we can go home now?"

"Becca, a man walked right out of the wall." I point. "I mean, a section of the wall opened like a door."

"Really?"

Stiffly, we both clamber to our feet and examine the mine wall.

"I don't see any kind of crack," she says.

"Me either, and I know where it should be. They've done a remarkable job on this." I run my hands over the stones, sensing a tiny bit of living-green in them, but locked away somehow, and step back to examine the whole wall, trying to remember exactly where the lines had appeared. "It doesn't make sense."

A lock of pale hair has fallen into Becca's face, and she hooks it behind her ear. "Talk to me."

"I saw it open here," I say, drawing a vertical line with my finger. "But that goes through the middle of several piece of stones."

"Maybe the stones are attached to the door and some extend over the edge?"

"Becca, you're a genius!" I feel my scowl dissolving. "That could be it! That would mean—" I run my hands over the largest protruding stone, which is about midway down the wall. "I can't get my hands around it far enough to pull on it."

Fishing in my pocket, I find my pocketknife and open it, prying it under the stone and using the handle as a lever. To my surprise, it opens easily and soundlessly.

"Oh my God!" Becca gasps. "What *is* this?"

"I don't know, but I have to find out. I want you to go back to the car." I pat my pocket. "If I'm not back in a couple of hours, call Detective Tracey Lohan and tell him where I am."

She draws up indignantly. "I will not let you go in there by yourself."

"Becca, I need you to be able to get help."

"You're just saying that to keep me from following you. We have my phone to get help."

I look down the slanting corridor as far as I can see, which is the first bend to the right. "I don't know that the phones are going to work in there."

"It doesn't matter," she said in her not-to-be-budged voice. "You are not going alone."

"I don't deserve you, Becca."

She rolls her eyes. "Let's go *la Rosa*."

Before we tromp off, I examine the door. It doesn't appear to have a lock. The secret of its existence is apparently what precludes unauthorized entry. To be certain, I make Becca stay in the mine while I step in and close the door behind me, confirming that a strong push from inside is all that is necessary to make it swing open. I have no desire to go exploring and trap myself inside. Me and close spaces do not do well together, and I am already sweating at the idea of going down the narrow passageway.

The lighting in the dank corridor is spaced widely, making long stretches where it is dim, and Becca swishes her stick against possible spiders. As we go, I scan the upper corners for camera eyes. This is part of an old mineshaft that runs underground, but it has obviously been upgraded and reinforced in areas. We've been gradually going deeper, and my compass says we are headed east.

We don't talk. As we go deeper, the tingling I felt in the mine entrance increases. Magic? It's not the living-green. I couldn't begin to explain how I know this; I just do. Whatever other magic exists here, we are getting nearer to a source.

The shaft turns through the mountain's heart, following the vein of ore its original diggers had searched for. The ground is rocky and uneven, and I suspect rails had long ago run through here and long ago been taken up. Although maps exist laying out the tunnels, they don't begin to mark all of them. It's a wonder the mountain doesn't cave in from all the worming of its belly. I have a brief (non-magic-induced) vision of the fancy condos along the ridge collapsing, and I shudder.

"What?" Becca hisses from behind me.

"Nothing." There is no point giving her more to worry about. I regret subjecting her to this, but another part of me is grateful for her presence. She has no motivation to be here other than to stand by me. We do not share a bloodline or even a history. Yet here she is schlepping down a dim, damp mineshaft with the possibility of nightmare creatures dropping on her head, on the trail of a murderer, solely because I am her friend.

We see no living creatures, not a salamander or a rat or even a spider web. That seems odd, because I doubt Mr. Black sends his housekeeper through here. Perhaps it is related to the growing sense of power I feel. The trickle has become a throb. I stop and slip my compass from my pocket at the next pool of light. The needle is making erratic shifts in direction though I'm standing still.

"Could we still reach Alice?" Becca asks, hopefully, but I think she knows better.

I shake my head and check the phone. "No signal down here."

"How much further, do you think?" She peers nervously over my shoulder.

"We have to go back," I say.

"Really?" Her voice brightens.

"Not all the way. I think we missed something."

"What could we possibly have missed? It's been absolutely the same since we came through that doorway."

"No." I shake my head. "That sense I had of something, it kept growing stronger, and now it seems to be fading."

"I feel like a blind person. I've no idea what you're talking about."

"I know. Just trust me on this."

She snorts. "Like I wouldn't be following you into a dark, spider-infested tunnel if I didn't trust you."

"There aren't any spiders," I say absently, as we reverse direction.

According to my watch, we return down the path about five minutes. I stop and go back a few feet. "Here."

Becca raises one golden arch. "Here what?"

I run my hand along the wall on our right. "The energy source is strongest here. It feels like a magnet is drawing my hand to the wall. There's got to be a door here too."

We both examine the rocky wall. If not for the experience of knowing how cleverly it could be hidden, we would never have found it, and it is more luck that one of Becca's tugs on a protruding stone opens it as soundlessly as the first door.

I motion Becca to move behind the protection of the open section, and I stand against the wall on the other side, out of the line of fire. Gun and flashlight scope out the area.

"Well, that's odd," I murmur.

"What?" Becca steps out from behind the door, her curiosity overcoming caution.

I move into the room and light envelopes us.

"Jesus!" Becca says, her hands flying to her chest at the sudden brightness.

"It's motion sensitive," I say, sliding my flashlight into my pocket and my gun into its holster. "No one is in here."

The small room is indeed empty, except for a hunk of stone roughly hewn as a chair in the center. There's no doubt the power I've been feeling comes from there, and it draws me like a mosquito to heat.

"What kind of stone is that?" Becca asks, following me.

"Iron," I say without any doubt. "It's made of iron and infused with some kind of power."

Becca eyes the chair dubiously. "Really? It's kind of ugly. What does it do?"

"I haven't the foggiest idea."

She's right. It's not a work of art by any stretch, at least not in my book. It is crudely made and rather than legs, the bottom is a solid pillar. The only pieces that are not solid are between the seat and the arms, which curve down and flow back into the seat. It looks more like a pagan throne than a modern chair.

Before I can stop her, Becca reaches out and touches the solid silvery-gray surface.

Nothing happens. She looks at me and shrugs.

Curious, I holster my gun, pull out the compass again and walk slowly around the chair. The arrow points to it from every position. At this point, I do something stupid: I sit ... and have my second awakening.

Chapter Thirty-Nine

The moment I touch the iron chair, a sensation cousin to the tingling I felt at the mine entrance, but greatly magnified, crackles through my body, raising the hairs on my arms and the back of my neck. It is different from holding the living-green, a feeling more like standing before a closed tunnel, sensing the building pressure of … something pushing, waiting for the door to open. *Is the chair the door?*

"Rose? Are you alright?" Becca puts a hand on the chair's arm and leans toward me.

"Don't!" I say, not sure why. "Don't touch me."

She backs off a couple of steps toward the doorway. "Why? What's happening?"

"I don't know. It's not the living-green; it's something else, but I don't know what it might do."

At that moment, a man made of sharp angles and dressed in black rolls an electric wheelchair into the doorway. I jump to my feet, drawing my gun, but Becca is between us. He glides to her and grasps her wrist. Instantly, her eyes roll back in her head, and she collapses into his lap.

"Not a good idea," he warns, nodding at my weapon, and I see he has a knife at Becca's throat.

I grit my teeth. "If you hurt her, I will kill you." It's not an idle threat. This is Theophalus Blackwell, the head of House of Iron. It is also, I realize, the younger man I saw in the gray and black of the past, the man who had not yet been confined to a wheelchair and left the mine through the hidden door carrying a gasoline canister; the man who threw a lit match into my house; and the man who has haunted my paintings and my nightmares. I would be happy for an excuse to kill him.

Becca is strangely calm, her mouth curved in a peaceful smile, as if she is content being held by him.

"What are you doing to her?" I demand.

"What are you doing here?" he counters.

"We were just curious."

"You felt nothing from the iron chair?" he asks, an edge to his question.

"What do you mean? I just wanted to sit down. It's been a long walk."

My sarcasm seems lost on him. He glances over his shoulder, still holding Becca pressed against his chest, as two men enter to stand beside him, one tall and muscular and another, shorter and heavier, a familiar figure.

"Paul!"

My ex-partner and lover has a gun pointed at my chest.

"I don't want to, but I will shoot you," he says.

"Why?" My heart is thudding in my chest.

"Because he wishes it," Paul says flatly. "Put your gun on the floor."

I don't see that I have any choice. Slowly, I lower the gun and lay it on the floor.

"Kick it aside," he instructs.

I do so.

"Now what?" I ask.

Black puts a hand on Paul's arm, and Paul's face glows in what strikes me as adulation. In that moment, I know if he is told to kill me, he will do it without hesitation. I want to vomit.

Black has withdrawn the knife from Becca's throat but keeps hold of her arm. "Give me the rose-stone," he says to me.

"Can't do that."

"Shoot her," he says causally to Paul, inclining his head at Becca.

"Wait!" I swallow. "I *can't* give it to you."

His face is as hard as the iron chair.

"I don't have it," I add quickly. "If you kill me, you will never find it." I can feel the sweat pooling in the hollow of my neck, despite the cool temperature of the mine.

Black releases Becca. "Go stand over there," he says, pointing to the far wall.

To my horror, she obeys him without a glance in my direction.

"What have you done to her?" I demand, anger overcoming my fear.

Black pushes a lever on the arm of his chair and approaches. I hold my ground. "What am I going to do with you?" he asks quietly and reaches up to cup my chin.

The pseudo-affectionate gesture turns my stomach. I recoil from him, but I don't have anywhere to go. Just behind me, the cool stone of the chair brushes the back of my thighs, spiking the hairs on my arms and neck.

"Sit," he orders, still touching me.

"Screw you."

He frowns. "So you *have* inherited at least the power of your mother's line."

"What are you talking about?" I'm not about to give him any information.

"Unfortunately, your aunt died before she could explain it to you."

I curb the reflexive desire to glance at Becca, keeping my gaze glued on him. In her state, if he asks her anything, I have a rotten feeling she will tell him. Hopefully, it won't occur to him to ask if Alice faked her death. If it does, I have no doubt that Alice will be really dead soon.

"Speaking of dying," Black says, cocking his head. "You are, you know."

I want to say something witty like, *Nope, sorry to disappoint. I quit brushing my teeth a month ago*, but I don't. Let him think I'm sick and have no idea what he's talking about. It occurs to me that if Angel hadn't put a hole in my toothpaste, I would indeed be dying, though I suspect it would take a lot to kill me. I am House of Rose.

I hold myself straight. "We're all dying," I say evenly.

The edge of his mouth quirks. "True." He nods at the thick-jawed man with Paul. "Search her."

When Jaws tells me to lift my arms, I consider ramming my elbow into his neck. Paul would have skinned me alive if I conducted a search like this bozo, but he's not a police officer, and Paul has a gun pointed at me. I submit to the search, which yields my compass and knife.

"No jewelry?" Black asks the man.

"No sir."

Black turns to Becca. "Where is the rose-stone?"

"I don't know." She looks unhappy at having to tell him this.

I'm grateful I didn't tell Becca what I'd done with the stone. If I had or if I'd brought it, there would be two bodies rotting somewhere in forgotten mine tunnels under Red Mountain.

"So." Black—as I still think of him—turns his chair back to me. "We have a little game to play."

"Come," he says motioning to Becca, who steps quietly to his side. "Walk in front."

Becca moves into the hallway, and I hear him tell her to turn to the right, the opposite direction from the mine entrance. Paul steps aside so I can follow her, keeping a safe distance from me. He knows I'm trained in how to disarm a gunman, but it only works if the gun is close. He doesn't give me that opportunity. Jaws follows behind.

The entire long walk down the tunnel, Becca doesn't say a word.

I'm worried sick about her, but my focus has to be on the weapon I know is pointing at my back. I want to scream at Paul, whom I have trusted with my life on more than one occasion, but I suspect he is as much under Black's spell as Becca.

It's Black who finally speaks. "Your friend," he says, "will not recover without my touch. But I will consider trading her for the rose-stone, if you can remember where you left it."

"Her name is Becca." Now I am angry that Black doesn't seem to see her as a person.

"Her name doesn't matter," he says. "She has no identity unless I give it back to her."

I grit my teeth but don't respond.

"Take your time," he says casually.

It's about forty minutes, according to my internal clock, before we arrive at yet another hidden door. This time it opens into a modern hallway. I'm trying to figure out where we are. I think we continued to move east. If that's right, we have to be somewhere on the east side of the Red Mountain expressway. Inside the corridor, we pass three doors on our right. At the fourth, Black says, "This one," and opens it.

Inside is a replica of a jail cell of the 1960s. The only way I know this is because a mannequin of Martin Luther King, Jr. sits on the bed staring out toward the bars ... or through them. I know where we must be—the lower levels of the Simpson mansion. We didn't get to this particular scene on Uncle Sam's tour, but I'm sure the other rooms along the hall hold snatches of time like this one. The coincidence of there being another underground museum like this is too far-fetched. The time period of the "jail" is later than the others I saw, but maybe someone picked up the hobby from the earlier builder.

I am not surprised that the bars are real iron, and the lock closing behind us makes an authentic *click*.

Chapter Forty

It's surreal to be sharing a cell with a mannequin Dr. King. I imagine this is a re-creation of the incarceration where King wrote his famous "Letter from Birmingham Jail" chastising the white clergy who wanted him to cease the marches and protests in favor of letting the court system force change. I am too worried about Becca to contemplate the irony. Our captors have left us, but Becca stands in the exact spot where Black directed her, gazing at the place where she last saw him.

"Becca?"

She doesn't answer. *What has he done to her?* I shake her, yell at her, plead with her. She is unresponsive, even when I slap her face as a last resort. I tug on her arm, and she follows me meekly, turning her head to keep her gaze on the door. At the edge of the cot, she stops. I move the mannequin to the corner to give her space, and have to pull down on her to get her to sit on the bed. I sit beside her.

"This is a fine mess I've got us into," I say, my throat closing.

No response.

With a stab of recognition, I realize this is the vision I saw in my back yard—Becca behind bars—but I hadn't dreamed that I would be in the cell with her. And if I had, would I have done anything differently? Can I change the future I see? Obviously I can, since I shot the man in the alley before he shot Paul, and I stopped that jerk at The Club from his verbal assault on the waitress.

I find little comfort in this. I didn't stop the vision I had of Becca here.

After a while, it occurs to me that the room might be bugged, and having nothing more constructive to do, I search it as thoroughly as I can.

Nothing. Not that surprising. We must have tripped some kind of alarm when we entered the tunnel. Unless Mr. Black is accustomed to keeping prisoners or has a similar ability to scry the future, there is no way he could have known I would show up in his hideaway and sit on his iron throne. What was that thing anyway? And what was the power it channeled?

Even though I've been over every inch of the place, I look around for something I might be able to use. We have to get out of here. I give the cell door a strong shake and a kick, hoping it might be more for show than security, but the owner of this bizarre collection of history snapshots had a penchant for realism. I can't budge the lock. Fortunately, the realism carries over to the toilet, which flushes. That means there is a source of water if we get desperate, gross as that might be.

I examine the cot again to see if there is a way to work off a leg and use it as a weapon or maybe beat my way through the wall, although I know we are below ground level. Maybe I could get to the sewer line—I'm thinking *Shawshank Redemption* here—but the entire cot is welded together.

This is the point where something happens in a movie, but nothing happens in my movie. The minutes crawl by, probably into hours. No one dims the lights, so my sense of time is measured only by when I have to use the toilet. I make Becca go when I do. I'm afraid if I don't, she would just sit in her own waste. I want to cry, to finally let go and cry. But I can't, and in any case, on the chance that there is a tiny camera I didn't find, I wouldn't want to give Black the satisfaction.

I SLEEP BESIDE BECCA ON the narrow cot, sharing what little warmth we can find under my jacket. Needless to say, it has not been restful. Twice, Jaws has brought a couple of bowls of scraps from a nice dinner, along with bottled water. He wasn't amenable to conversation and shoved the food through a small opening at the bottom of the cell door. I tried to get him to come inside, pleading Becca's illness, but he ignored me.

I don't think we're getting three meals a day, so my measurement of time, besides toilet calls, reflects the time I have felt the need for sleep, although that could be chalked up to exhaustion or sheer boredom. No way to tell. I don't have a watch; I used my cell phone to tell time, and Becca did as well. When I get out of here, the first thing I'm going to do is buy a watch. All kinds of interesting and potentially useful things might have resided in Becca's purse, but Jaws took that, too. I'm surprised he left me my belt, but probably he doesn't particularly care if I try to hang myself.

Becca has no interest in eating. I have tried everything I can to coax her into it. I'm even more worried that she has hardly touched the water, swallowing only what I've managed to get into her mouth. I've actually chewed the food for her and put it in her mouth, tilting her head back and stroking her throat the way I saw my father get a pill down his old dog. To my surprise, it works. She doesn't seem to mind. It's what I'm doing, sitting beside her on the cot, when the door to the room opens.

Mr. Black rolls inside, flanked by Paul. They stand in the narrow, empty space between the cell door and the door that leads out into the long hall.

I don't bother standing. My heart is thudding, however, dreading what he is about to say or do, but I won't give him the satisfaction of knowing that.

"So," he says conversationally, "have you given thought to revealing the stone's location?"

Relief floods me. He hasn't found it. I imagine my house is a wreck. What does he want with it? This is another item that has occupied my thoughts. Alice implied that the rose-stone would be useful only for a member of House of Rose, although I think the words she actually used were that she *thought* it wouldn't be useful to anyone else. In any case, I don't want it in his hands.

"Don't remember where I put it," I say.

He waves a hand at Becca. "Not even to cure your friend?"

"What's wrong with her?" I demand.

"She's lovesick." His expression doesn't change with the absurd declaration.

"That's ridiculous."

"Well, look at her." He waves a hand in her direction.

Indeed, Becca's eyes are fixed on him.

"She would do anything I ask," he says. "She craves my presence. What else would you call it?"

"Not love." I say.

He tilts his head, as if considering my comment. "Worship then."

"Is that what you've done to Paul?"

"More or less." He pauses. "Less actually. Paul can still act and think on his own; it's his will and memory that belong to me."

"Must be a fine line to achieve."

"It is, but I've had a long time to practice."

I wonder exactly when he "touched" Paul. Was it after I was assigned to him, or did Black do it before that? Did he "suggest" that Paul ask for me to train to make sure I worked the beat where Alice lived? That made the most sense. How? Was it a type of hypnosis? Something enhanced by the power of House Iron? I once saw a demo on TV where the hypnotist explained he couldn't make someone do something that was deeply against his principles, but when he told the subjects to forget about their instructions or what they had done while under, they seemed to. Did Paul forget he had ever done anything to hurt me or anyone else? I want to believe that. I *can't* believe the man who taught me street policing and watched my back, who gave out candy and smiles to children, who liked listening to fairy tales … and made love to me … could "know" he had put me in harm's way—*a bullet pings off the stone in the mine entrance*—or tried to kill me.

"What's going to happen to Becca?"

"It depends. If you continue to hide the stone, she will waste away and die in a matter of days. If you tell me where to find the stone, I will cure her."

"And—?"

"And what?" He spreads his hands in mocking innocence.

"And what happens after you 'cure' her?"

"I will release her."

"Cure her and release her first, and then I'll tell you where the stone is."

His mouth tightens. "Not in the bargain."

My heart sinks. "You don't intend to cure her, do you?"

He meets my gaze. Perhaps a modicum of respect burns in his pale blue eyes. Or is it hate?

"Of course I do." He tilts his head at Paul who immediately opens the door for him. "Think about it," Black says as he leaves.

"Paul!" I call out.

Paul, who was about to follow Black out the door, stops and turns.

"Did you set me up that night in the alley?" I ask quickly.

He blinks. "I arranged it."

"Zachary was supposed to shoot me, wasn't he?"

Paul frowns. "No, it was supposed to be Carrot Man who shot you, and then I would shoot him. That was the way it was supposed to happen."

I'm certain Carrot Man didn't know about the last part of the plan. "Carrot Man chickened out and gave the job to Zachary, didn't he?"

He blinks. "Yes, and Zachary panicked and screwed it up. *He* was not happy."

Black must have let Paul arrange this, because from what I have seen, if Black had done it himself, Carrot Man would not have been able to change the plan. There is no pleasure in learning I was right. But there is something else I want to know.

"And you killed Carrot Man to keep him from talking?"

"It was for the best."

"The best." I repeat flatly.

"Yes."

"You shot at me on Red Mountain and tried to poison me and killed two men … for the best?"

"Yes."

His forehead wrinkles momentarily, as if he believes that, but can't remember why. My stomach lurches. I can't wrap my head around this. Paul never appeared to be under someone's sway when we rode together. Maybe he wasn't so deeply under Black's influence then. Or maybe—I try to follow the line of thought out logically. If he would accept *anything* Black said, how would he seem if ordered to "act normal"? The hypnotist I saw got people to do weird things by putting them in a trance and making suggestions, but nothing as sophisticated as this. And all Black did with Becca was touch her. Was that why he put his hands on my chin and gave me an order? If so, I wasn't affected by his magic. And that told him more than any declaration of who I was. All this races through my mind before Paul can turn back to the door.

"Paul, *stop*. Fight him. This is not who you are."

He looks at me, his expression flat. "It's who I want to be."

Chapter Forty-One

I'm getting desperate, and I worry that means Black is, too. I don't know why exactly the rose-stone is so important to him, but that makes it imperative that he not get his hands on it.

Becca's condition is no better. I've been over every inch of the room multiple times and can re-create it in my sleep, something I actually do, dreaming there's a secret door or a panel or that Paul comes back and apologizes and unlocks the cell door. Then I wake up, and it's the same walls, and Becca is thinner and paler and drifting farther and farther away.

I consider pulling on the living-green and seeing if that will help her, but I'm afraid to. What if I make her worse? My efforts to scry have not produced anything more useful than predicting my next meal.

For the five-hundredth time I go over things, looking for something I may have missed. The cell is locked. I have nothing to try and pick the lock with, assuming I had a clue how to do it. The steel bars are too strong to bend and are sunk into the concrete floor. The ceiling appears to be as solid as the walls. There is no way to tear apart the bed for a weapon.

But something keeps prickling at the back of my mind, something I should know. I've never seen this room before Black opened that door. But … I have seen other rooms. Could there be a clue there? Shutting my eyes, I try to remember what those rooms looked like when Uncle Sam gave Paul and me an abbreviated tour, but I can only remember two. One was the first on the way down the stairs, the medieval scene, and the other was a room further down the hallway, a re-creation of pioneer days. I try to focus on the details—a woman in a bonnet stirred an iron pot hung over the fire; a man at the table sharpened his knife; log cabin walls; a small window through which golden light poured.

Wait a minute. *That window.* It looked real because a light shone behind a white shade. They couldn't have done that unless there was a space behind the back wall, a space for the light, for electrical wiring and … plumbing. And I am willing to bet that space goes all the way along the back wall of the rooms, which would include this one, even though there is no "window" in it.

Galvanized by a rush of adrenalin, I jump up to inspect the back wall, the one furthest from the door, tapping along it. My adoptive father built a walk-in closet into a section of the garage in one of the houses we lived in. He let me help and taught me to listen for the difference in the sounds along a wall. Nails go into the wooden stud framework that supports the sheetrock. My ears pick up where the studs are, but I can't tell if there is a hollow space behind the sheetrock. There is only one way to know. At worst, I would make a hole and encounter the foundation wall … and break my foot. At best—

My best imitation karate kick makes a dent in the sheetrock and hurts my knee, which I ignore. My next kick punches in, all the way to my shin. Elated, I tear at the sheetrock with my hands, making a space big enough for my head, and look inside.

Indeed, there is a long, narrow crawlspace housing the plumbing and wiring. With hands and occasional kicks, I work the hole big enough to squeeze through and return to Becca, who is, as usual, sitting on the cot's edge, her gaze perpetually on the place she last saw Black. There is no way to get her to crawl through the hole with me.

"If you can hear me, Becca, I'll come back. I promise."

She gives no indication she heard me, but I squeeze her limp hand. I choose to believe that somewhere deep inside, she understands.

The crawlspace is narrow and dark. I miss my flashlight and try not to think about spiders or rats or the ghost of Mr. Simpson's wife. While I was working on the hole, I shut one eye, a trick Paul taught me to give my night vision a head start at least in one eye. With that small advantage and the light seeping into the crawlspace from the hole I made, I can make out the shapes of pipes nearby at shin level. The narrow space barely allows me to move. I can feel the brush of the walls on my shoulders. My heart might as well be in my throat and ears. My hands are damp and slippery. I don't do close spaces. I would never have made it as an astronaut. An overwhelming need to *get out* tightens in my chest, building until I can't breathe. I am on the edge of losing it and going back to the cell.

With a wrench of willpower, I make myself stop and close my eyes, imagining I am standing on an open plain, wind in my face, stars overhead, mountains in the distance. Plenty of space. *I can breathe. I can breathe. In—* slowly, no hurry—*out.* Ignore the feeling that there is not enough air. It's an illusion. *In … out.*

A part of my mind knows I have hyperventilated, knows that I started breathing in deep gulps when I panicked and actually took in too much oxygen, even though it feels like I can't get enough air. I know this because once when I was first with my foster parents, before they adopted me, I decided the dryer made an interesting "cave" and crawled in. My mother walked by and seeing the door open, gave it a slam. I went berserk, screaming and banging my fist against the dryer door. What had to be only a few minutes felt like eternity, and when I was rescued, I thought I was drowning. I couldn't breathe. I didn't understand when my foster mother made me breathe in a paper bag, but I did it, and it helped because, after a few minutes, the oxygen level in the bag decreased enough to ease me. At the time, I didn't fully understand her explanation, but I listened carefully because I didn't ever want to feel like that again.

My chest finally calms. I still want to go back, to get out, but I think of Becca and open my eyes. My pupils have dilated enough that it doesn't seem quite as dark, and that helps. I squirm forward, concentrating on breathing.

When I come to a lighter square area, I am sure this must be the fake window I had seen in the pioneer cabin reproduction. The surface seems to be made of thin plastic. I work the light fixture out of the way and punch the material. Instead of breaking, it pops out of the wall. Good enough.

Climbing across the sill is awkward because of the height, but I use the pipes for a boost and worm my way into the room. There is not enough space to get my feet in, so I have to go head first, using my arms to break the fall. Even so, my head hits hard and I have to lie still for several precious minutes before I can move.

Inside, it is even darker than the crawlspace. Relying on my memory, I climb to my feet and square my back to the wall with the window, walking forward perpendicular to it, which, in theory, should bring me to the door that opens into the long hallway. But four strides into the room, I bump into someone. Even though I know there are mannequins in here, my heart lurches. From the material, I think it is the pioneer woman. I right her so I will know where she is and not trip over her again and move carefully around her, hoping I am still heading at the correct angle.

At last, I encounter a wall and feel along it until I find a doorknob. Thankfully, it is not locked, and I open it a crack. The hall is lit and appears empty. To my left are several more doors leading to other historical "display" rooms, including a room with a cell containing Martin Luther King, Jr. and my best friend. I remind myself that Black could appear at any moment, and I have no idea what else he is capable of, in addition to stealing a person's mind with a touch.

That is why, when I climb the round stairway up to the first floor, I do not slip out the front door or try to find a phone to call for help. I can just imagine trying to warn the responding officers not to touch the suspect. Someone would, of course, and that someone would be armed … and a lot of people would get hurt.

And I promised Becca I would come back.

I find my way to the kitchen and what I think must be the garage door. Hoping I'm not going to set off any alarms, I open it and flip on the lights, illuminating a Mercedes and a BMW convertible, both gleaming with polish. A table runs along the wall with some car maintenance equipment, but what I want is a crowbar.

Unable to find something to break Becca out of the cell, I reconsider my options. There is only one possibility of an ally in this house. The problem is finding him.

I back out of the kitchen and retrace my steps to the huge living room. One soft light glows, and I slip in to check the grandfather clock—3:45. The windows are dark, so that has to be 3:45 a.m., which mean Jason is most likely in bed asleep. That's good, but which room?

This is a puzzle for Sherlock Holmes, not me. I sit on a couch and bury my aching head in my hands. I can't give up now. What would Sherlock do? Ask logical questions like what do I know about Jason that might be a clue? I go over everything that was said between us here in this room the night of Hallows' Eve. Nothing helpful. What about our dinner date at The Club? We talked about my shoes, joked about someone trying to kill me, and—wait, what had he said when we were looking out the window at the city lights far below? *"I can see this view out my bedroom window. Sometimes, when I can't sleep I sit there."* That means his room is on the north side of the house and probably upstairs.

I do a recon of the upstairs. Three doors are possible candidates. I reach out to the living-green, thinking perhaps I can conjure up a vision of myself going into any of the rooms, but for some reason I can't even access it. Is it because I don't have contact with the ground?

Using magic might be a bad idea inside the walls where House of Iron resides, anyway. I have no idea if Black or anyone else could feel it, but I shouldn't take the chance. Maybe I can just go for a premonition. Alice had certainly done that, predicting I would show up for the rose-stone and later that she had better make herself dead before someone else did it for her. I close my eyes, imagining the three doors and try to sort out how I feel about each of them.

Nothing. They are just doors.

On impulse, I try the knob of the first one, holding my breath and hoping the hinges don't creak. Moonlight filters through a window that does indeed look out over the city, but it also illuminates a pair of high heels beside the bed that can only belong to Stephanie. So much for premonition.

With great care, I close the door and try the next one. Again, the window catches my eye, but only briefly, because sitting in front of it is Jason, bare-chested in the moonlight. Michelangelo's "David" has nothing on him. Despite the tension that strains every muscle in my body, I catch my breath.

I'm positive I have not made a sound, but he turns his head and looks right at me.

"Rose?"

Swallowing hard, I step into the room and close the door. If I have made a mistake, it could be the costliest one of my life.

Chapter Forty-Two

I stand in the doorway of Jason Blackwell's bedroom. It's about 4 a.m., the quiet punctuated by the measured *ticks* of the grandfather clock downstairs. Jason rises. He wears only a pair of boxer shorts. I have never seen a man so beautiful … and so deadly.

"Rose?" he says again.

His voice breaks into the clamp that holds me motionless. Before I can say another word, he is close, grasping my upper arms in his hands. As always, my breath shortens at his touch. Is this magic? If so, it is a kind I have no immunity for.

"What are you doing here?" he asks.

With a deep breath, I look up at him. His eyes are dark in the silvery light, unreadable.

"It wasn't exactly my idea," I say. My legs start to wobble.

He guides me to one of the chairs in front of the window. He sits in the other. There is a small, round table between us, and I find myself wishing desperately for a cup of Alice's tea.

"From the beginning," he says. And I am grateful that he isn't making assumptions about my presence in his bedroom in the middle of the night.

I tell him the highlights, leaving out the bit about Alice being alive. "Your uncle 'Theophalus' is Mr. Black, the man who killed my family. Why does he want the rose-stone? No games, please."

He shakes his head, his mouth a tight line. He has said nothing throughout my story.

"I haven't played games with you, Rose. I can't tell you very much. My uncle is a recluse. No one sees him much, and we don't even talk about him if we can help it. He's not a … pleasant man."

"I think you've all buried your heads in the sand. His fingers are everywhere—in the police department, the banks, in politics, I imagine."

"Theo has always been extremely secretive, but for what purpose could he want an artifact that has always belonged to House of Rose?"

"That's an excellent question. I was kind of hoping you could answer it."

He winces. "Fair enough." He pauses. "I do admit, when you told me the death of your family was not an accident, I wondered if he could have had anything to do with it. He hates your House so much, but there has never been any proof—"

"There is now."

"Theo has never hesitated to use his power whenever it serves him, but … genocide … of another House?"

"Why does he hate the House of Rose?"

"It goes back before I was born. My mother once got drunk and told me some things she had overheard about how my father's brothers—Theophalus and Samuel—had lost their sister at the hands of a woman from House of Rose many years ago before my father was born. She did not know the details and neither uncle would speak of it to me. She also hinted that there might be some 'contamination' in our House that had infuriated Theo. I didn't know if there was any truth to any of what my mother said or if she was trying to heal some wounds between me and my uncle."

"Wounds?"

He hesitates. "We have never gotten along."

I wait. I'm a psychology major, after all. I know how to listen, even though I can still hear the clock ticking downstairs. Maybe it's just in my mind. How much time do I have before Black returns to the cell?

But Jason doesn't continue.

In desperation, I lean toward him. "Jason, I came to you because you are the only person who can possibly understand what's at stake here and how to help me. I know I'm asking a lot of you—"

"Do you, Rose?" He takes a breath. "As terrible as my uncle may be, he is still head of the House of Iron. I had loyalty to House beaten into me from the time I could walk."

Something about the way he said "beaten" makes me wonder if he means it literally.

"What about your father? Did he beat you, too?" I ask.

Jason is quiet. Finally, he says, "No. My father died when I was four. My uncle Theo took it upon himself to ensure I was raised 'properly.' But he had little patience with children." His mouth twists. "The girls were not a problem; a touch from him, and they were obedient and quiet. But I was different."

"You have sisters?"

"Two older sisters. They're dead now. Mother, my birth mother, sent them away as soon as she could. I don't know how much you know, but the power of Iron runs in the male line. The women are as defenseless as the household staff."

"It's the opposite in the House of Rose, isn't it? Our power passes through the female line."

"That's right."

"So what happens if those two come together? You said at dinner it was forbidden."

He is staring at me. "I have always been told that a child of such a union would be a monster. That the magics must not ever mix."

My heart beats quicker. If what my mother and Alice told me is true, I might be a grandchild of such a union—

"Your uncle is the monster," I snap. "He killed my family."

"I understand that you believe that. I admit his actions with you are deplorable and inexcusable—"

"I was there, in the house. I crawled out the window, and I saw him leave. I was only a child, but I *saw* him."

"So you said, but well enough to identify him?"

It is my turn to hesitate. I look down at my fingers, twisting in my lap. I am asking Jason to trust me, against his own House; I owe him the truth. "No, not really, but—" Looking up again, I meet his gaze. "I'm a scryer, like my mother. I saw a vision of your uncle leaving through the hidden door in the mine. I'm certain it was the night my family was killed. He was carrying gasoline."

He doesn't question or seem too surprised at my ability. "And how do you know you were seeing that particular night?"

"I just know."

"You believe it."

"Alright," I concede. "I believe it. But the fact of the matter is that your uncle crippled my friend and imprisoned me at gunpoint. I have no doubt he will kill us both. The only reason we're still alive is that he wants the rose-stone. Are you certain you don't know why?"

Jason's brow furrows. "I was always told that the House of Iron couldn't use it."

"He must think differently."

"Unless he wants to destroy it."

"To keep a *Y Tair* from ever using it perhaps?"

"Perhaps. Yes. I was always told a *Y Tair* was a monster, the worst kind of abomination."

"I think that was a lie to keep the Houses apart."

He is silent. After a moment, he shakes his head. "The rumors of such are not just in my immediate family, but told by members of our House around the world. It seems very unlikely there is no truth at all to the stories."

My gut says Jason is not lying. *Was my mother?* Maybe the truth is somewhere between. "What did your mother tell you about the 'contamination'?"

He is clearly torn about telling me a House secret, but after a long hesitation, he says, "That there were rumors the head of our House before the Blackwells—Adam Greyson—had an affair with a witch."

Adam Greyson had an affair. With my mother? "Then," I say slowly, "you wouldn't be related to their offspring."

"No," he says, his eyes fixed on mine.

I find my earlobes and cheeks are burning and pull away from his gaze, looking out the window down into the jeweled lights of the valley. To change the subject, I say, "Even if Theophalus got his hands on the rose-stone, how do you destroy a diamond?"

He smiles. "There is a saying in my House. 'A blow of iron can shatter diamond.' "

"I thought diamonds were the hardest substance known."

"Not anymore, but the point is that although a diamond is very hard, it's brittle. It can shatter."

My hand reaches reflexively for my neck where the pendant has hung since I bought a chain for it, until I decided on a hunch I should protect it. *A blow of iron can shatter diamond.* I shudder, feeling as fragile as my vulnerable rose-stone.

"Or," Jason muses, "you could be right. He might think he can use it somehow."

Out the window, I notice a subtle shift in the color of sky. I stand, and so does Jason.

"Dawn is coming," I say. "I have to get Becca out of that cell and get out of here. Will you help me?" This is it. I need him. His answer will determine whether I can get Becca away from here, and I won't leave her. I can't even imagine what I will do if he says no.

For answer, he steps close. The intensity between us is so strong, it seems to have substance. We are like opposite poles of a magnet, and a field of electricity envelopes us, pulling us together.

"What kind of power do you wield over me, witch?" he asks.

I take a deep, shaky breath, holding Becca's image firmly in my mind.

"Will you help me or not?" I ask.

Chapter Forty-Three

The crowbar I was looking for turns out to be in the tool shed behind the house. For a moment, I think a barking dog is going to wake the entire household, but Jason puts a hand on its head and whispers to it, and it quiets immediately and lies at his feet.

"Handy," I concede. "Is the dog your slave for life now?"

"It will wear off," he says.

Wear off? Will what Black did to Becca wear off? Relief floods me, but I want to make sure. "Does it always wear off?"

"Eventually." He smiles. "It makes a marriage based on that kind of control very challenging, but there have been men who've tried it. I did myself when I was younger."

"I can imagine the temptation." I am thinking of Paul now and how Black would have to play a delicate game of control, having him come back to him periodically to refresh his influence.

"How do you control it?" I ask. I've never thought of regulating the living-green. I just … pull it in.

He hesitates, clearly uncomfortable talking about House of Iron secrets. "I was taught to imagine it as a dark stream running from the earth into me— the narrower the stream, the shorter and more precise the effect."

"Can you make the 'stream' wider?"

"Yes, the wider, the more power and the longer the effect lasts."

"Can you blow out someone's mind with enough power?" My stomach lurches in the silence of his hesitation. *Was that what happened to Becca?*

Again, he hesitates. "I imagine so."

"Is there a cure?"

"I don't know."

We enter the house through the same back door we'd used to get to the tool shed. Once again, the ticking of the grandfather clock dominates the quiet. It's 5:15 a.m. now, and I can feel the house on the cusp of stirring.

We slip down the curving staircase, Jason carrying the iron crowbar. I wonder if he can feel the energy residing in it. Physics has never been my strong suit, but I do know E=mc2, which means there is a lot of energy locked into the mass of ... everything. Rip apart just one atom of enriched uranium, and you've got a nuclear explosion. I can imagine what the governments of the world would think about someone who could do that with their mind, and I don't believe they would sit quietly and let us be. Suddenly, I understand on a visceral level why the Houses have maintained such secrecy about who they are and what they can do. And why Alice said it was dangerous that I had confided in Becca. In her normal state, Becca would never betray me, but she is far from being in her normal state. For the first time, I make myself admit that she might never be again.

"I have only been down here a few times," Jason says quietly. "Uncle Sam is always taking people through like it's some kind of museum."

"If he hadn't shown me the rooms, I'd never have figured out how to escape."

"Then I'm glad he did, but I find the whole concept of the mannequin rooms disquieting."

"Do you think your uncle created the secret doors into the tunnels and mines?"

He shrugs. "When he bought the house, the family was told there were rumors that the original owner had escape routes into the mines. I thought it was all sales pitch, trying to heighten the mystery and intrigue surrounding the house, like the story of the Simpson murder."

"That's not a story," I say. "It happened. And there *are* secret doorways and passages."

The hallway seems to stretch out forever, but finally we come to the last door.

"This one," I whisper.

I'm anxious to get Becca and get out of this house. But what if Jason can't manage to get into the cell with the crowbar?

As he pushes the door open and we step inside, I realize that I have asked the wrong question. The cell door is wide open. Martin Luther still lies on his side where I lay him, but Becca is not there.

"She's gone," I say inanely.

"Could she have gone through that hole?" Jason asks, pointing to the place where I had kicked in the wall.

"She could have, but I don't think she would have. I could barely get her to move. And that wouldn't explain the cell door being open. She couldn't have done that."

"So, my uncle or one of the people under his sway took her."

I bite my lip. "It's my fault. This is all my fault."

To my dismay, Jason pulls me to his chest. "I've never met Becca, but I know she is dear to you," he says in my ear.

My heart thumps with his closeness, but the intensity of my fear for Becca overrides any other thought. "She's my best friend. I never had one before." I sound like a blabbering idiot.

Anticipating tears, he produces a handkerchief, which makes my chest cramp, my mind jumping to Paul and how Black has used him to get to me. I'm responsible for the destruction of two people's minds.

"Rose, do you have any idea where he could have taken Becca?"

I blow my nose into his handkerchief. The inability to shed tears has never interfered with my nose running.

"Maybe," I say.

"Where?"

"His damn throne room."

"His what?"

"You don't know much about your uncle, do you?" I sniff.

"Apparently not."

The corridor's end is only a few feet beyond the door to the cell room. I put my hands on the wall. "This moves somehow."

Jason joins me in pushing on various places, with no results.

We step back and study the wall. Frustration builds inside me. I can't stand the thought of Becca being in Black's hands. I have to get through that door. I *need* to—

"Wait. I can do this."

"Do what?"

"Just wait. Be quiet."

Jason's lips form a tight line at this instruction. I doubt many people have told him to be quiet.

I sit on the floor and try to still my thoughts. It's difficult to pull the living-green, though I have to be closer to it than I was upstairs. I think this house must be built on a seam of iron, and I can't pull through it. But I have to find a way. Becca's life is at stake. I try to focus on breathing and imagine the rose-stone. *Watch the rock grow.* That involves getting in sync with the timescale of a diamond, which is very slow. Lifetimes....

Below, far below, I work my way around a seam of iron. It is wide. I search for a way through, but it is a solid barrier. Over and over, I try. *If you stop trying that is when you fail.* I don't stop trying. Finally, I find a tiny crack and follow it down to a small deposit of coal. To physical eyes it might be black or gray, but to my senses, it is golden energy. I pull from it, warmth entering my body from my legs and rear—the closest parts of my body to the ground—up into me, filling me, and I let my need guide it.

The world shifts into the now familiar black and gray, and I see Jason's uncle, my Mr. Black, as a wavering image, standing before the blank wall at the hall's end. He spreads his hands wide and presses two spots simultaneously against the wall and then pushes the left side. It swings open away from him and he enters the mineshaft, Becca behind him like an obedient dog. After her, Paul and Jaws follow.

The black and gray world fades into the present.

"I know how to get through the wall," I say, standing.

Jason lifts his brows but doesn't comment. I don't have to explain. He was raised on magic.

While the vision is still clear in my mind, I copy Black's motions and push on the left side of the door. Nothing happens.

"Damn. That is exactly what I saw your uncle do to open the door." I step back, scowling at the uncooperative wall and eye Jason's crowbar. "Let's try to smash through it."

"Let me try to open it first," Jason says. "Maybe he applied more pressure than you can do with your arms spread like that."

For him, the door shifts. Irritating.

Jason turns to me and puts his hands on my shoulders. I didn't think my heart could beat any harder, but it does.

"Rose," he says, and I hear regret in his voice. "I will help you escape, but I can't, I won't, help you destroy my family."

I swallow. "Right now, I just want to find Becca and get her somewhere safe."

Jason picks up the crowbar and says, "I'll go first."

Miffed, I start to mention something about me being the police officer, but I remember I don't have a gun and I shrug. "Be my guest," I say.

Jason steps through the opening. I am right behind him.

From a great distance, I hear a sound that might have come from me. I don't hear anything else, lost in a swirl of lights that fade abruptly into a deep darkness.

Chapter Forty-Four

An unknown time later, I awake to more darkness, but it is a different kind of dark. In this dark, I hurt. When I raise my head, it feels akin to lifting a boulder attached to my neck. My hands instinctively rise toward the pain, but a sharp pressure constrains them at my sides. I seem to be in a sitting position with a support at my back. My fingers can't reach whatever is holding down my arms, but it feels like ridged metal against my wrists. Handcuffs?

The pitch dark presses in on me. Over and over, I fight the fear that rises like bile into my throat, competing with the pain in my head. It's the same panic that assaulted me when I struggled through the narrow passage behind the scenario rooms, but it's harder to keep at bay this time. I wasn't constrained there; I had a choice and a little light. This is worse. I can feel my lungs filling. I'm going to hyperventilate again.

No, I will not allow it. Stop.

I have to stop the panic. What was that line from the movie, *Dune*? *Fear is the mind killer.* Already, I can feel the warm seep of blood from my wrists. Do I want to bleed to death because of my own fear? What happened to my promise to be a hard bitch to kill?

"Is anyone here?" I pant into the darkness.

Nothing.

But the sound of my voice widens the dimensions to my prison. I'm not in a tiny cylinder. There is space around me.

I have to think, to focus my mind through the throbbing pain on something besides imaginary walls closing in on me. Between deep, slow breaths, I try to remember what happened. The last thing I recall is following Jason into the old mine tunnel and then, not even pain, just falling and darkness. Someone must have hit me. Where is Jason? Becca? Where am I?

I don't have answers to any of these questions, but I can determine some places I am not. I am not back in the MLK cell, unless they added a very solid chair to the furniture. The air is cool, but not as cold as it is outside, so I am either in air conditioning, which would be weird for winter, or underground. I last walked into an old mine tunnel. It stands to reason I am still in the mine somewhere, and this chair is a very big clue. I must be in Mr. Black's "throne" room, handcuffed to his iron chair. Oddly enough, knowing this eases my panic further, confirming the dimensions to the room and the fact that my brain still functions despite the blow.

Free from the grip of my phobia, I become aware of the tingle in my body, confirming exactly where I am. The pain in my head radiates everywhere, but when I lean back, the concentrated explosion on the back of my skull locates the origin. I imagine a knot the size of an apple.

Instinctively, I reach for the living-green for comfort, but I can't connect with it. I know it is there, in the depths below, but again my access to it is blocked. Iron. The iron chair?

A brush across my leg sends an adrenalin jolt through me. I gasp. A rat? One of the spiders that terrified Becca? No, I wouldn't have felt that through my jeans.

With every bit of concentration I can muster, I strain into the dark, listening. At first, nothing, but then a sound, so faint, but regular—*Breath. Someone breathing.*

My heart thrums like a plucked string.

"Who's here?" I ask again into the blackness.

No response. Nothing.

Is it Jason? Is he unconscious? We were together. He was ahead of me when I stepped through the door into the tunnel. That's the last thing I can remember. Maybe they clubbed him, too … or was he leading me into a trap the entire time?

The breath at my feet catches. There is something familiar in the tiny sound.

"Becca?"

I get no more response than I have the hundred times I tried before, but I can't give up. "Becca, please. I just need you to stand up." With sudden inspiration, I say, "Becca, Mr. Black wants you to stand up." I hold my breath, straining to hear if she might react to that, like the old childhood game of "Mother May I?"

If only I can get her to respond. "I have a handcuff key in my bra," I say. "Remember? I just want you to get it. Mr. Black wants you to stand up and get the key."

Before I can further test the theory of whether "Mother May I?" works, the world explodes with light. I blink, trying to adjust.

Becca uncoils from a fetal position at my feet and stands. As Black rolls into the room, Becca goes to him, a moth mesmerized by light. With one arm he brushes her aside, and she trips, falling to the hard ground. She is so weak; it took no more effort to knock her down than to crush a moth.

"Stay," he says, as if speaking to a dog, and she freezes where she lies.

My bloody wrists strain against the cuffs, thirsty for his throat. But I immediately still them, forcing myself to relax. If he thinks I am moved by his cruelty to Becca, it will only encourage him to use her as a tool. No matter what, I can't let him do that. I don't understand exactly what is at stake, but I know as well as I know anything that as soon as he has what he wants, Becca and I are dead.

"You don't look well," Black says.

"I'm not happy about being in handcuffs or about the knot on my head." My mouth feels like it is stuffed with cotton.

"I brought you some water." He sets a plastic bottle on the ground. Droplets of condensation roll down the clear sides, bringing to my attention the parched desert of my mouth and throat. I stare at the bottle. I can't help it.

"Would you like a swallow?" he asks.

I nod, despite my desire not to respond.

"It's yours. As soon as you tell me what I want to know."

I'm glaring at him now. I didn't think I could hate him worse, but I was wrong.

"Why do you want it?" I rasp.

He rolls over to Becca, and that's when I notice a stick across his lap. At first I think it's a billy club, a police baton.

"Do you know what this is?" He holds up the rod, and I realize I'm wrong. It's a cylinder about two feet long with what appears to be a dial at one end.

I start to shake my head, but the sharp jolt of pain accompanying the movement nixes that plan. Words are better, despite my parched throat and tongue.

"No, I don't know what that is, but I'm sure you'll tell me."

"It's a modified cattle prod," he says.

Nowhere in any of the different places that my adoptive father was stationed did we live near cows. I know nothing about them, but I suppose they need prodding at times. It doesn't seem that impressive a stick.

He lifts the end so I can see the two prongs, and suddenly I get it.

My comprehension must have shown on my face, because Black smiles and lowers the end of the prod, briefly touching Becca's neck. I brace myself.

She screams.

"You're a beast," I say, struggling to keep my voice calm.

He sighs. "Actually, I find this rather detestable."

"Really?" I grit my teeth. "Is that why you're doing it yourself, rather than having one of your zombies do such 'detestable' work for you?"

"You think I enjoy inflicting pain?"

"Well here you are." I am desperate to keep him talking. If he's talking, he's not hurting Becca.

"Only because you are being unnecessarily stubborn," he says.

He lowers the prod to Becca's neck again, and she shrinks away. Her gaze is still fixed on him, but it is conflicted, puzzled.

"That's not necessary," I say.

He stops. "Excellent. Where is the rose-stone?"

"I'm not going to tell you that, no matter what you do to her. She doesn't matter to me."

I want to ask him where Jason is, but I'm afraid to let him know I care. Or maybe I'm afraid of the answer.

"Really?" he asks. "Then why is she with you?"

I shrug, careful to make it a small movement that won't jar my head. "I wanted someone to carry my stuff. She was convenient."

"I see, and why did you try to make a bargain to let her go?"

"I was just … testing the limits of your power." I try leading into a diversion: "She's not of my House. In fact, thanks to you, there is no one, beside me, left of House of Rose. Why is that?"

Thankfully, he seems to find my attitude reasonable, and he moves the prod from Becca's neck.

"The House of Rose is an abomination." The last word drips from his mouth like black sludge.

I swallow. I need a strategy, but what pops unbidden into my mind is a call Paul and I responded to my first week on the training car.

A man on the smoking deck at UAB Hospital was threatening to jump over the edge. He had climbed over the railing, nothing between him and the ground but a step and lots of air. I was nervous, having no idea what to do. "Just stay back," Paul instructed. "Unless he jumps on me."

"Then what?" I asked, my eyes wide with apprehension.

"Then call for help and get him the hell off me!"

I sincerely hoped the man would not jump on my partner … or over the edge.

Paul started by asking his name. Alfred Doyle. I'll never forget that name. They talked about everything except the fact that Doyle was on a ledge a few inches from death. Finally, Doyle looked down and said, "I have cancer. I'm going to die a very painful slow death."

"Well," Paul said. "That may be or maybe not. They find new treatments every day around here, but today is not a good day to die."

Doyle looked at him in surprise. "It's not?"

"Nope." Paul had scratched at his chin. "Why don't you wait and see what happens? When it's the right day, you'll know."

Doyle thought about it, nodded, and came down.

"He didn't really want to jump," Paul told me later. "He just needed a reason not to. You gotta keep 'em talking."

"Well," I said, "if he didn't want to die, he was standing in a weird place."

Paul had chuckled. "You're alright, Rose."

Those were magic words for a rookie.

I blink and find that Black is right beside me, cattle prod in his hands.

Chapter Forty-Five

Mr. Black is not a large man, especially from the height of his wheelchair, but the electric cattle prod he holds fills my world. I force myself to stop staring at it and meet his gaze, hearing Paul's whisper again in my mind. *Keep 'em talking. Get in his world.*

"I understand now how powerful you are, what you can do," I say.

"You understand nothing."

"No, I do. I know seventeen years ago, you were able to make all the investigators on an arson/murder case see something different than what was really there. That's impressive."

"Anyone from my House could have done the same," he says dismissively.

I follow the reasoning. Anyone from Iron can make someone believe anything, but they can't make it stick. Like the dog Jason quieted with a touch. He said it would wear off. Black couldn't afford to let that happen, so he killed everyone involved, a complicated affair that had to look like accidents or natural deaths.

"But what you did with Paul," I venture, "is not something anyone from your House could do, is it?"

"You are perceptive, as well as bold." He sits straighter in his chair. "Paul is the result of years of experimentation and effort. No one has ever come this close to maintaining long term control that is imperceptible to the world and the puppet."

The "puppet." A sour taste fills my mouth.

"What you've done to Becca is hardly 'imperceptible to the world,' " I say, keeping the emotion I feel from my voice.

"That is something entirely different, but still at a skill level beyond anything most living can accomplish."

Hope flutters. Maybe he is telling the truth that he can bring her back.

"Why do you think the House of Rose is an abomination?" I ask, trying to make my voice casual.

"House of Rose is the *source* of abominations," he says.

I'm not sure the distinction is helpful. *Now what, Paul?*

"I don't understand why you think that," I say. "Can you explain it to me?"

"It's quite simple. When the blood of the Houses mix, the powers are uncontrollable."

"How do you know that isn't just a myth?"

"It is no myth. I have seen it, seen my sister consumed in flames by such a one."

"Is that why you set my family's house on fire? Why you burned *my* sister?" I am trembling, but this time with anger. "I never hurt your family. Why did you have to take mine?"

"Too much is at stake. Sometimes the end justifies the means." His voice is quiet, calm.

I fight the emotions that are boiling in me. I can't let them overcome my reason. That's the only hope I have. I force myself to think about what I know, to search for some clue that will give me leverage with Black.

All I know is that Adam Greyson, who was head of House of Iron at some point, must have experienced the same intense passion with my grandmother that has afflicted Jason and me. Sparks from the two magics ignited into an inferno, the result was a child, my mother. Such a thing certainly happened more than once in the past. I know that from the little Welsh diary. And maybe the cultural *verboten* and fear is based on the fact that the offspring from those encounters didn't always turn out so well. If my mother was an "abomination," so am I. Is there something dark and sinister in me?

I don't know, but I know I want to live and I want Becca to live, so there is a more important question—*Why does Black care so much?* I don't believe this is just a matter of House zealotry. It's too personal.

I take a leap, pulling together what my mother told me in her letter and what Jason said his mother told him. "Was Adam Greyson part of the cabal sworn to eradicate House of Rose?"

Black freezes.

Bingo. Was Black jealous? Had he, too, felt that attraction to my grandmother?

His silence is a thin membrane over a brewing storm. I can see it in his eyes.

"Don't darken his name with your mouth."

His name. Then it was about Adam.

"Where is he?" I ask, trying to stay matter of fact, slip back into his world as Paul did with Doyle on that roof.

"He's dead." Black's voice cracks.

"Did you love him?"

To my relief, his reaction to my question is not anger. He turns his head away, staring at the cave wall as if he sees beyond it to the past.

" 'Love' is a word soiled by the world."

I risk another probe. "Was he like a father to you?"

"Far more than that," he says, still staring at the wall.

There's only one kind of relationship between Adam Greyson and Theophalus Blackwell I can imagine that would be "far more."

"Were you lovers?"

"We never had the chance to be. He chose *her*." Bitterness stains his voice.

I have no doubt that the woman Adam chose was my grandmother, Lilith. This is not good. Alice mentioned I looked just like her and so did Theophalus when I first met him at the Hallows' Eve party. When he looks at me, does he see her?

I am desperate to find some clue I can use. Magic drove Lilith and Adam together. Was there more between them? Did they fall in love? I suspect the truth was that Adam never returned Theophalus' desires. Spurned, he still blames my grandmother for taking Adam away from him. His hatred of House of Rose is not just philosophical. It's fueled by jealousy and revenge.

Black's voice raises, his calm crumbling. "It was House of Rose who betrayed us all!"

I leap to the next logical conclusion. When Adam died, Theophalus became head of the House of Iron. His word was law.

"That's why the House of Iron followed House of Rose to Birmingham, wasn't it?"

"Yes. I brought my House here. To be near her. To watch her. To stop her and her cursed House. No one else believed that Adam would have a love affair with a woman of Rose—but I knew. And I suspected the child she bore was his, an abomination."

"My mother was not an 'abomination.' "

Slowly, he returns his focus to me and the look in his eyes spills ice down my spine.

"Passion," I say quickly, trying to sound understanding, "is a powerful force. You felt that with Adam. How can you blame him or Lilith for what they felt?"

He clenches his teeth, his upper lip curled like a snarling dog. "The blame belongs to the House of Rose; the disease is the House of Rose, and the only way to cure it is to destroy it. I will destroy it. Even if I fail, others will not."

I try my ace card, my last chance, though saying it is a risk.

"If that child was Adam's, that would mean I have House of Iron blood too. I'm part of House of Iron."

Too late, I see I have made a fatal mistake. The rage in his eyes seems to explode, or maybe it's the prod he jabs into my neck that sends stars dancing in my head and effectively cuts off the conversation.

What I had thought was severe pain was merely a headache in comparison to the agony in that little stick. Its touch is a scorching, jolting shock. Every muscle in my body screams in protest. When he withdraws it, I smell burning flesh. My limbs twitch and cramp.

"Where is the rose-stone?" Black asks, his voice quiet and reasonable again, as if my suffering is a balm.

I am gasping, trying to draw breath, trying to find some position of relief. He lowers the prod to my eyelevel.

"Where?"

"I don't … know," I manage, having never thought about the fact that my tongue is a muscle that can cramp.

"Didn't you tell me that you hid it?" Black demands.

Desperate, I nod, hating myself that I will give him anything to keep him from zapping me again.

"I did." I pant.

"Then you know where it is."

"No," I plead. "I don't know."

When he touches the prod again to my neck, I wish with everything in me that I did know, so I could tell him. Death is a better option.

WHEN HE FINALLY LEAVES, I have no idea how long he was there. My world is pain. The dark he leaves me in is no longer a source of fear. It is the light I fear now, the light that brings hell in the form of a two-foot stick.

Time passes, and slowly the pain ebbs as my muscles unclench. I relish every moment of its absence. Why is it I have never appreciated the absence of pain?

For a long time, I am without thought. Finally, one intrudes: *What did I tell him?* I remember screaming words, anything to make him stop. What did he make of "Find the cat!"? Nonsense words. Hysterical words. Nothing is different. He will come back and bring the pain. Another thought: *What if he doesn't come back? What if he leaves me here to die?*

I have soiled myself in my agony. I will die in my own stink.

I am not going to die like that. I sit up, bearing the weight of my head over my shoulders. I am House of Rose. There is magic in me, *inside me.* I have to find it.

A whimper reminds me I am not alone, and I am not the only one who is suffering.

"It's okay, Becca," I say, my voice hoarse from screaming. "It's okay."

If I die, so be it, but I can't abandon her.

Holding the image of the rose-stone in my mind, I go deep into myself, searching for power, for magic. I don't know what. I don't know how. But something is different. For a while, it puzzles me. I realize that the tingling, scratching feeling is gone. The pressure that was trying to get through isn't there anymore. *Or is it?*

Instead, there is an emptiness ... a channel. Did the pain break some resistance inside me? Was I the closed door to it?

This channel isn't for the living-green, but something different. Carefully, I reach for it. Not the warm gold of the living-green, but an oily, viscous blackness rises up through me. It is like sipping the ocean from a straw. But it is power. My breath comes faster. Is this my heritage from the House of Iron? Only men could draw this power. But I can. I do. I am the abomination—a woman who is witch and warlock.

If I am right, anyone who touches me while I have the power of iron will be susceptible to my will. No, I correct, any "normal" person. As a witch, I am immune to this power, and it stands to reason that other members of the Houses will be as well.

So, what can I do with it? Hope that Black's next visit brings Paul or Jaws and that they come close enough to touch me, assuming I can overwhelm whatever Black—who has trained his entire long life with the power of iron—has done to them? It is a fragile hope, but it is all I have.

Chapter Forty-Six

When light shatters the dark, hope and terror mount with my quickened pulse. I don't think I can survive another shock. My limbs still twitch randomly, and my heart flutters and skips beats. I don't want to die like this, but the thought of enduring more is intolerable. Can one overdose on magic? Could I pull enough to kill myself?

The same chair that blocks me from the living-green is a connection to the vast reservoir of iron in the earth's depths. I have only cautiously sipped from it, but now I open the gates and draw as much as I can. Shaking with the effort of holding so much power, I sit on the iron throne, a fat, bloated spider waiting for prey ... or death.

My hope rises as Jaws enters the room, Jason's uncle behind him. It sinks when I spot the cattle prod Black carries. The nightmare is not over. What will happen to the energy I hold when he touches me with that rod? If it kills me, hopefully it will kill him too.

Black approaches me, but Jaws hangs back. I don't blame him. I'm sure I look and smell as horrible as I feel.

"I don't suppose you've changed your mind about the rose-stone," he asks, casually waving the prod.

"I've told you everything I know." My voice is little more than a whisper, my vocal chords inflamed from screaming and lack of moisture.

"You've told me a lot of nonsense," Black says.

"Just kill me and be done with it," I croak.

"I gave you my word that you would live if you gave me the stone."

Right. I don't voice my sarcasm aloud. I would spit on him, but there is not enough moisture in my mouth.

"You forget," I hiss, "I saw you kill my parents and sister. I know who the monster is." *Oh, good move, Rose. That will mollify him, for sure. What is wrong with you?*

His mouth hardens, and he lowers the prod. My eyes are locked on his, the power inside me a building pressure. He hesitates. Does he see death in them? He rolls back.

"I think you are beyond the point where more of this will help. And so I have asked your friend Paul for his advice." He motions to Jaws who turns and pushes open the door.

Paul walks in, a child in his arms. The boy's eyes are shut, mouth open in a small "o." *Daniel, oh God, no!* I can taste despair like the acidic vomit in my mouth.

Black frowns at the unconscious child. "Is he still out?" he asks Paul.

"I just gave him the dose you said," Paul replies. There is a slightly off-focus look to Paul's eyes.

I have to remind myself to breathe.

Paul gives Daniel a little jiggle.

Daniel's lids flutter open, and I can see it takes several moments for him to register his surroundings. When he sees me, his dark eyes widen in distress, and his fist goes into his mouth. Paul puts him on his feet. Daniel hangs onto his hand trustingly.

What did Paul do to Daniel's mother? Did he knock her out, kill her? She was an alcoholic with a habit of leaving the door unlocked. That was how Daniel got out the day I found him playing in the dust, and the day he wandered over to my house. Paul might have found her passed out and just walked into the kid's bedroom. I am shaking with rage at Paul, Black … and myself, and maybe with the effects of holding so much energy, like a keg of black powder waiting for a flame. If only my anger could ignite it—

"Bring him closer," Black says.

Paul steps closer.

Daniel hangs back. "No!" he says, his face crunched up in readiness to cry. I don't blame him.

Tightening his grip on the little hand, Paul drags him closer. Daniel starts to cry.

Black's eyes narrow. He lowers the prod toward Daniel.

"Stop!" *I can't let him torture that child.*

"Where is the rose-stone?" Black asks.

"It's on the cat." I pant, close to hyperventilating.

He moves the prod closer to Daniel, who is now wailing in fear.

"Don't!" I strain my hoarse voice to be heard. "I'm telling you the truth. I tied the rose-stone to my cat's collar."

Black turns to Jaws. "Was there a cat in her house?"

Jaws shakes his head. "No cat," he says. "But there were bowls on the kitchen window sill."

"So, where is this *cat*?" Black turns back to me.

"I don't know. I left the window open. She must have run away."

"When we are finished here," Black says to Jaws, "put out some fish or whatever tempts cats and wait for it."

Stay away, Angel. I'm sorry.

Jaws nods.

"Meanwhile," Black continues in a tone of voice he must use to direct the housekeepers, "we have no more requirement for these … complications." He reaches in his pocket and brings out a switchblade, which he opens and holds out to Paul, jerking his head toward Daniel. "Slit his throat first."

"No, Paul!" I plead with everything in me.

A puzzled look drifts over Paul's blunt features, much like the expression on Becca's face when Black shocked her. Paul looks at Daniel and the knife in Black's hand. He stands rooted.

Annoyance clear in his voice, Black reaches out and jerks Daniel from Paul's grasp. "I'll do it myself."

Everything slows in my blurry vision.

Daniel stumbles, almost falling, but Black pulls him up against his wheelchair. I do not have to scry to know what will happen: Black will slice the blade across the child's throat. A thin red line will follow its path, and Daniel will crumple to the red clay dirt.

That cannot happen. *I will not let it happen.* The power in me strains for release. I reach for more. I can't hold more of Iron's energy; I need the living-green. My hands reach toward Daniel. I barely feel the bite of the cuffs against my bloody skin.

Handcuffs. Handcuffs are made of steel. Steel is an alloy of iron … and *carbon.*

Black has pulled the sobbing Daniel up against him. The knife is moving horizontally toward Daniel's neck in an efficient, almost thoughtless motion.

I reach for the living-green that resides in the steel handcuffs. It is locked away, bound into an iron-carbon alloy, but it is there. I rip it from its bonds, feeling the suck of energy that takes, and pull it inside me. Iron and carbon coexist stably in steel, but not, apparently, in magic. Gold meets black; flame to black powder. It roars out of me.

For a moment, it is all I can do to draw a breath. Then I look up. *What have I done?*

Black and Daniel are encased in flames. I struggle to my feet, my hands slipping from the corrupted cuffs, and stumble toward them, but Paul is quicker. He throws himself on Daniel, pulling him out of Black's arms and throwing him to the ground, blanketing him with his own body, trying to smother the flames. The blaze spreads over Paul's back and head. He screams, but he doesn't roll over or release Daniel, keeping him covered.

"Paul!" I beat at the fire on him with my hands, rip off my sweat-soaked flannel shirt and cover the back of his head, working my way down. "Give me your coat!" I scream at Jaws, and, to my surprise, he does. I throw it over Paul, snuffing out the remaining flames.

Only then do I look up. An inferno still consumes Black, who has fallen from the wheelchair, every part of him burning, as if he's been doused in oil and lit. A horrible rasping sound emanates from the ball of flame that had been a man, a powerful warlock, now a dark vertical streak in the orange-gold—the way I have painted him over and over.

Then I realize the sound was a name. He was crying out a name—*Adam!*

I turn back to Paul. My stomach wrenches at the blackened skin and blisters on his neck and head. All of his hair has burned away. A folded edge of the handkerchief he handed me the night I shot Zachary is visible in his back pocket, untouched.

Carefully, I roll him off of Daniel. Paul winces as his burned back takes his weight. His face is also blistered and waxy, his breath ragged. From the sound, I think his lungs may have been scorched.

Daniel lies face down in the dirt, in shock if he is not dead. His clothes have burned off his back and large welts have risen on the exposed skin. There is no doubt that Paul saved his life … if he lives. One of Daniel's hands is trapped beneath him. I work it out and feel for a pulse. It's there, faint but present. I hold the small hand, restraining my desire to pull the child into my arms. I want him to know I am here.

Paul forces his burned eyelids open. "Did I?"

"Don't talk," I say, almost choking.

His gaze finds me, insists. "The kid?"

"He's okay," I lie.

"My fault somehow," he rasps. "Don't know why."

The why I want to know is why did he hesitate when told to kill Daniel? Perhaps Black's influence had worn thin, and something deep in Paul rejected the order to kill a child, an order so alien to who he was. His breathing is becoming more and more labored. I know he is dying, and I lean close to what is left of his ear.

"Paul, you did good. You saved the boy."

A catch in his breath makes me think perhaps he heard me.

"You're a hero," I whisper …. And he is gone.

Chapter Forty-Seven

It hardly seems real when the cave door opens. Tracey Lohan races toward me. I vaguely register that a large dog is with him.

"Rose, my God, are you all right?" Tracey asks, kneeling at my side.

I lift bleary eyes to him. *Am I all right?* I just killed Paul; I'm responsible for the loss of my friend's mind; and I may have killed, or at least maimed-for-life, an innocent child. How can I ever be all right?

"I'm okay," I mumble and start shaking.

At what seems a huge distance, I hear him calling for paramedics and an ambulance, which is pointless since they will never find us, and besides, his radio can't get to a repeater from here. He realizes this and barks an order to two officers who are standing behind us, though I have no memory of them coming in. One snaps a leash on the dog and disappears.

Another goes to Becca, who is huddled against the far wall, her hands over her head. Jaws is nowhere to be seen. The world is going fuzzy around the edges, and there is a strange buzzing in my ears.

ACCORDING TO MY DOCTORS—AND I have a legion of them—I will be stuck in the hospital for at least a week, hooked to an IV to replenish the liquid and the electrolytes in my body. I can't seem to get enough water, something I will never again take for granted. My hands are badly burned, but the medical staff are happy, even astonished, at the speed of my healing. "I'm a witch," I explain one night, a little high on pain meds, and the nurse laughs.

I am told that Daniel is in critical condition and heavily sedated and will remain so while they do skin grafts. Becca is in the psych ward, being treated for shock and post traumatic stress.

A homicide detective interviews me in the hospital. I tell him a version of the truth, splattered with lies—that I had gone back to the site of the shooting, determined to look for clues (true); that the secret door in the mine entrance had been ajar (lie), and Becca and I had gone through (true); that a deranged man had imprisoned me in the room in the mine with the iron chair and tortured us both (true). I told him I had no idea how the fire had started or why or how Paul had found us (lie). I do not suggest he try to find a rifle belonging to Paul and match the bullet found in the cave to one fired from it. I tell him that I don't have any idea why a madman kidnapped Daniel and tortured me with a cattle prod (lie), and I leave out the whole part about the cell in the basement of House of Iron. I can't risk exposing them to scrutiny. Like it or not, they are my family too.

The man is not stupid. My story is bizarre, but there is corroborating evidence—a burned dead body, the modified cattle prod. In addition to the severe burns on my hands, the evidence techs took photos of the abrasions on my wrists, supporting my story that I had been cuffed and tried to get out.

The one thing that the detective seems fixated on is what happened to the handcuffs.

"I've never seen anything like that," he says. "They look like they *melted* and stretched. The lab can't explain it either."

"I don't know," I say.

"The best they can come up with," the detective prods, "is that whatever caused the fire burned extremely hot and altered the alloy, but they say that would have melted your hands first."

"I'm not a physicist or a chemist," I tell him. "All I know is I worked my way out of them just before you got there. Maybe they melted after that. How *did* you get there, anyway?"

"Tracey Lohan kept trying to find you."

On cue, Tracey walks in.

"I guess that's all for now," the detective says and leaves us.

Tracey sits beside my bed and opens a bag of chocolate chip cookies, the kind he keeps in his desk drawer. He offers me one. "I figured this was better than flowers."

I can't help a smile and take one awkwardly in my bandaged hands.

"How did you find me?"

"After you didn't show for work and didn't call in, I went to your house. The door was open and I went in and saw it'd been ransacked, so I filed a Missing Persons on you. The only thing I could think of was that the person who shot at you, abducted you.

"I searched the area but couldn't find anything. So, I talked the lieutenant into asking the Sheriff's Department to bring out one of their search-and-rescue dogs. We used a piece of clothing from your house."

I wince at the thought of strangers going through my drawers.

"The dog found your scent around the house," Tracey continues, "but lost it in the street. So, I took them up the mountain."

I lift my brows and he answers my silent question.

"I didn't know what else to do. I knew that's where someone took pot shots at you and where a body was recovered. Something bad was going on up there, and I thought maybe our abductors had taken you there for whatever reason. It was a wild shot. But the dog eventually hit on the old mine entrance."

"Smart dog."

"Yeah. Then he kept alerting on one section of the wall in the mine tunnel. The deputy insisted you had leaned against it or something, but I thought it was more than that and kept playing around with it. More dumb luck than anything else, I figured out it was a door. The dog was very excited and took off through the tunnel."

"Did you find the other door the same way?" I ask.

"Yep."

"Thank you," I say, and mean it with all my heart. "If you hadn't showed up, I doubt that little boy would be alive."

I FALL ASLEEP WHEN HE leaves. When I open my eyes again, it takes me a moment to bring my new visitor into focus, but I don't have to see him. I know that zap of sexual electricity that happens whenever he is close.

"Jason."

I hardly recognize him, standing beside my bed, his grip on the handrails seems desperate. A wide bandage covers most of his head. One side of his face is swollen and bruised, the blue of his eyes almost obliterated by enlarged pupils so dark you could fall into them. *Drugs*, the sensible part of my brain says. *Opiates*. He looks like he needs them.

"Rose," he says with only a slight slur, "I am so sorry."

"Sit down before you fall, you idiot."

He sinks into the chair by my bed.

"What happened?" I ask.

"I don't know. I remember stepping into the tunnel and that's it, but I saw the news report on you, and I guess Theophalus' henchman hit me, thinking I was you."

"Well, he rectified that mistake shortly after," I say.

"I led you into that tunnel. If I hadn't—"

"Stop." I frown at him. "Does your nurse know you are here?"

His eyes close, and I think he has drifted off, but he sits up and looks at me. I imagine I am as lovely a sight as he is.

"Did you," he says and then hesitates. "Did you say anything about—?"

"No."

"Thank you for protecting my House."

I start to say I have the blood of Iron too, but despite his condition, I know his loyalty to House runs deep, and I don't trust him. I don't trust anyone, for that matter … least of all myself. Or maybe I just don't want to be an abomination in his eyes.

NOBODY KNOWS WHAT TO DO with Becca. I take responsibility for her when I check out, claiming to be a cousin, and take her home to Alice. Then I return to my own house. As reported, it was ransacked, and I'm afraid I may never see Angel again. Black's men searching the house must have traumatized her. They tore up everything, and I find I have an uncharacteristic desire to clean everything, perhaps because my internal world is such a mess.

One thing has straightened out. Tracey told me the state finally presented their findings to the D.A., and he presented the case to the Grand Jury while I was in the hospital. They no-billed the charges, so that, at least, is off my back. Grand Jury proceedings are secret and only the prosecutor gets to present the evidence, so he must have believed I was not guilty of murder or manslaughter. In the midst of all this, that seems a small comfort, but one I am glad to have.

On my first night back in my house, I open a can of tuna fish and leave it on the porch. The next morning, I open the door, and a gray streak darts through my legs. I am happier than I thought possible to see Angel, and also glad to see the rose-stone pendant still attached to her collar, an inspiration from the movie *Men In Black*. Replacing it around my neck feels like a step toward restoring my "normal" … whatever that is.

I want my space, and I need time to figure things out. Little things, like who the hell I am and what that means. Relationships—always a knotty, thorny thing to avoid—are now fraught with danger. I have Alice and the House of Rose to protect. For that matter, House of Iron, as well, like it or not. Surely, there are innocent people in Iron. I can't betray them, either.

But I have to be honest with myself. The intensity Jason stirs in me is as frightening as it is tantalizing, a vortex that threatens to consume. Once again, it comes down to trust. *How do we ever let another human being past that barrier to really know us?* We are all, in a deep, intractable sense, alone.

Fine.

WEEKS LATER, I SIT WITH my aunt at her kitchen table, sipping tea. No one will recognize Alice, I am certain. *I* almost didn't recognize her. She did not plan to stay cooped up in her house forever after her "death." A red wig, contacts, and a long flowing skirt guarantee no one will recognize her. She insists on wearing it all, even in her own house.

"You never know who might come to the door or look in the windows," she says. "My name is Irene. You hired me to take care of Becca, should anyone ask."

I nod mutely. My hands are still bandaged, though not as thickly as they were in the hospital. I welcome the pain. It's a kind of minuscule penitence for what Daniel must be enduring. Stupid, I know, and it makes managing the cup awkward, but the ritual of the tea is an anchor to sanity. Daniel, I learn from the newspaper, is still in the hospital in critical care. His wounds are bad. If he survives, he will probably bear massive scar tissue on his back and one side of his face.

I have not been declared ready for duty, either by the doctors or the city's shrink, so I spend my time here taking care of Becca and trying to right my own mind. Becca is still unresponsive. I have moved back to Alice's with them because all of my time is spent helping with her. I bathe and dress her and feed her. She will swallow when something goes into her mouth. Baby food works the best. I refuse to try and use Iron magic on her. She's had enough of that, but she will walk when I put a hand on her arm and guide her. It is exhausting and heartbreaking.

Paul, I have grieved for, but he has found his peace.

"You haven't told me what happened with that House of Iron man," Alice says, her silver brows knitted together.

"His name is Jason." I'm sure she knows exactly who he is. "He helped me escape."

She sniffs.

"I don't trust him," she says, echoing my own doubts. "How do you know he wasn't part of it all?"

"Aunt Alice," I say with a wry smile, "it will be a cold day in hell before you trust anyone in the House of Iron."

She sniffs again.

I think of Becca, and the curve on my lips fades. Guilt is a black stone in my belly. I drain the tea awkwardly.

"We have to help Becca," I say.

"I have tried," Alice says. "But my little match-flame of healing magic isn't enough. I don't know how you experience drawing the living-green, but I can only pull and hold enough to last a brief time. Usually that is enough to discover what is injured and boost the repairing, but it is Becca's mind that is injured, not a broken bone."

I stare at her. "You think having access to more of the living-green would heal her?" A tiny flicker of hope rises in me. "I can try it. Alice, I can draw a lot of the living-green."

Alice sits up straighter. "It is not that simple. Healing is a delicate art. It is not just about applying power. It's about coaxing the body to heal itself and supplying the energy for it to do so."

The image of Angel screeching and dashing away in terror when I tried to heal her ear reinforces Alice's words of caution. But maybe I just poured too much living-green into poor Angel. Maybe if I restricted the flow and knew what to look for, what to do—

"Can't you tell me what to do?" I ask.

"You're more likely to make it worse than help her."

I stare into the cup at the leaves in the bottom. They say a fortune-teller can read the future in tea leaves. I'm a scryer, but the last thing I want to see right now is the future. I want no part of magic ... except—"Alice, what if *you* had unlimited access to the living-green? Do you think you could heal Becca?"

My great aunt sips her tea, her expression thoughtful. "I don't know. This is not repairing torn tissue or coaxing white cells to fight an infection. I don't know what that House of Iron man actually did to her mind. It would be risky."

"You're right."

"But." She takes a deep breath. "We should try. She's such a sweet girl. It's not right."

We go the guest room where Becca is sleeping. Alice sits on the bed and coaxes Becca to put her head in her lap.

"Tell me when," I say.

Alice places her hands on either side of Becca's head. Compliant as always, Becca stares at the ceiling. Alice looks at me.

"Tell me if it's too much," I say to Alice.

Alice nods, and I kneel beside her and rest my bandaged hands on top of hers. With a deep breath, I close my eyes, seeing the facets of the rose-stone in my mind, and draw on the living-green. It's the first time I have done so since the nightmare in the mine. I've wanted nothing to do with magic since then, but the golden light is warm, a counter to the stain of iron. Maybe that is because most of my heritage is from the House of Rose. Whatever I got from House of Iron was from my grandfather. The living-green is a balm, and I don't want to let go of it, but Alice whispers. "I'm ready."

I remember what Jason said about visualizing the power as a stream. I trickle energy into her. She catches her breath. "Oh, how ... wonderful!"

After a moment, she adds, "I think I may be helping some. Can you give me more time?"

I almost laugh. It takes concentration to keep from letting it pour through me as a flood. So many rich seams of coal and iron run beneath this city. And now that Birmingham has traded the manufacture of steel for a world-class university medical center, all that wealth is just sitting there. It is no wonder that both Houses were drawn to the magnet of central Alabama. I can give Alice all the power she wants as long as she wants it.

When Alice finally finishes, Becca is asleep. Not the restless tossing and turning she has been doing, where she seemed to be fighting something … maybe trying to find her "self." This is a deep, peaceful sleep.

"Did it help?" I ask.

"I think some, but I don't know if I have undone what was done or just smoothed it over. I had to tread very carefully. Don't expect too much."

"We can try again if it doesn't help, can't we? I mean you couldn't make it worse."

"On the contrary, I could. I think we should let nature take its course now. I don't dare do anything more."

I am there, sitting beside Becca many hours later when she finally stirs. She blinks and stares up at the ceiling and then at me, puzzled.

I draw a breath and answer the unspoken *Where am I?* in her eyes. "You're in Alice's—" I stop. "You're home, Becca. You're home."

Her forehead wrinkles in confusion. She raises a tentative hand to my cheek, touching the wetness there. I wait, but she doesn't speak.

For the next few days, she follows me around, almost as if she has replaced her mindless obsession with Black for me. She eats on her own, but she utters not a word—*will she ever?* She seems like a child, newly born to the world. The pain of seeing her like this sears my gut every day, but there is nothing more I can do for her.

There is, however, one more thing I have to do for someone else.

A SCOWLING NURSE STOPS US as Alice and I enter UAB Hospital's intensive care unit.

"I'm sorry, but no visitors here, only one immediate family member."

I touch the nurse's arm. I am full as a tick with the power of iron, afraid it might drain out before I needed it. I could destroy her mind if I release too much, but we have to move fast. Alice can only hold the living-green so long. I visualize a tiny trickle flowing into the nurse, and whisper. "Just for a few minutes."

Her face softens. "Oh, well just for a few minutes."

I feel dirty and manipulative. This is the first time I've ever tried this. It is too easy. Will this kind of power over people eventually turn me into a Mr. Black?

After I give her Daniel's name, she leads me—and the short, redheaded, dark-eyed woman accompanying me—into the patient section. We incur a couple of disapproving glances, but apparently this nurse has clout, because the stern looks of the other medical staff dissolve when they realize she is escorting us. At room 1-A, she stops and pulls a curtain aside for us. I touch her arm again.

"Thank you," I say. "You can leave us. We won't be long."

Inside, I stand beside the bed that holds a small, unconscious mummy wrapped in bandages. Clear tubes run from a port in Daniel's neck into multiple bags on poles. He lies on his stomach. I'm sure they still have him sedated to keep him still and help with the pain. On the opposite side of the bed, his mother sits in a chair, her hands wrapped on the bed's hard safety bar. I'm not sure she even sees us.

Alice and I have experimented with holding the energies of Rose. For her, it works only about fifteen to twenty minutes before it dissipates. I can contain it longer, but I don't dare pull the living-green while I hold iron magic. Mixing the two is what caused … whatever happened in Black's throne room. Besides, we are several stories high and the only carbon in reach resides in the steel beams that support the hospital building, not something I want to disturb.

With a start, it occurs to me that there is another source for my magic, not as accessible as coal, but if I could strip the carbon from the handcuffs, I can use other forms of it. And one source is the human beings around us. We are all built on carbon atoms.

For a moment, I am frozen with the realization that I could have killed Mr. Black at any time during that torture session in the mine, just sucked the carbon energy from his body. No, he was a warlock; it wouldn't have worked on him, and I am not sure I could do such a thing selectively, anyway. Even if it's possible, I might have killed everyone in the room … at the least.

A chill courses my spine to know I could massacre anyone within my "reach" this instant with a shift of my attention "out" instead of down into the earth. No human being should have that kind of power, not to mention being able to turn a person into an obedient slave with a touch. *Am I really a human being any longer?* My journey to discover who I am has led me deeper and deeper into alien territory, like an android who thinks he is a person, until a deep cut in his skin reveals the machine beneath.

Alice reaches for Daniel's unburned hand, the same hand I held in the iron throne room.

He doesn't move. I hope Alice can heal him, or at least ease his pain.

I hope this is the right thing to do.

After a few moments, as if she heard my silent plea, Alice turns her head and smiles at me, giving a little nod.

Thank God, I breathe. I don't know how much she will be able to help him. I guess no one will know until those bandages come off, but Alice would not have given me that silent reassurance if he were beyond her help.

She turns back to the boy.

Daniel's mother looks up with bleary, reddened eyes that have shed too many tears. It's the first time I have been near her that I didn't catch the whiff of alcohol evaporating out of her pores. Her gaze drifts to the bandages on my hands and lifts to my face in recognition.

"Oh." Her voice is a breathy rattle. "Thank you."

At first, I am startled. How did she know what happened? Then I realize Tracey or a homicide detective must have told her I tried to help Daniel.

I just shake my head.

"No, *thank you*," she insists. "You pulled my Daniel out of that fire."

Her words sear. I want to scream at her: *I caused the fire!* But I don't. It is my burden to bear. Before me burns the vision of the man I will always think of as Mr. Black, ablaze with an unholy fire that came of mixing the powers of House of Rose and House of Iron. Being a warlock apparently offers no protection from such a conflagration. And it took only a tiny amount of the living-green—what I was able to squeeze from the handcuff's alloy. What would happen if I pulled more? What if I mixed the two unconsciously? Could it happen while I sleep? I could burn myself alive, not to mention anyone stupid enough to be with me. The Houses maintained their distance over the centuries for a good reason.

I climb the steps to Alice's house, more weary than I have been since the ordeal in the cave. *Black is dead*, I remind myself. *It is over. The cost was high, but it is over.*

At the top stair, I stop dead. A single rose lies on the threshold, a red so dark, it is almost black.

photo courtesy of Roger W. Thorne

T.K. Thorne retired as a captain of the Birmingham Police Department and as executive director of a downtown business improvement district in Birmingham Alabama. Both careers and a Masters of Social Work from the University of Alabama provide fodder for her writing.

Her fiction, poetry, and non-fiction have been published in various venues and have garnered several awards, including her two historical novels—*Noah's Wife* which won ForeWord Review's "Book of the Year" for Historical Fiction and *Angels At The Gate*, which won IBPA's Benjamin Franklin award for Historical Fiction and a silver IPPY award. Her debut nonfiction was *Last Chance for Justice: How Relentless Investigators Uncovered New Evidence Convicting the Birmingham Church Bombers* (2013), which the New York Post listed on their "Books You Should Be Reading." A short film from her screenplay "Six Blocks Wide" was a finalist in a film festival in Italy and was shown at other juried festivals in the U.S. and Europe.

Most recently, she is delving into the world of paranormal thriller set in the deep South. Her hobbies include classical piano, martial arts, and horseback riding. She lives on a mountaintop near Springville, Alabama, with her husband, a horse, two dogs and a cat.

Learn more at www.TKThorne.com